COLD FUSION

DOCTOR WHO – THE MISSING ADVENTURES

Also available:

COLD FUSION

Lance Parkin

DOCTOR WHO

THE MISSING ADVENTURES

First published in Great Britain in 1996 by
Doctor Who Books
an imprint of Virgin Publishing Ltd
332 Ladbroke Grove
London W10 5AH

ISBN 0 426 20489 1

Cover illustration by Alister Pearson

Typeset by Galleon Typesetting, Ipswich
Printed and bound in Great Britain by
Mackays of Chatham PLC

To my wife, Cassandra May:
as beautiful as Princess Leia and as smart as Yoda

Thanks to the usual Time Team: Cassie, Mark Jones, Mark Clapham and Michael Evans. Special thanks to Jonathan Evans and David Pitcher for fixing my computer when it broke halfway through Chapter Twelve. Thanks also to Lisa Brattan.

Drinking song lyrics courtesy of Mark Jones and John Binns.

Part One

Distant Music

1

Ghostwatch

High, high above the trees the night sky was creaking and clattering.

Out here, among the mountain communities and the farmsteads on the ice plains far from the Strip, people explained that it was the chatter of all the souls ever lost to the avalanche, drifting over the horizon with the clouds. The scientists claimed that it was simply the sound of the wind buffeting billions of snowflakes together and that everything could be expressed in terms of air currents acting upon frozen droplets of water.

Underneath the forest canopy, the Doctor was sheltered from the worst of the blizzard, and at last he knew that he had reached his destination. A month ago he had left his companions behind and trekked hundreds of miles out here, following rumours, searching for leads. Ahead of him, up through the trees, the warning light of the waystation was flashing lazily. As the Doctor reached the edge of the forest, he could see that the station had been built on a raised area of ground to improve telecommunications and transmat reception. The snow whipped around the corners of the dark building, reminding the Doctor for a moment of something that he couldn't place. Judging by the architectural style of the half-ruined station, it had been built early in the colony's history, during the pre-modernist revival of the mid-twenty-second century. Thick snow on the roof indicated that the building was heavily insulated. Now the Doctor could hear a jangling electronic drumbeat in the air, distant music from inside the station. Beneath that, the rumbling of a dozen conversations and someone's laughter. He was surprised how lonely the sound made him feel. How far from home.

He stepped up onto the path, shaking the snow from his

boots. A variety of battered snowships had been moored around the waystation, and there were a couple of twenty-year-old skimmers parked by the entrance. A skitrain track ran straight past the building and curved around, disappearing along the contour of the mountain. The Doctor walked a hundred yards down the cleared pathway. Standing close to the entrance was an elegant transmat pagoda, showing signs of ruin but still in working order.

'Who's there?' In his thick layers of clothing, the watchman stepping forward appeared misshapen, a hunchback with stubby claws for hands and blocks for feet. Steam swirled from his facemask, but this was just his breath condensing in the freezing air. He held a gun, a homemade laser burster that had probably once been a cutting tool of some kind. It would only really be effective at short range, and must be very difficult to aim. The Doctor stepped closer, into the light.

'I am the Doctor. I've come a long way.'

'Who sent you?' As the guard spoke, he waved a primitive energy scanner, searching for weapons. The Doctor didn't need to look up, he wasn't hiding anything.

'No one sent me. What's the matter? It looks as though you've seen a ghost.'

The guard stiffened. 'In you go,' he said hurriedly, indicating the doorway. The Doctor thanked him and walked inside into a tiny cubicle. At first he thought it was a lift, but there were no controls and the room was an irregular shape. There was a metal door ahead, but it didn't open as the Doctor approached it.

Behind him, the door to the outside world slammed shut, closing him in. The Doctor nearly reached it in time. He pressed his fingers against the hatch, but it was solid, at least an inch of armour-plating. The Doctor glanced up and saw the sensor on the ceiling that had registered his presence. Pressurized seals hissed into place and the whine of a heating system began warming up. It was just a snowlock, a system that ensured none of the bitterly cold air would be allowed inside.

There was a chime, and the inner door slid open. The Doctor stepped from the snowlock into oppressive warmth.

4

The room was long, narrow. There was a heater at either end, and the great hall was full of people eating from steaming plates. There was a thick haze of smoke in the air. The rich smells of food, beer and sweat were overwhelming after so long in the pine forest, and the room, although large, was almost claustrophobic. As the Doctor made his way to the bar a couple of the patrons glanced up, but most weren't paying him any attention. There were a couple of dozen here in this low-vaulted room, mostly local trappers, farmers and travellers, but also a few offworlders. The humans had shed a few layers of their brightly coloured clothing, but kept it close to them. A group of humans in full warpaint watched him suspiciously. There were aliens here, too. By the door, a small group of Wondarks from the Wateh Galaxy were engrossed in conversation. A couple of Shark People sat towards the centre of the room, nursing their drinks. Recalling what little he knew of their physiognomy, the Doctor could tell that they were rather glum, unsurprising given that the Shark People's homeworld of Shlima had a tropical climate. Despite their blank expressions, the small group of smartly dressed Kosnax at the bar would be rather more comfortable on this frozen planet.

'Excuse me, ladies.' Silently the Kosnax drifted aside, and the Doctor eased onto a barstool. The music was coming from the pseudolive band, a quartet of musicians from Eighty-One, the robot planet. They must have been on a tour of the coreworlds when the war started, and they would have been trapped here ever since. They seemed happy enough, singing that they'd always be together in electric dreams.

Another droid bobbed at the bar serving the drinks. It was a mass-produced SAM drone, much less sophisticated than the musicians. Its casing was a standard chrome sphere in which the Doctor could see his face reflected.

'wHAt's YouR POIson?' the robarman buzzed. Its vocoder hadn't been serviced for years and its hoverfield was slightly misaligned. It had probably been kidnapped from one of the big hotels on the Strip, decades ago, and had ended up here. The Doctor resisted the temptation to fix the faults himself.

'A Dexheimer Spätlese Rädecke, the '07 if you have it,'

the Doctor said. Normally, of course, he wouldn't touch a synthetic wine, but he recalled that the SAMs had no difficulty copying German eisweins. The programmers had no idea why, although there were a number of popular myths claiming to account for it.

'oN THe ROcks?'

'Like the planet,' the Doctor observed. There was an almost inaudible click from within the drone's casing.

'if you WOulD ComE WiTH Me, Sir?' The robarman drifted over the counter, and the Doctor followed it across the room. No one looked up. On the far wall was a door marked 'Private', which slid open as the robarman reached it. The Doctor followed it through, and the door slammed shut behind him.

'MInd THE Step, SIr.'

The Doctor tripped over the step.

'SORry, SIr.'

'Not at all. Might we have some light?'

'THe glowbe must haVE Gone, sIR.'

'So I see – if you'll pardon the pun.'

'Yes, I PARDon the PUn, Sir.'

'Is it much further?'

'HE Is IN HERE, sir.' A door rattled open to the left, and dull yellow light spilled over the Doctor and drone out in the corridor. The Doctor moved towards the light, and stepped through the archway into a small office that smelt of must. The young man sitting at the desk was clearly startled and he dropped his book. The Doctor had caught it before it hit the floor. It was a paperback novel in Mandarin, *Gānggāng Zhànzheng*. The Doctor recognized the title, but had never got around to reading it. He handed the book back to its owner.

Ziyou was a slight figure, a descendant of settlers from the Southern Chinese Union. There were streaks of blond in his black hair, and like most of the people living away from the Strip he was clean-shaven, as a beard would have broken the seal on his icemask. He wore a tightly buttoned tunic with horizontal navy stripes, there was a bold logo printed on the breast.

* * *

The Doctor introduced himself.

Ziyou remained on his guard. 'I've heard of you. A couple of teleminers were in here a month ago, they said you'd helped them.'

'Gemboyle and Narvalek,' the Doctor confirmed, smiling. 'Their skimmer fell down a crevasse, I fetched it out. They do a nice little sideline in servicing robarmen, and yours was one of the ones they reprogrammed for me.'

'Why me?' the young man asked suspiciously.

The Doctor smiled. 'I just want to hear your story. I've come a long way.'

The Doctor was shorter than Ziyou had pictured him, and older. He had an odd, sad face. Underneath a shabby fur coat he wore a crumpled linen suit and a waistcoat. He looked as if he had stepped from the pages of a history book.

'What do you mean "my story"? I'm a freeman, working here as an accountant.'

'But a year ago you were a prospector, weren't you? Back when you were a warranted man. I want to hear your story . . . your ghost story.'

'You won't trick me into incriminating myself.'

'It's against the law to tell ghost stories?' the Doctor asked.

'You know it is. When the story is true.'

'It happened. No law can change the truth.'

'Scientific law *is* the truth. Logically, what happened to me couldn't happen. Therefore it didn't.'

'There are more things in heaven and earth than are dreamt of in your philosophy, Ziyou.'

Ziyou couldn't remember telling the Doctor his name. He'd been careful not to tell him. Had the Doctor read his mind?

'No,' the Doctor said conspiratorially, 'I just read your name-badge.'

'I'm loyal, I'm not a criminal,' Ziyou declared. 'Doctor, I spent three months in a mental hospital. They started to wipe parts of my memory. I had to escape before . . . before there was nothing of me left.'

The Doctor gently touched his wrist and looked him

7

in the eye. 'You've done nothing wrong. You saw something, that's all. Something that you can't explain, something *they* can't explain.' The Doctor was staring at Ziyou with an intensity that he found frightening. 'It's a presence that science can deny, it exists outside the latitude of human minds.'

'Please. They can hear every heresy, you know. Even down here.'

The Doctor smiled. 'They've got most of the Strip covered, but this is a big planet. It's impossible to watch every inch of the surface all the time, especially out here beyond the frostlands. They only have two dozen spy satellites in irregular orbits, monitoring random sections of the planet's surface. There's a limit to the power of technology.'

Ziyou straightened, ignoring the last remark. 'I know all that: everyone knows it. But you can't predict which sections they're watching, that's the whole point.'

The Doctor took a small white box from his pocket and held it up. 'This little device picks up the telemetry of the satellites as well as military transponder signals. If anything artificial comes over the horizon, or there's anything military within a fifty-mile radius then it gives a series of short buzzes. We'd have a little under two minutes before we were within range of a scanner. Plenty of time to change the topic of conversation.'

Ziyou couldn't keep his eyes off the box. 'That something so small could be so . . . powerful. You stole it?'

'No,' the Doctor explained, 'I built it myself. I could build another one.'

'May I hold it?'

'I can let you have this one,' the Doctor paused, 'if you'd just tell me your story.' The Doctor handed the box over. Ziyou turned it over in his hand, before opening it up. There were a dozen metal plates, laid out alongside one another like a miniature piano keyboard, and a metal stylus slotted above them. Ziyou turned back to the Doctor, unable to hide his disappointment.

'It's a children's toy. A musical instrument.'

'Take the stylus,' the Doctor prompted. He showed

8

Ziyou where to tap the stylus and a discordant buzzing started up. It took a moment for Ziyou to decipher the signals, a detailed log of military movements over the last couple of days.

'It works. Now tell me what you saw.'

'I saw a ghost.' Ziyou said it before he could catch himself.

'Tell me more.'

'There's nothing more. I'm sorry. It was a year ago now, just before the peacekeepers arrived. In a deep cavern north of here, close to the Nightingale Facility.' He rattled off the grid reference. 'It never happened, there is no rational explanation. It must have been my mind playing tricks. My psychotherapist told me.'

'Is that what you believe?'

'There is no other explanation. She said what happened to me in the cave must have been an optical illusion, or a psychological disorder. I can't remember everything, I can't trust my own thoughts. What happened, what I *remember* happening, is just my brain trying to make sense of garbled information by piecing it together. A neurochemical imbalance, or –' He stopped, disturbed by the Doctor's expression. 'What do you think it was?' he asked angrily.

'Do you know what they used to believe on Earth?' the little man began. 'According to the old calendars, today's Halloween, the thirty-first of October. In pagan times it was the last day of the year, and men thought that Halloween night was the gap between the old year and the new. A break in time. Out of that gap on that night, evil forces would walk abroad, spreading their influence.'

'Superstitious nonsense. Proscribed gibberish.'

'Perhaps.' The Doctor's eyes told another story.

The box in Ziyou's hand started buzzing intermittently.

Ziyou's mind emptied. They had found him. He realized he was looking around, trying to find a non-existent exit.

The Doctor tapped the side of the drone. 'SAM, would you mind awfully counting down from two minutes? Give us a verbal reminder every thirty seconds.'

'AS you WIsh. TWO mINutes. MaRk.'

Ziyou scrambled for the tracking device and tapped away at the keys. He was rewarded by a series of buzzes and parps.

'There's a skybase in low orbit.' He tried to keep the panic out of his voice.

'What's wrong with the light in the corridor?' the Doctor asked softly.

'The glowbe has gone,' Ziyou responded automatically. It didn't seem important, somehow.

'But what if it hasn't?'

'What?'

'What if there's nothing wrong with the light bul– the glowbe?'

'Then the switch is faulty.'

'And –'

'If that's OK, then the wire must be broken, or the fuse has gone, or there's a power cut, or . . .' Off-hand, Ziyou couldn't think of anything else that could go wrong with such a simple piece of equipment.

'But what if they are all in good working order?'

'Then when you flicked the switch, the glowbe would come on.'

The Doctor nodded. 'Yes. But what if it didn't? Just once. What if there was no explanation?'

'There's always a reason.'

There was a commotion upstairs, the sound of tables being pushed, a stampede, even shots being fired. The band had stopped playing.

'They're here already!' Ziyou yelled.

'But they can't be,' the Doctor complained, shaking the tracking device vigorously and holding it up to his ear. 'The skybase won't arrive for another . . .'

'ONe MInute THIrtY seconds.'

'. . . one minute thirty seconds. Thank you, SAM. So, if *they* aren't here yet, then who is?'

The Doctor was already bounding towards the saloon. Ziyou found himself following. As they reached the door that led to the main hall, he grabbed the little man's shoulders.

'If they find us here, they'll kill us. Doctor, they've sent a skybase after you. Do you know what that means? A thousand ground troops, a hundred guncopters, twenty-five battletanks, ten wardroids. Neutron torpedoes, particle disruptors, cannon threads . . .'

The Doctor waved his hands. 'Yes, yes, details, details.'

The door slid open, and the Doctor stopped in his tracks, his jaw dropping. There was a tall figure hovering in the centre of the room. *Again*, thought Ziyou. Male, humanoid, he flickered, fading in and out of vision. He was wearing a long black cloak and a high-collared tunic, which flowed about him as if it was lashing in the wind. There was no breeze in the room – in fact, no one in the room was even daring to breathe, the Doctor included. The trappers and aliens just stood and stared. Once again, the silence was the strangest sound that Ziyou had ever heard. The figure was completely hairless, he didn't even have eyebrows or lashes. *It happened. A year ago, in the cave, it happened.*

'ONe minUTE.'

'Is he the same as you saw before?' the Doctor asked, striding towards the figure.

'No,' Ziyou said firmly. 'The same uniform, the same race. A different individual.'

The Doctor had reached the centre of the room. The apparition pitched round, as if on castors, turning to face the Doctor and Ziyou. It stared past them, as if it was having difficulty focusing. It began to speak. The Doctor leant forward, keen to catch the slightest sound.

No voice came from the thin-lipped mouth, which worked up and down. After a moment, the ghostly figure realized that the Doctor couldn't hear him.

The Doctor and the ghost looked into one another's eyes for a moment. There wasn't even a flicker of recognition.

'ThiRTY SEConds.' SAM's voice made Ziyou jump.

'We have to get out of here,' Ziyou warned gently. The Doctor shooed him away, then stepped back from the figure, screwing his eyes shut. Ziyou could almost feel the Doctor's thoughts screaming at the apparition.

It lifted a hand, slowly, then its fingers danced for a moment.

11

'What is that? Sign language?' The Doctor's eyes were open again, he was staring at the figure, frustrated.

'Come on, Doctor.' Ziyou grabbed the Doctor's shoulder, but the little man shrugged him off.

'I . . . It has something to do with my past. You go, I . . .'

'Come on!'

'*Ferutu.*' The voice came from all around them, a scratchy sound like a quill on parchment.

'My past. My future. I . . . don't know. I've never . . . It's so *alien.*'

The apparition watched the Doctor's pained expression with scientific interest.

Simultaneously they reached out to touch one another. Their fingers brushed together.

'Is it solid?' Ziyou asked, after a moment.

'Yes,' the Doctor noted. 'But like a wall, not like living flesh. There's a wall.'

'arrivAL —'

The snowlock exploded inwards, most of the supporting brickwork above it cracking into rubble and crashing to the floor.

'– IMMinent.'

'DO NOT ATTEMPT TO MOVE. EVERYONE HERE IS IN VIOLATION OF PLANETARY EMERGENCY DIRECTIVE THREE. DO NOT ATTEMPT TO MOVE,' a monotone voice boomed. Something huge stomped in, over the wreckage of the doorframe.

Ziyou had seen pictures of wardroids, he'd seen them march past in parades, but this was the first one he'd ever seen in action. It was seven feet tall, and almost as broad. It had heavy armour-plating on the shoulders and chest, but only spindly legs. Its cylindrical head swung from side to side, a single camera eye registering everyone in the room. Behind the robot, the bitter night air was pouring through the new hole in the wall. Ziyou found himself wondering how the wardroid had arrived here. It must have transmatted in.

The waystation patrons were scrambling for cover, or grabbing their possessions and running for the emergency exit on the far wall. In front of Ziyou, one of the Shark People was raising his pistol. Before the gun was even waist-height, the robot's arm had whipped up and straightened. A mechanical fist clenched, and knuckle cannons fired, once. The Shark Person lurched back, sinking to the floor. There was a neat bullet hole above one of its eyes.

A panel on the robot's shoulderpad flipped open and a grenade *choomed* from it, arcing over everyone's head, almost touching the ceiling, before falling to the ground in front of the emergency exit. When it detonated, it brought down the roof, trapping half a dozen people in the wreckage.

Now everyone was blocked in, and there was no option but to stand and fight. Those with weapons reached for them, scrabbling through thick coats to get at them. Before anyone had found their gun, the robot's arm swung around the room in a carefully measured circle, firing single shots. Each bullet hit its target: a headshot for the humans, the dragonheart in the case of the Kosnax. Now everyone was screaming and diving for cover.

Everyone except the Doctor. Unnoticed, the ghost had disappeared. The Doctor stood his ground, deep in thought while the room exploded around him. Ziyou stayed close, hoping that some of the little man's calmness would rub off.

'Doctor!' Ziyou warned.

'Although the robot has laser ordnance at its disposal, it is using only projectile weapons,' the Doctor noted with fascination.

'Er . . . yes. Very interesting.'

'It leaves us in no doubt that lethal force is being employed.' A bullet whizzed past the Doctor, hitting a snowship captain square in the chest. 'An onlooker might mistake an energy beam for a stun ray, but a bullet is a bullet is a bullet.'

'Doctor, people are dying.'

The little man's head snapped around, taking in the carnage for the first time.

'Well, I'll soon put a stop to that,' he promised. He whirled to face the robot, and waved his arm in the air.

'Coo-eee!'

The wardroid lurched forward, the ground reverberating to its footfalls. It had fixed its gaze on the Doctor and

13

Ziyou. As it began stomping towards them, Ziyou felt surprisingly calm, almost serene. Nothing could prevent him from dying now. After over a year waiting for the authorities to catch up with him it was almost a relief.

A square shadow loomed over the Doctor. 'IDENTIFY YOURSELF.'

The little man raised his hat. 'I am the Doctor.'

The robot's torso twisted, its eye peering directly at Ziyou. The lens extended, focusing on him. 'IDENTIFY YOURSELF.' But before Ziyou could stammer out his name the Doctor had grabbed a bowl of soup from a nearby table and rammed it hard in the robot's camera eye. For a moment the wardroid stood still, thick soup dripping from it. Then it tried to wipe the lens clean with its hand. It wasn't equipped for such a delicate task, and crushed the camera with its fingers.

The Doctor bowed theatrically. 'There you go. As you can see, when the visual receptors are disabled, it simply shuts down. Now for my next trick, I'll

!'

g

r

a

a

W

Steel fingers grabbed the Doctor by the scruff of his neck and yanked him four feet into the air. But as Ziyou watched, the Doctor had slipped out of his jacket and slid down the wardroid's arm. Establishing a foothold on the robot's pelvis, grabbing on to its shoulder, the Doctor pulled himself around the robot's vast torso. He wedged himself between steel shoulderblades and wrapped his legs around the narrow waist.

Gun barrels welded to the robot's hips burst into life, spraying the room with bullets and almost taking off the Doctor's feet.

The wardroid lurched to one side, then the other, trying to shake him off, but the Doctor was lodged into place. 'REMOVE YOURSELF.'

'Shan't.' The Doctor had located an access panel on the

14

robot's flank. He tapped it hard on one side and a small keypad popped out.

A hydraulic arm swiped past the Doctor, trying to grab him. It found only thin air.

'I'm an itch you can't scratch, I'm afraid,' the Doctor shouted. He stabbed at a control, and winked triumphantly at Ziyou. The robot pitched forward, almost throwing its piggyback passenger against a nearby wall. It swept its free hand around the room, firing a salvo of micro-shells.

'ABOUT MECHINF,' it bellowed. 'SAAB-ROYCE MECHINF. VERSION FOUR POINT ONE TWO. COPYRIGHT COPYRIGHT SYMBOL TWENTY-SIX-EIGHTY-ONE TO TWENTY-SIX-NINETY-TWO SAAB-ROYCE CORPORATION.' It levelled its arm once more and the knuckle cannons blazed into life, splintering a heavy wooden table that a group of trappers had been using as cover. They scattered, and the robot picked them off one by one, again just firing single shots.

The Doctor blinked, and he dived back to the keypad. The massive robot swung its fist, swatting aside one of the trappers. Frantically, the Doctor began tapping commands into the keypad. 'MECHINF HELP,' the wardroid roared. 'PLEASE SELECT: GETTING STARTED. HELP INDEX. INTERACTIVE HELP. ABOUT.' The Doctor's hand hovered over the keypad for a moment before he selected a control. The wardroid's fist rotated through ninety degrees and a miniature rocket battery popped from its wrist. It fired, apparently indiscriminately, into the crowd. Ziyou turned away before they hit, but he couldn't block out the sound of the explosions or the screams.

'HELP INDEX. PLEASE SELECT: BEGINNER. STEP BY STEP. REFERENCE. YOU HAVE SELECTED REFERENCE. THIS SECTION OFFERS DETAILED INFORMATION ABOUT A VARIETY OF TOPICS. PLEASE CHOOSE. NO ENTRY: EMERGENCY SHUTDOWN. NO ENTRY: SELF DESTRUCT.' A guard shoved past Ziyou, levelling his rifle. He stood his ground as the robot stomped towards him, glancing down to check the energy levels of his burster. 'NO ENTRY: SHUT UP. NO ENTRY: SHUT DOWN. YOU HAVE SELECTED: DISARM. IF NON-LETHAL FORCE IS REQUIRED, YOUR MECHINF CAN BE PROGRAMMED TO DISARM ITS TARGET, RATHER THAN

ELIMINATING IT. DEMONSTRATION FOLLOWS.' The robot reached out, plucking the burster from the guard's hand. 'THE MECHINF DEFAULTS TO THE "SHOW-OF-STRENGTH" OPTION, A DEMONSTRATION OF PHYSICAL SUPERIORITY THAT MOST PSYCHOLOGICAL STUDIES IN THE AREA –' Its fist clenched, crumpling the rifle. There was a flash of light as the powerpack burst. '– AGREE HAS A DEMORALIZING –' the trapper staggered backwards, falling over a broken chair in an attempt to get away. '– EFFECT ON AN OPPONEN– YOU HAVE SELECTED: CANCEL. REFERENCE. THIS SECTION OFFERS DETAILE– NO ENTRY: DEACTIVATING ARMAMENTS. NO ENTRY: DEACTIVATING WEAPONS. YOU HAVE SELECTED: ARMAMENTS, DEACTIVATING: AN OVERVIEW. IN CERTAIN CIRCUMSTANCES.' The robot's fist connected with the trapper's jaw. He fell. 'YOU MAY CHOOSE TO SHUT DOWN SOME OR ALL OF MECHINF'S WEAPONRY SYSTEMS. THIS PROCEDURE IS RELATIVELY STRAIGHTFORWARD: –'

One of the Kosnax swept forward. She raised her claw, preparing an energy blast. The robot caught her wrist and broke it, punching her hard in the stomach with its other hand. The fist withdrew slightly, then the robot extended a finger and plunged it into her torso, puncturing the chest wall. She froze, energy crackling over her pale skin. The wardroid had short-circuited her dragon energy, forcing it to backlash. Ziyou watched, fascinated, as the young Kosnax woman boiled away, disintegrating in wave after wave of blue light. Her expression hadn't changed the whole time. The wardroid pulled back its hand.

'FIRST PRESS COMMAND SEVEN. NOW ENTER YOUR PASSWORD. PASSWORD INCORRECT, PLEASE TRY AGAIN.'

'SIr, IF I might INTErvene?'

'Yes, SAM?'

'THe MecHInf version 4.12 has A RESet swiTCH, SIR. Just TO the LEft oF YOUR HAND.'

The Doctor pressed the control, and jumped clear as the robot sunk to its knees and crashed to the floor.

'So it has. Thank you, SAM.'

'SIr, tHREE ARMourED HOVErcopters HAVE JUSt enteREd THE WAysTATIoN'S DEFEncE Perimeter.'

'ETA?' Ziyou asked.

'IMMinent, sir.'

There were sounds from outside of skimmerfields dying down and marching: boots pounding against the pathway. Ziyou heard shots. It sounded like a burster. Then a couple of rapid bursts from a machine pistol. Half a dozen shapes advanced through the hole torn in the wall by the wardroid. One grabbed Ziyou's hair and pushed his head down. Another was behind him, forcing him into handcuffs. Ziyou could hear the robot guillotine trundling itself into place.

'Ziyou Wanle, you are under arrest. You are charged with violating Planetary Emergency Directive Three, disseminating propaganda with treasonable intent and terrorist acts. There are also a number of less serious misdemeanours against you. Judgement has been passed in your absence, and you have been found guilty on all counts. Do you have anything to say in your defence?'

'I saw a ghost,' he spat. 'I saw a ghost, everyone here saw a ghost, and killing us won't change that.'

2

On the Rocks

G radually, light dawned in the chamber.
Prospectors had entered this cave system a year ago
looking for palladium and jabolite. They had found a vast
rock gallery only slightly smaller than the Carlsbad Caverns
back on Earth. The mainly sedimentary rock had been
eroded away over millions of years by the stream that still
ran through it. It seemed unreasonable that such a vast space
could have been carved by such a tiny thing, but it had
taken tens of millions of years to do so. Each year, the water
had only dissolved away an amount of rock the volume of a
sugarcube. Time had done the rest. The cavern itself wasn't
the discovery that excited the miners.

The Machine almost filled the cavern. A thick central
column as tall as a skyscraper pierced the roof and floor of
the chamber, at a slight angle. It was an oily gunmetal grey.
Yellow and orange lights flickered dimly along its sides.
Gleaming panels spilled from it over the floor and were
splashed across the ceiling. Vast power couplings and ten-
metre-thick cables loomed from the cavern roof like jungle
creepers. The sheer size of the Machine was disconcerting,
too large for the human mind to take in. Imagine, then,
how the scientists felt when the dating techniques they used
showed that the Machine was *older* than the rock that
surrounded it. A few panels were showing signs of corro-
sion, there was evidence of fossilized organic material in
places, but the Machine itself was almost intact after millions of years. The archaeologists said there was no indica-
tion of building activity: indeed there was no evidence that
there had ever been intelligent life on the planet before
the arrival of humanity. There was nothing else like the
Machine anywhere in the Empire.

Scientists had managed to quantify the Machine: they

18

measured exactly how tall and broad it was and they could calculate its mass and weight. They knew that it was built from metals that weren't found on the planet, and so logically it must have originated elsewhere. They discovered evidence that the Machine had grown over time. By scraping away at some of the surrounding rock, they had determined that the Machine had roots and branches, like a tree, and some of the panelling appeared more recent than neighbouring sections, almost like scar tissue.

But the scientists still didn't know what the Machine was *for*.

The two-storey dome from which the scientists conducted their studies was on a more mundane scale than the Machine, an oasis of normality in a mile-high subterranean chamber. Now, thirteen hooded figures swept across the observation gallery, taking their allotted places. They moved in unison, their hands grasping each wrist in turn, then the neck clasps, as they checked the seals on their radiation suits. Even this far away from the Machine, regulations demanded that thick protective clothing was worn. At a signal from their leader, they brought down their visors and began their work. Gloved fingers pulled down levers and tapped at control panels, twelve individuals moving in a carefully choreographed ritual. As they began chanting their reports, the babble of voices sounded like a church congregation.

Outside, the Machine responded. The lights on its side brightened almost imperceptibly. The earth was beginning to hum, pulsing every couple of seconds. The scientists sat back, awestruck. They were in the presence of a power beyond their comprehension, something that a more primitive race might descibe as 'divine'. The leader gave another signal, and they returned to their controls. After another moment's frantic activity, the Machine died back down.

A printer in the corner of the room chattered into life, spooling out several feet of computer paper. One of the scientists was already standing over it. When the printout had finished, he tore the last sheet off and handed it to his leader, who raised the visor on her suit. She studied the report for a little under a minute.

Finally, she looked up. 'First stage has been achieved. Hypothesis confirmed. Estimated time before second stage completion?' she asked her deputy.

'Unknown, Chief Scientist. We predict that the second energy peak will occur within sixty minutes.'

'Proceed.'

Nyssa found the Doctor in the TARDIS cloisters. He was sitting on a stone bench, absent-mindedly playing with a frond of ivy.

'That's a *Hedera helix*. You really shouldn't be touching it,' she said.

'It's perfectly harmless, to a Time Lord at any rate.' But the Doctor released the creeper, which sprang back against the wall. He gestured around. 'I wasn't sure whether these had been ejected or not. Much of the TARDIS has gone: so many memories, so much of my past.' A few days ago, to escape a trap devised by the Master, it had been necessary to remove much of the TARDIS's mass. This had been a straightforward operation which had saved their lives, but now a quarter of the interior had simply ceased to be. As far as the Doctor and his companions could ascertain, nothing of significance had been deleted. The cloisters were a hexagonal colonnade, part of a tranquil area not far from the console room. The sound of trickling water was coming from somewhere, its rhythm infinitely more soothing than the normal background hum of the TARDIS engines.

'It affected me.'

'Of course it did,' Nyssa consoled him.

'It's more than sentiment: you might say that the TARDIS is an aspect of me, just as I am an –' The Doctor glanced into an ornamental pool and his attention stuck there. 'Do you think it's changed?' He looked up at his companion. 'My hair I mean?'

He turned his attention back to the water, as if he was trying to scry the answer. Nyssa was unsure how to respond. Three days ago the Doctor had been a middle-aged man, with a craggy face and curly, greying hair. She had watched him fall from a gantry many hundreds of feet in the air, run over to him, seen his broken body, wept for him. Then, for reasons she still didn't fully understand, his body had changed: melted, then resolved into a new form. Now the Doctor appeared half a lifetime younger. Nyssa sat beside him, and looked over his shoulder into the pool. The Doctor's face appeared reflected in the water, smiling at her.

'It's just that I'm sure that my hair was *longer* yesterday.' The Doctor tugged a strand down from his fringe. 'It's probably a side-effect of the regeneration . . . or perhaps a trick of the light. Never mind, eh?' He poked the surface of the water experimentally, and his face rippled and dissolved. The Doctor turned his attention to Nyssa, apparently untroubled.

'You seem to have made a full recovery,' she observed. Immediately after his transformation the Doctor had been unable to walk unaided and his memory had been erratic. Within hours he had regained most of his faculties. Now, a few days after the event, his personality had stabilized. Nyssa could see much of the old Doctor in the new version. He had lost none of his wisdom and benevolence. It exhilarated Nyssa, reminding her of Tremas, her late father.

'I'll never fully recover,' the Doctor said matter-of-factly after a moment's silence. 'I died, and death is not something you recover from. As you have learnt, at far too young an age.'

Nyssa stared at the ancient stone ceiling. 'Traken has gone. My people celebrated life, and accepted death. I intend to continue that tradition. I am not a morbid person.'

'No,' the Doctor admitted, 'you aren't.'

Nyssa changed the subject. 'Why are the cloisters made from stone?'

The Doctor seemed to consider the question for a moment, puzzlement on his face. 'Why shouldn't they be?' he asked finally.

'But all the other walls in the ship are made from . . .' Nyssa faltered. 'What are they made from?'

The Doctor smiled forgivingly. 'The cloisters are among the very oldest parts of the TARDIS. Everything else grew round them.'

21

'Metaphorically,' Nyssa noted.

'Yes, that's right, metaphorically. And literally too, of course. Now, I think it's high time we got Tegan home.' The Doctor stood, dusting his frock-coat down and adjusting the vegetable pinned to his lapel. 'The TARDIS will seem very different without her. In a way, of course,' he noted softly, 'she's been here for a lifetime.'

Before Nyssa could reply, the TARDIS lurched, throwing her off the bench and into a thick stone pillar. The TARDIS righted itself, once again sending Nyssa sprawling. The Doctor bent down to help her up.

'Are you all right?'

Nyssa nodded, brushing her hair back into place. 'What happened?'

The Doctor's brow furrowed. 'I'm not sure.'

Tegan's eyes were fixed on the TARDIS console. Her heart was still racing. She didn't pretend to understand what had buffeted the TARDIS. The ship still appeared to be in flight: the readouts were constantly changing and lights were flashing, the crystalline column in the centre continued to rise and fall rhythmically. Most telling of all, there was a real sense of motion. They must have hit a pocket of turbulence, just like planes did every so often. Yeah, right.

The truth was that Tegan didn't want to think too hard about exactly what the TARDIS was doing. The ship was way out of her league, an alien technology millions of years ahead of Earth in the twentieth century. Tegan was getting used to the impossible. She couldn't even begin to understand why the TARDIS was bigger on the inside than the outside, but had little choice but to accept it. She could get her head around that, anyway. Once you were inside the gleaming console room, it was easy enough to forget that you'd stepped into what looked like a battered old British police box. But what really unnerved Tegan was that she couldn't begin to imagine how a time–space machine moved, what precisely it was travelling through. The only way she could picture it was as a police box flying through space, like a rocket, but the image seemed faintly ridiculous.

Tegan wasn't the Astronomer Royal, but she watched the telly: space probes from Earth were beginning to explore the solar system. The new space shuttle could orbit the Earth in ninety minutes, that was ten times faster than Concorde. But it would take the space shuttle hundreds, perhaps thousands of years to reach the nearest star. According to Einstein, the fastest that anything could travel was the speed of light: 186,000 miles a second. Her year twelve science teacher had said that the speed of light was a constant that underpinned the way the universe worked. If the shuttle could fly that fast, it would be able to whiz around the Earth nine times a second, which seemed plenty fast enough for Tegan. But it would take a spaceship travelling at the speed of light four years to reach the nearest solar system. The TARDIS travelled to other galaxies, even other universes, in a matter of moments. The Doctor had mentioned once that his ship had a 'lightspeed overdrive', and with just those two words he had casually invalidated the whole of human physics.

'You can't fly it, you know. It was the Master who guided the ship to Castrovalva.'

'I'm perfectly well aware of that,' Tegan replied curtly.

'From what I've seen of Earth in your time, I doubt you even begin to understand how the ship works.' What infuriated her most of all was that Adric wasn't trying to be cruel, he thought he was making a reasonable point. He was sitting cross-legged on the floor by the hatstand, scratching equations into a notebook with a stubby pencil.

'And you do, I suppose?'

Adric looked up from his notepad for the first time. 'Gallifreyan technology is very advanced, but if you understand block transfer computation and realize that TARDISes have an infinite amount of mass and energy at their disposal, the maths involved is surprisingly straightforward.'

Tegan bristled, determined to say something perceptive. 'The TARDIS isn't infinite any more, we jettisoned a quarter of it.'

Adric just chuckled.

Before Tegan could reply, the Doctor and Nyssa bustled into the console room.

'Good, good. You've not touched anything.'

'I wouldn't know where to start.'

'No, you wouldn't.' When the Doctor said it, the remark was almost comforting.

'What the hell happened?' Tegan demanded to know. 'Are we still heading for Heathrow?'

'To answer your questions in order: I don't know and I don't know.' The Doctor dashed around the console, glancing at settings, flicking levers. 'But at least now we've stopped. Um, that's odd: a syonic pulse.' He cancelled the readout with the flick of a switch.

Adric had shuffled to his feet and reached the console. 'So where are we?'

The Doctor's eyes flashed. 'See for yourself.'

He twisted a control, and the scanner shutter slid open. Together they watched an alien world as it rolled beneath them. Tegan gazed at its image on the scanner. The TARDIS imaging system gave a very good impression of scale. This near, they could only see a section of the planet. It was a brilliant soap-powder white. Meteorites tumbled into the gravity well, incandescing as they hit the atmosphere. Aurorae danced in the ionosphere. Below, grey clouds drifted by, looking as if they had been daubed onto the atmosphere with a thick brush. She watched awestruck as a hurricane swept across a wide plain. Despite these isolated examples of violence, the overall impression was serenity, timelessness.

'That isn't Heathrow,' Tegan noted. No one listened to her. The planet was beautiful, it was a sight that no other Earth person had ever seen before, nor would they in Tegan's lifetime. But it wasn't home.

Information was pouring across one of the readouts on the console. Nyssa began to examine it. The Doctor joined her.

'Why don't you read out loud?' he suggested.

'I'm not sure I understand it yet.'

'You'll never know unless you try,' smiled the Doctor.

Nyssa started reading, 'Distance from star 107.9 Million Miles, Gravity 98% Earth Normal, atmospheric density slightly thinner, radiation slightly higher, the year is 413

Earth days long, local day is 16.9 hours. A very low surface temperature. Some evidence of industrial pollution.'

Adric was at another control panel. 'We're way off course, Doctor.'

The Doctor bobbed across and peered at the indicators. 'So we are.'

'Do you know where we are?' Tegan asked.

The Doctor was at the scanner controls again. The picture zoomed out, and now the whole planet was visible, not just a section.

'Still in Earth's galaxy, many centuries in your future. That planet has been settled by your descendants.'

'How can you be sure?'

'You see that narrow black band?' The Doctor indicated the screen. The equator of the planet was marked out just as it would be on a globe, a neat line dividing the planet into northern and southern hemispheres. 'The planet is extremely cold. At the poles elements like oxygen and nitrogen that are gases on Earth are solid: they've become frozen into ice. If you were to set foot at the pole, the temperature of your body would cut through the ice like a blowtorch and you'd burn down hundreds of metres. Now, at the equator, the planet is much warmer, just like it is on Earth. When humans arrived here, naturally they settled at the equator. Over the years, the settlements grew from villages into cities, but new building only spread out along that narrow strip where the climate is comfortable for humans. Now it's just one big urban area.'

'And people can't live anywhere else?' Now it was Nyssa and Adric's turn to look confused. From what Tegan could gather, they'd both come from planets with stable, Mediterranean climates.

'Sure,' Tegan said, looking at Adric in particular. 'It sounds like Australia.'

The Doctor frowned. 'In what way?'

'All the big cities lining the coast, everything else a desert. Too hot, too cold, what's the difference?'

The other three opened their mouths to explain, but before they could two men were standing in front of them, an inch or so from the ground. They wore identical stiff

25

black robes, their faces were angular. One moved a little closer to the Doctor, and made an odd gesture, a stroke of the hand that could have been a greeting or a salute. Their robes were flapping, as if they were standing in the middle of a storm. They turned away and then they were gone.

'Did you see them?' the Doctor asked, striding over to where the apparitions had stood. Everyone had. The Doctor waved his hand over the exact spot. There was no lasting trace of them, and it was already tempting to believe that they were a trick of the light.

'Doctor!' Adric called, clearly worried.

The Doctor was bending down, examining the floor. 'Mmm?'

'We're moving again.'

'No, no. Quite impossible.' He didn't look up.

'The column's going up and down,' Adric insisted.

The Doctor glanced over his shoulder. Within a second he was at the console. 'The TARDIS has automatically initiated landing procedures and locked out the controls. Extraordinary.'

The column ground to a halt and there was a resonant chime from deep beneath the floor.

The TARDIS had landed in a narrow alleyway. The Doctor stepped out into an inch of snow. He pulled his overcoat tightly around him and ventured out a few feet. Nyssa, Tegan and Adric emerged in turn. They had all managed to find winter clothing that fitted them in the TARDIS wardrobe: Nyssa was in a tailored cashmere coat, Adric had found a parka and a fur hat with earmuffs, Tegan was wearing a fur coat over her air hostess uniform.

'This is as warm as it's going to get, then?' The air was dry, desiccated by the bitter cold, and it almost hurt to breathe it. How much colder it must seem to a human.

'Yes, Tegan,' the Doctor said patiently. 'We've landed at the equator, in that city I showed you. It's late afternoon by the look of it.'

'I'm glad I packed my legwarmers. So what do we do now?'

The Doctor held up his wristwatch. 'This is a time sensor,

26

it detects disturbances in the time field. With it I ought to be able to track anything capable of deflecting the course of a TARDIS.'

'Do you have another sensor?' Nyssa asked brightly.

The Doctor frowned. 'Yes, in the TARDIS. Why?'

'If we split up into two groups, we could cover twice as much ground.'

The Doctor brightened, admiring such a practical approach. 'You're right of course. Adric and I will go, er, that way. You girls can go the other.' He fished his key from his pocket and slotted it into the lock. It didn't turn. He tried again.

'Is it frozen?' Tegan asked. 'Try heating up the key.'

The Doctor stepped back. 'Thank you, Tegan, but I rather think the TARDIS has shut us out.'

'Why would it do that?'

'I don't know. TARDISes are telepathically linked to their owners, but the old girl isn't giving me any clues.'

'Well, she wouldn't,' Adric remarked.

'And why not?' the Doctor asked sharply.

'Well, you're not its owner, are you? Not really. Romana told me that you stole it.'

The Doctor bristled. 'That was a long time ago.'

'Has the TARDIS ever locked you out before?' Nyssa asked quickly.

'Never.' The Doctor looked up, and then around. 'But I can take a hint. She's trying to defend herself against something.'

'Those men we saw in the console room?' Adric suggested.

'Possibly,' the Doctor said guardedly. 'Likely, in fact. I have the feeling they have something to do with my past. My future, or my past. I've never . . .' His mind raced, trying to place them. He'd never seen them before, but something about them reminded him . . .

'Are you all right, Doctor?'

He shook his head, as if to clear it. 'The sooner we find those time disturbances, the sooner we can leave.' The Doctor walked to the end of the alleyway, his companions trooped along behind him.

They looked out over a city densely packed with tower-blocks, none of them more than a couple of dozen storeys high. The ground was criss-crossed with roadways and monorail tracks. The city thinned out quickly, it couldn't have been more than a couple of miles wide, but stretched out over the horizon. There was a range of mountains on the horizon in the other direction, and just before that great factories were belching out plumes of black smoke that drifted towards the city across the grey sky. Snow billowed across the landscape, all but blotting out the pale winter's sun. Little else appeared to be moving. There was the smell of gasoline in the wind.

Acting as a focus, drawing the eye across the city towards it, there was a statue of a young woman with a staff in one hand, an orb in the other. She was tall and broad-shouldered, like an athlete. The overwhelming impression was of power. A stone cloak wrapped over her shoulder almost preserved the statue's modesty, but also emphasized wide hips and a generous bosom. The statue's shadow reached the raised roadways at the edge of the park in which it stood. It wasn't the largest structure in the city, some of the newer tower blocks were almost twice the size, but somehow it dominated the skyline. The Doctor brought it to his companions' attention.

'It's about the size of the Statue of Liberty, wouldn't you say, Tegan?'

'I wouldn't know.'

'What, never been to New York on a stopover? I thought that was the sort of thing that air hostesses did as a matter of routine.'

'I never got the chance to be an air stewardess, if you remember,' Tegan replied scornfully. The Doctor looked away feeling guilty.

'She's beautiful. Who is she?' Nyssa asked.

'That, Nyssa, is a statue of the Divine Empress, Glory of the Earth Empire, the most powerful single being in the galaxy. It's a somewhat idealized portrayal,' he added. 'The memorial architecture of the mid-Imperial period is a fascinating subject. Believe it or not, most colony worlds have a statue of the Empress on a similar scale. They all use a similar iconography: the orb is a representation of the Earth, as one might guess. If one looks carefully, you'll see the cloak is patterned with an elaborate map of the galaxy. The staff represents the various –'

'Fascinating,' Tegan observed dryly, cutting him off. The Doctor glared at her.

'What's the brooch?' Adric asked. Now the Doctor looked, he saw that the cloak was loosely fastened at the right shoulder by a circular clasp. He peered at it carefully. 'It's a heraldic device. A chequy disk, plain annular without. I recognize the design from somewh– Is something the matter, Tegan?'

Her arms were crossed firmly over her chest and she was stamping her feet. 'Doctor, it's freezing. Couldn't we continue the lecture inside somewhere?'

The Doctor was genuinely concerned. 'Yes, yes, of course. There's a hotel just up the road,' he pointed it out, 'so why don't you and Nyssa head there, and book us all some rooms?' He reached into his pocket and tossed over a drawstring purse. Nyssa caught it.

'What will you two be doing?' Tegan asked suspiciously. Although she was shivering, the Doctor could tell that she still didn't want to be left out of any action.

'Well, Adric and I will be looking for the time disturbances. We'll start the search here, in this block, and then we'll work our way systematically over to you at the hotel. It should take about an hour or so, but if we're late then don't worry about us.'

Nyssa opened her mouth, presumably to volunteer her services, but Tegan had grabbed her arm. 'Come on.' The Doctor watched Tegan drag away her companion.

Tegan only let go of Nyssa's arm when they were at the foot of the hotel steps, nearly ten minutes later. The building had an imposing façade, in an almost Art Deco style. Although it had been built centuries in her future, Tegan found it almost old-fashioned. Like most of the buildings, the hotel had dark patches staining the brickwork and the windows that weren't boarded over were dirty. She had expected the city to be futuristic: bold glass and concrete with sweeping curves and huge towers and clean roadways. More like Canberra. She looked up at the colourful words that hung in the air in front of the building as if by magic.

'The Imperial,' she observed.

'Who are those people?' Nyssa asked. Tegan turned. Three figures in chunky blue uniforms stood at the corner of the street. They looked like medieval knights, with shoulder and wrist guards. They wore full helmets, and black, half-length robes. They were talking amongst themselves, shifting from foot to foot. All the time they were looking away from each other, watching the street. They wore sidearms. Tegan found them a little unnerving.

'They must be the local police,' Tegan concluded warily.

'The what?'

'Don't tell me: there weren't any policemen on Traken.'

'I . . . think so. We called them Fosters.'

'Now you're making *me* feel homesick,' Tegan muttered. 'Let's get inside.'

They climbed the stairs and stepped through the revolving door. It was warm inside, enough to make Tegan dizzy for a moment. She shrugged off her coat and looked around. Centuries in her future a hotel lobby still looked like a hotel lobby. The room was a picture of faded grandeur: the weak sunlight had begun to bleach the rich maroon and gold wallpaper, a couple of crude electrical junction boxes had been fastened to the ceiling. The smart businessmen huddled around the low tables seemed out of place. Over the years a path had been worn in the carpet from the door to the reception desk. Tegan found herself trudging along it.

A row of metal torsos, like shop window dummies, but with smooth egg-shaped heads, were fixed to the desktop. Sculpture, Tegan thought, until she and Nyssa reached the desk and the nearest frame spun on its axis, its arms opening in a gesture of greeting. It was an automaton of some kind, a robot.

'Welcome to the Imperial Hotel, ladies. How may I help?' It had a plummy masculine voice which was slightly too upbeat for its surroundings, and a little too supercilious for Tegan's liking.

30

'We'd like to book two twin rooms please,' Nyssa announced, apparently unfazed by a mechanical concierge.

The robot's head twisted, and it registered both of them in turn. 'But there are only two of you.'

'We have two companions.' Tegan explained, getting into the spirit of things. 'They will be joining us shortly.'

'I understand,' the robot said. There was a brief whirring noise. 'Your rooms are being prepared. Would you like a meal or beverage while you wait?'

'That would be lovely, thanks,' Tegan replied. A holographic arrow pointed them to a table in a nearby alcove. They followed it, and sat squashed together on a white leather sofa. A spherical drone bobbed over and served them coffee.

'Do robots do all the work now?' Tegan asked. She knew that Nyssa was from a different galaxy, and so she'd never been to this place or time, but she didn't seem half as bewildered as Tegan was feeling.

Nyssa smiled. 'Most civilizations have a phase in which they are dependent upon machines. Traken outgrew that stage around eleven thousand years ago, but on many planets, robots develop sentience and are granted full citizenship. That isn't always the way it happens, of course: the six-million-year-old civilization of Troxos 4 collapsed when their robot servants –' Tegan's mind began to drift. Her attention had been drawn by a man sitting at a nearby table. He was only a couple of years older than her, and was tall, well over six foot, with a bodybuilder physique and square jaw. He wore a neatly tailored, collarless, grey suit. He looked like a pilot, or an actor. She peered over her menu at him, half-trying to catch his eye.

'– but, of course, it doesn't take much intelligence to provide drinks, serve simple meals and ask if people want their cushions adjusting,' Nyssa concluded.

'I'll try not to take that personally,' Tegan said. 'What do you think that man is doing?'

'He looks as though he is calling over a waiter,' Nyssa suggested prosaically. 'Yes, look.'

A man – a real human man – in a grey tunic was bringing over a steel box that looked a bit like a telephone.

31

He placed it on the blond's table then left him to his business.

'Cheers mate,' the large man called out cheerfully. 'Catch yer later, cobber.' He chuckled nasally to himself.

'Tegan!' Nyssa exclaimed. 'That man's an Australian!'

3

Off the Rails

'It's very odd.'

After over an hour of trying, the Doctor had failed to locate even the slightest trace of temporal disturbance. They had ended up sitting on a bench under the lengthening shadow of the Empress Statue. They were on a raised platform in the middle of the park, with a peculiar icy u-shaped roadway running straight through it and on in a straight line as far as the eye could see in both directions. The platform must have been about fifty metres long. The whole length was covered with a transparent canopy which kept off the snow, but this hadn't prevented a layer of ice from forming on the platform or moss growing on the roof of the canopy. Adric reckoned that the canopy was relatively new – built in the last decade or so – and that the rest of the platform was a lot older, although how much older he didn't want to guess. The Doctor shook the time sensor, but it remained stubbornly silent. He slipped it from his wrist and reached into his frock coat for the sonic screwdriver.

'It isn't broken is it?'

'No.' There was a streak of impatience in the Doctor's voice. 'I'm simply trying to recalibrate it.'

'Sorry I spoke.' Adric decided it was time to stretch his legs. He was used to the cold by now, but night was drawing in, and temperatures were falling. He didn't particularly feel like staying outside any longer than he had to. The park appeared in evening shades of pale blue and grey. Around the park, the city itself was bathed in the grey-orange of sodium lighting.

There was only one other person around, a middle-aged woman in a grey fur coat standing at the other end of the platform. She was carrying a large bag, and kept walking out to the edge of the platform, looking down the roadway and checking the chronometer on her wrist. Adric briefly considered walking over to start a conversation with her, but decided against it. Instead he looked at one of the brightly coloured posters mounted on the canopy walls.

'Nyssa and Tegan will be getting bored of waiting.' The thought amused Adric.

'I'm sure they'll cope,' the Doctor responded automatically.

Adric's attention was drawn by a camera mounted on a stubby post about three metres away. It rotated, following Adric as he walked along.

'We're being watched,' he announced.

The Doctor didn't look up. 'So we are. Try not to do anything illegal.'

Adric walked towards the post. The camera continued to follow him.

'About time, mate. I thought I'd been stood up.'

The loud Australian had met up with another colleague, a local who was looking around nervously. Luckily he didn't notice the two young women in the corner staring at them. The colleague was a small, rat-faced man, wearing a grey tunic. He was pacing nervously on the spot, his head turning from side to side.

'G'day mate. Calm down, you look like you're dying for the dunny. Pull up a stool. D'ya wanna drink? Something to wet yer wallaby?'

Tegan had been watching all this, her arms folded over her chest. She was getting redder and redder by the minute. Nyssa could feel anger radiating from her. 'He's not an Australian,' Tegan insisted, not for the first time.

'But his accent is —'

'It's nothing like mine,' Tegan snarled before Nyssa could even finish.

'Your speech patterns share many characteristics,' Nyssa pointed out reasonably, as she poured Tegan a cup of coffee and unwrapped another packet of complimentary biscuits. 'The nasal whine, the use of colourful idiosyncratic colloquialisms and neologisms.'

'Rack off! That performance is a crude, racist . . .' Tegan's voice trailed away. Nyssa had learnt that Tegan – and perhaps all humans – often found it difficult to put their emotions into words. 'I'm surprised he's not wearing a cork hat and hasn't brought a sheep along to shear. "Wet your wallaby"?'

'But why would he *pretend* to be an Australian?' Nyssa asked soothingly.

'That's what I plan to find out.' Tegan moved to get up.

'Tegan!' Nyssa gasped, pulling her back down. 'What exactly do you intend to do?'

'He's up to no good, I know it. He keeps pretty shifty-looking company.'

Nyssa turned her attention back to the two men. The Australian was passing over a small paper bag. The rat-faced man weighed it in one hand, opening it up and sneaking a look before pocketing it. Finally, he handed over another package. Within seconds he had scurried away deep into the hotel, following a sign marked 'Public Transmat'.

'Whazza matter, cobber?' the Australian shouted after him, making a few of the other guests turn. 'Don't ya trust me, sport?'

Tegan fumed.

'What possible motive has he got?' Nyssa asked again.

The question did not appear to concern Tegan. She stood, shaking off Nyssa's grip and stormed over to the Australian's table.

But he had gone.

Staring up at the camera, Adric walked straight into a little man with a pinched face, who glared at him. Adric stepped back nonchalantly. The man stuffed his hands in the pockets of his tunic and walked up the platform. The woman had been waiting for him, Adric realized. Adric turned back to the Doctor, idly wondering where the man had come from.

'It's very high security for a . . . what is this place?'

'It's a skitrain station. That pedestal that the camera's mounted on has the signalputer in it. The local network and points are controlled from that little box. I would imagine they've had a problem with vandals in the past.' The Doctor

35

waved a hand in the general direction of the roadway.

'What's a skitrain?'

'It's a cross between a bobsleigh and a steam train.' Adric was none the wiser. The Doctor explained that a train was an engine that pulled a series of carriages behind it. On Earth, they would have had wheels, here everything ran on sleds and ski blades.

'But what's it for?'

'Moving people and materials around.'

'It sounds a very primitive form of transport.'

'Mostly obsolete now,' the Doctor said nostalgically. 'But one can't transmat everything.' He indicated an ornate hut set in the park, fifty yards or so away from the platform.

'I'll take your word for it.' Adric still found it difficult to picture a skitrain, but he could see the advantages of propelling a vehicle along a frictionless runway. The Doctor had returned to his tinkering.

In the absence of anything better to do, Adric trudged towards the hut. It had a dull metal door, with a control panel. There was also a notice:

PUBLIC TRANSMAT – Please read the instructions. This facility is provided by HKI Industries, Phobos, and is subject to their terms and conditions (copies available on request). This transmat must only be connected to Pentalion-compatible teleportation devices by an approved engineer. Failure to do so will invalidate the warranty. In such an event, HKI will not be liable for the consequences. If in doubt, ask your dealer. This does not affect your rights under the Particle Matter Transmission (Deregulation) Act, MMCXX. If in difficulty please ring our helpline.

It didn't give the number. Next to the panel was a brightly coloured directory of other Transmat sites. Adric peered at them. This station was 'Empress Park', predictably enough. The other names ('Scientifica', 'Imperial Hotel', 'Offworld Zoo', 'Spaceport Terminal One') meant nothing to him, and many of the other locations were simply identified by serial numbers. A couple had been scratched out. Adric managed to read one of the obliterated names: 'Pryanishnikov Way-station'.

The Doctor was stepping over to join him. Adric's boot scuffed against something on the floor. A metal object was lying at the base of the pedestal. He bent down. Whatever it was had fallen to the ground and become half-buried in the snow. It could only have been there for a short time, as hardly any new snow had fallen on it. It was a metal object, the shape and size of an egg. He picked it up. There was a plug on one side, and it looked like a component of a machine, a computer peripheral perhaps.

'Doctor, what do you think this is?'

'Mmm?'

As the Doctor came over, there was a high-pitched whine from inside the pagoda. The metal door slid open with a pneumatic hiss, and there was a blast of warm air. A huge figure wearing blue armour was framed in the doorway. Instinctively Adric pocketed the silver egg.

'Excuse me,' the new arrival said, stepping from the booth. He wore a helmet that electronically filtered his voice. The armour was trimmed with gold. 'Could you move on, please?'

The Doctor looked up at him. 'Of course, officer. Might I know why?'

'Security, sir.'

'Of course. What other reason is there?'

'There's been a bomb scare, sir.'

The Doctor perked up. 'Well, might I help?'

'That's quite all right, sir, there's a team on the way. A team of *experts*.'

'Come on, Adric.' The Doctor led him away, down the platform, towards the exit.

'Who is that?' Adric asked as soon as they were out of earshot.

'He's an Adjudicator. The Adjudicators' Bureau is the intergalactic police force, committed to fairness and justice. A member of the Bureau is often called in when an intractable legal dispute develops. They are renowned throughout the galaxy for their impartiality. All parties know that the Adjudicator will come to a just decision.'

'One Adjudicator can sort out an entire planet?'

'One Adjudicator. That's all it needs, generally.'

Adric would obviously have to spell it out for him. 'So what's so important about this one little skitrain station?'

The Doctor stopped in his tracks and looked down at Adric. 'I'm not sure.'

'And why did he want to move us on?'

'Well, I'm not sure about that, either.'

'You seem to be saying that rather a lot since your regeneration,' Adric suggested sulkily.

The Doctor pretended not to hear. 'I intend to find out, though.'

He stopped in his tracks, glancing over his shoulder at the Adjudicator, who was making his way towards the man and woman. 'That's far enough, I think. Can you feel the vibration?'

'No.' But now the Doctor had mentioned it, Adric could hear a new sound, a slight rumbling.

'It's the train.'

The Doctor tiptoed over to the camera pedestal, concealing himself from the Adjudicator. He motioned for Adric to follow. Once in place, they peeked around the corner. Adric looked past the Adjudicator, past the couple at the other end of the platform. In the distance, the headlamp of the skitrain was visible, a single round disc of white light growing steadily larger. The train was still tiny. Adric watched it winding its way towards them.

Presumably to camouflage it as it travelled through the Arctic wastes outside the city, the train was a mottled grey with white patches. The engine had a solid squared-off shape designed for functionality rather than aesthetic appeal. It wasn't streamlined, but wasn't fast enough that it needed to be. There were half a dozen carriages, featureless boxes in the same colour scheme as the engine. They didn't have windows.

The train clattered towards them, almost sedately. Adric estimated that it was a kilometre or so away, travelling between sixty and seventy kilometres an hour. It was still about a minute away.

'What's it carrying?' Adric asked.

'Nuclear material?' the Doctor said. 'Military equipment? Something that can't be transmatted, at any rate. It's also', he added thoughtfully, 'something that the authorities don't want people to see.'

Adric glanced up at the platform. The Adjudicator had reached the people at the other end, the woman and the rat-faced man. He asked them to move on.

The woman drew a lightweight pistol from the folds of her coat and shot him. The armoured figure was bathed in light, and Adric almost believed that he saw the man's nervous system flashing through the armour as though he'd been pumped full of barium sulphate. The Adjudicator slumped, groaning as he fell, so he was unconscious rather than dead. The woman secreted the gun, and began scanning the area. The Doctor pulled Adric behind the camera pedestal, and clamped a hand over his mouth.

A conversation had started between the man and woman, and both the Doctor and Adric leant forward, straining to hear over the ever-increasing noise from the train. All they could catch was a sense of urgency. Panic in the case of the man, efficient concern from the woman. At about the same time it dawned on both the Doctor and Adric that the two were heading towards them.

They couldn't speak, so they resorted to gestures and mimes.

Adric held out his hands, palms upward and looked from side to side helplessly.

The Doctor shrugged.

Adric leant forward and silently mouthed a question.

The Doctor frowned.

Adric's shoulders slumped. A moment later, he pointed a finger towards the pedestal, then tapped his bottom eyelid, indicating his eye. *Should we take a peek?*

The Doctor shook his head quickly, then winced.

The woman's footsteps had stopped.

The Doctor pressed himself against the base of the pedestal.

Adric did the same.

'I'll get the access panel open.' Her voice was so close it startled Adric, but he managed to keep his lips squeezed together.

There was a mechanical whir. They must have opened

up the pedestal to get to the workings inside.

'Come on!' she insisted. 'The train is nearly here.'

'I can't find the override.'

The Doctor looked puzzled, but Adric knew what the man was looking for. He tugged the Doctor's sleeve and held up the silver egg.

The Doctor raised an eyebrow.

'I think I must have dropped it,' the man concluded. 'Without the override I can't tell the computer to stop the train, we'll have to abandon –'

'No,' the woman said firmly. 'This is our last chance to get in before the train reaches the pyramid's defence perimeter. I'd much rather try and stop the train now than have to mount a frontal assault.'

'You said that your friend had set up an escape route.'

'Yes, but it's a lot safer to stop the train here. We'll have a lot more time to play with here, and a lot less armed guards.'

'But without the override . . .'

'Shut up, Gemboyle. Better still, make yourself useful and jam that transmat. That'll buy us a little more time.'

The Doctor and Adric eased themselves out of the man's path as he scurried towards the pagoda. He turned back to the woman. 'Remember, it's carriage three.'

There was a crunch and scrape from behind the pedestal.

Adric leant round to catch a glimpse of the woman, to see what she was doing. She was kicking the park bench, trying to dislodge it. Adric watched her for a moment. She aimed a couple of powerful kicks at the leg of the bench, but it didn't budge. She bent down to examine it, to see how it was fastened to the platform. She began scrabbling at the base of the leg. Finally, she gave up, standing, turning to face the oncoming train.

To Adric's astonishment the Doctor was standing in front of her. 'Hello,' he said cheerily, 'I'm –'

He was bathed in light and fell.

'I don't care who you are, as long as you weigh more than twenty-five kilos, you'll do,' the woman scowled, pocketing her pistol. She rolled the Doctor's body off onto the icy track. He sloshed down the side, his

40

momentum causing him to slide a couple of metres down the track.

The Doctor was in the path of the train.

It was vast now, the front engine a rounded cylinder ten metres in diameter. The headlamp now poured light over the whole station, the clattering of the carriages reverberated around the platform. It wasn't travelling very fast, fifty kilometres an hour at most, but it was relentless: so big, so wide. The ground was shaking, the roar from the engines was blotting out every other sound, the glare from the light was dazzling now, almost bleaching out the Doctor's prone body. Adric calculated that the train would reach the Doctor in eight seconds.

'No!' Adric screamed, rushing forward.

Seven.

Adric leapt after the Doctor, trying to pull him clear.

Six.

The woman grabbed his shoulder.

Five.

She pulled him away from the edge of the platform.

Four.

'Not smart,' she yelled, restraining him.

'But the –' Adric's mind was racing, trying to open up possibilities. Thinking of a way to save the Doctor.

Three.

The Doctor was beginning to stir. Adric opened his mouth to shout. Anything he said was drowned out by the noise of the train.

Two.

The Doctor squinted in the glare of the train's light. He raised his hand, half to shield his eyes, half in an attempt to protect himself.

One.

The train had stopped and the engine noise was beginning to die down. Vents on the engine's roof opened and steam hissed from them, billowing across the park.

The woman said, 'Relax, kid. I needed to stop the train, but I managed to misplace the override. The train's able to detect an obstruction on the line. It brakes automatically when there's anything that weighs more than twenty-five

41

kilos in front of it. I tried using the park bench, but it wouldn't move. Your colleague was much more co-operative.'

'And you knew for a fact that it would be able to stop in time?' Adric demanded angrily.

'Yes, she did, Adric,' the Doctor's groggy voice drifted up. 'The train has an inertial damping system, using the same sort of gravitronics fitted to warships to stop people being squashed flat by superlight velocities.' Adric leant over the edge of the platform. The Doctor stood, centimetres from the front of the train, the light from the headlamp framing him like a spotlight. He prised off one of the array of small discs clipped to the front of the train in a triangular pattern and handed it to the woman. 'I was never really in any danger.'

'Gravity discs are one hundred per cent reliable,' the woman noted, holding up the disc so that Adric could see it. 'Well, almost. If they were totally reliable, I'd have jumped down myself.' The Doctor's face fell.

'I'm afraid I can't stop to chat. Please don't get in my way again.' The woman sprinted down the platform. Adric moved over to help the Doctor up.

'Well, don't just stand there, Adric, try to stop her.' The Doctor skated over to the edge of the platform and tried to gain enough footing to hoist himself back onto it. Adric nodded, and headed after her, slipping a little in the ice.

She had already reached the carriage, and was examining a sign on the side. Adric moved to get a better look at it, and her. She was small, no taller than he was, and was much slimmer. She was perhaps three times his age, but had spent the time well – her body was lean underneath that fur coat, and every action she made looked like a martial arts move. The woman was aware of his presence, but was untroubled by it. That in itself was enough of a deterrent to prevent Adric from trying to get any closer, let alone trying to stop her. On the third carriage, and only on that one, there was a sign bearing the same circular design that had appeared on the statue of the Empress. Next to it, there were a couple of smaller notices, bold geometric designs that were almost certainly hazard warnings of some kind.

The woman had reached into her bag, and was removing a

small reel of white tape. Expertly, she unwound about half of it, attaching it to the side of the carriage in a rough square.

'This is laserwire, so stand clear and look the other way,' she warned him, taking a couple of steps back. She had a control box in her hand, some kind of remote control.

Adric glanced up at the sky.

A pale blue slab was hovering just above the canopy. It was about six metres long, and three metres wide. Along its underside ran a word in large white letters: JUSTICE.

Adric instinctively shoved the woman aside. They both lost their footing in the ice, and tumbled over.

It saved their lives. An energy bolt sliced through the canopy above their heads, before punching a chunk out of the edge of the platform. A second bolt did the same, only closer. Shards of transparent plastic began clattering and plinking to the ground.

They half rolled, half scrambled to their feet. A third bolt smashed into the floor where they had been.

The woman's pistol had fallen from her coat. It was a chunky thing, with an oddly shaped grip. It appeared to be made from red plastic.

Adric grabbed it and aimed it at her.

The woman stepped back defensively, shaking her head, her eyes flashing with concern. Not for herself, but for him. Without knowing why, Adric dropped the gun.

An energy blast hit the side of the carriage. Whatever metal the train was built from absorbed the energy, but the sound was enough to shake Adric back to his senses.

A hatch opened on the side of the hovering object – an anti-gravity vehicle of some kind, Adric realized. Three armoured Adjudicators jumped from it into thin air. They were wearing jetpacks, the retros firing orange against the night sky. Ignoring gravity, they drifted through the hole in the canopy, landing as one on the platform, not even losing their foothold on the ice. They carried drawn blasters, and fanned out in a well-rehearsed move. Before their feet touched the ground, the air was full of light and pulsing chirps: blaster fire exploding on the platform and along the side of the train.

Behind Adric, the woman had scooped up her pistol and

dived into the gap between two of the carriages. Three energy bolts tried to follow her through, but couldn't, and they impacted on the side. The three Adjudicators hurled past Adric, ignoring him. One skidded to a halt, and knelt to check the Adjudicator that the woman had stunned. The others continued after his attacker. The two Adjudicators reached the gap between the carriages. They hesitated before moving to either side of the gap. One raised his gun to his shoulder, the other moved into a firing stance.

The woman appeared from behind the carriage, grabbed the nearest Adjudicator's wrist and kicked his feet from under him. He fell backwards onto the track. His jetpack fired, and in less than a second he had been propelled down the runway.

The other Adjudicator watched his colleague vanish, so he didn't notice the woman knocking him out with a swift chop to the back of his neck, right at the base of his helmet.

Adric viewed all this with his mouth open.

The third Adjudicator, having made his colleague comfortable, was on his feet now. The woman leapt for him, and a high kick to his breastplate knocked him back down. He didn't rise. Now she had beaten all three of the Adjudicators, but there were sirens sounding. Three more hovercopters were converging on the park, hurtling low over the snow. After a moment's consideration, the woman changed direction, spinning on her heel and rushing down the platform.

The Doctor hoisted himself out of the runway, pulling himself upright. Within seconds he had jogged past the woman and whirled to face her.

'Hello again.' This time, the Doctor caught her wrist before she had a chance to draw her stun pistol.

'Oh, get out of my way,' she scowled, bringing her knee up hard between the Doctor's legs. He gawped at her for a moment before sinking to the floor. Adric stepped forward, blocking her way. Before he could react she had tossed him over her shoulder. He landed heavily on his companion.

Adric scrabbled to his feet. 'Are you all right?'

'No,' the Doctor groaned. Adric moved to help him up.

'Where's she gone?' the Doctor demanded.

44

Adric spun around. 'She's vanished.'

'People don't just . . . unless!' The Doctor pulled himself up and raced over to the transmat pagoda, losing his footing a little on the ice. The rat-faced man was beckoning the woman. She was moving as fast as a sprinter, and she jumped the last six feet, right into the transmat cubicle. The Doctor was close behind her. He narrowly avoided trapping his fingers in the door as it slid shut. There was a high-pitched whine from inside the booth. The Doctor beat a fist at the door with frustration. Adric reached the pagoda just as the dematerialization cycle completed and the door slid open again.

The Doctor stepped into the tiny cubicle and rapidly located the control panel. A plastic box the size of a packet of cigarettes had been attached to it. The Doctor tapped it.

'A security override,' he said, unplugging the box and turning it over in his hands.

'What does it do?'

'It gives whoever has it priority clearance on the transmat network. Adjudicators and maintenance engineers use them in emergencies.'

'So where did that woman get it?'

'I have no idea,' the Doctor said, slipping the box into his pocket. 'I imagine she stole it from an Adjudicator.'

'And where is she?'

'The device was set to delete the co-ordinates when she'd gone. I imagine it's wiped the whole log. She could be anywhere on the planet, or even on a ship in low orbit.'

'So what can we do?'

The Doctor looked around. 'Nothing. For the moment.' He stepped out of the cubicle, shaking the dust from his shoes.

'*Gah!*'

The Doctor felt a sudden stabbing pain in one of his stomachs. Another attack? No, the only person around was . . .

Adric loomed over him. 'What's the matter?'

The Doctor couldn't breathe, he couldn't speak. An insistent bleeping started up.

'What's that sound?'

The time sensor on my wrist going haywire, the Doctor didn't say.

The Doctor was on his knees, trying to force air into his lungs.

Three men in stiff black robes were surrounding them. They moved slowly, carefully. One raised his hand. The Doctor could see the city lights in the distance, shining through the apparitions.

'Can you see them?' the Doctor rasped at Adric. They were looking down at him curiously, regarding him with disdain. They seemed oblivious to everything else, including his companion. There was cruelty in their faces, but something else, too. Concern?

'See who? Doctor! Who?' Adric asked. His voice seemed to be echoing. The signals from the time sensor were coming so close together now that they merged into a continuous tone. It seemed to be getting louder, but the Doctor knew that the device was set at a constant volume and pitch.

It drowned out the sounds of the wind, the city, the voice of his companion, the beating of his hearts, his thoughts, his and others' memories.

'Blood, blood on my hands,' the Doctor bawled. He could see it, thick red blood dripping from his fingers, soaking into the sleeves of his overcoat. But whose blood? His own? His companions'?

'Doctor, please say something!' Adric shrieked.

They had gone. The Doctor screwed his eyes closed, summoning all his mental resources, trying to shut out the pain. Only then did he realize that the pain wasn't there any more and that the only thing he could feel was the cold seeping through his clothes where he had fallen into the snow. There was the sound of distant music drifting across the city. A mile away a hovercopter sounded its horn in a sluggish river of moving air traffic. Nearer, dogs were barking. Nearer, there were people heading home after a night on the town, singing and laughing. Nearer, there were the sirens.

The Doctor could hear the sound of energy weapons

46

powering up. The Doctor's eyes snapped open. Adric was kneeling in front of him, a gun to his head. The muzzle of another weapon was pressed to the Doctor's temple.

A dozen Adjudicators surrounded them, their sidearms levelled.

Part Two

Scientifica

4

Take Me to Your Leader

A dozen Adjudicators surrounded them, their sidearms levelled.

A couple grabbed the Doctor's shoulders from behind, and hoisted him to his feet. The Adjudicators weren't speaking, but communicated via tiny hand gestures and movements of their heads. These physical signals seemed to constitute an elaborate language in itself, one the Doctor didn't fully understand.

One of the armoured figures signalled that Adric should also be pulled up.

The Adjudicator that had given the order stepped forward. The gold trimming on his shoulderplates was more elaborate than his colleagues'. The Doctor couldn't determine his precise rank, but he was very senior, far too important for field operations. Half the Adjudicators seemed to be his bodyguards. They were preoccupied with the surroundings, on the lookout for assassins.

Another Adjudicator searched them for weapons. They weren't carrying any.

Satisfied, the senior officer reached up to his neck and, with a pneumatic hiss, removed his helmet, handing it to a subordinate. Underneath the armour he was a middle-aged man, with thick jowls and pale blue eyes. His brown hair was thinning and his face was heavily lined. He looked more like a bank manager or a stockbroker than a military man. He held out a gloved hand. 'Adjudicator Provost-General Tertullian Medford.' A Provost-General would be in command of several thousand men, equivalent to a planetary garrison, so Medford must be one of the two or three most powerful people on the colony.

The Doctor smiled. 'I am the Doctor, and this is Adric.'

'I must apologize for any distress you might have

51

endured, and I'm afraid that you will have to remain here for a little while and answer some questions. Are you hurt?' The Doctor opened his mouth to speak, but Medford had already moved on. Before the Doctor could protest, the Provost had motioned for a medic to come forward. The Provost-General left them behind in order to survey the scene. Drones were circling the skitrain station, setting up a tape barrier – 'Do not cross'. Within the cordon, a dozen Adjudicators had set to work. Memory droids waddled around recording images of the scene, forensics experts dusted up samples. A couple of engineers were resetting the signalputer. Adjudicator Provost Medford moved among them.

'Are you all right now, Doctor?' Adric asked.

'Yes,' the Doctor said distractedly. The medic held a portable medical scanner just above his head.

'You collapsed,' Adric reminded him.

The Doctor hadn't forgotten. 'It had something to do with the time disturbance.'

'You could feel it?' Adric winced as the medical officer took a blood sample from his forearm with a tubular instrument.

'I'm sensitive to the subtlest distortions of the temporal field. That was more like being caught in a hurricane.' The medic took a tissue sample from the back of the Doctor's neck.

'And it was that distortion that knocked the TARDIS off-course?'

'We're jolly lucky it didn't dash us against the planet like a sailing ship against the rocks,' the Doctor said rubbing the back of his neck. 'But before you ask, no, I haven't a clue what caused it. There are very few forces in the universe that can deflect the course of a TARDIS. Very few.'

The train was beginning to edge forward. It gradually began picking up speed, and it was soon out of sight and earshot. This time it was escorted by a couple of armoured hovercopters.

'Like what?' Adric prompted the Doctor once it had gone.

'Well, off-hand I can't actually think of anything,' the Doctor admitted.

'The Keeper of Traken did.'

'I think we can safely rule him out as a suspect.' The Doctor turned his attention back to the clean-up operation unfolding around them. A holographic figure walked along the platform, like a ghost. Not like a real ghost, though. This was just a simulacrum, a computer's estimate of the woman, based on the size and depth of her footprints in the snow. It jumped from the platform, between imaginary carriages and derezzed. A forensic scientist made a note on an electronic notepad.

Medford was walking back towards them. He checked their condition with the medic, who was satisfied that they had suffered only superficial injuries.

Another Adjudicator began to take down their statements. Once again, the Doctor and Adric gave their names.

'What are your occupations?'

'Well,' the Doctor began, 'I am a scientist and Adric is a mathematician.' The Adjudicator took this down, without betraying a flicker of interest. Medford, though, leant closer to listen in. Adric related the events of the last quarter of an hour or so; the Doctor was content to stand back and listen. Adric did an admirable job, carefully omitting certain details that might be difficult to explain: quite why they were on the platform in the first place, the Doctor's time sensor and so on.

'What do you think the aim of the attack was?' the Adjudicator asked.

'An attempt to steal the train's cargo?' Adric suggested. 'I don't know to be honest. I think they were thieves.'

'A little more than that, lad,' the Provost-General smiled. 'This attack is part of a terrorist campaign to disrupt our peacekeeping operations on this planet. We've become used to the bomb threats and minor acts of sabotage.'

'There was a bomb warning?' the Doctor asked. He'd just noticed that the Provost wore a badge on his breastplate with the same grid design as the Empress statue and the skitrain carriage.

'No.'

'And there wasn't a bomb either, was there?'

Medford looked around thoughtfully, as if he was trying

53

to spot it. 'The bombers probably took it with them.'

'A rather risky strategy, surely. They could have been hoist by their own petard – literally.'

'They were removing the evidence.'

'Really? So if the bomb had gone off, they'd have stayed around to pick up all the bits? Your forensics team could have found all the clues they'd need in the debris.'

'Then they've kept hold of the bomb so that they can use it to murder more civilians. These people are killers, don't forget.'

'No one died here,' the Doctor noted. 'Indeed the woman was only carrying a stungun. I think she was more interested in getting a look inside the train than blowing it up.'

'That is your opinion.'

'With respect, Provost, you weren't there.'

'And with respect, Doctor, you weren't there when they bombed civilians and when they forced my flagship down in the mountains.'

'One way of settling the argument would be to look at the recording of the event,' Adric offered.

The Doctor and Medford both turned to face him. 'I beg your pardon?' the Provost asked quietly.

Adric pointed upwards. 'That camera must have had a pretty good view of the whole attack.'

With a gesture, the Provost ordered one of his men over to the pedestal to retrieve the recorder. After a moment, the technician returned, a mangled mass of plastic and metal in his hands.

'It was hit by a stray blast, sir. The memory cubes have been completely destroyed, the recording has been lost.'

'Oh, nonsense,' the Doctor insisted, taking the bundle from the technician. 'It needs a little work, that's all.' A couple of metal components clattered out of the Doctor's grasp onto the floor.

The Provost eyed him suspiciously. 'You could fix this?' The technician was also looking sceptical.

'Oh yes,' the Doctor said cheerily, turning it over in his hands, shedding more of the pieces. 'Given the right facilities and a little time.'

'We have state-of-the-art laboratories back at the Scientifica. We'll continue our investigation there.' Medford indicated an armoured hovercopter resting by the side of the transmat pagoda. They began making their way towards it, over the rubble. The Doctor looked back at the station, now a shattered metal framework and piles of concrete chunks.

'I wonder what Tegan and Nyssa are getting up to,' he said aloud as he rolled up his hat.

>GUESTS APPROACHING: IDENTIFY>GREET< 'Hello Miss Jovanka, Miss Nyssa.' >AWAIT RESPONSE< 'Er, hello. That man who's just been sitting over there.' >ROTATE 45 DEGREES<>IDENTIFY< 'Is he a guest at the hotel?' >CROSS-REFER: CURRENT REGISTER<>SPEAK< 'Yes, miss.' >AWAIT RESPONSE< 'Could you possibly tell me his name?' >SPEAK< 'His name is Bruce Jovanka, miss.' >AWAIT RESPONSE< 'I beg your pardon?' >REPEAT LAST< 'His name is Bruce Jovanka, miss.' >AWAIT RESPONSE< (Pause) 'That does it. Which room is he in?' >CROSS-REFER: PRIVACY PROTOCOL< >SPEAK< 'I can not give out that information, miss.' >AWAIT RESPONSE< 'Can't you, indeed?' >SPEAK< 'Personal information may only be given to close relatives, miss.' >AWAIT RESPONSE< 'I'm his (Pause) wife.' >ASSESS VERACITY: 95% PROBABILITY TRUTHFUL STATEMENT, BASED ON SURNAME AND VOCAL PATTERNS<>ACCESS GRANTED<>UPDATE CURRENT REGISTER<>SPEAK< 'Your husband is in room 74, Mrs Jovanka.' >AWAIT RESPONSE< 'May I have a key for that room, please?' >ISSUE KEY< >AWAIT RESPONSE< 'Thank you.' 'Tegan, come back.' >AWAIT RESPONSE<>NO RESPONSE<>TIME OUT<>STAND-BY<

The hovercopter hurtled over the city. They were about two hundred metres up, roughly following the route of the skitrain track. This high, it was clear how narrow the Strip was, only about a dozen blocks wide. The city was a mish-mash of architectural styles, centuries-old concrete buildings jostling with more elegant stone and brick structures. Adric was surprised how many of the buildings had fallen into ruin. A number of window panes had been boarded over, and it seemed that every other building had some scaffolding erected around it. In this climate, the people here must be constantly renovating buildings against frost-damage.

The Doctor was sitting beside him, looking ahead through the windscreen. The Provost-General and his aide were seated opposite, discussing a report. Adric could only catch snatches of their conversation over the roar of the hovercopter's engines.

'– ansmat network shut dow–'

'– dea how they –'

'– kov Waystation –'

'– traced the call back to a publi–'

Adric gazed out of the window. At the moment they were flying above a sluggish brown river. Adric could see black barges, their prows heavy triangular icebreakers, working their way along the waterway, loaded up with something underneath thick green tarpaulins. The river was half-frozen: Adric imagined that the pollutants that turned the water brown had also lowered its melting point. Either that, or the river had been thawed out by warm water discharged from factories or power stations.

There was a burst of conversation from the cockpit. The pilot was talking to air traffic control, broadcasting their security codes. Ahead of them, Adric could see the reason why: they were entering the airspace of a vast spaceport. It was a flat expanse of tarmac filling a circular area that spilled out over the edges of the Strip. In all it must have been about five miles in diameter. Hangars and docking pits ringed the perimeter, runways and launch pads criss-crossed the rest of the area. Among an armada of service craft, shuttles, workpods and tugs there was a handful of larger ships. Adric didn't recognize the designs, of course, but he appreciated their beauty. One of them in particular resembled a massive dragonfly, the winter sun glancing off the fluorescent metallic greens and blues of the hull and the translucent solar sails. Another ship was a long white tube, with green lettering up the side and a red docking clamp at the top.

56

'A Wondark ship,' the Doctor noted.

In the centre of the spaceport there was a cluster of needle-like spires, hundreds of metres high. They glinted pure white in the pale sunlight. Air traffic control, Adric guessed, and the buildings probably incorporated the departure lounges and office space for the spacelines. As they passed between two of the spires, the buildings changed, became more squat and functional. There were more spaceships docked on this side of the spaceport, but they were of a more uniform design. These were military ships. They were just as elegant as the others: the laws of aerodynamics dictated the shape that a ship travelling through an atmosphere had to be, but despite the streamlining they were less aesthetically appealing. Most were of the same oily blue as the Adjudicator's armour, although some of the smaller craft had been painted a camouflage grey. Virtually all had weaponry: laser cannons, missile batteries, bomb bays. In all, there were between two and three hundred vehicles.

Adric glanced across at the Provost-General, the man in command of all this hardware. The Adjudicator was studying their reactions carefully. Adric realized for the first time why they hadn't simply travelled across the city by transmat: this flight was a demonstration designed to impress upon them the might of the Adjudicators, and particularly the power and authority of their leader, the man sitting opposite them.

Then the spaceport was behind them and they were back in a residential area. They caught up with the skitrain. It was the same one the terrorists had tried to stop, there was little doubt of it: the mottled white and grey paint scheme made it stand out against the bolder brown and chrome buildings. Besides, it still had its armed escorts, two hovercopters like their own flying alongside. Their vehicle was on a higher flightpath, and it overtook the skitrain and its entourage now, surging onwards.

Medford leant over to the pilot and asked him something. Then he turned back to them.

'ETA at the Scientifica in one minute.'

Adric peered out of the windscreen. A pyramid had appeared on the horizon and was growing ever larger. Its

57

smooth black sides were broken by flat terraces – docking platforms and hanging gardens. The pyramid dwarfed the surrounding buildings, it was a couple of kilometres high at the apex. There was something regular about its construction that spoke of architectural perfection. If its dimensions had been even slightly different, Adric could imagine how incongruous, or even threatening, the dark structure might appear. Yet somehow the building achieved harmony with its surroundings, as if the most natural thing to find in this flat, snowblown landscape was an ebony pyramid the size of a mountain. As they got closer, Adric saw that a number of skitrain tracks ran inside the structure, disappearing into discreet tunnels. The Doctor was studying the pyramid, and although he would never admit as much, he was clearly impressed by it.

Beneath him, Adric felt the undercarriage of the hovercopter deploy and lock into place. The engine whine lowered in pitch and they began to slow down. He could hear the chatter of traffic control in the pilot's earphones now.

'Justice Alpha, slaving your autopilot to Scientifica Traffic Control.'

'Copy that Scientifica Traffic Control,' the pilot responded, releasing the controls. The Provost-General was already unfastening his safety harness.

'Docking chamber thirteen selected.' The hovercopter passed under an access stairway and into the body of the pyramid.

'It's a good job we're not superstitious,' the Doctor remarked cheerfully. Medford glared at him.

The hovercopter was flying through a large hangar area, one big enough to be holding around a dozen similar vehicles. Many sported Adjudication Bureau colour schemes, a handful had a more drab grey livery. The personnel milling around had a similar divide: there were a dozen or so Adjudicators here, many in full armour, but some in a lighter version of the same uniform – presumably technicians or administrative grades rather than combat troops. There were civilians here too: men and women in colour-coded tunics. Some were technicians, others appeared to be messengers or couriers.

The traffic control computer had allocated a space for them about halfway into the hangar. Landing lights began flashing there, more for the benefit of the hovercopter's passengers than for that of its flight computer. The vehicle eased into place, and a buzzer sounded.

'Docking procedure complete,' a synthesized female voice said. 'Welcome to Scientifica.' A light above the hatch lit up green. With a hydraulic hiss, the door slid open and a step unfolded itself. The Provost-General's aide left first, and even here he scanned the crowd for danger. The Provost-General was next, followed by the Doctor and Adric. The pilot detached himself from the controls and brought up the rear. An Adjudicator wearing the lightweight uniform hurried forward, holding out a black cloak for his commanding officer. With practised ease, Medford clipped it to the hooks on the collar of his armour.

'Justice by your side,' Medford intoned.

'And fairness be your friend.' Some sort of ritual greeting. The Adjudicator bowed his head. They moved out from the parking bay into the hangar itself.

In complete contrast to the dark exterior of the pyramid, the hangar was an airy space, painted in delicate pastels and greys. Natural light spilled into the room, dancing off the ceiling. The heavy machinery being used was clean: the cranes and lifters were electrically driven, drifting silently along on hoverfields. It was so clean in here, so free of the oil, grease and dirt usually associated with this sort of place, that much of the floor was covered in a plush carpet. Pleasant music, a gentle electronic rhythm suggesting busyness and efficiency, wafted across the hangar. The Provost-General led them to the lifts. Half a dozen Adjudicators saluted their commander as they crossed the room. Adric fought the urge to salute back.

'Excuse my ignorance,' the Doctor was saying, 'but what is the Scientifica?' It was about time someone asked that question, Adric thought.

Medford raised an eyebrow. 'You don't know?'

'My friend and I are visitors to the planet.'

'Even so . . . the Scientifica are the rulers of this colony.'

'A ruling elite of scientists?' Adric asked. In his experience, most advanced civilizations eventually adopted this structure. Both he and Nyssa came from such worlds, and from what he could gather about Gallifrey, so did the Doctor.

'That's right,' the Provost-General grunted. 'It dates back to when the planet was first settled as a mining colony. Life here can be harsh; food and energy resources are scarce, even here at the equator. The settlers discovered that they could survive using computer modelling. They used scientific principles to determine everything from recycling and crop rotation to widescale social engineering. The Computers assess a child's genetic potential, and provide an education and facilities tailored to individual need. The Scientifica were ahead of their time in many ways: they were one of the first planetary governments to reintroduce slavery.' It was the Doctor's turn to raise an eyebrow, but Medford continued. 'Thanks to the Scientifica, this planet is one of the most harmonious in the Empire.'

'Yet they need a peacekeeping force.'

The lift arrived, and they stepped inside. Without anyone pressing a control, the lift car began moving upwards.

'Indeed. Recently, the planet's economy has suffered: the palladium and jabolite have begun to run out. Robots can work mineral seams that human miners couldn't even reach, and so have all but replaced them.'

'With economic hardship the rule of law has begun to break down: rioting in the streets, an increase in petty crime, that sort of thing?'

'The criminal psychologists rapidly identified the problem.'

'I'm sure they did.'

The lift door opened onto a terrace garden. They were high above the city here, near the summit of the pyramid. The garden was protected from the snow flurries and wind outside by an elegant plastic dome, but it was cold here. The floor was tiled, in a black and white chessboard pattern, and white pots and troughs had been carefully arranged around the terrace. They contained a variety of plants. Each was different: some leaves were grey,

60

some bright green, some had delicate fronds, others sharp needles. In each plant pot there was a nameplate pushed into the soil giving the common and scientific name of each plant and a two-line description. They were walking too fast for Adric to stop and read.

Around the corner, a woman was tending one of the plants. She was small and somewhere between middle and old age. Her blonde hair was white at the roots and she wore a collarless white tunic and leggings. The pale tunic made her face appear flushed, although anywhere else her skin would have been papery. She had green eyes which were so piercing that Adric found them almost disconcerting. As they approached she straightened.

'Chief Scientist Whitfield,' she announced formally. Her hands remained by her sides. Adric and the Doctor exchanged looks.

'The governor of the colony?' the Doctor asked. She nodded her head. He held out his hand. 'I am the Doctor, this is Adric.' Adric smiled pleasantly, but knew that the Chief Scientist was more interested in the Doctor than him. It was the same the universe over. The Provost-General took his place behind Whitfield, looming over her like a bodyguard. Did he outrank the Chief Scientist? Adric wasn't sure what the protocol was, who would be in charge. They seemed relaxed around each other, at least as relaxed as either of these rather formal people ever would be.

Behind them, the lift door opened. Adric turned to see a young man in a red tunic approach. 'The medical report is complete,' he announced.

The medic handed an electronic notepad to the Provost-General. He glanced at it, then handed it to Whitfield. 'Proceed.'

'The two subjects are free from infection, and in good health.'

'I'm glad to hear it,' the Doctor piped up.

'The first subject,' the medical officer continued in the tone of a prosecuting counsel, indicating the Doctor, 'has two hearts, mirror images of each other. Both are equally developed. The electric activity of the subject's brain is at a

61

higher level than ever previously recorded. His body temperature is a constant fifteen degrees. The blood is of a completely unknown type. The respiratory pigment is not haemoglobin, but has many of its structural characteristics and its capacity to carry oxygen is much greater. There is a wealth of further evidence pointing to one conclusion: although they resemble humans, both the Doctor and his friend are aliens.'

'Yes,' the Doctor said patiently, 'I know.'

'You don't deny it?' Whitfield said, surprised.

'Of course we don't, why would we want to? Adric here is an Alzarian, I am from Gallifrey.'

'Neither of those worlds are protectorates of the Empire,' Medford declared. If the Earth Empire was really as large as the Doctor had said, the Provost-General must have been guessing – no one could possibly remember the name of every single planet out of millions.

'There has only been . . . only limited contact between our peoples,' the Doctor declared cheerfully. Adric admired the Doctor's ability to conceal the truth without actually lying, and his ability to change the subject of a conversation. Before the Chief Scientist could ask why they had come to the planet, how they had arrived or if they were alone, the Doctor had said, 'Speaking of aliens, it's a marvellous collection here.'

The Provost-General looked puzzled. 'The vegetation here has been imported from the arctic areas of over a hundred worlds,' the Doctor explained.

Whitfield held up a leaf from the bush she had been tending. It was light brown, elongated. It was not an immediately appealing plant, indeed it looked distinctly shrivelled, but there were little fruit growing underneath the leaves. 'This is a winter berry from the Mare Sirenum. A gift from the Martian government.' She plucked one of the fruit and handed it to Adric. It was a colour somewhere between tawny-orange and scarlet. It had a strong, acidic smell. 'It's edible,' she assured him.

Adric bit into it. The skin was surprisingly soft, and juice squirted from it. It was a little bitter for Adric's taste, but it was refreshing enough.

'It grows in a low-temperature, high radiation environment that would simultaneously freeze and fry any Terran plant. It thrives here. Unlike Mars, this planet has no native life of its own, except for a small barnacle-like species found in some of the deeper caves.'

'Some of my best friends are small, barnacle-like creatures,' the Doctor objected.

Whitfield ignored him. 'The Scientifica introduced some plant species to this world centuries ago as part of routine terraforming, but they faced problems. What little soil there is on this world has poor drainage and aeration. It's very acidic. Organic decay and bacteriological action are also slow. Plants here survived by becoming less colourful, harder.'

'Like the Scientifica?' the Doctor asked.

'Exactly,' the Chief Scientist answered. 'Offworlders sometimes find us impersonal, unemotional. We are merely shaped by our environment, as are they. We have become . . .' She searched for the word.

'Cold?' the Doctor suggested.

'The very same. But we've adapted to our climate. Evolved to fit this particular niche in the universal environment.'

'Like pets growing to look like their owners?'

'No,' the Chief Scientist answered, apparently unaware that the Doctor was making a joke. The Provost-General laughed, though. He clearly wasn't a native.

The Doctor leant over to Adric. 'That seems to have broken the ice,' he observed. Adric rolled his eyes and groaned. The Doctor was strolling over to the edge of the terrace. Adric joined him. The sky was a mass of black and grey clouds, bold shapes that twisted and reformed as they watched. This high, it was easy to see where the Strip had got its name. The city was a narrow line, a belt of orange and white lights disappearing to a vanishing point on the horizon. Beyond the city, there were hills and mountains, all coated with snow and ice. At night, the snow appeared a pale blue. There was the odd light twinkling out there on the snowfields – skitrains? isolated settlements? It was impossible to say.

'The city is beautiful,' the Doctor concluded. For just that moment, the Doctor's tone of voice reminded Adric of the Doctor he had known first. His words carried the weight of the ages.

Whitfield stood at his shoulder. 'It is far from perfect, especially now, but we continue to seek harmony.'

'I left my own people to search for the ideal society, a place of ordered peace and civilized values. Instead I found blasted wastelands, tyranny and intolerance. I came to realize that I would never find perfection, but that fact should never stop me from looking.' The Doctor paused for a moment, then turned back. 'Forgive me, Provost-General. This is hardly solving your problem. I volunteer my services: think of me as a scientific advisor, it's a role I've played in the past.'

The Chief Scientist and Provost-General shared a look that Adric would have given anything to decipher.

'Now, first question: what are so many Adjudicators doing on this planet? You told me before about the breakdown in social order,' Adric noticed that the Chief Scientist frowned at that, 'but that's hardly a reason to justify the expense to deploy three entire legions.'

'You sound like the Imperial Defence Select Committee,' Whitfield observed drily.

'At the station you said that the terrorists attack the peacekeeping force. To what end, though, mmm? What do the terrorists want?'

'They object to the presence of the Adjudicators. They have targeted Adjudicator Lodges, transporters, even attacked bars and clubs frequented by the peacekeepers.'

'I see,' the Doctor said thoughtfully.

'We're beginning to win the war, now. The terrorists are all but beaten – they have only a few snowships remaining. We are on the verge of capturing Adam, their leader. The attack on the train might be in revenge for recent defeats.'

'What was the train carrying?' the Doctor asked.

'That information is classified,' the Chief Scientist declared.

'Would it be considered a military or a scientific target?'

'Yes,' the Provost-General and Chief Scientist said in unison.

'Both?' the Doctor mused.

'You said before that you could recover the recording,' Medford reminded the Doctor.

'And you said that there were state-of-the-art laboratories.' The Doctor had realized that they were changing the subject, but was playing along.

'There are indeed. If –' The communicator on Medford's wrist bleeped. He glanced at it. 'I'm afraid I must leave you,' he apologized. 'There is an intersystem call waiting for me in my office.' He bowed his head to the Chief Scientist and hurried to the lift. Adric watched him leave.

'I am due elsewhere shortly,' Whitfield said. 'There will be time only for a brief tour of Scientifica. Following that, I shall show you to your laboratory.'

The Provost-General double-checked that no one had seen him enter the antechamber, then slid the door closed behind him. He flicked the switch that soundproofed the communications chamber. Finally, he swept the room for bugging devices using the sensor on his wrist computer. Only when he was satisfied did he sit in the padded chair in the centre of the small room. Green letters appeared in the air a metre or so in front of his face. '++Incoming message, secured warplink++' a synthesized voice announced. Medford reached for the control unit and selected 'Visual Only'.

An eyepiece whirred up into place, lighting up. It would check his retinal pattern before releasing the message. The Provost-General placed his eye against it.

'++Identification confirmed, Adjudicator Provost-General Medford, T S. Message follows++' There was a brief delay as the encrypted files were decoded, then decoded again. '++From: Admiral Dattani, J, commanding officer: Ark Royal: flagship Third Fleet++Message reads: my forces placed at your disposal. Assembled at grid reference nine-six-eight-zero-nine-two-nine.++' Medford calculated that at battlespeed the fleet was less than an hour away. Twenty thousand of the finest astronauts in the Empire, including support staff. '++Estimate can hold this position for a week without complications.++' Medford smiled at that. He'd known Januscek for thirty years, come to appreciate his Pakislovak gift for understatement. There were few sane men that could contemplate high treason with a smile on their face. He memorized the grid reference, then erased the message, making sure that he purged all the servers, buffers and back-ups it had ever been through. Then he typed in the reply.

'++Confirm Ark Royal. Hold position and await further orders. Thank you++'

That done, Provost-General Medford sat back. They would hang for this, if they survived. But if they didn't survive . . .

5

Behind Closed Doors

'Please stop and think about this.' Nyssa's voice was beginning to get on Tegan's nerves now.

'No.' The lift had deposited them on the eighth floor. Now they could only be moments from 'Bruce Jovanka' in Room 74. Tegan began mentally composing what she would say to the man.

'You're not acting rationally.'

Tegan didn't slow down. 'How would you feel – dragged across time and space in a flying phone box that's on the verge of falling apart. Instead of Heathrow, I end up on a planet cold enough to freeze the beak off a penguin only to find there's some crim booked into a hotel using my name. Forgive me, Nys, if I don't feel like acting rationally.'

'There is a possible explanation that you have over-looked.'

'And what might that be?'

'I'll tell you if you slow down,' Nyssa insisted.

Tegan stopped, and turned. 'OK.'

'This is your future.'

Yes, Nyssa, I know that. 'Go on.'

'He could be your descendant: your great-grandson's great-grandson.'

Tegan considered the possibility. Nyssa wasn't to know that her surname would change if she got married, but that didn't detract from the basic argument. Centuries down the line, there could be hundreds of little Jovankas running around. There was one snag, though, 'If he's for real, then why the phoney accent?'

'Speech patterns change and evolve over time. Who knows, that may be how Australians sound now.'

'I suppose it's possible,' Tegan conceded grudgingly. Secretly, she found the thought quite comforting. However long it took her to get back to Heathrow, she'd get there in the end, have a life, raise kids. Best of all, it had happened centuries ago. Her grandchildren would end up here, among the stars, just as her grandfather had emigrated from Yugoslavia to start a new life. He'd always called Australia 'The New World'. Perhaps space travel was in her genes, part of the indomitable Jovanka spirit.

'You could be right,' Tegan conceded.

'And it's certainly not good etiquette to call in on your relations while time travelling,' Nyssa continued knowledgeably.

'Who says?' Tegan was suspicious again.

'The Doctor,' Nyssa said, just a little too quickly.

'When did he say that, then?'

Nyssa was silent.

Tegan set off again, her pace slightly brisker than before. 'You had me going for a minute there.'

'What if he tells you something about your future?' Nyssa was saying. 'He might know all sorts of things about you. He might know what your future husband was called.'

Tegan was leaving Nyssa trailing behind. 'As long as it isn't "Adric" I'm sure I'll cope,' she called back to her companion.

Medford entered the surveillance suite. The room was darkened. In the centre, a bearded member of the Scientifica sat in a padded chair. He had a green tunic, denoting that he was a member of the technical service grade. He wore a neat turban, also in green.

'What's your name?' Medford asked him.

'Falconstock, sir.' His voice was resonant, he had a straight, almost military, bearing.

The Provost-General bent his arm and raised it to his temple. 'We are not alone in the universe.'

Falconstock repeated the action. 'Earth is under constant threat from alien attack.'

The Provost-General lowered his arm. Hesitantly, Falconstock did the same. 'You remember the oath.'

'Of course, sir.'

'Marvellous. Repeat the rest for me.'

68

' "Ours is a top secret organization set up to investigate extraterrestrial forces at large in our existence. Our mission is to keep a constant search for anything mysterious so that HQ can be immediately alerted to an attack from the stars. We pledge to keep our planet free from the perils of the universe." '

Medford smiled. 'Good. Word-perfect. Show me the Chief Scientist.'

Whitfield appeared on the monitor, heading away from the camera. She was neat as ever and beautiful, to his eyes at least. The Doctor and Adric trailed behind her, taking in their surroundings. The fish-eye lens distorted them, like a fairground mirror. In the darkened surveillance suite, the colours of their clothing appeared even brighter.

'Those gentlemen with the Chief Scientist are aliens, the vanguard for an invasion force. We've been expecting the attack for just over a year now, and we are ready for them.'

Falconstock seemed startled, unsure what to do. The Provost-General rested a hand on his shoulder.

'No need to worry, for the moment at least.' He eased into the other chair. 'They are unarmed, and have no immediate hostile purpose. We're going to watch them: record every word they say, log every gesture they make. I want you to cross-refer every name they use with the main database. Anything that isn't in there, access the Imperial Datanet.' He sat alongside the technician.

'Yes, sir. Recording started.'

'I want to find out exactly what they are planning, what they already know.' Medford leant back, intently watching the monitor.

They were in the lift.

They were in the lift. A map was mounted on the far wall. Whitfield stepped up to it, and tapped the transparent plate protecting the diagram of the building. 'Scientifica is a tetrahedron, each side is two kilometres long. Therefore it is –'

'One thousand seven hundred and thirty –' the Doctor began.

'Seven millimetres short of one kilometre six hundred

69

and thirty-three metres high at the apex,' Adric interrupted quickly.

Whitfield looked at him properly for the first time. 'Yes. Elementary trigonometry, of course.'

'Two root two over three.'

Whitfield was beaming. 'You are a mathematician by training?'

Adric brightened. 'Yes, I am. The star I wear is a sign of mathematical excellence among my people.'

The Chief Scientist stepped forward, and examined the badge. 'It is good that your people and ours share certain values.' Adric nodded, accepting the compliment.

'If we could get on?' the Doctor complained. He never liked being left out, and Adric could tell that he was itching to explain what a tetrahedron was to someone. He'd only just finished counting out something on his fingers.

Whitfield had returned to the map. 'It has been laid out upon purely logical lines: there are exactly seven hundred and fifty floors above ground, a further two hundred and fifty below. The subterranean levels contain archives, generators, heating equipment and the like. Each floor has its own hypocaust, fed centrally from a furnace in the basement. Most large buildings here have similar systems. The top two hundred and fifty levels contain the government offices, as well as living quarters for the civil service and government officials. The higher up the pyramid, the more senior the official.'

'With yourself and the Provost-General in joint charge, does that mean you bunk up together on the top floor?' the Doctor asked flippantly.

Whitfield chose not to answer, looking away. The Doctor turned to Adric and shrugged. Adric rolled his eyes: the Doctor really should have realized by now that the Chief Scientist lacked a sense of humour. Besides, from her slightly embarrassed reaction, he suspected that the Doctor might well have been right.

'The middle two hundred and fifty levels are for administration,' Whitfield continued, 'the inworld revenue computers, the genetic database, serfnet, the police mainframe.'

'The machinery of state,' the Doctor noted dismissively.

Whitfield looked as if she was about to lecture him on the importance of such an infrastructure, but she changed her mind, instead indicating the lowest third of the pyramid. 'The two hundred and fifty levels below that concern pure research.'

In an instant the Doctor had perked up. 'Really? Scientific research is done here?'

'Of course. The principal aim of Scientifica is the knowledge of causes, and secret motions of things. The enlarging of the bounds of human empire, to the effecting of all things possible.' The words came out like a mantra. 'In other words, we want to reach an understanding of how the universe works. That is why so much floorspace is dedicated to the subject. At the moment, there are over a thousand state-funded projects underway, in every field from particle physics to applied artificial extelligence.'

'Extelligence?' Adric asked.

'Computer telepathy,' the Doctor muttered. 'Exploring the surconscious mind is something of a long-term project for human science.'

'– *for human science.*' The Doctor's face filled the monitor. Medford raised an eyebrow. 'They know of our aims. The boy is no threat, but the Doctor is dangerous. He masks his knowledge behind those jokes.'

'Do you think the aliens are in league with the Adamists?' Falconstock asked.

'He claims to know little of the struggle,' the Provost-General answered. 'But the Adamists have used alien mercenaries in the past: Shlimans, Wondarks, even Kosnax.'

'None of those races is a match for the Imperial Navy, sir. A single war rocket could subdue them.'

'Oh yes,' Medford agreed, a wicked smile on his face. 'But have you ever faced a Shliman in hand-to-hand combat?'

'No sir,' Falconstock shuddered.

'I could tell.' The Provost-General paused. 'You're still alive.'

'I had heard that the Shark People were cannibals.'

'That's not true, Falconstock. They don't eat their *own* kind . . .'

'*I must say, this is all very impressive.*'

'I must say, this is all very impressive,' the Doctor told Whitfield.

'Thank you.' She seemed genuinely happy that the Doctor approved. They were out of the lift now, walking down a corridor on floor one-zero-zero. The decor was spartan, as it was everywhere else in the pyramid. Rather than looking bare, the lack of ornamentation gave the place an elegance, a pleasing simplicity. It came as quite a shock to see the statue. It was in an alcove, to the right of a large set of double doors. Adric didn't recognize the stone figure, or the manner of his dress. It was of a bearded man, wearing ruff and baggy pantaloons. The nameplate read 'Francis Bacon'. They paused there for a moment.

Whitfield looked up at the statue, almost reverently. 'One of the first of our modern human scientists.'

'Yes, I know,' the Doctor said.

'You are aware of our history?' Whitfield asked.

The Doctor looked into the eyes of the statue as though it were an old friend. 'Yes.'

'How?'

The Doctor turned back to her, suddenly wary. 'Oh, you know, travellers' tales.'

Whitfield was watching him, assessing what he was saying. Testing him.

'I know little about the history of this colony, I'm afraid,' the Doctor admitted disarmingly.

'This system was discovered when the hyperdrive on a science ship misjumped. The engines vented, and the ship drifted into the planet's gravity well. The scientists put ashore here. The science team were marooned for three years, and set up a survival station. The planet had a breathable atmosphere, the temperature was tolerable, there was potable water. When the rescue ship arrived, over half the colonists elected to stay. As the colony became a little more established, scientists from throughout human space began to flock here to conduct research.'

'But surely the conditions here —'

'Don't forget, Doctor, this was one of the earliest colonies. It was a lot more hospitable here than on Venus or Callisto. Or Earth, for that matter. At first, much of the scientific effort was spent just surviving: developing fertile soil from barren rock, building solar cells that would work even in the weak sunlight we get here. But within a century the plantations were established and the planet was energy self-sufficient.'

'So you have become a galactic centre for scientific research. You must get a lot of grants from Earth.'

'We pride ourselves on our isolation — our detachment from such concerns. We earn hard currency by exporting minerals.'

The metal doors ground open, leading through into a high-ceilinged chamber. It was a laboratory of some kind, with testbeds and benches. A couple of men and women in grey tunics were assembling some heavy equipment in the centre of the room, ready for a test. There were about a dozen people present. The Doctor watched, fascinated. The scientists moved quickly, in concert.

They walked past a tall glass cylinder full of metal beads. 'Is that a cold fusion generator?' the Doctor asked.

'Yes.'

'And that's a warp field stabilizer,' the Doctor noted, as they passed what looked like a metal tennis net.

'It is, yes.'

'A rather expensive piece of laboratory equipment.'

'It is a prototype built by our research team here.'

'But why are you building a dimensional observatory in the first place?'

'— *a dimensional observatory in the first place?*'

Medford's eyes narrowed.

'This is the cutting edge of science, Doctor. With this device we will be able to probe other dimensional states. One of our scientists believes that we will even be able to tap into "dimensional energy". If that was possible, then humanity would be able to generate almost infinite power supplies.'

73

The scientists made their final adjustments and stood clear of the test area.

Whitfield measured the Doctor's response. The young man looked sceptical, but he didn't dismiss the idea out of hand. His companion, the mathematician, was asking something, 'The red tunics are medics, the green are . . . technicians. You have the white tunic. What does grey signify?'

'They are warranted men.'

'Ah yes,' the Doctor piped up, 'slaves. I've been meaning to talk to you about that.'

Whitfield was happy to change the subject. The warranted labour system was a familiar topic of contention between her government and the galaxy at large, and the arguments for and against had become well-trodden pathways. 'Slavery, if that's what you want to call it, is part of the natural order of things – Aristotle himself said as much. Many of the advanced races use slaves.'

'Races like the Daleks?' the Doctor said accusingly.

'They use slaves, yes. They are also brilliant scientists.'

A spherical area in the middle of the apparatus began to pulse and phase through six dimensions. The globe of air seemed to spin, then twist itself inside out before settling down into a regular pulsing reminiscent of a heart beating.

The Doctor seemed hardly to have noticed. 'In this day and age, couldn't you just use robots?' It was the argument used by the offworld mining companies: robots were more 'efficient', apparently, and there were no 'civil liberties complications'. Such arguments had put a million of her citizens out of work: in some former jabolite mining areas unemployment – a word that hadn't been used on the planet for centuries – was almost total.

'Human slaves are self-replicating, self-repairing. Are you seriously suggesting that machines make better agricultural workers than people?'

'No, I'm suggesting that you are treating people like machines.' They were leaving the lab now, the doors closing behind them. Once again they were in a bare corridor.

'The Scientifica provides for them. A slave receives full education and training, food, housing, medical care –

74

we have state-of-the-art hospitals, available for the entire population. The problem with social equality is that it places the lower classes at a disadvantage. Chief Scientists, mathematical geniuses . . . doctors, we find it easy to reach the standard. But those below average have to struggle just to reach what society demands of them, if they ever can. They end up exploited, or starving. Under the warranted work system, there is full employment. Not only that, but the supply of resources can be regulated: no one has less – or more – than they need.'

'You make it sound attractive,' Adric said. 'Mathematically speaking,' he added quickly, when the Doctor glared at him.

'People might seem free under other systems, Doctor, but they are forced to sell their labour for the least amount of money to guarantee their jobs, and they spend what little they do earn trying to scrape together enough to pay for "luxury" goods. Under our system, resources are distributed fairly. Our economy has been stable for hundreds of years.'

'I disagree,' the Doctor said, as if he needed to.

'I disagree.'

Medford was tapping his fingers on the arm of his chair.

'Is this a diversion?' he asked.

'The Doctor appears genuinely interested in our social structures here.' Medford had not expected Falconstock to reply, but the technician had confirmed his own observations.

'They are on level one-zero-zero, we'll see what.they make of the security door. We'll find out if they know about the Patient.'

Set into the wall was a great round hatch.

Set into the wall was a great round hatch, the size of a bank vault door. It was a dull grey colour. Adric didn't recognize the precise alloy, but imagined that it could withstand virtually all attempts to force it open. 'What's behind there?' the Doctor asked as they passed it.

'Classified research,' Whitfield said. They had already

walked past it. The Doctor gazed back at it. Adric tugged his arm, indicating the door. The Doctor nodded. Whitfield was watching them. The Doctor stopped in his tracks and smiled. 'Heavy security for a science project. Is it military?'

'No. Scientifica was once involved with weapons research, but such projects were banned centuries ago. We are a pacifist people, involved in pure research with no military applications.'

'The Earth authorities are clearly interested in your work, and for an establishment committed to peace, there are a lot of guns around.'

'That has proved necessary, due to the terrorist threat.'

'Three legions to fight a bunch of terrorists? There are more Adjudicators here than on all of the Outer Worlds put together.'

'The peacekeeping force has proved very effective.'

'I bet they have – they probably outnumber the terrorists by one thousand to one, and they have state-of-the-art weapons and armour.'

There was a bleeping from the Doctor's pocket. He took his hand out to see what it was. The bleeping continued, now at his wrist. The time sensor! Quickly, the Doctor shut it off.

'– *state-of-the-art weapons and armour.*'

'Sir?'

Medford leant over. 'Yes?'

'We're registering a scanning device.'

'Where?'

Whitfield frowned. 'What was that noise?'

'The Doctor's right wrist, sir.' Falconstock pulled a lever, and the monitor zoomed in. It isolated the scanning device, and mapped it onto another picture. The device became a technical drawing, the location of the power source and the receptors marked out in red.

'Just my watch alarm. It's Adric's bedtime.'

'What is the function of the device?'

'It is working on principles unknown to human science, sir. It has created a scanning beam, but it is unclear precisely what it is looking for.'

'The Doctor has been probing the entire building? Mapping it?'

'*May I see?*'

'No, sir. The device activated itself, and only as they passed the security door.'

'*If you insist.*'

'So, he does know . . .'

'If you insist.'

The Doctor slipped the sensor from his wrist, and handed it over. Adric frowned, but the Doctor shook his head.

'What is the purpose of this device?'

'It tells the time.'

Whitfield examined it warily for a moment, before handing it back. They continued down the corridor for a few more minutes, then entered the lifts again.

'Your room is on the level above this.'

'Here we are, room 74.' Nyssa watched Tegan taking the keycard from her pocket and trying to locate the keyhole.

'Tegan, you're clearly not in the best frame of mind to talk to him,' she whispered.

'So what would you suggest we do?' Tegan was holding the card the wrong way up, and back to front. Nyssa chose not to correct her.

'I think we should go back downstairs and wait for the Doctor.'

'No.'

'Well in that case, I suggest that *I* go in.'

'You?'

'You wait here, I knock on the door, have a civilized conversation. There's no evidence that the man is armed or in any way dangerous. If there's a problem, then I will call for you.'

Tegan considered the offer for a minute. 'Done,' she decided.

Nyssa knocked on the door.

They waited.

Nothing.

'He's not in.'

'Try again.'

Nyssa knocked on the door.

There was still no reply.

'I'm going in,' Tegan announced.

'Tegan!' Nyssa gasped, shocked by the idea.

'If he's not even there, who's to know? If I'm caught, I'll just say I'm the maid, or something.'

'I refuse to let you.'

'Well, one of us is going in.'

Nyssa snatched the keycard. 'Then I will do it.' She slid the card down the reader and the door clicked open. 'You wait here,' she ordered.

Nyssa closed the door behind her once she was inside. The lights automatically blinked on. The room was quite large. A double bed took up much of the space, there was also a large wardrobe in one corner, an entertainment unit in another. There was a dressing table with a mirror, and a door – presumably leading to the water closet. She passed a patch of wall that had been plastered over. The decorator hadn't quite managed to find a paint that matched the original colour. The bed had been slept in already. She checked under the pillows, and found nothing but a pair of yellow pyjamas. As Nyssa crept around the bed towards the wardrobe, she caught sight of the suitcase. It was large, made of a black fabric. She ran her fingers along the top, pausing at the combination lock, but decided that it would be improper to open it. Instead she folded back the wardrobe door. Three identical business suits hung from the rail. A smaller bag rested on the floor. Nyssa hesitated for a moment before deciding that the only way to prove the man's innocence to Tegan would be to violate his privacy. She checked his jacket pockets. There was a stack of business cards in the side pocket.

BRUCE JOVANKA
NSW Solar ITEC
Regional Sales Representative

The card seemed genuine enough, with a magnetic strip down the side, which presumably contained encoded information – his address, how to contact him, perhaps even a little about the company. Simple technology, but effective enough. He wouldn't miss a business card – in fact the whole point of having them was so that he could distribute them. Satisfied that she wasn't stealing, Nyssa pocketed one of the cards and carefully replaced the remainder. Now there was only the water closet to check. Nyssa stepped through carefully.

There was someone in the shower. She saw a large shape behind the translucent shower curtain, his head bent forward so that he could wash his hair. Water was splashing around him. Nyssa hadn't heard the shower from outside – the room must be soundproofed. It was Jovanka, of course, she could tell that even through the curtain.

Nyssa edged back towards the door, fumbling for the handle, all the time keeping her eyes on the man behind the curtain. Her hand brushed against the handle.

'Off!' he shouted, making her jump. She realized he was talking to the shower. The water died down.

'Towel!' The towel rack swung out and extended.

'Curtain!' The curtain flung back and Jovanka stepped out, blinking, groping for the towel. Nyssa blushed and looked away, turning only to face a full length mirror. He filled it. Unsure where to look, Nyssa turned back. He kept his distance. His muscular development was extraordinary, with broad biceps, developed pectorals and abdominal muscles. His calves and thighs were toned, and . . . now he had covered the rest with a large towel. Nyssa looked down at the floor.

'Did ya want something, sport?' Understandably, he seemed a little confused by her presence, but clearly didn't seem too worried by her. Why should he be? He was twice her size. Despite the physical advantage, Nyssa sensed no hostility from him, only curiosity.

After a moment composing herself, Nyssa looked up, straight into his eyes. She took a deep breath.

'I'm the maid. My friend says you aren't Australian!' she blurted, before flinging open the bathroom door and fleeing the room. Jovanka protested, moved to stop her, but she was out and across the bedroom before he could reach her. Without looking back, she opened the door and leapt out into the corridor.

Tegan was waiting for her. Nyssa grabbed her arm, tugging her around the corner and down the corridor.

'What's going on?' Tegan demanded.

'Sssh!' Nyssa pulled them into an alcove.

The door to Jovanka's room opened again.

'He's coming after us?' Tegan hissed. She was ready to get up and confront him.

'Don't worry, he won't come far, he's naked,' Nyssa assured her.

Tegan boggled. 'You were only in there for two minutes!' Nyssa reddened.

The door closed again.

Nyssa stood up, and helped Tegan to her feet.

'What was all that about?'

'It's a long story.'

'Did you find anything sus?'

'No, he's a solar panel salesman.' She handed Tegan the business card. Tegan turned it over, examining it thoroughly.

'What exactly are you looking for?' Nyssa asked. She was beginning to run out of patience. 'He's a good man, Tegan, I can sense it.'

'I don't know really. I guess he could be genuine.' Tegan seemed almost disappointed.

'What's NSW?'

'New South Wales,' Tegan explained. 'One of the Australian states.'

'Can we go back to the bar, now? Quickly?'

'OK,' Tegan conceded. As they headed back to the lifts, Tegan looked back in the direction of the room.

The room that Whitfield had led them to was quite small. A heavy metal testbench sat along one wall, its surface packed almost solid with scientific instruments and monitoring equipment. A flatpanel computer terminal was hanging on the opposite wall, next to the built-in bunk bed. The room smelt of antiseptic. Someone had placed a box in the middle of the tiled floor containing the remains of the camera from the skitrain station. The Doctor strode into the middle of the room, taking it all in.

'I am afraid that I must leave you now, Doctor, Adric,' Whitfield said softly. 'If you need anything, you may page one of my staff. Breakfast will be brought for you at zero seven hundred.' She bowed her head slightly, and stepped from the room. The door closed itself behind her.

The Doctor took the top bunk. Normally, Adric wouldn't have cared less, only the Doctor seemed to be particularly pleased about his achievement. As he sat on the bottom mattress, he could hear the mattress creaking above him as the Doctor shifted around. He had begun to tinker with the remnants of the security camera: every so often Adric would hear the whine of the sonic screwdriver.

'Can you really fix it?' Adric called up sceptically.

'Oh yes, I could, given time,' a voice drifted down.

'How long do you think the Scientifica has been here?'

A pause. 'Whitfield implied that they have been around for centuries. Remember? When she was talking about weapons research.'

'The pyramid's much newer, though, isn't it?' Adric remarked. 'The paint's still fresh.'

'You know, I think you must be right.' The Doctor jumped down and paced over to the nearest wall. Adric shuffled over to join him. The Doctor was peering at the paintwork, the remains of the camera eye cradled in his hands.

'Spick and span,' he concluded. 'I'm not sure whether it's new, though, it might just be very well maintained.'

'It's odd that the government spends so much money on its offices, but outside everything's falling into ruin.'

'Well,' the Doctor admitted, 'there's nothing too remarkable about that. Strange that there aren't *any* signs of cutbacks here. No drawing of purse-strings or tightening of belts. It's not very good public relations.' He was looking around the room again, now, seeing it afresh.

'It doesn't add up,' Adric muttered.

'You're the mathematician: go on.'

'If all the jabolite and palladium has gone, they can't be exporting very much. That spaceport was almost empty apart from Adjudicator battleshuttles. Well, where does the money come from these days?'

The Doctor furrowed his brow. 'And, for that matter, why would Earth bother to send a peacekeeping force? Colonies fail all the time. Whitfield said herself that the planet keeps itself to itself – why would Earth defend it? Since the Dalek Wars Earth's fleet has been operating on reduced capacity. This colony doesn't have any mineral wealth any more and it's not in a strategic sector.'

'*– strategic sector.*'

The Provost-General was watching the Doctor's expression closely.

'He doesn't know,' Falconstock said.

'He's heard of the Daleks.'

'*Perhaps it has to do with those ghosts?*'

Falconstock turned back to the screen in horror, trying not to meet the Provost-General's eyes. Medford hadn't taken his eyes off the Doctor.

'*Perhaps.*'

Medford kept watching the screen, tried to see the slightest sign that the Doctor knew more than he chose to reveal.

'*Doctor, I really do think we should get in touch with Nyssa and Tegan, let them know that we are all right.*'

Without realizing it, Falconstock began working at his console as soon as he heard the names.

'*Adric, they are booked into a hotel, what could possibly happen to them there?*'

'There!' Medford declared. 'Check all hotel, hovtel and simtel registers. Cross-refer the names to the linguistics processors for spelling and phonetic variations.'

Falconstock's hands danced across the keymat. 'The Imperial Hotel, sir. Empress Park sector. Two women booked in last night under the names "Nyssa" and "Jovanka, Tegan M". A "Jovanka, Bruce C" is also booked in.'

'Five of them. Good work. Can you get identiphots of them?'

'Accessing the hotel security grid.'

The screen went dark for a moment, then head-and-shoulders shots flashed up, one after the other.

An attractive-looking girl with brown hair and an aristocratic, somewhat haughty air.

A slightly older girl with auburn hair.

A blond-haired, blue-eyed young man with broad shoulders and a square jaw.

Falconstock looked at each of the faces in turn, memorizing them. They were all so young, none older than twenty-one. Difficult to imagine that they represented a threat to the entire human race: they were little more than children. Throughout the galaxy, whatever species they might be, children looked the same: they had softer skin and bigger eyes than their parents. Somewhere along the way, evolution on a million planets had conspired so that sentient beings found it difficult to kill the young of any creature. He glanced over at Medford, who was dialling something into his wrist communicator. Seeing him sitting there in his armour, Falconstock knew that Medford had murdered children before, in the name of justice.

'Do we have their room numbers?' Medford asked. At a touch of a control, a framework map of the hotel appeared, the suspects' rooms marked out in yellow.

'There are no records of them arriving at the spaceport. They must be false names, or here illegally.'

'Thank you, Falconstock, that will do for now,' the Provost-General said quietly. He keyed in a final sequence, then left the room. The door slid shut, and Falconstock was alone once more. For a moment, he couldn't bring himself to move. Something primal inside him was protesting. He'd just helped a man to kill children.

Disgusted with himself, Falconstock reached forward and deactivated the viewer. For a moment, before the lighting level automatically readjusted itself, he was alone in the dark. After a moment, he turned the viewer on and forced himself to look at their faces again.

6

The Patient

The large man sauntered up to the reception desk and propped himself up on an elbow. 'G'day cobber.'

The nearest robot concierge rattled around to face him. 'Good evening, Mister Jovanka.'

'Call me "Bruce", mate, everyone else does.'

The robot's head tilted to one side, and it seemed to consider the request for a moment. 'Thank you, sir, but no.'

'Suit yerself. About half an hour ago I was down here in the lobby.'

'You entered the lobby at 19.43 and left at 20.47.'

Jovanka waved a hand. 'I'll take your word for it, sport. Now, two sheilas came in –'

The robot leant back, in simulated distaste. 'I assure you, sir, that the Imperial Hotel operates a strict "No Shlimans" policy. We frown on all of the man–eating races.'

'Nah, you drongo, I'm not yabbering about sharkies. Hell, you won't find an Aussie in God's green galaxy who's worried by something as run-of-the-mill as a man-eating mutant shark. I'm talking about something much more dangerous: Sheilas – wimmen.'

The robot relaxed. 'Ah, yes, sir. In the period while you were in the lobby, some fifteen females entered the hotel.'

'Two of them came in together. Both about my age, one in a fur coat, the other in a tailored jacket. They cracked a couple of tinnies in that chair over there.'

The robot turned its head. 'You are referring to Miss Nyssa and your wife, Mrs Tegan Jovanka?'

'My better half?' Jovanka spluttered.

The robot produced an identiphot of the two from its chestprinter. The young man studied it for a moment. 'She's a fine woman, isn't she?'

'She is indeed, sir, but if I might offer a suggestion, I would not let your wife hear you say that.'

Jovanka studied the pictures again. 'That one's Tegan? She's quite a looker, I reckon, but haven't you got a photo of her smiling?'

The robot whirred and clicked. 'No, sir,' it concluded.

'Rabbits. Where are they now?'

'I am afraid the privacy protocol of the Imperial Hotel prevents me from informing you of Miss Nyssa's whereabouts.'

'Fair enough, I suppose.'

'Mrs Jovanka has ordered dinner in the restaurant, and will be joined by her companion there shortly.'

'Ripper! Book me in there, mate, would you?'

'As you wish, sir. A table for one?'

'A table for two, mate.' He winked at the robot. 'I'm feeling lucky.'

Chief Scientist Whitfield stood perfectly still in the lift car as it shot upwards. There was only the barest sensation of movement – and even that had been put there by the engineers. The human brain found it psychologically difficult to cope with a lift which could travel as fast as an aircraft without apparently moving.

The lift had reached the apex of the pyramid. The door chimed and opened. Between the two actions, Whitfield knew that she had been scanned and identified by an array of sensors, cameras and computers. She stepped from the lift and into the arms of the only other person allowed on this level. The Provost-General was wearing his pale blue nightrobe, the one she had bought for him on Drenbrandis fifteen years before. The material was a little frayed at the cuffs now. He held her for a moment, running a hand down her back.

'I can't stay,' she told him, burying her head in his chest. 'There's been a development at the research dome. I'm going to pack, then beam straight over.'

He was disappointed. She could feel him pull back. After forty years he still wanted to spend every possible night with her. 'What sort of development?'

Whitfield clutched his hand, then let go of it. 'Something that the Prorector won't tell me over a commlink.'

She walked through into the bedroom. The walls in here were sloped, making the double bed look even larger than it actually was. 'Lian's armour stood in one corner. Without its occupant, the armour was hunched and the helmet sat at a twisted angle. Had she a less logical mind, Whitfield might have imagined it watching her, or even moving. As it was, she still found its presence disturbing.

Whitfield packed a spare tunic and a couple of simchips into a travel case. That done, she walked back out into the living area. Medford was sitting, half-slumped in the easy chair, a drink in his hand. Whitfield walked past him to the food dispenser alcove, pulled the lever and the hatch dilated open. Her food pill and glass of artificial winterberry juice were sitting in the middle of the tray. As the plastic cover pulled back into place over the drip tray, there was a sound just behind her ear.

The Chief Scientist turned, but the alcove was empty.

'Is anything the matter?' Medford asked her. He hadn't heard it.

It hadn't been the heating system: when the hypocaust was warming through, the panels expanded slightly, but the heating had been on for hours. It wasn't a water pipe. The pyramid was fully soundproofed, so it wasn't coming from outside. For a second, before dismissing the thought as ridiculous, she considered the possibility that it was a burglar. She chose not to ask 'Lian whether he had heard it.

Whitfield swallowed the pill and washed it down with her drink. The winterberry juice tasted as it always did: cold and bitter.

The noise had been very quiet. But she hadn't imagined it.

'Shall we explore?'

Adric forced his eyes open, he didn't want to move. 'What, now?'

'No time like the present,' the Doctor declared cheerfully. He was fully dressed, of course. He'd even found a fresh stick of celery from somewhere.

Adric slipped out of the bunk and stood. He looked around, furtively. 'I thought you said we were being watched,' he said softly.

'Oh, we were,' the Doctor continued, in his normal voice. He held up the wreckage of the surveillance camera. 'But after a quick look at this, it was pretty easy to find out how the security around here works. The security grid receives and processes information from a camera in every room in the building, and can holographically reproduce every point in the building in microscopic detail. Meanwhile, interpretative software analyses everything that is said and warns the operators if it hears anything worrying. The system can be set to recognize key phrases or to follow an individual around. It's all very sophisticated, but that just makes it all the more easy to fool it. I've hacked into the grid, and told it to ignore us. We'll be invisible.'

'There are bound to be guards. We won't be invisible to them.'

'The Scientifica trust their instruments and their computers. No doubt if we drew attention to ourselves then they'd send a squad of Adjudicators after us, quick sharp, but as it is, they won't realize that they need to. The system encourages complacency. We'll have to be quiet, of course, but it's the middle of the night.' He was already pacing towards the door. Adric followed.

'So where are we going?' Adric said.

The Doctor raised a finger to his mouth. Adric asked him the same question again, in a slightly lower voice.

'That's better. That hatch on the level below us, er, level one-zero-zero, seems the obvious choice.' The Doctor set off down the corridor at a brisk pace. Adric had little choice but to follow him.

Unlike most people, Whitfield kept her eyes open while she travelled by transmat. Psychologists recognized the condition of 'transitphobia', the fear that some people had of teleportation, but such beliefs were irrational. Most phobias had deep-seated origins. Spiders, snakes, rats, fire, high places and enclosed spaces, the causes of the six most common fears, had all been genuinely dangerous thousands of years ago. Cavemen who were wary of spiders or fire were at an evolutionary advantage over those that didn't. Their genes survived. In a similar way, centuries ago, the first transmat systems had carried an element of risk. Phobics realized that the safety features built into modern transmats had statistically eliminated the dangers of accidents or signal distortion, but they were still scared. To rationalize their fears they now claimed that the designers had not managed to eliminate psychological damage to those teleported. They said that men had been driven mad, that people suffered flashbacks, hallucinations. That was all nonsense. Transportation was instantaneous – less time than it took to blink. There were no proven cases of mental instability resulting from transmaterialization. The people who came out of a transmat with a mental illness already had it when they went in.

As a child, Whitfield had found the sudden change of surroundings disconcerting, but now she was used to it. She still remembered how strange she had felt when her father had explained how the transmat worked. They had teleported from the family home to an orbiting starliner, the first stage of a trip to Earth. Daddy bought her an ice cream and explained that a computer had broken up her entire body into dust and moisture. Then it had broadcast a radio signal, telling another computer tens of thousands of kilometres away how to rebuild her from the dust and moisture stored up at the other end. Whitfield remembered how strange it had felt that night looking at herself in the mirror. Now, her little body was made from bits of other people. She had tried to imagine whose dust and moisture she was made from now and had stared at her reflection trying to see if she looked at all different. Everything was exactly in place: each mole and hair. Even that tiny scratch on her finger where her last body had caught itself on a pin. She didn't feel different, she didn't look different. Her memories were all there: she could still recite the whole periodic table and the Tolvey equations. She was still the same person. Over the years, she had come to realize that there was much in the mundane world that could be presented as disturbing to a child. There were microbes that crawled across her skin and tiny mites in her eyebrows and skin. When magnified they were spiky, antlered creatures with massive mandibles, the stuff of nightmares or science fiction. All food is full of insect carcasses and dung, the tapwater in your drinking glass has been recycled from urine. The dust that danced in the sunlight and settled on the furniture was mostly dead flakes of human skin.

The transmat cycled once, and Whitfield appeared in the materialization cubicle, wearing a new body built from someone else's dust and moisture.

'Welcome back, Chief Scientist.' The Prorector bowed his head as a mark of respect. He was thirty-three, a slightly built young man. He had been her deputy here for three years, after impressing her with a paper on Einstein's twin paradox. His name was Henga, but she rarely used it. They walked through into the observation dome.

'Why was I summoned?'

'One of the extrasensors in the cavern is registering what we think is a datastream on a very high frequency psionic wavelength. It's coming from the Machine.'

Whitfield stepped over, looking out into the cavern. The Machine loomed there, as ever, lit by spotlights on the roof of the observation dome.

'It's still being broadcast?'

'Yes, ma'am.' The Prorector continued his report. 'By analysing the signal, our computers have made contact with the operating system of the Machine.'

Whitfield didn't look back at her deputy. 'Is it trying to communicate with us?'

'Not in any way that we can recognize. We've run every first contact protocol on file, and we've got hold of some new translation software. Some patterns have emerged: "letters" in the machine code "alphabet". After an hour, our computers have already identified over ten million individual "letters". If it is a language, it's the most complex one we've ever encountered.'

'English-speakers can compose every word they need with twenty-six letters,' Whitfield whispered. 'What sort of mind needs over ten million letters to express its thoughts?'

'It could be a language that uses pictograms: Chinese has

89

nearly fifty thousand characters. On the other hand it could be an incredibly inefficient system.'

It was an interesting suggestion. 'A primitive language with very long words? Possibly it's not a language at all, but a Lacanian pre-Oedipal communication.'

'A stream of consciousness?'

'Possibly. It's not my field. I'm not sure how we would test for it. Is there any evidence that the operating system is sentient?'

'Possibly. It's adaptive, certainly. If it uses that much energy, it's got to be powerful enough to . . .'

'That's supposition. The first computers filled a room, needed their own special power supplies but could only do simple maths. The Machine's force field and self-repair systems alone must take up much of the energy.'

'That is true, Chief Scientist. What do you think it is?'

It was not the first time they had asked that question, but they were no nearer the answer. Whitfield continued to stare out of the window. 'Have you heard of Stonehenge, Prorector?'

'No, ma'am,' he admitted.

'It was one of the earliest scientific instruments, on Earth. A prehistoric method of predicting solar eclipses, and other astronomical events − stones arranged in a circle, marking off points in the heavens. On certain days, at certain times, the sun and moon would appear between the gaps in the stones. The blocks it was built from were imported from Wales, several hundred miles away. It doesn't sound far now, but it took fourteen hundred years to finish. The equivalent now would be to ship a billion tonnes of material to Andromeda to build an autobservatory.'

'Who built it?'

'The priest-scientists of ancient Britain, so that they could know how the universe worked just a little better. Every primitive society from the Mayans to the Egyptians spent centuries building structures that allowed them to make astronomical measurements. Ever since, there has been an unbroken line of men and women dedicated to that task, willing to defy authority, to risk death, because of what they knew to be true. Our methods have changed, become infinitely more sophisticated, and now we walk among the stars, but we are the descendants of those druids.'

'Is that what the Machine is for? To explain how the universe works?' The Prorector's face was reflected in the plastic window. Outside, the Machine stood, vast as ever. It was a thousand times older than Stonehenge, built before man was walking upright.

'Yes,' she concluded.

The Doctor plucked the sonic screwdriver from his pocket, and levelled it at the lock. After a moment he withdrew it and adjusted the setting.

'Is it working?' Adric asked him.

The Doctor stepped back, beaming. There was a snap as the bolts drew back. The Doctor looked around, but no one had heard the noise. He reached forward and tapped the handle. The hatch drifted smoothly open on power-assisted hinges. Through the circular portal it was dark. Adric stepped in first, the Doctor following closely behind.

'We'd better close the door,' the Doctor advised. The corridor outside was the only source of light. He pulled a couple of torches from his pocket and handed one to Adric. They were in an anteroom, ahead of them was a smaller metal hatch. The Doctor opened it and stepped inside.

The room was full of medical equipment and scientific instruments. Half-covered in shadow, they looked like twisted masses of cables and panelling. There were a dozen readouts glowing in the half-darkness. Adric was moving towards one of them when he stumbled into a metal frame. It crashed to the floor, there was the sound of glass breaking.

'Shush, Adric,' the Doctor insisted. But his companion had found something.

In the centre of the room there was a cylinder, two metres tall, a little less than a metre in diameter. At first it had looked like a supporting column, but it fell just short of the ceiling. It was made from a dull, burnished metal. A control box was connected to the side. Adric was studying the readings. 'There's someone inside, but their lifesigns are weak,' he concluded quietly.

The Doctor ran his fingers along the metal. 'Well they would be: this is a cryosleep tube. It slows down the metabolic rate of the person inside it. They used to be used for deep space travel, nowadays they mostly have medical applications — if someone is critically injured they can be frozen until they reach a hospital.'

'Whitfield said that the Scientifica had some of the finest medical facilities in the galaxy,' Adric reminded him.

'It makes you wonder why he's still in there and not in a hospital,' the Doctor said in a low voice.

'Perhaps he's beyond help,' Adric offered.

The Doctor took his glasses from his coat pocket and unfolded them. 'Then why keep him alive at all? Why allocate all this equipment, hmm?' There was an electronic notebook clipped to the back of the cryogenic tube. The Doctor lifted it off, and it flickered on automatically. He slipped on his glasses and scrolled through the report. 'Almost a year's worth of medical data. And he was only moved here earlier today. Do you know, I think we might have just found out what was onboard that skitrain.'

'Does it say who it is in there?' Adric asked.

The Doctor peered at him over his lenses. 'He's only referred to as "the Patient".'

'There's only one way to find out who it is, then.' Before the Doctor could stop him, Adric had touched one of the controls. A low whine started up. Slowly, the lid of the cylinder slid back, and a pale blue light spilled out.

A figure hung inside the tube, suspended in thick blue liquid. It was emaciated, with skeletal limbs and claw-like hands. A tattered cloak hung from angular shoulders, floating in the fluid, caught around the figure's torso. Skin the colour of rotten fruit was pulled back over the large skull, exposing pearl-white teeth. Its eyes were closed, covered with leathery flaps of skin. It looked like an exhumed corpse. The liquid bubbled. The body was supported by wires, electrodes running from the spine, the chest and the back of the head. It bobbed in the life support fluid like some kind of macabre puppet.

'It's the Master!' Adric exclaimed. The Doctor furrowed his brow. His arch-enemy had reached the end of his natural life long ago. Although long-lived when compared with humans, the Time Lords were not immortal. Their minds and bodies could only withstand the stresses of regeneration twelve times. After that, their fate was inevitable. Most of his race stepped willingly from the red circle of endless death and rebirth. They spent their last years in meditation, contemplating the state of timelessness that lay ahead. It was a choice that the Doctor knew he would make one day, distant millennia from now, but he was not nearly ready for it yet. Some of his kind sought to prolong their existence. Many of them had succeeded: Gallifreyan science was among the most advanced in the universe, and even the lowliest acolyte possessed the mental resources to keep himself alive by sheer force of will, if he so wished.

The Master was one of the Time Lords greedy enough to defy the inevitable. As his last body began to die, he had made his plans. He needed a vast energy source to fuel a new regenerative cycle. Across time and space he had tried to harness such a force: he'd tried to capture the Eye of Harmony on Gallifrey. When that failed, he'd attempted to rend asunder the constellation of Mandusus using a segment of the Key to Time. He'd even entered a pact with the Embodiment of Gris. Each time the Doctor had beaten him, and saved billions of lives. Finally, on Traken, Nyssa's home planet, the Master had captured the Source, the font of power for an entire galactic Union encompassing a million star systems. The Doctor had thought he'd defeated the Master there, but his old enemy had survived and stolen the body of Tremas, Nyssa's father. Over the years the Master must have gradually accumulated the energy he had needed. Perhaps he had summoned some reserve of strength from his own body. Whatever the case, the Master now had the new lease of life that he had desired for so many centuries.

Revitalized, more deadly than ever, the Master had attempted to hold the entire universe to ransom. Once again the Doctor had foiled his plan. The Master sought revenge, but he became caught in his own trap. The Doctor saw gloved hands flailing as a Castrovalvan mob pinned his arch-enemy to the floor, watched as a world, a civilization, a people dissolved, fragmented. Castrovalva had been a beautiful place of endless libraries, filled with some of the kindest, noblest men the Doctor had ever had the privilege to meet. All of it – all of them – had been created by the Master.

'The Master is dead, Adric,' the Doctor concluded sadly.

Adric stepped back from the life support tube, looking up at its occupant. 'Then who is that?'

The Doctor pressed his palms against the transparent tube and peered inside. 'Humanoid. About five foot six. No immediate sign of injury or disease. The subject is ancient, however, and in an advanced state of physical degeneration.'

The Doctor looked into the cracked, gnarled face. It looked more like the bark of an ancient oak tree than skin.

The eyes snapped open. Green eyes.

The Doctor stared into them, unable to look away.

Contact

So ancient.

I.

'Doctor!' Adric shouted.

Who are you?

Mental barriers. Inside them already. I.

A woman's voice. Catlike. An eye in his head.

Older than you can imagine, I . . .

Doctor who?

Concentrate.

A familiar female voice spoke: 'We must think . . .'

He crashed through the brittle metal. Romana was surrounded by leather-clad guards. A couple of them moved forward, their whips raised.

'Hello everybody,' the Doctor grinned, throwing his scarf back over his shoulder.

'Doctor are you all right?' Romana rushed forward. The guards stepped forward to restrain her.

'Yes, I'm fine,' he assured her.

'I was so worried about you.' She was grinning from ear to ear. K9's tail was wagging.

The Doctor picked a piece of metal from his hair and examined it absent-mindedly. 'Oh, you shouldn't be worried, Time Lords have ninety lives.'

'How many have you got through?'

He thought for a moment. 'About a hundred and thirty.'

I was joking.

Tell me more. You are a Time Lord? How old are you?

Inside my mind. Probing my memories. Searching for secrets from cradle to grave.

I have no cradle, I have no grave. I was born at Otherstide through the Loom of the House of Lungbarrow in Southern Gallifrey.

Waiting to be born. Strung out, spread really thin. Unable to think, unable to assemble my thoughts. I couldn't wait to get out. They were there. All forty-five of my cousins. Satthralope smacked me so hard I could barely walk and –

You are Loom-born?

Yes, I think so.

Are you a scientist?

'Let me tell you, sir,' the Doctor bawled, 'that I *am* a scientist and I have been for several thousand –'

'The man's mad,' Kettering declared. The Doctor glared at him, before striding from the room, his cape swirling behind him.

You left Gallifrey? Why?

'I was bored.'

'Bored?' Jamie and Zoe chorused.

The Doctor caught his breath, gathered his thoughts. 'The Time Lords are an immensely civilized race,' he explained. 'We can control our own environment; we can live forever – barring accidents; and we have the secret of space–time travel . . . we hardly ever use our great powers. We consent simply to observe and gather knowledge.'

The Time Lords allowed you to leave?

I . . .

The young teacher, whatever his name was, wouldn't stop asking questions. The Doctor whirled to face him. 'Have you ever thought what it is like to be wanderers in the fourth dimension? Have you? To be exiles . . . Susan and I are cut off from our own planet, without friends or protection. But one day . . . we shall get back. Yes, one day . . . one day.'

These accounts contradict one another.

Memories often do.

I want to know what is happening.

'If you would be so kind as to come with me?'

'Who are you?' He was so old, but there weren't any old people any more. He walked through the cloister with the aid of a stick, a knobbled stick with strange writing on it. There was a dark shape drifting behind him in the shadows. Outside the Capitol was burning.

'I couldn't possibly tell you that, oh no.'

'You wear my husband's ring.'

He held it up to the candlelight, examined it, then clutched it to his chest. 'Yes. So I do.'

'Please stop them – they are trying to find my daughter-in-law, they are going to kill her child.'

He placed a reassuring hand on her shoulder. 'Your granddaughter was born ten minutes ago, I was there at the birth. She is safe, quite safe.'

'A girl? Where is she?'

'She will be taken away from here, away from this madness. I will take her far from this world of vampires and valeyards. First, however, we must get *you* to safety.'

'Me?'

He took her hand. 'Come, my dear.'

This memory is faint.

It was a long time ago. I'm not even sure it's one of mine.

The truth.

A lot of what happened before my second regeneration is hazy. Great chunks of my life are missing. It was all so very long ago.

Your second regeneration?

'How far, Doctor? How long have you lived?' An over-sized claw snapped open and shut, a human hand clasped a rail. A brain within a tank, red eyestalks glaring at him. A patchwork monster with a gurgling voice. 'Your puny mind is powerless against the strength of Morbius. Back! Back to your beginning!'

You can't . . . not that far . . . I won't let you. . . . Not even I . . . Here and no further.

A cold wind.

A mountainside.

It is dark.

An old man stands there, alone.

He raises his fist.

'Is this how it began, or how it will end?' the female voice asked without breaking the silence.

A third voice spoke. 'It is both. Time is relative. History repeats itself, and repeats itself again. Father to son.'

The Doctor turned to see who had spoken. There was no one else there. Just him, the woman and the . . . the other.

When did this happen? Tell me!

But the Doctor was staring at the other.

'You!' the Doctor shouted.

The other smiled.

'You!' the Doctor shouted.

Adric leapt over to him, clamping a hand over his mouth. 'They'll hear us,' he whispered into the Doctor's ear. The Doctor struggled free, his hand thrashing out towards the cryogenic tube. A crack had appeared along its length, and spread along the transparent plastic. It splintered. Blue fluid exploded across the room. Adric ducked instinctively, felt himself pelted with shards of plastic, great gobbets of cryogenic fluid. When the last fragments had clattered to a halt, Adric turned. The Patient had sloshed from the tube, and now lay on its back like a broken heap on the floor. The wires had snapped, and hung twitching in the shattered metal tube. Foul-smelling blue liquid was congealing over the floor and medical equipment.

The Doctor was slumped against the tube. Adric's hand was wet. He pulled it away from the Doctor's face. Blood was dribbling from the Doctor's nose. He seemed oblivious to his surroundings.

A bony claw caught Adric's wrist. The Patient's head creaked around, its jaw dropping open. It rasped, a sound like a child's rattle. Its lipless mouth was curled into a sneer or a smile.

Adric stared at it, saw the expression of raw fear in the Patient's eyes. He tried to speak, but couldn't.

The Doctor screamed.

Part Three

Patience

7

Changing Faces

The Doctor screamed.

Adric scrabbled over to him. 'They'll hear you,' he hissed. 'The Adjudicators will hear you.' He wasn't getting through. The Doctor continued to cry out, staring wildly ahead of him into thin air at some invisible threat. Adric tried to restrain the Doctor but couldn't. With a growing sense of panic, Adric turned back to look at the Patient.

The body was lying on its back. It didn't appear to be breathing. The veins that stuck out on the cadaver's neck and arms were no longer pulsing. Adric felt compelled to get a closer look at the corpse, and leant over. He hesitated before he touched the withered skin. Although it had just been suspended in cryogenic fluid, the body was dry as an autumn leaf. Adric found it hard to believe that such a stunted, desiccated thing could ever have been alive. He swallowed, and found to his surprise that he was fighting back tears.

The door slid open. Adric spun around to see three Adjudicators marching into the room, their blasters raised. The Doctor had stopped screaming, but only because his mouth had dried out. He continued to moan hoarsely.

'Stand away!' one of the armoured figures ordered. They were keeping their distance from the corpse. Adric wondered for the first time whether it was in quarantine.

Adric turned back to the Patient. A chink of light had appeared on its neck. Adric leant forward, fascinated.

'Get back!'

'Look,' Adric insisted.

Cracks were appearing all along the body. The one at the neck had surged along the Patient's torso, finally running out of momentum at the hip. Another shot down from the

101

fingertips to the elbow. Tiny slits began appearing all across the face, spidery lines were criss-crossing the Patient's skin. Within moments, the Patient's body looked as if it was made from shattered panes of brown glass. It was beginning to crumble away into nothing.

A gloved hand clamped on Adric's shoulder. 'You were ordered to stand away!' an electronic voice warned. Adric refused to budge. Rather than pulling him back, the Adjudicator faltered, mesmerized by what he saw.

The cracks were glowing now, the rough skin was melting into wax. The skin was bubbling, flowing. As they watched, light began pouring out of the Patient's body, radiating around the room. A couple of the Adjudicators were looking up, watching the beams of light dancing across the ceiling. Adric's attention was focused on the Patient. A new body was beginning to appear, bathed in the brilliant light. Withered limbs were growing longer and more supple, hair was sprouting from the scalp. The skin was lightening and becoming baby-smooth. The rate of change was building to a crescendo: the entire body was rippling with frantic activity as though water was streaming over it.

Adric had seen this happen once before.

A new face was appearing, fading up into view, a new set of features superimposed over the old.

There was a final burst of light, and then the room was dark once more.

The metamorphosis was complete.

The Patient's eyes snapped open. They were a piercing blue. The gnarled face had been replaced by high cheekbones and full red lips. Long blonde hair cascaded down slender shoulders, and over a delicately curved chest, but left a flat stomach and long legs exposed.

'It's a woman,' Adric whispered redundantly. She had propped herself up on her elbows, wincing. Adric moved to help, but one of the Adjudicators, the officer in charge of the small group, yanked him back. The woman clasped her forehead. She was clearly in great pain.

'Get a doctor in here,' the Adjudicator-Lieutenant ordered, 'and seal off this floor.' He unhooked his cloak and draped it

102

over the young woman's shoulders to preserve her modesty. She was unselfconscious, unaware she had been naked, but accepted the cloak gratefully. She rubbed the material between her fingers, and peered at it with curiosity.

The medical team arrived, an Adjudicator paramedic and a couple of Scientifica physicians. They began unclipping medical scanners from their belts and readying autosyringes.

'Where's the Patient?' Medford was here now as well, anxiously examining the remains of the cryotube. The room was becoming crowded. At a signal from the Provost-General, a couple of the Adjudicators took up positions outside.

'That is her.'

The Patient was looking around the room, clearly unsure of her surroundings. In human terms, she appeared to be in her early thirties. 'Nonsense,' Medford concluded.

'I saw her change,' the Adjudicator-Lieutenant insisted.

'She's regenerated,' Adric added. 'She must be a Gallifreyan.'

Medford tilted his head towards Adric. 'One of the Doctor's people?'

'Yes,' Adric said. Medford nodded, as though his suspicions had been confirmed, then turned back to the Patient. One of the physicians was aiming a medical scanner at the Patient. She shook her head again, wincing. The light source beaming from the scanner seemed to be causing her pain. Finally her eyes closed and she slumped.

'She's in a self-induced coma,' the Doctor's voice announced. Adric had almost forgotten about him. The blood had dried on the Doctor's lip, but he appeared pale, shaken. He remained slumped in the corner.

'Are you all right?' Adric was acutely aware that the Doctor had collapsed twice in the last twenty-four hours. Seeing the process again reminded Adric just how recent the Doctor's own regeneration had been. The Doctor ignored him.

'She is of your race?' Medford demanded before the Doctor had time to answer.

103

'Yes,' the Doctor said quietly. 'But I had no idea,' he added.

'We will discuss that elsewhere. Take them away.' Adric was grabbed from behind. The Doctor was pulled out of his vision, clearly too weak to resist.

'She needs my help,' the Doctor shouted. 'Regeneration is a traumatic experience and I am the only person around here who is qualified to help her.'

Medford tapped a button on his wrist computer. 'This is the Provost-General. Security alert. Activate the defence grid.'

The physicians had loaded her onto a trolley. The Doctor tried to break free to reach her, but was dragged back.

'The psionic beam has cut off,' the Prorector announced. Whitfield joined him at his monitor.

'It happened suddenly. There was no reduction in the datastream until the moment of termination. Then everything flatlined.'

'It's been there for a million years.'

'If only we had a time machine: we could go back and see it arrive.'

'That is hardly a practical suggestion, Prorector.'

'No, Chief Scientist, I apologize.'

Whitfield looked out of the observation port. The Machine stood there, silently as ever. There was no outward sign of activity, and nothing about it had seemed to have changed. She banged her fist against the plastic window.

'Chief Scientist?'

'It's so frustrating. The moment we make a discovery, it's snatched away from us or it completely contradicts what we already know.' She stood straight, tugging her tunic back into shape. 'I am sorry. This is not the place for such an emotional outburst.'

The deputy was clearly a little unsure how to react, beyond embarrassment. 'What shall I do next?' he asked after a short pause.

'We continue. Prepare the third stage.'

* * *

The decor in the restaurant of the Imperial Hotel was light, but this only served to emphasize how many cooking stains there were on the ceiling. The carpet by the swingdoor to the kitchens had been worn bare, and around the tables it was little better.

Tegan sat at a table towards the centre of the room, watching the comings and goings while she waited for Nyssa. Quite what her companion was doing, she wasn't sure. Tegan didn't particularly want to order yet another cup of coffee – in fact, she was worried that the restaurant would be closing for the night any minute. Most of the diners were the usual mix of couples: married, unmarried and not-married-to-each-other. Everyone here was human, although the variety of clothing was a little bewildering: everything from tailored tunics to what almost resembled eighteenth-century pirate gear. Most were on their best behaviour. The only exception was a party of laboratory technicians in the middle of a night on the town who were sitting behind Tegan singing an incomprehensible drinking song. They were clearly very amused by it. The lyrics consisted of the same line repeated over and over and over again.

> 'We're in a chronic hyst-er-esis.
> Yes, we're in a chronic hysteresis!
> We're in a chronic hyst-er-esis.
> Yes, we're in a chronic hysteresis!
> We're in a chronic hyst-er-esis.'

And so on.

The volume fell from a loud roar to a low whisper, picking up again at the end of each line. The lab technicians were enjoying themselves, but the other diners were less than thrilled. Most were content to scowl at them from time to time. It had been carrying on for three or four minutes. Tegan was just about to turn around and give the men a piece of her mind.

'Excuse me,' a male voice asked. 'Could you keep it down? Some of us here are trying to eat.'

They laughed rowdily at first, made exaggerated *shushing* noises. But they didn't resume the chant. A number of fellow diners made a show of looking grateful. Tegan twisted around to thank the man, only to face the Australian.

'Hi honey, I'm home,' he drawled. Without waiting to be invited he walked round and took the seat opposite her. He had changed out of his suit into a tuxedo, complete with bow tie. It served to emphasize his broad chest and shoulders.

A spherical robot bobbed over, a large green bottle in its claw. 'The champagne you ordered, Mr Jovanka,' it purred in a perfectly modulated voice. The cork popped, and the robot began pouring.

'Now, wait just a minute,' Tegan began.

'Relax. Have a drink. I'll explain.' His smile was almost reassuring, and there wasn't an ounce of menace in the voice. He was almost the definition of clean-cut: like a fifties movie star or an Olympic athlete. He passed her the glass.

'Why should I trust you?' she asked, already half-willing to do so. She sipped at the champagne.

The young man smiled. 'Now what sort of attitude is that? A wife not trusting her own husband?'

Medford had taken them to one of the medical suites on level three-three-zero. He stood in the corner now, as the Doctor lay on the diagnosis couch, a medical scanning beam passing down his body. The chief medical officer of the Scientifica was tapping instructions into a computer terminal. His flowing red uniform reminded the Doctor a little of the robes of the Spanish Inquisition. On the screen at the head of the bed the results of the scan were being translated into images. The Doctor cricked his neck to see his own vital organs, skeletal and nervous systems resolving into a detailed plan.

'Are you all right now, Doctor?' Adric asked. He was sitting on a bench, an Adjudicator standing over him.

'There's no need to keep asking me that question. Don't fuss.'

The chief medical officer unhooked a simbook. Holographic pages unfurled, diagrams and charts filled themselves in. He stood engrossed in them for a couple of seconds. 'These are the details of the female patient.'

106

'Where is she?' Adric asked, before the Doctor could.

'In another suite like this one,' the medical officer informed them. 'You say that you and the Patient are members of the same race?'

'That is correct. We are both Gallifreyans. Er, you don't happen to know her name, do you?'

'No. My colleagues have asked her, but she seems to be suffering from selective amnesia. It is difficult to say, she doesn't appear to speak any language known in this galaxy.'

'She banged herself right on the back of the head.' The Doctor sat upright, tapping the appropriate spot on the anatomical diagram. 'The structure of the brain is more specialized in Gallifreyans than in humans. There's a lobe at the back of the head, the hippocampus, that helps to regulate the short-term memory. Or is that the lindal gland? I forget. The regeneration won't have helped clear the mind.'

'She underwent total cellular restructure.' It was a statement, not a question, but the scientist clearly wanted to know more.

'Selected members of my people, the Time Lords, have the ability to regenerate. As long as our brain survives to initiate the process, we can grow an entirely new body when the old one is mortally injured or wears out through extreme old age.'

'Convenient,' Medford noted.

'Not always. The process is not without its dangers, and is never easy. Special mental preparation is usually required, the regeneration itself should ideally take place within an area subject to a low-grade telepathic field. If possible, another one of my race should be there to assist in the case of difficulty, to coax and guide the regenerative process. After regenerating, total tranquillity is required for a short time, while the mind and body readjust.'

The medical officer didn't acknowledge the last remark. 'When we discovered the Patient, she was in extreme old age – it's impossible to say how old, but it was many, many centuries. She must have been on the verge of death for a long time, but hadn't "regenerated". Was it your presence that triggered the change?'

The possibility hadn't occurred to the Doctor. He took a

moment to think about it. 'Yes,' he concluded, 'I think you must be right. I didn't know that she was from Gallifrey until just before she regenerated.' She'd initiated telepathic contact. The Doctor remembered that now. He couldn't recall the details, but she had tried to communicate with him. What had she said? He tried to piece it together.

'But you are sure that she is a Time Lord now?' Provost-General Medford prompted.

'Only we can regenerate,' the Doctor assured him.

'And members of your race all have the same bio-chemistry, genetic make-up and physiological structure?' the medical officer asked.

'Well yes,' the Doctor replied, a little confused by the question and where it was leading.

'Provost-General,' the medical officer announced, 'the two subjects are from different species.' He touched the screen, and a diagram of the Patient's body appeared alongside the Doctor's.

'As you can see, she only has one heart. A number of other organs are a different size, configuration or shape.'

'Is it a gender difference?' Medford asked, but both the medical officer and the Doctor were shaking their heads.

'Their blood has a completely different composition, as do the hormones and pheromones. Her DNA is closer to the Doctor's than to a human's, but it is in no way identical – they are about as different as human DNA is from that of a chimpanzee.'

'They *are* from the same planet?'

'It is a strong possibility that they have a common ancestor, Provost-General, but I cannot confirm or deny that at this stage. As an interesting aside, the Doctor's own DNA has been subject to genetic manipulation at some point in his past, many generations ago.'

'My people sought to improve on their physical form, long ago. Advances in medical science helped to prolong our lifespans, to make us more resistant to disease.'

'And all . . . Time Lords were altered in this way?' Medford asked.

'Well, yes,' the Doctor said. 'Any other way would have been terribly unfair.'

'The female subject shows no evidence of such genetic engineering.' The medical officer announced triumphantly. 'The only conclusion is that she is not of your race.'

'Oh,' the Doctor said softly. He gazed at the diagram of the Patient again, trying to find a clue in the gentle musculature of her stomach, the swirling patterns of her arteries, the delicate network of capillaries or the flowing curve of her clavicle. 'I have to see her. Ask her myself.'

'That is out of the question,' Medford stated.

'I demand the right, on medical grounds if nothing else. I am a doctor, after all.'

'You don't have any rights,' Medford told him softly.

The Doctor stopped. 'What?'

'You're an alien and a spy,' Medford explained. 'Under Imperial Law, espionage is a capital offence. Alien spies don't have any rights, you don't have any rights. Remember that. Remember that I can have both you and your friend here executed here and now. Now that your medical examination is complete, we shall continue this interrogation elsewhere.'

Despite his brash exterior, Tegan was finding Bruce Jovanka good company. The champagne was also rather fine. He was still sitting opposite, studying her. Whenever she was speaking, Tegan got the impression that he was listening. The conversation had been pretty much confined to small talk so far. They had discussed the champagne, the weather and the decor. His accent was a bit softer, now, the Ocker slang had all but disappeared. Tegan hadn't forgotten, though. She was leading up to the killer question.

He leant forward. 'You've got pretty eyes, you know?' His voice was lilting, hypnotic. His eyes were blue. He was about her age.

'Thank you,' she said. 'Your eyes are nice, too,' she added, rather wishing she hadn't.

'Tegan's a lovely name, you know. I've always thought so.'

She arched an eyebrow.

'I know it's an unusual name, but there was a "Tegan" at my school when I was very young. We used to hang

109

around together, go for bike rides, swim in the creek. There wasn't anything more to it than that, even though our parents seemed to think we'd get married one day. We were only eight.'

Tegan smiled at his innocence, then blinked, remembering the killer question.

His hand brushed against hers. Tegan glanced down. There was downy blond hair on the back of his hand, running up to the wrist. It stood out against the tanned skin.

Tegan roused herself. It was time to ask it. 'So whereabouts are you from?' she asked sweetly.

Bruce chuckled. 'I'm from a lovely city by the name of Australia, back on Earth.'

'Really?' Tegan said. 'Is it a big place?'

'Oh yeah, but despite that it's a really close-knit community,' he said wistfully. 'The weather's beautiful and sunny and there's a swimming pool in most back gardens. Everyone knows one other, and we're all in and out of each other's houses all the time, making each other casseroles and lammingtons. Everyone talks through their problems at the local coffee shop, or over a nice cup of herbal tea. That's the thing, isn't it? With a little understanding, you can find the perfect blend, and that's when good neighbours become good friends.'

'Excuse me while I throw up,' Tegan said in a still, level voice. She didn't withdraw her hand.

Bruce blanched. 'I beg your pardon?'

Tegan leant forward, her eyes narrowing. 'You're a liar. You've listened to a couple of Barry Humphries LPs and brewed up some ludicrous half-baked racist stereotype to cover up what you're really doing here. But I've caught you out. Look, mate, I don't care what you're doing here, because you've insulted my country and you've insulted me. Apologize. Now. Then explain why you've done it. And make it good.'

'What does LP stand for?' Bruce tried to ask.

'Answer me!' Tegan snarled.

'You're right,' he stammered. His voice had shifted to something resembling Canadian. 'Of course you're right,' he added. He struggled to regain control of the situation. 'Sorry,' he said finally.

'Good start. Now, why?' Tegan demanded.

'I'm here on special business.'

'If you're about to spin me some bull about being a solar panel salesman, I'll go straight to the police.'

'No, look, don't shout, I'm trying to explain.' He straightened, his entire body language changing from a swaggering lout into something altogether more disciplined in bearing. 'I'm working here undercover.'

'You're a spy?' Tegan asked.

'Yes.'

'OK. So I take it your name isn't really "Bruce Jovanka".'

'No, my name is Cwej, Chris Cwej.'

'A likely story.'

'It *is*,' he insisted.

'Prove it.'

'How? I'm here undercover, so I've not brought any ID.'

'Well, forgive me, but I don't believe a word of what you say.'

He reached into his pocket and pulled out a small grey box. 'Here. I've got a friend –'

'You surprise me.'

'– a friend who'll be able to tell you what my name is.' He tapped the button.

Nothing happened.

He tapped the button again.

Nothing happened.

'I'm impressed,' Tegan told him.

'Look, why don't we go up to my room? The reception up there will be a lot better. We'll talk this over, then I'll try this again.'

Before he could react, a splash of champagne arced through the air towards him. It sloshed along the length of his forehead, streaming down his face.

'Pervert!' she shouted. 'Of all the lousy excuses.'

By the time Cwej had wrung the champagne from his eyes, Tegan had vanished.

Another volley of energy bolts shot past, red this time.

Gemboyle bit his lip.

There was a huge explosion.

Roslyn Forrester dived into the space behind one of the buttresses at the base of the western face of the Scientifica pyramid, dropping her heavy bag to the ground.

'Was that your communicator bleeping back there?' Gemboyle asked nervously.

Forrester was hunched over, her hands on her knees. 'Possibly. I was too busy trying simultaneously to outrun a wardroid and dodge through a minefield.'

'Wardroid?' he stammered. 'I didn't see the wardroid.'

'Don't worry about it. Ancient history now.'

'What happened?'

She looked up. 'I dodged a plasma mine, the robot didn't.'

'It must have been a version four: the new MechInfs have bigger feet than the earlier models, but the software didn't take that into account at first. They've turned on the defence grid, haven't they?'

'Yes.'

'They know we're coming?'

'Gemboyle, don't flatter yourself. There are two of us. The measures they've set up there would stop a small army.'

'We got through.'

'Not yet we didn't. We're still on the outside.'

Forrester and Gemboyle looked up. The ebony surface of the Scientifica swept up at a steep incline, too steep to climb.

'So how do we get in?' Over the last couple of weeks, Gemboyle had learnt that Forrester could do the impossible almost as a matter of routine. She'd acquired a digital map of the Scientifica from somewhere, for one thing, one that included all the security points. She was consulting it now.

'The nearest way in from here is that window – it's a long way up.'

Gemboyle couldn't even see it until she pointed it out to him. 'Either you've got a pair of wings underneath that coat or you've got a plan.'

His companion shrugged and reached into her bag.

She removed a chunky pistol, then zipped the bag up. 'I haven't got wings, I haven't got a plan, but I have got this service issue grappling hook and line. With integral rangefinder.'

She raised the gun above her head and flicked a switch. After a moment, she brought it back down. There was a luminous readout on the butt of the gun.

'Two hundred and fifteen metres.' She checked the map for confirmation. 'It's an observation room on level one-zero-one, for civilian use. Civilian is a Xhosa word meaning "no guns".'

'How long is the line?'

She checked the panel on the side. 'Two hundred metres.'

Gemboyle grimaced. 'We can't do it, Roz, not this time. We'll have to go back.'

'Not necessarily. We've also got this,' she reminded him, pulling what looked like a discus from her waistband.

'One of the gravity brakes from the train. What use is that?'

'It has its own power supply, it can be adjusted.'

'So we can stop trains. That didn't work last time and there *was* a train then.'

'Could you set this to maximum range?' She handed him the brake. Gemboyle took a small tool from his breast pocket and fiddled with the innards of the machine for a couple of seconds. 'Maximum range,' he announced, handing the disc back to her.

Forrester laid it on the ground.

'You've got a plan now, haven't you?'

'Yes. It's a bunjee jump, only in reverse and without the rope. The brake fires, reversing the gravity field in a column two hundred and fifty metres directly above it. Anyone standing on the disc at the time would be propelled up that distance at around fifty metres a second.'

'And then you'd be stuck in mid-air.'

'No, because at maximum power the disc's batteries run down after five seconds.'

'So, what you're saying is that it's like jumping off a cliff a quarter of a kilometre high, only in reverse. Then the

113

power cuts out, and it becomes exactly like falling off a cliff a quarter of a kilometre high.'

'Yes.' Her eyes flashed. 'Are you coming or not?'

'I'll pass, if you don't mind.'

'OK. You remember the escape route?'

'Of course. Skitrain station, northern face.'

'Get back to the Imperial. Give Adam my regards and tell him what I'm doing.'

She stepped onto the disc, as if it were a diving board.

'Good luck,' Gemboyle called over.

Gemboyle watched as Forrester composed herself, drawing her hands to her sides, pulling herself straight, tucking her head down tight to her collarbone. She brought her breathing under control. When she was ready, she looked up at the black slope that vanished into the clouds. Gemboyle kept his eyes fixed on her.

She clicked her heels together and shot into the air.

8

Angels and/or Devils

Falconstock stood at the edge of the terrace. It was the middle of the night. He had wanted to come up here, to reflect on what had happened tonight. Soon those young people would be dead. Through the thick plate glass, the city looked serene as ever. The air was thin up here and the sound of babies crying and barking dogs rarely drifted this far up. Falconstock remembered a story he'd been told by one of his teachers, decades ago. Once upon a time, an old man who had been born blind was cured. When he had looked at the world the first time, he saw all the cracks in the plaster, the chips in the paint, the mould on the walls, the missing roof slates, discoloured tarmac, the dirt, rust, mange, acne, grime, discoloration, filth, all the little imperfections that he had never imagined were there, that he had never pictured. Unable to live in an imperfect universe, he took out his own eyes the very next day. The story probably wasn't true, not in the usual sense.

Nowadays, restoring sight was simply a routine operation, not the miracle it might once have been. The Scientifica could cure cripples and lepers here with their medicines. They could walk on water and part the seas with artificial gravity. Molecular processors could turn water into wine, lead into gold, people into columns of salt. Food poured from nutrition synthesizers. They'd abolished poverty. They'd proved conclusively that Father Christmas didn't exist, that there were no such things as fairies and that angels were simply metaphors. They could kill children in the name of justice. Everything could be explained away.

A woman wearing a grey fur coat fell up past the window. She held in mid-air for a moment, raising her arm straight out in front of her. Falconstock had time to register that she was holding something before there was an explosive blast and the plate glass shattered into shards. Falconstock stumbled back, covering his eyes. Something whizzed past him, and the viewscreen bolted to the back wall exploded into sparks.

The intruder alarm was buzzing, it had been ever since the glass had shattered. The sound shook Falconstock, convincing him that he hadn't been dreaming. He whirled round. A metal hook was embedded in the monitor, a taut metal line led from it and outside into the cold night air. Falconstock rushed over to the window. The woman was dangling five metres below him, the line wrapped around her right hand. As he watched, she began to pull herself upwards. Her eyes were closed, she was out of breath, but she continued, hand over hand. Beneath her, fragments of glass were twinkling against the lights from the Scientifica, they still hadn't reached the ground. In almost no time, she was hauling herself over the window frame, her leg swinging over for momentum. She was sweating, trying to catch her breath. She grunted something. She was old, no more than ten years younger than him.

Falconstock punched her in the face. She reeled, but in the same movement had lashed out, forcing him back. He grabbed a piece of metal piping that had fallen from the frame and swung it at the woman's head. She caught his wrist, squeezed it, prised the pipe from his hands and kicked his legs from under him, all in one movement.

The alarm continued to blare. Why hadn't anyone answered it yet?

As he fell, Falconstock slipped. A sound like a whipcrack passed through him.

A headless body fell into his field of vision alongside him.

She wasn't pressing her attack. Why were her eyes wide? Why was she staring at him? Why that expression of horror? And why was the body wearing his tunic?

Alarm bells ringing.

It's my body. Alongside me. A clean cut, right through the neck. A shard of glass from the window. I didn't even feel it, only heard it. The blood supply to my brain has been

116

cut off but for just one calm moment before the blood already in my head is used up I am still

'Excuse me, have you seen my friend?'

The young man lowered the napkin. It was Jovanka. 'G'day.'

Nyssa looked away, blushing. 'I'm sorry.'

'Cripes, it's Nyssa isn't it? I didn't recognize you with my clothes on.'

'How do you know my name, Mr Jovanka?'

'Call me Bruce, everyone else does. To answer your question. I made it my business to. As soon as I'd finished my shower, I went downstairs and asked the concierge about the lovely young maid who'd been in my room. He gave me your name. D'ya want a drink?' He pulled back a chair for her, and Nyssa took her place at the table.

Bruce poured her a glass of champagne and leant forward. 'You've got pretty eyes, you know that?' His voice was earnest, and his eyes sparkled as he spoke. He was a number of years older than she was.

'Thank you,' Nyssa replied, blushing slightly. It was the first time she had tasted Terran wine. It compared well with those of Traken.

'Nyssa's a lovely name, you know. I've always thought so.'

She frowned.

'I know it's unusual,' Jovanka said quickly, 'but there was a "Nyssa" at my school when I was very young. We used to hang around together, go for bike rides, swim in the creek. There wasn't anything more to it than that.' He chuckled. 'Our parents thought that we'd get married one day. We were only ten years old.'

His hand brushed against hers. Nyssa started, and looked down. He had very large hands and well-manicured nails. As before, she sensed only goodness from him.

'I'm sorry about . . . you know,' Nyssa began. 'I understand that human etiquette regarding the display of genitalia is very strict. My people have similar taboos. For an unmarried woman to see a man's er –'

'Listen, Nyssa, I'd rather not talk about it in public.'

117

Nyssa reddened. 'No, no, I quite understand. Neither would I. Why don't we go up to my room for a little more privacy?'

'Are you sure? You hardly know me.'

'No, no, I insist. It's the least I can do.'

Tegan slid the keycard down and the door to her room clicked open. She stepped inside, and the lights flickered on. She kicked off her shoes, rubbing the heel where it was sore. The curtains hadn't been drawn over the glass door leading out to the balcony. Tegan saw herself reflected in it, looking exhausted. Alongside her were two chunky blue shapes.

She was shoved against the wall and frisked, a gun to her head. There were two of them – armoured figures like she had seen outside the hotel. The smaller one was patting her down, looking for guns. The other had a box in his hand.

'Don't kill me,' she said, trying to keep calm, trying not to panic them into shooting her. All basic tactics when dealing with hijackers and armed nutters.

The one frisking her was a young woman, she realized. She caught a glimpse of curly red hair.

'Clear!' she called when her search was complete.

'Turn around.' Tegan did so, very slowly. They stood watching her closely. The blue armour was made from some plastic-looking material trimmed in gold. Nyssa wasn't here, there wasn't any sign that she had been. The taller one, a middle-aged Asian man, said one word: 'Record.'

'Hands behind you,' the woman demanded. Without protest, Tegan crossed them behind her back. She felt something pressed to her wrist. It secured itself around her. Automatic handcuffs.

'You are Tegan Jovanka?' His voice was weary. He had seen better days.

'Yes,' she said quietly. How did they know that?

'You are under arrest for conspiracy to commit treason.'

'I've only been on the planet three hours,' she objected. 'All I've done in that time is book into this hotel and had a pot of coffee. You've got the wrong woman!'

The man wasn't listening. 'I am obliged to inform you

118

that your words, gestures and postures are being recorded and may form part of any judicial action taken against you. You have the right to consult legalware.'

'You're recording my posture?' Tegan echoed, standing up straight.

The elder one was searching the room. Drawer after drawer was empty, neither of the beds had been slept in. 'Where are your belongings?'

'I'm wearing them all,' she said brusquely. 'Apart from my shoes.'

The woman bent down to investigate them: a pair of cheap white high heels that Tegan had bought the week before from Freeman Hardy and Willis. The young police officer picked them up and dropped them in a plastic bag.

Tegan had regained some of her composure, now that her life was not in immediate danger. 'Do you mind telling me exactly what I'm meant to have done?'

'We will deal with all that back at the Lodge.' The man moved to lead her away.

'We'll deal with it here,' Tegan told him. At the same time she was worrying about Nyssa: try to get them away from here before she comes looking for me.

The male Adjudicator faced her. 'You have been consorting with aliens,' he stated.

Tegan couldn't deny it.

Roz Forrester was on her knees, trying to get her breath back.

The headless corpse of the man she had killed lay beside her. There was blood everywhere. She had tried to stop it from happening, Roz told herself. It was an accident. The alarm was still ringing, and she had to get moving. Reaching into the pocket of the dead man's tunic she found an identity card, a Unitatan coin and a couple of keycards. She palmed them and left the room, closing and locking the door behind her with a standard Adjudicator override code that she knew was already in use now, a couple of centuries before her own time. From her Academy days the Bureau had used a mnemonica to tuck all that sort of information away in her mind. Every single code that she was

119

authorized to use, including all the ones that had been declassified centuries ago.

It was the middle of the night, and there were few people around. The lighting was dimmed. She needed to find a security terminal. Before that, she'd have to stop and consult her map. She came to a halt by a statue of an Asian man in a long kaftan: 'Chun Sen'. It looked out of place in an otherwise bare corridor. She'd heard the name before, but couldn't remember in what context. Her breathing was a bit more even now, but her lungs were still sore and her wrist was burning where the metal line had dug into it. She was surprised how exhausted she felt. Ten years ago, five years ago, she'd have been fine. Now she needed to take a painkiller before she blacked out. She slumped at the base of the statue, pulled herself out of view and slipped the dispenser from her pocket.

Three Adjudicators in full combat gear ran past, travelling too fast to see her. From behind the statue, Roz strained to hear what they were saying.

'Door's locked.'

'Open it.'

A pause as the door hissed open. Then horrified cries.

'A Scientifica technician.'

'Lots of glass. Killer must have jumped out the window.'

'Must have had a jetpack.'

'No, look, he used a hook and line. Climbed down.'

'Crime scene, officer, don't touch it.'

'Alert security control: killer at loose in the city.'

'Get a memory droid in here.'

'I'm glad the killer's not in here any more.'

Roz was a little light-headed now that the pills were taking effect. She stood and made for the end of the corridor before the Adjudicators had finished. The liftshafts were concentrated towards the middle of each floor. She was only one floor away from level one-zero-zero, her objective.

Whitfield watched as the dozen research scientists moved into place. They performed the normal checks on their radiation suits. Once this was done, she gave the signal to begin, and pulled down her visor. The technicians at the first console began the start-up procedure. Beneath the observation dome, fusion generators were roaring into life. If you were aware of that, you could feel the floor hum very slightly. Other technicians began their work, murmuring reports into their recorders.

'Stage three in five seconds,' she heard the Prorector call.

Outside, the Machine responded. The lights on its flank began to gain in brightness. For the moment, there was nothing that she could do: her people knew their jobs. All she could do was watch the Machine. The lights were almost dazzling now. The cavern was filled with a brilliant radiance. A couple of the vast power cables were beginning to twitch. At the base of the Machine, a crack of white light had appeared. It grew wider.

Whitfield's eyes were fixed on it.

'It's a doorway,' she whispered.

The Doctor and Adric were being frogmarched to the detention cells on level three-zero-eight. Adric was in front of the Doctor. Each had an escort. Behind them there were half a dozen Adjudicators, four of whom were holding up laser pistols. Medford was in front of them with another three troops. It was midnight, and the Provost-General had just been informed of a successful military operation against Pryanishnikov Station, an enemy stronghold to the north.

'Provost-General to security control: clear corridor three-zero-eight-zed.'

'We are not spies,' the Doctor insisted.

'Then you should have no objections to undergoing a mindscan.'

The Doctor was about to reply when there was a buzzing from his wrist.

'Hand me that,' Medford ordered.

The Doctor slipped the time sensor off and passed it over.

'What is it?'

The Doctor clearly felt that he had nothing to lose. 'It detects disturbances in the time field. I arrived on this planet to track down such a temporal anomaly and every time that sensor has buzzed it has meant that –'

Five of them were in the corridor, their stiff black robes blowing in some alien breeze. They were advancing, fading in and out of reality with every step.

The Adjudicators levelled their weapons.

'Don't shoot!' the Doctor warned them, trying to step forward. The Adjudicators ignored him. Bright red energy bolts sliced through the air. The apparitions stopped, but the energy passed through them, hitting the wall behind them.

'Cease fire!' Medford ordered.

There was a pause. The ghosts were drifting forward, but more slowly than before. Then the lead one held his hands out, palms flat.

'*Chal'Ar, Cha!*' He swept his right arm down. The Adjudicator to the right was swept off his feet and was hurled against the wall as if he'd been caught in a tornado.

'Telekinesis,' Adric observed.

The Adjudicator to the left aimed his blaster and fired. The bolt reached the ghost, but stopped before it hit him. The ghost took the energy of it in his hand, examined it for a moment, then hurled it back. The Adjudicator was hit in the chest, dying instantly.

The Provost-General was barking orders into his communicator, 'All Adjudicators, respond. Priority: Scientifica has been invaded by hostile alien forces. All officers in the area to take up defensive positions.' The Adjudicators behind them rushed forward.

The Doctor tugged at Adric's arm. 'I think we might use this diversion to escape, hmm?'

They slipped away.

'Where do we go now?' Adric asked. Behind them, the Adjudicators were firing their guns again.

'We try to find the Patient.'

The hatch on room one-zero-zero was sealed with tape, and there was a guard on it. Forrester was still unarmed, and didn't want to kill a member of the Bureau unless she had to. She certainly didn't want to try when he had a gun and she didn't.

What happened next was almost too good to be true: the officer's communicator buzzed and before the radio message had been completed, the Adjudicator had left his post. He was still clattering down the corridor as she arrived at the metal door. She broke the tape with the sharp edge of one of the keycards and opened it up using another security code. The bolts drew back with a crack and the hatch swung open. It was dark inside. There seemed to be an anteroom of some kind leading to the life support chamber proper.

That door was open already. Roz moved into it. The life support chamber was full of smashed medical equipment. Every piece of glass in the room was cracked, all the metal was twisted. Everything was covered in thick blue slime.

The cryotube was there, but it was open, and empty. Forrester paced around it, ran her fingers over it, but there was still no one inside it. The blue slime was cryogenic fluid, she realized. Things were not going according to plan.

She needed time to think, and so needed to know whether anyone was looking for her. There was a computer terminal hanging from one wall. Roz booted it up and dialled the security grid. The main news was a military action to the north. It sounded bad, but she couldn't worry about it just yet. There was also a priority call to level three-zero-eight, something about intruders. It was a busy night. Beneath that, easy to ignore, was an APB with identiphots. She recognized one of the perps.

Forrester read the whole message before unclipping her communicator.

Nyssa slapped Chris on the face.

'I am not that sort of girl,' she told him.

'I didn't say you were. I'm not that sort of . . . All I said was –'

'When I agreed that you could come up to my room, it was to talk, nothing more. Now you try and . . . you hardly know me. Out!' She pointed at the door. Chris slunk out, closing the door behind him. Out in the corridor, he stared back at the door for a moment. He ought to go back and apologize.

'*Forrester to Cwej. Forrester to Cwej.*'

He reached into his tuxedo and pulled out his communicator. 'Where have you been?'

'*Busy. There's no time for small talk, they're coming for you.*'

'Who?'

'*Who do you think? They've got your room number.*'

Chris's eyes widened.

'*Congratulations on your wedding. The bad news is they've just arrested your blushing bride and now they're coming back for you and a girl called "Nyssa".*'

There were two bulky shadows at the end of the corridor. Chris spun around. Two Adjudicators moving into position. He flicked off the communicator, drew his pistol and kicked down the door.

Nyssa had removed her jacket, and was halfway to unlacing her blouse. She whirled to face him. 'How dare you?'

Chris grabbed her, and flung her over his shoulder.

'Put me down!'

He blew off the lock to the balcony door with a well-aimed shot.

'I said put me –'

He sprang over the railing and off the balcony just as the first energy bolt sizzled past.

'– down.'

It was only then that Chris remembered that they were on the fifth floor.

There hadn't been a guard on the door, although how the Doctor had known exactly which room they would find the Patient in was a mystery. She was lying on a diagnostic couch, still unconscious. She was wearing a flowing gown, presumably hospital issue. It was white, and reached her ankles. The Doctor hurried over to the bed, bending over her.

'Ανδ I τυρνεδ αρουνδ ανδ τηεψ ωερε αλλ ωεαρινγ εψεπατχηεσ,' he burbled. The syllables were almost musical. It sounded like a nursery rhyme to Adric.

The Patient's eyes flickered open. She seemed more at ease than before. The Doctor touched her face tenderly. She smiled. Whatever pain she had been in just before her regeneration had clearly worn off.

124

'What did you just say?' Adric asked.

'It's Gallifreyan,' the Doctor explained. 'And she recognized it.'

The Patient began to stir. With a little assistance from the Doctor, she was able to swing her long legs over the edge of the bed. Finally she stood, unsteady on her feet, like a new-born calf. Adric hadn't realized how tall she was, almost exactly the Doctor's height. As they stood together for the first time, it struck Adric that they looked like brother and sister: they both appeared to be in their early thirties, they had fair hair and a slim build.

Already the Patient was more sure of herself. She stood straight, her head lifted. She made her first tentative step. The Doctor smiled encouragement.

'Hello,' said Adric slowly. 'What is your name?'

She smiled at him, but clearly didn't understand what he was saying.

The door pulsed, and suddenly it was glowing red.

'The Adjudicators have found us.' The Doctor stood back. Adric could already feel the heat coming from the door.

'Is the door strong enough to hold?'

'I doubt that they'd be trying to cut through it if it were.'

The Patient appeared alarmed. The Doctor moved to reassure her. He caught sight of something on the skirting board. 'A ventilation duct!' He moved towards it, taking the sonic screwdriver from his pocket. He loosened the grille and pulled it away from the wall.

'They're nearly through,' Adric told him. Sections of the door had almost melted away.

The Doctor led the Patient to the open vent. She understood what he was trying to do, and the hole was just large enough for her to squeeze through. She dropped out of sight.

'You next, Adric.'

'There's only time for one more person to get through. You go.'

'They'll kill you,' the Doctor yelled.

'Go!' Adric shouted. The Doctor turned on his heel, and dived through the hole. Adric moved the grille back into place. By the time he had finished, the door had evaporated.

Adric raised his hands, turning his palms forwards so that they could see he wasn't carrying anything.

The middle-aged woman from the skitrain station stood in the doorframe, still wearing her fur coat. She looked around. 'I take it that I've missed the Patient?'

Adric nodded dumbly. There was the sound of clattering boots from outside.

'Here we go again,' she said wearily. 'Well, come on if you're coming.'

Adric scrambled to his feet and joined her. They jogged down the corridor.

'Where to?'

'Not far.' She stopped at one of the doors. 'Just in here.' She tapped a combination, and shoved him through. The door hissed shut behind them.

It was pitch black. He could hear the woman wheezing, out of breath. His own heart was still pounding against his ribs. Adric reached out, his hand brushing over what felt like a tortoiseshell, and then he found a touch-sensitive plate. The light winked on.

She had stripped down to her underwear, a pale green haltertop and tight shorts that looked odd next to her skin. Rivulets of sweat were running down her spine. She looked exhausted, but hadn't even sat down, stuffing her coat and other clothes into her bag.

'Well, don't just stare,' she said in a low voice. The walls of the room were lined with suits of Adjudicator armour. The curved shape next to the light switch had been a shoulderpad. The woman was reaching down a pair of leggings for herself.

'What's your name?' he asked. 'I'm Adric.'

'A what? I'm Roslyn Forrester. You can call me Forrester.'

She bent over, clipping strips of armour over her shins. 'Find one your size,' she prompted. Adric nodded, and began looking. By the time he had found a breastplate that he thought would fit, she was looping a bulky utility belt around her waist. Forrester must have been on the verge of collapse: she was old enough to have greying hair, and although her arms were muscled, her face was lined.

'Why did you save me?' he asked, trying to get her to slow down.

Forrester paused. 'I was returning a favour.'

Adric struggled to remember. 'You mean when I didn't shoot you at the station?'

She chuckled. 'No. The stungun is keyed to my thumb-print. If you'd tried to fire it, then the whole powerpack would have discharged down your arm. You saved me just before that when the armed response hovercopter turned up.'

'Oh yes, I'd forgotten that.'

'Lucky for you that I didn't.'

Adric was wrestling with one of the shoulder-catches of the armour, and Forrester came over to help. She reached over him, and slapped it hard. Adric caught a glimpse of dark hair underneath her arm. The catch snapped into place. Forrester returned to her bench to pull on a pair of boots. As they were buckling themselves, she selected a pair of leggings for him. Adric pulled them on over his trousers and fastened them. She was tugging on a thick pair of mittens, and flexed her fingers. She held out her right hand for Adric's inspection. A stubby metal tube ran from the back of the hand down into the fabric swathing her upper arm.

'Have you ever used a guntlet before?'

'No. I'm not even sure what it is.'

She clenched her fist and a high-pitched whine started up. She flicked her fingers out in turn, as though she was counting. Every time another finger snapped out, there was a clicking sound and the whine changed pitch. 'It's a stan-dard Adjudicator weapon: a wrist-mounted laser cannon. You change the settings by making hand gestures. You fire it by miming pulling a trigger. If you've not used one before, then you'd better take the standard issue gloves. These things are dangerous if you're not used to them. Especially if you're playing charades.'

Adric put on a pair of dark blue gloves. They were fingerless, but had strips of plastic woven into the knuckles. They were nearly finished. Forrester passed over a portable computer. He'd seen Medford with one before, so knew where it slotted into his armoured wrist-guard. He booted it up to check that it was working. Forrester was doing the same. Finally, they put on the helmets, a one-piece affair with a mirrored visor. Holographic eyecons flashed up to indicate the status of the suit's systems. Forrester appeared as a bright map of pressure points and vital organs. The room's shadows and corners flashed yellow as the tactics computer warned him that danger could be lurking there. The doorframe was picked out in red. Earcons buzzed warnings and prompts – 'Suit integrity at 100 per cent' 'Intruder alert' 'Defence grid active'. Adric used the controls on his wrist to simplify the displays. Forrester was doing the same, by the look of it. They looked up at precisely the same moment to confirm that they were ready.

'How do we get out?'

'There's an escape route planned.' Her voice was electronically modulated. Adric realized that his voice was also being filtered through a helmet microphone. 'We'll have to get to a designated cell.'

'Which one?'

She was dialling up something on her computer. 'The one that the computer "randomly" allocates to anyone brought in with the surname "Jovanka". It's all part of the plan.'

'Jovanka, but that's –'

'Cell 289-G. First, though, we have to try to find the Patient and get her to the Doctor.'

'The Doctor has already got her.'

Roz turned. 'What? How long have you known the Doctor?'

'Only a couple of weeks,' Adric admitted, 'but we've been through a lot together in that time. I was there when he regenerated.'

'He what? No, it's all right, I heard you.' Forrester considered this new information for a moment. 'Wait a cotton-picking minute: that young man at the train station with pyjama bottoms and the gormless grin . . . the guy I shot, he was the Doctor?'

Adric nodded. 'He did try and tell you. You escaped, but

we were arrested and brought to Scientifica. We got out and rescued the Patient from the medical centre. When you found me I was covering their escape.'

'Fantastic,' she replied, with more than a hint of irritation in her voice. 'I wish he would tell me these things. There's a complete lack of communication, so we get the usual misunderstanding and confusion. No one knows who's who or what's what. Right: change of plan, we head for level two-eighty-nine and get the hell out of here.'

'Good plan,' Adric agreed. He placed his hands on his hips. 'Do I look like an Adjudicator?'

He couldn't see Forrester's expression behind her visor.

9

Escape to Danger

The Doctor's foot probed thin air for a moment before it found the girder. Slowly he released his hand, easing his weight onto that foot. The girder held.

The Patient was making faster progress: she was five or six metres below him, and almost out of sight. It was dark in the ventilation system, even for Time Lord eyes. The hypocaust system was quite simple: hot air from the furnaces in the basement rose up the flues and channels that criss-crossed the pyramid.

'Wait,' he called down, his voice echoing along the metal ducting. They had already established that there were no monitoring devices in here and the system was relatively soundproofed. The Patient stopped, gracefully balanced on a metal support. She swept her hair back over her forehead as the Doctor caught up with her. The Patient still seemed a little distant, constantly distracted by something. The Doctor put this down to the new surroundings and the language barrier. She watched him step down level with her with something that in anyone else would have almost been indifference.

As if to confound him, she broke into a smile as he came to a halt.

'I think we've climbed down about twenty levels,' he told her. She nodded, as if she understood.

She was pointing at something coiled around the girder. The Doctor edged towards it. A red ribbon was dangling from it. The Doctor took it in his hand, then gave it a tug.

The rope ladder unfurled, dropping down and down until the end disappeared into the shadows.

'Good heavens,' the Doctor said.

'Doctor? Is that you?'

The Doctor looked around. 'Tegan?'

The Patient indicated the wall. Tegan's unmistakable voice was coming from the other side. The Doctor shuffled over, foot over foot.

'What are you doing there?' the Doctor asked her. A reasonable question in the circumstances.

'I was arrested. It's a cell.' The wall between them was made from elongated strips, each about fifty centimetres wide.

'Wait, I'll use the sonic screwdriver to loosen one of these panels.' The Doctor moved across to the metal panel, looking for screws. One of the strips came away in his hand. 'How odd,' he concluded.

Tegan almost toppled out of the cell. Between them, the Doctor and the Patient managed to catch her. She found her feet, and clambered out into the ducting. It took her a moment to adjust to the darkness, the warmth and the tenuous footholds.

'Hello, Doc,' Tegan said as she looked around. 'Who's your friend?'

'She's a Time Lord. If she has a name, she's forgotten it.' The Doctor removed Tegan's robocuffs with the sonic screwdriver. The cuffs fell, squealing, down the ducting.

'Why do I get the feeling that this is going to be a long story?'

'The explanations will have to wait, I'm afraid.' The Doctor replaced the panel, screwing it shut. It wouldn't do for an Adjudicator to find it.

Tegan eased across the girder, careful not to look down. 'I'm impressed. You've got an escape route planned for once. Is there a getaway car at the end of that ladder?'

'Where's Nyssa?' the Doctor asked softly.

'She's back at the hotel, safe as far as I know. Adric?'

The Doctor looked away.

'Adric?' Tegan repeated.

'I'm sure he'll be fine. We had better get going before the Adjudicators miss you.'

The battle was going badly.

Adjudicator armed response teams had sealed off level three-zero-eight. Evac teams had moved the civilians out

131

and shut down or rerouted the lifts. They'd set up barri-
cades and force barriers, brought in wardroid units and
broken out the energy rifles and full combat armour.
Hovertanks were converging on Scientifica, some units
were already massing in the piazza on the western face.

The ghosts had responded by dropping through the
floor.

Now they were on level one-zero-zero. There were
five, six or seven of them, the exact number shifting from
moment to moment. They weren't carrying any weapons
or other technology. Although they uttered harsh alien
syllables every so often — echoey noises that sounded more
like grunts and snarls than words — they didn't appear
to be communicating with one another. The extrasensors weren't even picking up any telepathic signals. That
wasn't conclusive: the various sensors and scanners were
only picking up the intruders intermittently. They weren't
inhaling or exhaling air, or displacing it as they moved.
Computer analysis offered no explanation as to where they
went when they faded from view. They weren't responding
to the negotiating team, they didn't even acknowledge
them. A couple of the Scientifica xenopsychologists had
been drafted in, but they were just as baffled by the ghosts'
behaviour.

The scanners continued to amass information: the exact
nature of the weaving on their cloaks, their retinal patterns,
their height, their average rate of movement. The creatures
didn't have any visible hair, skin pores or nails. Their shoes
appeared scuffed, indicating that they didn't always float:
they had walked on the ground. They moved through level
one-zero-zero with intent, only bothering to attack if they
were attacked themselves.

They were heading for the life support chamber.

Medford guessed this as soon as he had discovered which
level they had ended up on. It was a big floor, but it was too
much of a coincidence that the Patient was on that level.
The ghosts seemed to be heading directly for the room,
managing to beat the computer map's optimum route by
passing through a couple of the walls and partitions. They
seemed to be navigating by instinct. They moved at a

steady pace and ignored their surroundings.

Medford beat them to the life support chamber by running. Two of his officers came with him.

As the ghosts floated through the security hatch, they registered his presence. There were only three now. Three of us, three of them.

Medford looked at them closely. It was odd: they might be male, they might be female. He had assumed they were the former, judging by their height and build, but there were many human women of their size. If they were aliens . . .

Adjudicators spent a lot of their training learning not to make culturally specific assumptions: the Klulaki didn't raise their hands to surrender, it was merely a greeting; if a member of a felinoid race smiled, it was baring its teeth; the Balvanians of Balvar were masters of delicate irony and sarcasm − everything they said was the opposite of what they meant.

The ghosts' leader − the one in front, not necessarily their senior representative − drifted towards him. It tilted its head, watched his reaction closely. Medford stiffened, looking him straight in the eye. The other two circled the room, looking for the Patient.

If Medford could end this peacefully, then he would. He took a step forward. 'I am Provost-General Medford, the leader of the human forces on this planet and the official representative of Glory, the Divine Empress of Earth and all her dominions. We are the major space power in this galaxy. Please identify yourself.'

The wraith didn't appear to hear the words, but seemed fascinated by the movements of his mouth. Medford turned away, a little self-conscious. Another ghost was passing its hand through the wall of the cryotube.

'I must ask you, sir, to state your business or leave this world.'

And then they snapped out of existence. The time sensor stopped buzzing.

Tegan grasped the rung below and lowered herself, grasped the rung below and lowered herself, grasped the rung below and lowered herself . . . Her arms and calves were getting stiff now, the rungs were digging into her feet. She had given up trying to prevent the steady flow of air that blew upwards from lifting her skirt. At least the air was warm. The Doctor was above her, with the mysterious woman above him. The Doctor still hadn't explained who she was.

'How many levels have we climbed past?' The Doctor's voice called down. What sort of stupid question was that? If he wanted her to keep count, why didn't he say so? She wasn't even sure how long they'd been climbing. She told the Doctor as much.

'Do you know which level your cell was on?'

'No.' Tegan paused. 'There was a statue of Galileo just outside for some reason.'

'The Scientifica honour the great human scientists by –' the rest of the Doctor's words were swirled away up the ventilation ducting.

Tegan's feet touched solid ground.

'I've reached the bottom,' she called up. She'd also laddered her tights.

The Doctor and his friend caught up with her after a couple of seconds. Neither of them had a hair out of place.

'It was exactly the right length,' the Doctor observed. The ladder was perhaps two inches short of the ground.

There was a rumbling sound that built up to a crescendo, then died back down. The woman was whirling around, alarmed.

'It sounded like a tube train,' Tegan said cheerfully. When you get nostalgic for the Circle Line, you really must be homesick, she realized. They were centuries in the future: surely everyone travelled around in electric cars and jetpacks by now.

'You know, I think you're right,' the Doctor said. He set off in the direction of the noise.

'I think I've twisted my ankle.'

'You were lucky you didn't break both our backs,' Nyssa replied. They had fallen twenty metres through the air, Nyssa screaming the whole way down. They'd hit a pile of ploughed snow, rolled over one another onto the icy pavement. Bruce had pulled her into cover behind some waste bins. When she had heard the shooting from her room, seen the flashes of laser energy, she'd realized that he'd saved both their lives. Now Nyssa stood, brushing the snow from herself. He also pulled himself up, clearly in pain.

'Are you all right?' he asked her.

'It knocked the wind out of me, and I'm cold, nothing more.'

Her blouse was long-sleeved, but low-cut. She had pulled it on as tightly as she could, but her shoulders and collar-bones were still exposed.

'We'll take this.' He hobbled over to an anti-gravity vehicle, a hovercar. It was painted a dark metallic green, and was streamlined. Jovanka unlocked the door, apparently without using a key, and ushered her inside. Nyssa sat in the passenger seat, trying to ignore the voice in her head which was asking who the car really belonged to. Panels inlaid into the doors and dashboard were made from a dark wood, the seats were hand-stitched leather. It was the first piece of human technology that Nyssa had seen that displayed one of the fundamental creative virtues: elegance in functionality.

Jovanka was sitting alongside her, starting the engine. The car began lifting gently into the air. The dashboard lit, holographic dials and warning lights rezzing up.

Jovanka was clearly happy. 'Fantastic. This is the latest model Austin Martin. Good old British craftsmanship.'

'You've lost your Australian accent,' Nyssa observed.

'Yes,' Jovanka admitted, 'I'll explain all about that on the way.' He pressed a switch by the gearstick and his window slid smoothly open. He took the blaster from its shoulder holster and dropped it out of the window. The window slid closed and the car moved off on a cushion of depolarized gravitrons.

'Why did you do that?'

'You'll see.'

'Where are we going?'

'My apartment.'

The car sped into the night.

'So what's the escape route?' Adric asked Forrester.

Her voice came back over the helmet radio. 'We get into

the ventilation ducts and climb down to the cellars.'

'I take it that this has all been arranged by the Doctor?'

'Uh-huh.'

They passed an Adjudicator. 'Justice by your side.'

'And fairness be your friend,' they replied automatically. Forrester had already coached him in basic Adjudicator behaviour: how to walk and stand, who and who not to salute, a few of the ritual responses.

They left the Adjudicator behind, turned the corner and walked past a statue of Galileo.

'You're a natural,' Forrester told him, and Adric thought that he detected the hint of a genuine compliment behind the sarcastic tone.

'Is it much further?'

'No. Here we are.'

It was the door to a prison cell.

For a fleeting moment, Adric half-suspected that this had all been an elaborate ruse to get him into gaol. That thought had already dispersed by the time the door had slid open.

Together, they stepped inside. The room was small, with a retractable bed and latrine.

'There's a loosened panel on the back wall. Press it at a certain point and it opens up.' Forrester pushed her hand against the wall. It remained in place. She tried another of the panels. And another. She tried the last panel.

'They're sealed. Stand back.'

She clenched her fist and raised it. She flexed her fingers and the guntlet fired once. A devastating bolt of energy spat out, splashing against the wall.

The cell wall was barely scratched.

'Not one security camera registered the ghosts? We don't have a single image?' Medford knew the answer already. The banks of monitors that filled the room were only displaying corridors, empty rooms and workrooms. It was the familiar frustration that always followed this sort of action. After thirty years, Medford should have been used to it.

'We have a great deal of information about them,' a young Adjudicator-Lieutenant told him. 'So much that we will need several hours to process it.'

'Get the forensics team to scan everywhere the ghosts went.'

'They have still not finished in the observation room, sir,' a pretty young female officer told him. He didn't recognize her.

'What are they doing there?'

'The murder investigation,' she explained, referring to her simbook. 'His name was Falconstock, a member of the Scientifica's technical service grade.'

The Provost-General nodded, unsure how to feel. 'I knew him. How did he die?'

'Beheading. It appears to have been an accident, during a struggle. The Freudroid reckons that the killer was so racked with remorse that he leapt through the window.'

Medford found himself looking at the holographs of the crime scene. 'The window is two-point-five-four-centimetre-thick platestic glass.'

'The ballistics computer estimates that the suspect weighs three tonnes and is capable of moving in excess of one hundred kilometres an hour.'

'So we're looking for a guilt-stricken rocket-powered robot elephant.'

'The computer trying to build up an identiscan is having difficulty,' she admitted.

'What's the news from Pryanishnikov Station?'

'The site is secure. Twelve judicial executions. The MechInf was deactivated, but the first response teams arrived soon after. Some people managed to escape into the woods, but they've been recaptured now.'

'Adam?'

'No sign of him, but we captured a couple of his men.'

'Good. I authorize the use of the mind probe.'

The female officer made a note of this before continuing. 'A traitor, Ziyou Wanle, was executed. There were Shlimans and other aliens there.'

'The place clearly earned its notoriety. Keep hovercopter units in the area. Anyone returning to the scene will –'

There was a burst of activity in one corner of the room.

'Sir! Energy discharge in the detention area.'

'Visual.'

Two Adjudicators standing in a cell, one firing a guntlet at the wall.

'Who are they?'

'They are not Adjudicators. All our officers are accounted for.'

'That one is combat trained. Close the cell door.'

The cell door slammed shut.

Adric and Forrester exchanged worried glances.

Forrester grabbed the door with the guntlet, then slipped it from her wrist. The glove was still clasping the door handle. A holographic eyecon flashed up in front of Adric's face: a bird with an elongated beak, a green head and grey wings. He frowned, trying to decipher it.

'Down,' Forrester warned him. Adric turned around, just before he was thrown against the back wall by the force of the blast.

The door had vanished, as had most of the floor and surrounding wall. Forrester grabbed her bag and dropped it down to the next level. She jumped after it. Adric followed.

'Where are we going?'

'We try to make our own escape route,' Forrester called. 'A job made harder by the fact I've just lost my wrist computer.' Adric dialled up a map from the armour's tactics menu.

'Head left!' he shouted. Forrester did as she was told. They were in a communal area, empty except for another one of those statues. Doorways led away in every direction.

'Can you open that door?' Adric pointed to the one that he meant.

'Give me a second.' She produced a keycard from somewhere, slid it into the lock. Adric had time to look at the statue. It was a man called 'Paul Dirac'. He must have been another human scientist, one from around Tegan's time judging from his clothing. Forrester had opened the door. Through it, the room was small and virtually empty. A pentagonal area was marked off in white on the floor, there was a bulky control unit in the centre of the room.

'A transmat,' Roz declared, closing and locking the door behind her.

Adric beamed, 'So we can go anywhere on the planet.' He moved over to the control panel. All the lights and indicators were deactivated. 'It's dead,' he told her.

'I don't know the override codes for the transmat network.'

'But before, you had a transmat override. Have you still got it?'

'No, I left it behind at the station.'

'Of course, the Doctor has it now. Do you know how it worked?' Adric asked her.

'Not really.' She didn't seem sure whether they were wasting time or not. 'Do you?'

'Most computer programs have a "back door",' Adric explained. 'Even in programs with high security, the programmers leave a way in so that they can access it if things go wrong. It's usually a mathematical encryption.' He turned to the console and tapped in a couple of commands. A small part of the panel lit up. Roz raised an eyebrow, clearly impressed. 'I don't have time to free the whole network – there are millions of nodes in there. If I had a set of co-ordinates I'd be able to bypass the system for one transmission, to that location.'

Roz was looking at another readout. 'Here: this is the log. These are the last co-ordinates that were used. About an hour ago. It doesn't say anything else.'

Adric looked over her shoulder and did a quick calculation. 'North of here. Over a thousand kilometres.'

'That's out in the frostlands. It must be a garrison of some kind, or a waystation. It could be dangerous.'

'Anywhere has to be safer than here,' Adric said.

'The Adjudicators tend to steer clear of the frostlands,' Roz agreed.

Adric twisted a dial on the console. The pentagon on the floor lit up. 'I've set the timer for ten seconds,' he told her. They moved onto the pad, Forrester standing to attention.

Adric tensed.

'Relax, you won't feel a thing,' Roz assured him. 'See?'

They were somewhere else.

A maintenance robot buzzed past. It was dark here, colder

than elsewhere in the building. They were in an area like a hangar, or a multi-storey car park. The floor was concrete, it was cold and rough beneath Tegan's feet. There were dim floodlights mounted on the ceiling, but it was still only twilight in here, a real contrast to the overlit corridors of the Scientifica.

'Where are we?' she whispered.

'A stockyard,' the Doctor replied.

'For trains? Real, solid trains?' Trains were something that Tegan could understand: they didn't defy gravity, travel through time or anything weird like that.

'Skitrains, yes.'

Tegan was wary at first, but a quick look at them confirmed that they were just trains that ran on skis. The carriages were like American box cars: great squared-off shapes made from slabs of dark grey metal with large sliding doors on the side. At last, some technology that she understood.

'They still use trains in the future, then?'

'Tried and trusted methods, Tegan. The technology might be centuries old, but it works. These days, on most worlds, people travel using transmats – matter transmitters that teleport –'

'It's all right, Doctor, I've seen *Blake's Seven.*'

'Well, anyway,' he continued, more than a little irritated, 'the Scientifica have clearly decided that the skitrains are more suited to these conditions. Perhaps the storms and other atmospheric phenomena make large-scale transmat platforms uneconomic.' The Doctor was examining a noticeboard with a display like a digital watch. 'This one is leaving in two minutes. We're in time for our connection. We'll head for the engine.'

'Won't the driver object?'

'There isn't a driver, it's all computer-controlled.' Again, this was technology that Tegan could cope with.

A vent opened on the roof of the engine and a cloud of black smoke blasted out. The noise made them quicken their pace. The Doctor reached the cabin door and ushered the Patient and Tegan inside.

He had barely closed the door when the train had started

to chug into life. The cabin was small. There were two seats, functional things with only minimal cushions. There was a control panel in front of one of them, with a steering wheel the size of a dinner plate and a row of big square buttons. There was also something that looked like a radar box – possibly an electronic route map. There was a door on either side, and they were almost identical to the doors on a jumbo jet: heavy and airtight. There were little square windows in the doors, and a narrow strip of double glazing in front so they could see where they were going. Doctor was in the corner of the cabin, turning up the thermostat. By his knees there was an equipment locker. Tegan vowed to get a look at it once they were properly underway, but she imagined that there was a first aid kit in there, along with thermal blankets, an icepick, a flare pistol. The Doctor finished his adjustments and opened up a folding door in the back wall that led through to a little kitchenette and chemical toilet. Tegan experimented with a little box above the door, and discovered she could control the cabin lighting.

The cabin was about six feet high, meaning that the Doctor and his Time Lady friend couldn't quite stand up straight. The woman moved to sit in one of the chairs, the Doctor indicated that Tegan could sit in the other. She did so before he began feeling less chivalrous. It wasn't very comfortable, but it took the weight off her feet.

'This is all very civilized, isn't it?' the Doctor piped up. Tegan found that she could almost agree with him. The woman was smiling. Oh, this was hopeless . . .

'Doctor, who is this? What's her name?'

'I don't know. I'll see if I can find out.' He shuffled over to the other woman. 'May I?' he asked her, brushing aside the hair at her temple, touching the back of his fingers to her head. It was a tender move, almost a caress.

'Contact,' the Doctor said. As she watched them, Tegan realized that the Doctor was communicating with her on some mental level. She could almost see his thoughts passing down through the fingers, down the nerves and veins of the woman's body, into her brain. He was smiling at some intimacy, and then so was she.

141

'Is she cold?' Tegan asked, slipping her coat off. The cotton gown the Time Lady wore was thin enough to see that she wasn't wearing anything warmer underneath it.

'No,' the Doctor responded.

'Can she speak?'

'Her memories are fragmented.'

'Can you find her name?' Tegan asked as she tugged her coat back over her shoulders.

'No.' The word hung in the air for a moment. 'No need to worry,' the Doctor continued cheerily. 'Her memory has been damaged, but it should heal. That must have affected her language and speech centres. In the meantime we'll just call her "the Patient".'

'Patience?' Tegan asked.

'No, "the Patient". It's the only identification given on the medical report. Although, come to think of it, Patience is a better name.'

'What happened to her?'

'She has just regenerated for the first time.'

'You are certain? You know it's the first?'

He nodded again, looking puzzled that Tegan needed to ask a second time.

Realization only dawned as she spelt it out for him: 'She remembers that much. So she's not lost all her memories. Is there anything else in there?'

The Doctor grimaced, trying to piece together something. 'She was born of Blyledge, one of the Senior Houses of Glorious Gallifrey,' he said after some hesitation.

'Anything more useful?' Tegan asked, a little bemused. 'Can she remember anything about the house? Can she describe it?'

The Doctor closed his eyes, letting the memories come to him. 'The House is old, older than the hill on which it stands. It is angular. Dark. A small dark building beneath an orange sky. Inside it is large and the walls are white, with a regular circular pattern on the floor. There is a walled garden in the centre of the House, a quadrangle filled with silver trees. The birds sing a pretty song and there's always music in the air. Our youngest children play in the court-yard.'

142

'Our?' Tegan asked.

'*Their*,' the Doctor corrected. 'I'm sorry, it's sometimes difficult to disentangle my thoughts from hers. She has thirteen children.' Tegan was shocked by this, until she remembered that Time Lords lived forever, and that, despite her appearance, this woman wasn't really in her early thirties. 'I . . . can't find their names. She can't remember the names of her own children. I should be able to . . .' The Doctor seemed lost again.

'Can she remember anything about the father?' Tegan prompted.

The Doctor said his name, then paused. 'No, no. Quite impossible,' he declared.

'You've heard of him?' Tegan asked him.

'Oh yes, but it's a name I've not heard in a long time. He was a pioneer and leader among my people, one of the first Gallifreyans to enter the time vortex after it was discovered. He came from a family of explorers: he led an expedition into deep time, returning with charts and trophies from every corner of the universe. He brought back with him travellers' tales of monsters and lost civilizations.'

'How long ago was this?' Tegan asked.

'That's just it: Patience says that her husband has only recently returned from his journey. He took her as his wife the very day after his return. He was hailed as a hero, and many honours were bestowed upon him. She didn't see much of him at first: he was busy shaping the new future. He is still caught in the midst of the rebuilding, using the wisdom and experience acquired on his travels, but now he is beginning to find the time to see his family.'

The Doctor was rattling off the information, while also wearing that puzzled expression of his as he tried to assimilate the information. Tegan asked him what the matter was.

'Something terrible has happened here. To me the Odyssey was thousands of years ago. Everyone from that time is long dead. In fact, little survives from the period, including historical records. While my people honour her husband, they no longer even know his real name.'

'But you recognized it,' Tegan noted.

The Doctor faltered. 'I . . . I did, didn't I?'

143

He shared a puzzled look with Patience.

'Departure imminent. Start-up complete,' a voice announced. They realized it was just the computer, and relaxed again.

The train lurched into life and began to move off. It was travelling at walking pace at first. It nudged its way out of the stockyard, towards an archway. Tegan gazed ahead for a moment, seeing where they were heading. The engine cleared the archway and they were outside at the base of the pyramid, heading away from it along a concrete piazza and into the city. Tegan caught a glimpse of a futuristic tank, one that seemed to be floating a couple of feet from the ground like something from *Star Wars*. A small group of Adjudicators were massed around it, questioning a nervous-looking civilian. A few of them looked round as the train ran past them, but none paid it too much attention. The train began steadily picking up speed.

'Do you know where we are heading?' Tegan asked, looking away.

'That departure board said "North". I imagine that we'll find out who planned this escape route there.'

'What? You didn't set up that rope ladder?'

'No. Someone here has been manipulating events ever since we arrived on this planet. He's been co-ordinating terrorist activity on this planet, and he's attacked the Scientifica. I imagine that he also knows all about the ghosts and time disturbances. It was that person that arranged the escape route, including this getaway train.'

'You knew all that but walked into his trap anyway?'

'Yes,' the Doctor said simply. 'How else would we get to meet him?'

Part Four

A Bit of the Other

10

Snowfall

The car radio was announcing that the peacekeeping forces had stormed an enemy stronghold to the north. Many terrorists, aliens and other criminals had been captured, or executed resisting arrest. A commentator told them that the war was nearly over now, but that people couldn't be complacent just yet: they would have to remain vigilant against the threat of terrorist reprisals. The next story concerned energy rationing.

There was a checkpoint ahead.

Nyssa squirmed in the leather bucket seat, and looked across at Jovanka to see what he would do. He was already applying the brakes. A couple of humanoid robots moved forward, one at each side of the car. The drone on the driver's side had a sign on his chest that flashed on, indicating that the driver should turn off his engine and wind down his window. Bruce pressed the control, and the window coasted down.

'Where are you heading, sir?'

'Hello, my name is Christopher Cwej,' he said in a new voice, one softer and more measured than before. 'I was planning to head along the ring road. I've got an apartment in Sector Seven, close to the spaceport. I'm taking this pretty young lady I've only just met back there to cook her a romantic breakfast of champagne and oysters. I'm going to apologize to her, after that I hope we're going to get to know each other better.'

'Very good, sir. Mind how you go.' It waved him on.

Jovanka thanked it, wound the window back up and started the engine.

'How did you do that?' Nyssa asked.

'This far from the Scientifica, there's only low-level security and the droids aren't very sophisticated,' he explained. The Australian accent hadn't returned. 'That droid was looking for a married Ozzie called "Jovanka" who's armed. I didn't fit any of the search parameters, and the weapon and lie detectors didn't find anything either.'

'So your name is really Cwej, then?'

'Yes. Call me Chris, it's easy to pronounce. The "Bruce Jovanka" act was a cover. A friend of mine suggested it, he said it was a classic case of misdirection. Good old Bruce has probably outlived his usefulness now, though. Any more questions?'

'Yes. What are champagne and oysters?'

Cwej smiled, revealing a row of pointed teeth.

The train had left the city limits after only a few minutes' travelling. That wasn't surprising, of course. The Strip was only ten or twenty miles wide. After an hour travelling north, the blizzard was more severe than ever. As far as Tegan could tell, dawn was breaking, but the sun was still barely above the horizon and the light outside was still a pale blue somewhere between night and day. Lining the track were endless rows of greenhouses the size of football pitches. Tegan had already seen maintenance drones sweeping off the snow from the outside, and people in grey tunics busy wiping down the condensation on the inside. The soil in there was rich and brown, and all manner of veggies and crops grew there in neat lines.

'Astonishing,' the Doctor said. 'They've ground up barren rock and made soil. They must recycle their organic waste to make compost. That's how the Scientifica keep the population fed. A triumph of man over nature.'

The buildings looked old, but well-maintained. They reminded Tegan a little of the pictures she'd seen of Crystal Palace: lots of iron girders and panes of glass. They passed through a train station without stopping. Ahead of them were more and more of these greenhouses, the weak sunlight glinting off them.

Patience was looking outside with the sort of inquisitive look usually worn by children. She had become even more subdued since the train had left the Scientifica pyramid. For

148

much of the time she didn't even seem to notice Tegan, only reacting to what the Doctor said or did. At the moment, he was bent over the instrument panel, studying the controls.

'Do you know what we are carrying?' Tegan asked him.

'According to the manifest, we are pulling twenty carriages of "building materials". The journey will take ten hours.'

'How fast are we going?'

'Not very: about two hundred kilometres an hour.'

'Two thousand kilometres?' Tegan spluttered. 'I thought you said that no one lived that far north.' They would end up a long way from Nyssa, Adric and the TARDIS, and it was cold enough at the equator.

'There are isolated settlements, research centres and the like. We must be heading for one of those.'

'What are we going to do when we get there?'

'Meet whoever has arranged all this,' the Doctor concluded.

The sun was clear of the horizon when the hovercar pulled inside the garage. The door automatically lowered itself shut behind it. Chris smiled at Nyssa, deactivating his safety belt. She did the same. On the back wall of the garage there was a thin metal door, which was slowly opening.

Chris stepped out of the car, wincing slightly as he put weight on his twisted ankle. He opened Nyssa's door for her, and supported her arm as she pulled herself out of the bucket seat. In turn, she steadied him as he hobbled towards the exit. Behind them, the garage door slid open again, letting in bitterly cold air.

'What's going on?' Nyssa asked.

The car began reversing itself out.

'The car isn't ours. I've programmed it to return to where we found it. It'll stop off on the way and fill its tank with fuel. While it's there, it'll also get an autovalet – so not only will the rightful owner get his or her car back but they won't find our fingerprints.'

Nyssa nodded her approval.

They stepped into the apartment.

It was neat, with a white leather sofa and thick carpet. A holofire raged in the middle of the room. It was the first place she had been on this planet that wasn't in urgent need of repair. Everything looked new, and expensive. It was also warm. Chris was standing over a matt-black holographic entertainment console in one corner. After a minute changing channels and consulting holotext Chris turned his attention back to her.

'The action at Pryanishnikov Station takes up most of the coverage. There are no reports that they've found Tegan,' he concluded. 'You can sit down, if you want to.'

'Thank you.' Nyssa knelt on the plush rug by the fire. Chris hesitated before sitting down on the sofa.

'If you've got this apartment why did you need to book into the hotel?'

'I was meeting someone. Haven't your clothes dried out yet?' They had been soaked through when they'd landed in the pile of snow.

'Very nearly.'

'You can take them off if you want,' he told her. She stared at him. 'There are more clothes in the spare room,' he explained hurriedly.

Nyssa smiled and stood.

The skitrain had slowed as the gradient increased. Now it was travelling no faster than thirty or forty miles an hour. The views more than made up for it. Patience had spent much of the last three hours asleep. Tegan and the Doctor had sat and talked as the plantations had given way to foothills and finally jagged mountains that would put the Alps to shame. Tegan had only been travelling with the Doctor for a few days, and they'd had few chances to sit and talk like this. She told him about her ambitions, her career plans. Then he'd told her a little about himself and his people, the Time Lords. He still hadn't explained about the celery, though. The train track clung to the mountainsides, about halfway up. The blizzard was worse now, but the sunlight reflected from the snow and ice on the ground, giving them a good view of their surroundings. Below there was a steep drop into a rocky valley. Above them the mountain peaks were shrouded in blue fog which the Doctor thought might be condensing oxygen. He had turned the thermostat up three times in the last twenty minutes.

As the train cleared the corner, Tegan saw a settlement ahead. There were dark grey shapes clinging to the mountainside, standing out against the snow. They were just above the treeline. Pine trees. Tegan wondered about that for a moment, finally deciding that they must have been planted by the colonists. There was a thick column of smoke rising from the centre of the buildings and drifting over the valley. It must be a factory or refinery. Perhaps a power station. They were a couple of miles away.

'How could anyone live out here?' Tegan asked.

The train was beginning to slow down.

'We are approaching Pryanishnikov Waystation,' the computer voice announced, making them all jump. 'Please prepare for unloading.'

'Something has happened here,' the Doctor announced.

He peered out of the window. They were inching through the outskirts of the settlement. The first outbuilding they saw was blackened: there had been a fire. The next structure resembled a shipwreck – the skeleton of a fishing boat with all its windows smashed. The next twenty or thirty feet were just a rubble-filled crater. Some of the great pine trees at the edge of the forest had been felled, some had been splintered.

As they made their way into the centre of town, Tegan could see that whole streets had been levelled. Thick gashes had been cut into a narrow roadway, even into the underlying rock. There was a vast crater, and Tegan saw that there had once been an underground building there, the hole punched through it allowing her to see it in cross-section. That's how people lived here: by burrowing into the ground to keep out of the snow. It was at least two storeys deep. Fire had swept through it. Snowfall had covered the worst of the damage. There were no signs of life.

'Who did this?' Tegan asked.

'Perhaps they know,' the Doctor concluded. An Adjudicator hovercopter was floating above the devastation, a searchlight probing the ruins. Unlike the one in which

Tegan had been taken to the Scientifica, this vehicle had a cannon fitted to its side. It rotated in its mounting, tracking something she couldn't see on the ground.

The centre of the encampment was a large brick building. Presumably this was the waystation that the computer had referred to. The roof had collapsed, seemingly under the weight of the snow. A great hole had been torn in its side. The skitrain had come to a halt at a small platform by the side of the waystation. Something had scooped the roof off the ticket hall, and great cracks ran down the masonry. The line itself showed signs of repair.

There was a clanking noise behind them. Tegan was alarmed, but a quick glance at the control panel assured the Doctor that it was just the back four carriages detaching themselves.

'Building materials,' the Doctor said simply. Outside, a dozen chunky yellow robots with fork-lift prongs for hands bobbed past. Tegan wondered whether they had been passengers on the train all this time, or whether they had been waiting here for the train to arrive.

'We are pulling twenty carriages, Doctor. Does this mean there are another four bombsites like this?'

'Possibly.' The Doctor was getting to his feet and pulling on a pair of mittens that he'd found in his frock coat.

'What are you doing?'

'Going out there to get a better look. I need to find out what happened here.'

'You are joking, I take it?'

'No.' The Doctor pulled down on the handle and the door hissed open. He jumped down out of sight. Tegan ran over to the doorway and looked down. The bitter air struck her like a whipcrack, and she stepped back.

'You stay here,' she told Patience, before lowering herself onto the track. It was slippery, and she almost lost her footing. The Doctor was more used to the terrain. He was heading down to the back end of the carriage, keeping his head low.

He turned to Tegan and looked down. 'Aren't your feet cold?'

'Freezing,' Tegan informed him. Her shoes were still

152

locked away in some evidence drawer back at the Scientifica. The Doctor seemed untroubled by the subzero temperatures that were turning her legs blue and tightening the skin on her face.

'Old Edmund told me a mountaineer's maxim: "If you lose your gloves, you lose your life." You really can't stay out here like that.'

'What's that?' she asked, trying to take her mind off the temperature. There was a crashing sound all around them in the distance. It was rhythmic, but it wasn't soothing, just the reverse. 'It sounds like the sea.' She knew it wasn't. If there was an ocean around here it would be a block of green ice the size of a continent.

'Avalanches. Glaciers. Snow thawing then instantly refreezing.'

Tegan reached out to lean against the carriage. The Doctor pulled her hand away. 'Don't touch the metal with your bare hands. It's so cold your skin will come straight off.'

'It all looked so peaceful from the train cabin.'

'Then you shouldn't have left, should you?' the Doctor said professorially. In the distance, there was a sound that Tegan recognized from the TV news: artillery bombardment.

There was a high-pitched pulsing noise much closer, just above the waystation, then the sound of brickwork collapsing.

'The hovercopter is shooting at something.' The Doctor was already heading in the direction of the sound. Tegan trailed after him. They reached the waystation itself, but just as they were about to turn a corner, the Doctor lurched back, pressing himself flat against the wall. Tegan did the same. There were footsteps clattering over rubble, presumably the person that the Adjudicators were looking for. Tegan craned her head around the corner and saw a short man in a black fur coat hurtling towards an outbuilding.

Suddenly, a bright light was shining in her face, transfixing her.

The Doctor pulled her back round the corner. 'That hovercopter has motion sensors. Stay still.' A searchlight probed the area, but it hadn't seen them. It returned its attention to the other target.

153

'What if the train leaves without us?' Tegan whispered.

'The unloading will take ten minutes,' he assured her. 'Plenty of time.'

There was another burst of fire, then a different sound.

'He's got away!' the Doctor exclaimed. 'That was a transmat activating. That copter will start to come this way now, we'll have to find better cover.' The circle of light was getting nearer again. The Doctor edged back, and Tegan was forced to crab along the wall. There was a gaping hole a few metres away in the direction they were travelling. Tegan gingerly stepped inside over the rubble, her pace quickening when she realized that inside she would be sheltered from the wind. The Doctor strode in after her, and together they moved to one side of the hole out of the range of the searchlight.

It looked like the ruins of a restaurant or service station. It was dark, cold. The tables and bar had been splintered in a frenzied attack. Tegan's throat was sore, it was all that cold, thin air that she had been breathing. She wiggled her toes and stamped her feet, trying to get her circulation going.

The floor was piled with bodies.

'Oh god,' Tegan murmured, unable to say anything else.

There were dozens of them. They could have died recently, but they might just have been well-preserved in the cold, thin air. Food and dried blood were smeared over the walls and floor in equal measure. It looked like a scene from the TV: images from Belfast or El Salvador.

In the centre of the room there was a vast statue, a humanoid form that looked like the result of an unholy union between a suit of Samurai armour and a Chieftain tank. The Doctor examined it briefly, then he began moving about the room, covering the bodies, closing their eyes. All the time he was checking for lifesigns, even though it was fruitless. Tegan saw him remove something from around the neck of one of the corpses, but couldn't see what, as the body was in the shadows. Tegan realized that she was staring, and looked away.

She found herself face to face with a head impaled on a silver spike.

It was a young Asian man. His eyes were staring, pleading with her. The pole had been thrust into the man's neck. Blood was still dripping down, but it wasn't fresh.

She opened her mouth, but no sound came out.

There was a plaque hanging from the spike. Tegan strained to read it.

ZIYOU WANLE

EXECUTED BY ORDER OF THE ADJUDICATION SERVICE

FELLOW TRAITORS TAKE HEED

A hand planted itself on her shoulder. She jumped, even though intellectually she knew it could only be the Doctor.

'The massacre took place six or seven hours ago, judging by the state of the bodies. There are a lot of blaster flashes and bulletholes, and many of the dead people were armed. They managed to deactivate that MechInf, but then the reinforcements arrived and sprayed the room with bullets.'

Tegan was sobbing.

'I'm sorry. I shouldn't have brought you here.'

'No,' she said quietly. 'If this is happening I need to know about it.' She looked into the face of the dead man.

'The Adjudicators are generally good men. If they did this, they must have been scared.'

'And what could this man possibly have done to deserve this?'

'Nothing.'

'I thought this was the future, I thought that we'd be civilized by now.' My god, Tegan thought, humanity has spread across the universe. Trillions of us, with flying cars and laser guns and nuclear fusion and videophones and space rockets and solar power and robot servants and colonies in space. But despite all the *Tomorrow's World* technology we haven't really progressed since the days when the Aborigines were shot for sport and children could be hung for stealing a loaf of bread.

Tegan looked up at the Doctor, and she saw something in his eyes that she would never forget: an expression of an emotion more deep and intricate than any human could possibly feel, or even put into words. Her rage and frustration

155

seemed so *small* beside it that she found herself averting her eyes.

'Can you feel it?' he asked.

'Yes,' she said, still not daring to turn round. A sense of foreboding, of history in the making.

The Doctor consulted his watch. 'We have to get back to the train.'

The lock on the transmat chamber door was proving particularly stubborn. It hadn't responded to any of the Adjudicator codes that Forrester knew, and she had abandoned it to search the room. Adric had set to work, using his wrist computer to hack into the lock's operating system. The combination seemed to be an entirely random sequence, and it looked like they needed a keycard. None of the ones that Forrester had with her worked.

Roz was standing on tiptoes, peering out of a skylight. 'Adric, come and have a look at this. Bring that chair over here.'

'What did your last slave die of?' he asked her.

'I accidentally beheaded him.'

Without another word Adric pulled one of the chairs over and clambered onto it.

He saw something that was too big, too awesome to take in at once.

'What is it?' he asked, already aware that Forrester couldn't possibly know the answer.

'Alien,' she said.

Everything about it defied description or explanation. Vast sections of it hung over the cavern floor, in defiance of gravity. It was made of a material that was solid and shifting, oily and burnished, curved and angular. It wasn't a building, a sculpture or a spacecraft. They stared at it, tried to work out how tall it was, what it could possibly be. The sensors in their armour had gone dead, unable to interpret what they registered.

'People,' Adric said simply. At the base of the artefact there were tiny white dots. Increasing the magnification on the visors, they saw a dozen men and women in radiation suits. The Machine was even further away than they thought. The scientists were preparing some heavy equipment, floodlit by a pure bright light.

'Look above them,' Roz responded. Adric turned his head, his view of the Machine lurching at even that tiny movement. He corrected himself, bringing his head down and lowering the magnification. A portal was open on the side of the Machine, the only visible entrance to the structure. The scientists had fed cables through the doorway, and those cables were connected to monitoring equipment.

'What are they doing?' Roz asked impatiently. 'They look like the bomb squad.'

'I recognize some of that equipment,' Adric realized. 'I saw it in the Scientifica. It was a research programme into –' he racked his brains '– dimensional energy. The Doctor said it was a dimensional observatory.'

'Meaning what, exactly?'

'It allows them to look into other dimensions,' Adric explained. 'Perhaps that's another Gateway.'

She looked away from the Machine for the first time. 'A what?'

'At the mathematical boundary of E-Space and N-Space the Doctor found a pan-dimensional structure that allowed transference between Minkowski Space to other quantum states, access to non-Euclidean geometries, post-mathematic spatio-temporal co-ordinates and extra-universal –'

'Yeah, OK, I get the message: inside that thing you think there's a doorway to another dimension.'

'Yes. Or perhaps just to another universe.'

'A doorway that's open,' Roz observed.

There was a chime from behind them. They spun around, and saw that the transmat platform had lit up.

'The rematerialization cycle has started up,' Forrester said. 'Someone's coming through.'

Nyssa knelt on the floor in front of Chris. She was wearing a towelling dressing gown loosely tied at the waist. Her clothes were drying on a rack by the holofire. Steam rose lazily from them. At her side there was a plate with half a dozen empty oystershells on it. Chris was still wearing his tuxedo. Nyssa sipped at her champagne, then leant over and

157

tugged off Cwej's left shoe and sock.

'What are you doing?' Chris asked, apparently a little disconcerted.

'It is nothing I haven't seen before,' she said primly. 'You can relax, I am only examining your ankle.' She began to massage the foot.

Chris settled back in his chair, looking down at her. Nyssa pulled her dressing gown tight around her.

'You must be tired,' he said after a little while, clearly keen to start a conversation.

'No. My people don't need as much sleep as yours.' Her fingers stroked his ankle. It was red, but no bones had been broken.

'Where are you from?' he asked.

'Traken. You won't have heard of it.'

'I have,' Chris told her. 'It used to be in Mettula Orionsis, but it was destroyed centuries ago. So, you must come from the Trakenite colony on Serenity?'

Nyssa's heart quickened. She had watched on the TAR-DIS monitor as her entire home galaxy was blotted out, as everyone she had ever met or even heard about had been killed. But now, here of all places, she had discovered that at least some of her people had survived. Serenity had survived the destruction unleashed by the Master.

'Tell me what you know of it,' she insisted.

Chris recounted the sketchy details that he could remember: Serenity was the only surviving colony of the Union of Traken, a verdant garden world with advanced biotechnology, whose people lived in peace and relative isolation. They believed that at the time of the cosmic disaster that obliterated the entire rest of their galaxy, something called 'the Source' had protected them, at the cost of its own existence.

'The Source was first constructed there, ten thousand generations ago,' Nyssa told him. She felt odd. It must be the wine or the oysters affecting her.

'We Adjudicators learn about Serenity as an example of a peaceful and just society.'

Nyssa straightened. 'You are an Adjudicator?'

Chris didn't move. 'Lapsed,' he admitted.

'What does that mean?' she demanded.

'The Adjudicators are meant to be impartial, committed to the law and justice. A year out of the Academy, I discovered that the Lodge was corrupt. I uncovered a conspiracy that went right to the heart of the Empire. I was forced to flee Earth. Since then, my friends and I have discovered that a handful of secret organizations have covertly been controlling human scientific research and defence policy for centuries. These are dark forces with their own agenda, and they must be fought. We have been aware of them for some time.'

Nyssa listened to him, sensed the truth in his words. The hairs on the back of her neck were prickling. 'I will help you in any way that I can.'

The Doctor hadn't said a word since they had left the station, neither had Tegan. Patience was staring ahead, apparently not even slightly curious about what had happened at the waystation. She still sat in her chair. Tegan had preferred to squat by the heater vent rather than take the other. The Doctor took the seat, then, and continued to consult the control panel.

'We are now at full speed,' the synthesized voice informed them. Tegan was warm again now. Standing, she opened the side window blind.

The Adjudicator hovercopter had pulled level with them.

'Doctor!' she warned.

He glanced in her direction, turned his attention to the instrument panel, then was staring out of the side window.

'Relax, they don't have any reason to think we are here.'

Pattern recognition software in the hovercopter targeting computer booted itself up and focused on the face of the woman. Within a second it had identified her. It moved on to the young man at her side. They were two fugitives who had escaped from the Scientifica earlier that morning. A warning buzzer sounded in the cockpit.

'DOCTOR! SURRENDER. THERE IS NO ESCAPING JUSTICE,' a modulated voice boomed from the speaker.

'We'll have to outrun them.' The Doctor turned his attention to the controls and began assessing his options.

'You just said that we're travelling as fast as we can, and that plane isn't even trying,' Tegan complained. Their room for manoeuvre was a little limited: forwards or backwards. Patience joined him at the controls, and she began studying them with a calm efficiency that Tegan found rather reassuring.

'Cheer up, Tegan, I've been in worse scrapes.' He stabbed at a control and there was a clank behind them.

Suddenly the train was travelling twice as fast as the hovercopter.

'How did —'

'I detached the carriages we were pulling. Without that weight dragging us we've bought ourselves a little time.'

The hovercopter was bearing down on them again.

'Not very much time, Doctor.' The Adjudicator aircraft was level with them again. The gun mounted on the side of the hovercopter swivelled. Tegan was staring down the muzzle. The cannon fired once. Tegan braced herself, but the gunner was aiming too high. Tegan heard a reverberation as the shot hit the rockface above them. Rather than dying away, the noise was growing louder.

'They've triggered an avalanche,' the Doctor shouted. 'Of all the irresponsible —'

'We'll lecture him when we see him, eh, Doctor?' Outside, the hovercopter had peeled away. It took up position a safe distance away.

'Of course. Brace yourselves!'

The engine lurched, throwing them all against the door.

'Hold on!' the Doctor shouted, but it was too late. The engine had been swept off the skiblade, and now it tumbled over. Flung against the ceiling, the Doctor's knee pressed into her chest, Tegan saw the tops of the trees roll past the window. They were in freefall, floating like astronauts.

'Gravity brakes,' the Doctor coughed, straining to get to the controls. Tegan shifted across, freeing him.

The Doctor yanked one of the controls.

'The lever you have pulled — "Brakes" — is not in

service,' the synthesized voice informed him. 'Please make a note of it.'

The train bounced off a prominent rock and they were tossed across the cabin. The Doctor cracked his head against the windscreen, and his head slumped. Patience screamed. The wind was knocked out of Tegan.

They hit the trees which splintered as the train ground against them. Great jarring noises surged through the cabin. The train was falling, the branches were getting thicker, but were still cracking and tearing under the momentum of the engine. They were still travelling fast, but much slower than they had been. The train hit the bottom, turned over onto its back and pitched until the cabin was pointing uphill. They had come to a halt.

Tegan and Patience looked at each other. They broke into smiles. They had survived. Patience moved over to tend to the Doctor.

Something blotted out the sunlight.

Tegan cricked her neck, looking up and out of the windscreen.

Ten tonnes of rock and ice were surging down the mountainside towards the skitrain.

11

Fusion

Ten tonnes of rock and ice were surging down the mountainside towards the skitrain.

The targeting computer onboard Adjudicator hovercopter Justice Kappa had tracked the trajectory of the engine as it fell down the hillside, through the trees. The avalanche was only a fraction slower, and the gunner watched as the wave of snow ploughed through the trees, pulling them from their roots. The tsunami hit the skitrain engine, carrying it away. The gunner looked up, satisfied that the target had been destroyed, but the targeting computer wasn't sure. It flagged up its concern, raised the definition on the sensors and began searching the area for lifesigns. The gunner frowned: when he'd fired, the computer had registered three lifesigns onboard the train. Assuming that those three people had survived the fall – and he doubted that – they would be in no state to get up and out of the cabin. Even if they had, they'd have been swept away by the avalanche. Targeting computers were always pedantic about these things. If they hadn't seen the bodies themselves they were always reluctant to declare a 'kill'. It used to be easy to trick a computer into thinking you were dead, and if you managed to do that, it would take you out of the tactical equations. Battlefields were complicated places, and the fewer variables the better. There was no point wasting processing time worrying about planes that had been shot down, dead troops or write-off wardroids. Viewed electronically, the combat zone started off complicated and got simpler and simpler as more pieces were removed from the board.

The gunner turned his attention away from the monitor. The ravine was filling up with rock, snow and other debris. A great cloud of snow rose, obscuring the more delicate sensors. The gunner switched to a lower definition. The carriage was still mostly intact, but it had half a mountain on top of it. After a couple of seconds, the targeting computer conceded that the target had been killed. The mission directives were complete and they could head for home.

Chris flipped open the sim-map. A three-dimensional plan of the spaceport sprang out like a picture in a pop-up book. Chris turned his attention back to Nyssa. 'I have been here for a month, trying to discover exactly what the Adjudicators are doing. At the moment we're not even sure how big the "peacekeeping" force is. If I can get into one of the Adjudicators' ships at the spaceport I can access the secure databases, uncover their sealed orders.'

'They must be well guarded.'

'Oh yes, troops and droids on the ground, full electronic surveillance, transmat bafflers, the ships' crews are on full defensive alert.'

'So how do we get in?'

'We don't.' He tapped the side of the book, and an orbital platform appeared above the spaceport. 'Skybase One, local name Icarus Station. It's where the ships too big for atmospheric landing dock. It's also where the hyperlink relay is based. Although the Adjudicators have a garrison up there, it's owned by the Scientifica.'

Nyssa looked at the station. It resembled a molecular model – spheres linked by thick tubes. The structure was roughly square. In all, judging by this hologram, each side was about a mile long. 'It looks heavily armed.'

'The skybase is a flying fortress: the first line of defence in the event of an attack from space. During the Third Draconian War, bases like that proved they could keep back an entire warfleet long enough for reinforcements to arrive. They can outgun a battlecruiser, but inside the security is relatively light. They won't be looking out for a young, unarmed, married couple. We buy spaceline tickets, transmat up there and then sneak into the Relay Room. A couple of minutes monitoring transmissions and tactical data and I'll know what's going on here. Then we just beam back down.'

Chris smiled and snapped the sim-map shut. 'Easy, really.'

Before Adric could even brace himself, the transmaterialization process was complete. A little man stood on the transmat platform, facing away from them. He wore a scruffy fur coat and carried a long black umbrella with a red handle. Although he was clearly rather bewildered, he was aware of their presence. He turned around warily, then broke into a broad grin. He raised his hat and took a theatrical bow.

'Wait a moment,' Forrester frowned, 'it's you.'

The man's thick eyebrows furrowed. 'Of course it's me. Hello, Roz.'

She removed her helmet. 'No, it's *you* you.'

'That's right,' he said a little impatiently.

'No, no. You changed. Remember, you became all . . .' she did a little mime.

'What, all frock-coat and youthful appeal?' he scowled. 'Well, perhaps I did but I haven't yet.'

Forrester whirled to face Adric, stabbing a finger in his visor. 'You told me that he had regenerated,' she snarled.

Adric took a step back. 'That's the Doctor?'

'Oh, for heaven's sake,' the little man said, turning around to face him, 'how many times do I have to –' he stopped in mid-sentence. 'Isn't he a bit short for Cwej?'

Adric struggled at the catches to his helmet, finally managed to unfasten them. 'Forrester, I don't recognize this man.'

The new arrival cocked his head to one side, and this 'Doctor' gave him the strangest expression. 'Hello, Adric,' he said finally. 'I'm not sure the armour suits you.'

'Well, he knows you,' Roz told Adric.

'Adric used to travel with me, a long time ago,' the little man explained to Roz. 'I'm from what you think of as your future,' the Doctor beamed at him. 'If you are here, then I take it that one of my past selves is, too. Which one: Boggle or Bland?' There was something about the man. Once again, he didn't look like the Doctor, his voice and mannerisms were different, but there was something there that Adric recognized.

'The younger-looking one,' he answered.

'And that's why he thinks I regenerated: Adric here saw me regenerate, only a couple of days ago in his timeline, but centuries ago in mine.' The Doctor smiled, satisfied that he had explained the situation sufficiently clearly.

'So there are two of you on this planet, at this time?' Adric asked.

'Yes,' the Doctor admitted. 'I've crossed my own time-stream. Oops.' He didn't seem unduly concerned.

'It's a temporal paradox, then?'

'Well, at the very least it's a pair of Docs,' the Doctor chortled at his own joke. Adric and Roz glanced at each other.

'Don't the Time Lords have a law against this sort of thing?' Forrester asked.

'Oh yes, but laws like that are there to be broken. Don't scowl, Roz. There are all sorts of loopholes. I'm not meant to meet myself, but I haven't, have I? Not yet. Anyway, these things happen. It's no worse than having a boy from another universe or an Adjudicator from nearly four hundred years in the future wandering around. Now we know there's been a mix-up, your Doctor can return to the TARDIS and pop off somewhere else. Is he still trying to get Tegan back to Heathrow?'

Adric nodded.

'Well, just find him and say that the situation here is all under control and he's not to worry about it.'

'The situation's under control, is it?' Forrester asked.

'Just about.' The Doctor's grave expression discouraged Adric from pursuing the matter.

'So you know what that thing out there is?'

The Doctor bounded up onto the chair and peered out of the skylight. 'Good, it's here. Thought so.' He jumped down again, his face set in an expression of determination.

'Why should my Doctor leave?' Adric asked. 'He was here first.'

The Doctor and Forrester hadn't heard, or were pretending not to.

'Do you know what it is, then?' she was asking.

'We have to get down there,' the Doctor said evasively.

165

'The door's locked,' Adric told him. 'We'll need the sonic screwdriver.'

'Oh no we won't.' He moved over to the keypad and tapped one of the controls. The door slid open. The Doctor looked back over his shoulder, grinning. 'When in doubt, always press the big green button.'

'Camera Twelve: Booking Office. Look at her. She's not concealing any weaponry, that's for sure.'

Adjudicator Haigh twisted one of the dials on his console, and the bare back of the young woman lurched towards him. Adjudicator Lewis returned to study the same image on his own monitor. The girl in question wore a full-length dress in green silk. It was low-cut at the back, any lower and she would be facing an indecency charge. On a planet with an Arctic climate there weren't too many dresses like that, even in the buildings with climate control. She was petite, with a finishing-school walk.

'She looks good from the back,' Haigh confirmed. 'But that's no guide. Some of the ugliest women I know look good from the back. Remember that gorgeous blonde who turned out to be a Maalri? Lovely bum, but the face of a warthog.' Lewis wondered, not for the first time, how his colleague had passed the rigorous psychological profiling at the Academy. He also worried briefly about neglecting their duties – they were meant to be on the lookout for terrorists and illegal aliens – but then he remembered the banks of computers behind him that were covertly sweeping the entire complex for guns and bombs. If any Adamists made it into the terminal, then Haigh and Lewis would be the last to find out – the computers informed Security Command before getting around to them. Looking out for pretty girls was one of the more entertaining ways of passing the time while nanoprocessors did your job for you. Besides, there hadn't been any Adamist attacks here for over a year.

The girl turned around, and smiled at something. The dress wasn't as low-cut at the front, not quite, but it shimmered around her as she moved.

'OK, I admit it, she's beautiful,' Haigh said.

'She's very young.'

'Nothing wrong with that. I like the virginal type.'

'You're disgusting.'

'Oh look.' A young man had joined her. He was tall and broad, built like a gravball player. He wore a designer suit – it probably came from Earth itself. They made a show of kissing.

Lewis felt a twinge of jealousy. 'Still think she's the virginal type?'

'My turn. Camera Three: main concourse. Those three Kalkravian nuns.'

'So where are we going?'

Chris held up the tickets. 'We're taking a linking flight to Beta Five, then picking up a Hyperion for a three-week safari on Heurippa, one of the Rimworlds.'

Nyssa slipped her arm around his waist. 'It sounds wonderful.'

They joined the queue for the offworld transmat. Chris was still hobbling a little on his twisted ankle. There were only about a dozen people ahead of them. This planet was a little off the beaten track, and had strict rules about foreign travel. Most of the people in the spaceport were offworlders, and that included the armed Adjudicators patrolling the concourses. Although the spaceport was large, it had to support the entire population of the planet.

The Adjudicator removed someone from the queue, the only apparent reason being that he had warpaint on his face.

It was only a minute or so before it was their turn. An Adjudicator scanned them and Chris's suitcase for weapons and checked their ID. He moved them on, indicating that they should stand side by side on the transmat platform.

And then they were on the Skybase. The transmat chamber was fairly featureless, although there was a customs information hologram hovering from one of the walls. A Scientifica administrator conducted another weapons scan, more cursory this time, and then they were ushered down the transparent walkway to the departure lounge. As they walked along the corridor, the planet filled the view beneath them, revolving at a leisurely nineteen miles a second. Even the hardened space travellers were taking a moment to stop and stare at such a magnificent sight. It looked just as it had from the TARDIS monitor, with thick blue-grey clouds at the poles, thinning out over the dark equator. At this distance the Strip was about as wide as Nyssa's finger.

They reached the end of the corridor. A man in a grey tunic bobbed towards them.

'Good afternoon Mr and Mrs Cwej. Booking in for your flight will take place in around twenty minutes. Please feel free to look around and order any drinks while you wait.'

'Thank you,' Nyssa replied, but the man was already drifting over to the next in the queue.

Chris tapped her on the shoulder and inclined his head towards a side door marked 'Staff Only'. They moved over to it as casually as they could. It was unlocked. They stepped inside, Nyssa carefully closing the door behind them. It was a staff room of some kind, with droid recharging points in one corner and a kitchenette in the other. A holographic noticeboard hovered above one of the tables, apparently displaying a timetable of some kind. Nyssa's attention was drawn by the room's viewport. It pointed away from the planet into deep space.

'There won't be any ventilation ducts, will there? I'm not really dressed for those.' Nyssa glanced down. 'I'm not really dressed at all.' Chris had provided the jade green dress from somewhere, assuring her that she ought to wear it. Although it was an exact fit, Nyssa wasn't used to clothing that clung to her with quite so much dedication.

'Don't worry, it's all walkways and carpeted corridors. And you look great.'

'Where are we?'

'This is one of the pilot ready rooms. That hatch', he pointed to a big square plate on the floor, 'leads straight down to the hangar.'

There was a burst of light from outside.

Chris stepped carefully over to the window. Nyssa was already there. A gunmetal slab had appeared in the distance, and was heading towards them. As it got closer Nyssa could

168

make out more details: points of lights that were viewports, vents and pipes running along the side. Writing and other markings.

'It's an Earth ship,' Nyssa concluded.

'Yes, a Type Twelve freighter.' Chris screwed up his eyes as he tried to recall what he knew about the model. 'Crew of eight, light armaments, hyperdrive capable. There are hundreds of them in service, most of them used as medium-range couriers.' He moved over to the arrivals/departure board. 'It's not listed.'

'It must be a military flight.'

'No, they're all listed, too.'

'It's docking at the port just below us.'

'Let's get down there.'

Nyssa hesitated. 'What about the relay room?'

'We can do that afterwards.' He was limping for the hatch, despite his ankle. Nyssa lifted her skirt to free her feet and followed. Chris had opened up the hatch and found a metal ladder. He began climbing down. They couldn't hear the freighter, of course – it was travelling through a vacuum – but it must be very close to them now.

There was another hatch at the base of the ladder. Warning lights were flashing over it. Nyssa helped Chris to release it, and had dropped down through it with him even before it had finished hissing open. They landed heavily on a metal floor, Chris wincing a little. The freighter was heading directly towards them. They looked up, but the hatch had closed and there wasn't a release handle on this side. The docking bay was pressurized. Presumably a force wall kept the vacuum out, but let spaceships in. Hatches ground open all along the underside of the vehicle. Flat undercarriage clanked out, unfurling. The roar from the engines blanked out every other sound, echoing around the docking port. It filled the docking port. Her eyes were shut now, the sound of rocket motors passing through her. Chris took Nyssa, pressed her to him, pulled her down. The freighter's docking clamp punched the air above them, then locked into place.

There was a subsonic whine and the cabin lights flickered

back on, a great deal dimmer than before. The Doctor stood back from the control box. The heating was on, but at one of the lowest settings. He moved over to Patience, checked her pulse and steadied her. After that, he opened up the equipment locker and pulled out the two thermal blankets he found there. He draped one over her, tucking it in. Tegan groaned and rose, clutching her head. She looked cold. The Doctor thought that he could almost see goosebumps beneath the thin material of her airline uniform. He sat alongside her.

'I thought we would be killed,' she said, composure already returning to her voice.

'Oh, we have been,' the Doctor said. 'We might have survived the fall, but we were caught in an avalanche.'

'It's just snow. We can dig our way out.' She pointed over to the shovel in the equipment locker.

'It's not that simple. The snow has frozen solid above our heads. An inch-thick barrier made from ice mixed in with rock can stop the path of a bullet: it's as strong as concrete. The ice above us must be a hundred metres thick, and there are boulders and trees mixed in with it. We'd need heavy equipment.'

'So we wait until the air and heat run out?'

'Yes, basically. Heat loss isn't an immediate worry – snow is an excellent insulator, and our body temperature will keep the cabin heat tolerable. Air is more of a problem, but I've opened the vents. We really need to hope that whoever arranged the escape route cares enough about us to come along and dig us out. Patience and myself will place ourselves in a coma, to conserve our supplies.'

'What about me?'

'I can hypnotize you, slow your breathing. First I need to revive Patience to prepare her for sensory withdrawal.'

'Is she injured?'

'She's unconscious, and we need to get her to a hospital. There are no signs of injury, but there might be internal wounding or bleeding. Her head is bruised.'

Tegan leant over. 'You are concerned for her?'

'Yes.'

'You know that there is nothing more that you can do for her here?'

'Yes.'

'Then relax.'

He couldn't. 'I'll try and make telepathic contact.' He stepped over to Patience, and sent out some thoughts. Familiarity. Warmth. The beating of a single heart, then two, then three.

'Contact,' he said and their recent thoughts were intertwined. The Gallifreyans excelled at *entrelacement*. The luxury of immortality, the ability to take time over things. Elaborate thoughts and conversations expressed in million-letter alphabets. Each word unique, each tense and inflection specific to one moment in time and space. Jump cut. Freefall, bone-jarring crashes. The skitrain hurtling down the mountainside. The cabin spinning from two perspectives, disorientating enough from one.

He touched her memory, brought something calm out and focused on it. A hand rising, brushing a wave of blonde hair away from the forehead.

I know about today, they said together, we were there. Let's think of yesterday, before we met. What happened yesterday?

A woman dreaming of archways and glowing powerlines. Simple, comforting images. Around her, womb-warm blue fluid, bubbling. The Doctor smiled at a passing thought. She was doing the same, remembering the cloister room. A tranquil room of slate-grey stone and running water. Fingers stroking an ivy leaf. It was dry. A stone space, Loom-calm.

Before that? No need for thoughts or memories, no need for secrets. Just emotions, feelings and impressions. There was just a spark, a few ergs of energy in the brain. Nothing at all for so long. An exhilarating rush backwards through the years. Frozen solid, in a deep coma, but alive. Experiencing the world as a redwood tree might, not moving, not seeing or hearing. The planet spins on its axis, day and night strobing, each season like a frame of an epic film. The planet circles its sun, the sun circles the galactic core, the galaxy moves ever outwards. Mountain ranges

171

and rock strata come and go, I was there for it all, doing nothing more than being alive.

Then a sea of memories and emotions. Mustering will-power as the ice started to bite into legs and arms. Unable to move or feel toes and fingers, all the sense at the base of the spine freezing away, as the body begins to shut down. Neurochemical messengers in retreat, fighting a rearguard action against the frost. Skin cells crystallizing, bloodbergs in the veins and arteries. The contents of the stomach and intestines solidifying, cracking the gut walls as they expand. The lungs are tight, but they have already stopped. The heart is slowing.

I'm dying.

No, this is the past. These are just your memories of being on this planet. Cast your mind back to before then.

Memories of springtime sun on bare skin. A dark-haired woman straddles her husband, his unfamiliar hands beneath her shoulder blades. He rolls her over onto the grass, strok-ing her side and kissing her belly. As he kisses it again an owl flies through the amber sky. The sun is overhead, so it's a little after noon.

'I'm getting old.' He pulled himself up to his knees, resting a hand on her thigh.

She sat up, laughing, tickling his beard. It was darker and coarser than the blond curls growing on his head. His new body was so much taller and hairier than the last.

'You said that when we were expecting our firstborn,' she replied.

'And by this time tomorrow he will be a father himself. Perhaps then he will start feeling his age.'

'Perhaps he'll start acting it.' She kissed his cheek. He cradled her head, running his fingers through her short black hair and down her neck to her collar-bone.

Power lines and shock-webbing. Something wrong.

That memory shouldn't be there.

I know, the Doctor replied. It's your memory, isn't it? Where does it fit?

Brainscream, something wrenching itself out of her mind. It hits her, the pain hits her again. Again.

No. Wouldn't you rather be here?

172

Turning her over onto her front, kissing the back of her neck, his hand running down her body. His thoughts dipping into hers, tasting her emotions. She was propping herself up on her elbows. Her body was familiar, he'd known it for centuries, seen it age ever so slowly. The birthmark on her ankle, the pattern of freckles on her shoulderblades. Only he had ever had those thoughts.

I am intruding here.

He lay alongside her, examined her spine as though he'd never seen it before, ran a finger right down from her neck to the back of her knee.

I want to stay here.

Pressing her down, nuzzling her cheek and shoulder. Memories and bodies intertwined in a beautiful, intricate design. Her body moving with a rhythm both familiar and utterly new to him.

I'm so sorry, but I shouldn't be here, not now.

There are buried memories here: your memories.

A woman screaming.

Can't you see? You've undergone a trauma. Your memories have been blocked. We can find out what it was, and help you to come to terms with it. I know it's unpleasant, but it's all in the past now, and we have to find out what it was.

It's to do with those ghosts, isn't it?

Ghosts? No.

Here.

The sun is low on the horizon. It is the early evening and the house is screaming. Guards in full ceremonial dress are advancing down the corridor with stasers drawn and swords at their sides. The horizon is flame-red.

'Search the bedchambers.'

'You can't –' a staser blast, killing the housekeeper. The house screams again, its lights flicker. We all feel its pain. Screaming children. The eldest son, dragged with their mother by the hair into the courtyard. His twelve brothers and sisters there already, all in blue. Where is his wife? Where is her husband? The youngest are crying, like their mother.

The eldest son stood tall and faced the captain, the guard

173

in the plumed helmet. 'I am a Cardinal, and a Time Lord of the first rank. My father sits on the Supreme Council, as his father did before him. On whose authority are you acting?'

The guard captain unfurled a scroll. 'By Presidential decree, only the Loom-born shall inherit the Legacy of Rassilon. There shall be no more children born of woman. We have authority to search this House for the spawn of the Pythia.'

'Let me see that.' The guard captain handed the scroll over.

The eldest son read the hieroglyphs, examined the seal. 'It is genuine,' he concluded. 'They have issued a warrant for father's arrest. They accuse him of consorting with aliens.' Something had broken within him as he had read it. When he spoke again, his voice contained none of its former resolution. 'My wife is expecting her child tomorrow. What do you propose that they do?'

Doctors were moving towards the bedchambers.

'The law is clear, sir. Her pregnancy is to be ended at once. Your wife will be examined here, then taken to a medical centre. I must ask you to lead me to her.' As if to add emphasis, the guard captain placed his hand on the hilt of his sword. Numbly, the eldest son nodded and began to walk towards the living quarters.

His mother screamed, begged them to stop.

'Why are you doing this now? Where is my husband?' she demanded. 'Please wait for my husband. He is a

'Doctor!'

Tegan shook him. He'd been unconscious for at least an hour. The Doctor looked happy enough, and Patience was curled up beside him, some inscrutable expression on her face. There had been a number of times when Tegan had felt like snapping the Doctor out of it. Now there was a pressing reason why he should be awake. Tegan slapped the Doctor on the face. His eyes snapped open. 'Tegan?' he said groggily. 'You're all right?'

No, her head was spinning and she felt dizzy. The cabin was stuffy. Tegan suspected that Time Lords didn't sweat, and so she was entirely responsible for the muggy atmosphere. 'Never mind that: look at the door. We're being rescued.'

The hatch was glowing red, there was a mechanical pulsing coming from the other side. The Doctor was scrambling to his feet, waking Patience. The heat from the door was almost unbearable now. Tegan felt faint.

The door was grasped by powerful claws that didn't even flinch when they grasped the red-hot metal. The door was torn from its hinges and hurled back. They could hear it hissing and popping in the snow outside. The Doctor moved to greet their rescuer. It was humanoid, squat and powerfully built, wearing a close-fitting matt-black spacesuit. There was a rope tied around its waist, like a leash. It had a device that looked like a blowtorch grasped in one claw, and levered itself into the cabin with the other.

It had the head of a shark.

A nightmare creature: a Great White's head grafted onto the body of a shotputter. Darth Vader and Jaws rolled into one. Its skull was out of all proportion to its body, twice the size it should have been. Tiny lidless eyes stared at her, one on each side of the pointed head. It moved with a lurching grace, towering over them. Tegan couldn't imagine anything worse, she hoped that it was just the heat and the dizziness making her hallucinate. And then it hissed, opening its vast circular mouth to reveal three rows of teeth, dripping with saliva. The room was filled with the smell of rotting meat. It lunged towards her, snarling and roaring as it came.

Tegan screamed.

12

Staring into the Abyss

Tegan screamed, her eyes wide open. Suddenly, the monster and cabin pitched to one side. The Doctor had tackled her, throwing her to the ground. Her head spinning, she began pushing herself upright, her back against the wall. What happened next confused her: the Doctor was holding out a medallion and roaring, so loud that the creature stopped in its tracks. The monster swung around to face him and snarled something. The Doctor barked back, and handed the medallion over. The creature turned towards Tegan.

'My apologies,' it said in a gravelly voice, bowing its head ever so slightly. 'I am Quint, of Shlima.' It held out a claw.

After a moment's hesitation Tegan shook it. His skin was rough, like sandpaper. 'Tegan Jovanka, of Earth.'

'I had thought you grave robbers, or murderers.' He clipped the medallion to his tunic. 'This was worn by my brother, and only by him. It bears his name. He was killed last night by the savage humans. The Doctor, however, is Gallifreyan, and a man of honour. He retrieved the medallion so that the Shliman funeral customs might be observed.' His face wasn't capable of human expression, but the cadences of his voice were almost poetic in their subtlety.

'The Doctor told you all that in a few snarls?'

'Shliman is a very concise language,' the Doctor informed her. 'Be thankful for the Shliman homing instinct — without it, Quint would never have been able to locate the medallion, and us.'

'Doctor, this Gallifreyan female is injured.' Quint was kneeling to examine Patience. Tegan half hoped that the poor woman didn't open her eyes. Friendly or not, Quint

176

wasn't what you would want to see looming over you when you'd just woken up.

'Yes,' the Doctor said, hovering at Quint's shoulder. 'We need to get her to a medical centre.'

The Shark Person tugged at the rope around his waist.

'Signalling a colleague?' the Doctor enquired.

'A primitive method of communication, but not one that spy satellites or monitoring stations can intercept. Can we move the unconscious female?'

'I think so. We will have to be careful about sudden movements to her head.'

Quint inclined his head to one side. 'As you wish.' Together, he and the Doctor eased her up, carrying her.

'You go first, Tegan.' The Doctor prompted. Tegan went over to the door, a blanket draped over her shoulders. A circular corridor had been carved in the ice, leading up. It was narrow, just enough for one person – or Shark Person – to clamber through. The skitrain's door was half-melted into the side of the corridor. A little light was percolating through the walls, but it wasn't really enough to navigate. Tegan located the rope attached to Quint's waist – she could just make it out, leading up through the tunnel – and used it as a handrail. Her other hand drifted up the wall of the corridor. The floor and walls were smooth where the ice had melted then instantly refrozen. The ice stung her bare feet as she climbed. Behind her she could hear the Doctor and Quint entering the tunnel. The rope was slackening, but that didn't matter so much any more, because as she climbed more sunlight was getting through. Ahead of her was a circle of light: the end of the tunnel. As she reached it, four powerful hands pulled her up and out. There were two humans, dressed in bulky furs to protect them from the wind and cold. Protected only by a light blanket, Tegan buckled.

'Get her inside,' one of them shouted over the gale. The other led her towards a dark shape, surrounded by snow. It was perhaps five metres away, but almost obscured by the snow. Recent events started catching up with her: the horror at the waystation, and of seeing her first Shark Person, the intense heat as Quint burnt through the door, the cold now, the dizzying fall and jarring crash-landing. As she began to pass out, Tegan fancied that she saw Noah's Ark standing there in a snowdrift, a great wooden boat with a big door on the side. Her eyes were closed now, it was too cold to open them again. Everything went white.

Nyssa could hear the warning sirens again and the approach of loaders. Together, she and Chris eased themselves round the wall of the docking port until they were concealed behind a pile of fuel drums. The robots moved into place, supervised by Adjudicators in light body armour. A cargo ramp unfolded noisily from the belly of the freighter. The robots drifted up the ramp and disappeared inside, while the Adjudicators remained on guard outside.

Nyssa was just about to move forward when she saw someone coming their way. She pulled Chris back. An Adjudicator strode past, an aide at his side.

'That's the Provost-General, Medford,' Chris whispered, 'the commander of all the Bureau forces here. Why has he turned up to see a space freighter being unloaded?'

They peered over the tops of the fuel drums for the answer. The first robot loader had emerged from the ship carrying a metal container the size of a coffin.

A human military officer followed the robot down the ramp. He wore a glittering silver spacesuit, a sashtop computer draped over his shoulder. He stopped in front of the Provost-General and the soldiers saluted one another.

Medford ordered the droid to stop, then opened the box and looked inside. Satisfied, he sealed the container up again and motioned for the droid to continue.

'How many in total?' Medford was talking to the human pilot.

'Twenty-four.'

'Excellent. Thank Captain Dattani for me on your return.'

'Aye, sir.' The officer saluted him. 'We're taking something back – a cryotube?'

'There's been a change of plan. We'll send that to Earth directly, in one of our cruisers. While the cargo is being unloaded, your crew might as well take advantage of the facilities at the Skybase.'

178

'Thank you very much, sir.' The officer saluted again, and then moved to an intercom post at the base of the ramp. After a short conversation, half a dozen astronauts emerged from the ship, smiling and laughing amongst themselves. They clambered up the ladder that she and Chris had used, heading to the rest room.

'We have to follow that loader,' Chris told her, 'see where they are taking the cargo.' The first of the yellow robots was heading through an archway into the main part of the station. A couple of Adjudicators with rifles and full armour were guarding it. The military officer was climbing the ramp back up to his ship. Under the watchful eyes of half a dozen Adjudicators, another droid buzzed past them towards the ship.

'First of all, let's find out what the cargo is. There is still some onboard,' Nyssa said, standing and straightening her dress. Before Chris could argue she had ducked behind the droid, putting it between herself and the Adjudicators. Chris followed. They climbed the ramp, careful to keep level with the loader. After a couple of seconds, they were on a flat surface again. The loader executed a neat ninety-degree turn, then set off at the same brisk pace as before. Chris and Nyssa followed it.

'It's heading for the hold,' Chris told her. He was rubbing his leg, clearly still in pain.

'I'll follow it, you take your time.'

Chris shook his head. 'Don't worry about me.'

Nyssa hurried after the loader. It passed through a couple of hatches before arriving at a set of double doors marked 'Cargo Bay Three'. They slid open automatically. Nyssa followed the robot inside. The room was full of warehouse racking. The row nearest the wall was stacked high with metal containers, like the one the Provost-General had checked outside. The rest of the shelving was empty. The robot's arms extended and it removed one of the containers. After a quick reckoning, Nyssa could see that there were another twenty-two of them left in place. Chris had arrived by now, although he had to move aside to let the robot leave. Together, Nyssa and Chris took one of the metal boxes down and laid it on the floor. It was bulky, but

179

surprisingly light. Nyssa opened up the case. Inside there was a lot of grey foam padding, a material that Chris told her was designed to block sensor beams. The foam was swaddling a metal cylinder the size of a cigar, featureless apart from a green cap and a seam exactly halfway along it. She placed it on a nearby workbench.

'It's a fusion bomb,' Chris announced, a hint of awe in his voice.

'A device that creates an uncontrolled nuclear fusion reaction?' Nyssa was horrified by the thought of such an indiscriminate weapon. 'The energy created would be huge. An area would be totally vaporized.' The device was tiny – but it didn't need to be very big. The principle behind the bomb was simple, just an adaptation of an everyday cold fusion generator, but what sort of person was capable of thinking of such an application? Nyssa felt cold. This was science gone mad.

Chris nodded. 'Each one of these charges is enough to level a city and kill fifty million people.' He accepted the existence of such a device without question. This *thing* had been designed and built by his people, Tegan's people. Chris was clearly fascinated by the device, like a fly by amber.

Nyssa tried to keep her voice steady. 'The Adjudicators and the Scientifica rule this planet. Why would they want to destroy it?'

'That's not the worst of it.'

Nyssa opened her mouth, unable to conceive of anything worse than being in a room packed with bombs powerful enough to kill a billion people instantly. Then she realized. 'If these were set to go off in sequence then there would be a chain reaction. The blast area would increase logarithmically.'

Chris nodded grimly. 'Fusion tests were done out on the Rim in the twenty-third century: five of these charges are enough to destroy a planet. Eight will shatter every solid planet in a solar system and ignite the gas giants. These things were banned before they could try testing nine or ten. The human race has never used them in war, even as a last resort. The Provost-General thinks he needs twenty-four – and what's more, whoever is supplying him can get hold of them.'

'Hands in the air.'

A space pilot was covering them with a slim pistol. He had followed them into the hold without them noticing. He was calm, aware that he could gun both of them down.

'A crew complement of eight,' Nyssa noted, trying to keep her voice steady. Cwej had said that back in the rest room. They'd seen one pilot, then six astronauts. This one hadn't been accounted for. They raised their hands. The pilot was in his thirties. He was tanned and although he didn't have Chris's physique, he clearly kept fit. He was watching them both, but his attention was drawn by Nyssa, particularly the neckline of her dress. On the edge of her vision Cwej was slipping forward. For the first time she understood why Chris had insisted on the silk dress. The pilot's eyes met hers. The lascivious expression he wore repelled her, but she forced herself to smile.

Chris lurched forward.

'Stay back,' the pilot warned, bringing the pistol round. Chris stopped in his tracks, surprised how quickly the pilot had been able to react. Without taking his eyes off them, the pilot reached out for the communications panel on the wall.

Nyssa's hand found the table behind her. Her hand crept up the surface until she found what she was looking for. Chris was edging forwards again.

The pilot twitched the pistol. 'Stay still. One more move out of you and –' He turned, distracted by the faint digital bleeping from the other side of the room.

Nyssa made a show of looking puzzled. 'How long is fifteen seconds?' she asked sweetly, holding up the fusion bomb. She was surprised how light it was.

Both Chris and the pilot had gone very pale. The pilot dived for her first. Nyssa stepped back clutching the bomb to her chest. Chris's fist swung up, intercepting the pilot before he could grab at her. The blow connected with the side of the pilot's head. He reeled, but kept hold of the pistol, and shoved himself hard into Chris, knocking him

181

off-balance. As the smaller man pressed home his advantage with a swift kick to the solar plexus, Cwej lost his footing as his weak ankle gave way. He recovered fast enough to deflect the next kick and turned, putting his whole weight behind a punch. The pilot dodged it, bringing his elbow down hard on Chris's shoulder. Chris flinched, and the pilot kneed him in the back. Cwej fell to the floor, his face dripping with sweat. The pilot pulled himself up and caught his breath. He glanced over at Nyssa, and dabbed at a spot of blood on his lip.

That was all the time Chris needed. Now he was looming up behind the pilot. He grabbed his shoulders, spun him around and punched him on the jaw. Pulling the pilot up by the collar, Cwej slammed him into the bulkhead, knocking the air out of his lungs. Another couple of punches and the pilot had stopped moving. Cwej loosened his grip, guiding him to the floor.

'Unconscious,' Chris assured Nyssa. His forehead was running with sweat and he was out of breath. 'Haven't you forgotten something?' Hurriedly, Nyssa twisted the cap, disarming the bomb.

'That was a nice trick. Let's get the bombs out of here.'
'How?'

Chris patted the bulkhead. 'We'll take this shuttle. It'll buy some time. They'll have two of the fusion charges, but we'll have the other twenty-two.'

'They could kill hundreds of millions of people.'

Chris shook his head. 'They need every single one of these for some reason. They want to kill tens of trillions of people.' He stopped, realizing what he was saying. 'Someone said once that the human mind finds it difficult to comprehend numbers above one hundred. It's too much to take in. We see them as a "crowd" or an "audience", somehow as some entity in its own right, rather than something made up of individuals. It's difficult to imagine six million people watching a holovid or dying in a war. It becomes less personal, harder to relate to. Ten trillion people . . . there *aren't* that many people to kill.'

'I come from Traken,' Nyssa reminded Chris sharply. 'Which means both that I don't have a "human mind", and

182

that I can comprehend what it means for a trillion people to die. These weapons are evil and we must destroy them.'

Chris gestured helplessly. 'I agree. I don't know how, and I don't want to risk a guess. The Doctor will know what to do, we must get them to him.'

Nyssa frowned. 'You know the Doctor?'

The Doctor was climbing quickly hand over hand. Adric's progress was slower. The plateau was steep-sided, but the rock face was rough and uneven and there were plenty of hand- and footholds. Unlike the Doctor, though, Adric had no experience in rock-climbing: there was little call for it on Alzarius.

The Doctor reached a ledge, and waited for his companion to catch him up. Leaving the observation dome had been easy: the brightly lit building had been all but deserted. He had told Roz to head into the Machine, and instructed her what to do once she got there. He'd pointed out the plateau, a stump of rock rising about two hundred feet above the cavern floor. It was tiny compared to the Machine, of course, but it was the largest natural feature here. It would serve as the landmark he needed. Roz went off on her mission, while Adric came with him.

Now Adric had caught up with him, reaching the plateau. He looked exhausted, but he would do. He was still wearing his armour. Smiling sympathetically, the Doctor produced a Paisley handkerchief from thin air and passed it over. Adric finished mopping his brow with it, but it had vanished before he could hand it back.

'You don't need the armour,' he told Adric. The boy nodded, and together they removed it, unclipping and unclasping. Finally Adric stood surrounded by a pile of blue and gold metal pieces. Now he looked exactly as the Doctor remembered him: a bright yellow outfit with a little blue and gold star for mathematical achievement pinned on the bright red pocket on the front.

The Doctor gazed across the cavern. He could just make out Roz. At this distance she looked just like a bluebottle in her armour. She hadn't been challenged so far, but was still only halfway to the doorway. He fished out his pocket watch and checked the time. That done, they began climbing again.

Tegan awoke surrounded by fur. She was lying flat on her back on a fur-lined bed, underneath a fur blanket. Her head still hurt. There was a sensation of movement, as if they were on a boat or a plane. There was a creaking noise above her and a rich smell all around. She opened her eyes, and found herself looking up at a wood-panelled ceiling. She shifted onto her side, pulling her arm out from under the sheet. She was wearing an unfamiliar white garment made from a material that felt like cotton. It was a one-piece outfit with a polo neck, stretched tight as a second skin except at the cuffs and ankles. A leotard, the sort of thing an aerobics instructor would wear.

A young man was sitting by the bed, stirring a steaming mug. He was in his mid-twenties, with high cheekbones.

Tegan sat up, pulling the blanket over her chest. Although she was covered from neck to toe, the outfit she was wearing left absolutely nothing to the imagination. It must have been quite a feat getting her into it while she was unconscious. 'Who undressed me?'

The man smiled knowingly, reaching out with the mug. Tegan didn't take it. He wore plenty of clothes: a blue tunic with gold buttons down the side, and breeches. He looked as if he had stopped off here on the way to a fancy dress party with a pirate theme. 'You've got a lovely couple of moles, you know? Just above your left –'

'Do you have a name?' she demanded, angry now.

'Adam,' he said. 'You may have heard of me.' His accent was somewhere between Welsh and Scottish, a gentle lilt.

'No.'

'Take this, it'll warm you up a bit more and help with that sore head. Take it from me that you're covered in bruises.' She recognized him from somewhere, but couldn't place it.

The drink smelt of citrus fruit. Tegan sipped at it. When she spoke again she was a little calmer. 'We're on a ship?'

'A snowship.'

'Like a skitrain: a boat that runs on skis?'

184

'That's right.'

'Made of wood?'

'Pine, stolen from government plantations. It doesn't show up too well on sensor scans and you don't lose your fingers if you touch it in cold weather.'

Tegan poked her foot out of the bed and found the floor. Varnished wood, like the walls and ceiling. She stood, finding it easier to balance than she had thought. She stretched, Adam studying her the whole time. He did his best to look like a connoisseur rather than a voyeur. She faced him, her hands crossed over her chest. 'Where's the Doctor?'

'He's with Quint in the map room.'

'I want to see him.'

'Would you be wanting to put your clothes on first?' Adam indicated behind her, where the Air Australia uniform, handbag and coat were hanging. Her underwear and jewellery were lying on a bench by the hook, even her laddered tights. There was also a pair of plimsoles. A curtain hung there, making that corner of the room look like a changing cubicle at the swimming baths.

'You can pull the curtain across if you want some privacy.'

'I'm not stupid,' Tegan informed him.

'Shame,' Adam said. 'In my experience the stupid are OK. It's the clever ones that you have to watch out for.'

Tegan drew the curtain across.

'I wouldn't put that ring back on, you were lucky you didn't get a nasty burn from it.'

It was good advice, and it explained why her ring finger was so sore. She slipped the jewellery into her jacket pocket. Tegan started to remove the leotard, then it dawned on her that she didn't know how to: it was a one-piece outfit with a polo neck that wouldn't stretch. There wasn't a zip, a row of buttons or a strip of Velcro. She turned, ready to ask Adam how it was done, but she could imagine the smirk on his face, and so decided not to. Instead she pulled her skirt and blouse on over what she was already wearing. Once she was wearing her jacket, she pulled back the curtain and picked up her mug. Adam was standing. He was shorter than Tegan had thought, and thin. He had picked up a black fur coat and draped it over his arm. He opened the door for her.

Together they walked along a long wood-lined corridor that must have run the length of the ship. There wasn't a window in sight. Tegan found herself wondering where all the droids and holograms had got to. She got the sense that they were deep in the bowels of the ship. She had a dim recollection of the outside: a vessel the shape of Noah's Ark, the size of a cross-Channel ferry. She couldn't hear or feel the snow, but wasn't missing it. Inside here it was cooler than she would have liked, but it was comfortable enough. She hadn't quite finished her drink.

'I remember where I've seen you before,' she told Adam as she supped the dregs. 'You were at the Imperial Hotel. In the restaurant.'

'You were sitting on your own,' he replied. 'I'd have come over and bought you a drink, but I was waiting to meet a couple of people. They didn't show.' They passed through a small anteroom, possibly a little chapel: there were benches and a crucifix hanging on the wall. Beyond that was a heavy door. Once again, Adam opened it for Tegan. She stepped through into a room with a fire in the corner. The Doctor was sitting in a high-backed leather chair, lit by the glow of the fire. There was a chart in his lap, and he was studying it through his half-moon glasses. Quint was hunched over a table, consulting a ream of maps. Behind them, Patience was lying on a bench, covered with a fur blanket. She was deathly pale.

'The nearest hospital is the Nightingale Facility,' the Doctor told Quint. 'An hour or so from here with the wind behind us.'

'That's in hostile territory. The heart of the warzone.'

The Doctor looked up at Adam. It was clearly the first time they had met. They studied each other carefully.

'Hello again, Tegan,' the Doctor said. 'I take it this is Adam?'

Adam nodded graciously.

'As in "notorious leader of the Adamist terrorists"?' Adam nodded again. Tegan shifted away from the young man with-

186

out realizing she had done it. 'You're a wanted man, Adam.'

'And so are you, my friend,' Adam responded. 'I've heard a lot about you. You *are* the famous Doctor who has been travelling the planet looking for ghosts?'

It was the Doctor's turn to nod.

'Found any?'

'One or two,' he said warily. 'My friend is very ill – I must get her to a hospital with or without your help.'

'I know. We've already changed course.'

The Doctor thanked him.

'She is the Patient?' Adam asked.

'Yes.'

'Have you found out anything more about her?'

'I have communed telepathically with her, twice now, but although she is telepathically adept her thoughts are still fragmented, unreliable. It's like a dream: I can only half-remember what I saw, and my own memories are mixed in now for good measure.'

'Surely you must have enough clues to be going on with by now? How did she arrive?'

The Doctor paused, considering the question.

'Doctor, are you all right?' Tegan asked.

'We must hurry,' he said.

'How did Patience arrive?'

'In –'

The Doctor paused as he reached the top of the plateau.

'Doctor, are you all right?' Adric asked.

'We must hurry,' he said.

'What is that Machine?'

'It's –'

The cavern floor was damp, it glistened with water. The scientists had laid duckboards down from the research dome to the Machine, and had programmed a drone to paint a white line marking out the route. Roz Forrester felt exposed walking along them, but it was the quickest route, and this way her boots didn't get wet.

A group of scientists were setting up some scaffolding along the side of the Machine. They hadn't seen her. There

187

were two options here: act as if you own the place or sneak past. Roz was just at home doing either, but some instinct made her choose the latter. She checked the cavern floor – there was no one else around. There was just enough scientific equipment lying around to act as cover. Dodging from energy cell to floodlight pylon to a computer the size of a wardrobe she found herself only a couple of metres from the doorway. The technicians were still occupied, and so she crossed the threshold unchallenged.

She was surprised how cramped the antechamber was after the vast dimensions of the exterior. The walls were night-black, but there were glowing powerlines and coloured wires criss-crossing the room. Glass cones (capacitors?) ran along one curved wall. There was a machine in the opposite corner that looked like a random collection of electrical components. A big red lever stood in front of it. Next to that was a glass dome about a metre in diameter, full of twinkling lights. There wasn't another way out of this chamber, at least not one that Roz could see.

There was an old wooden rocking chair on a rug in the middle of the room. A middle-aged woman in a white tunic was sitting in it consulting a notepad. She was staring at her. Forrester recognized her from the holonews as the Chief Scientist.

'What are you doing in here, I gave strict instructions –'

Roz drew her stungun. 'Take me to the control room,' she ordered.

'This is all that there is,' Whitfield replied. 'It's disconcerting, isn't it, that the place is so much smaller on the inside than the outside?'

'I'm rarely disconcerted.' Forrester checked the chronometer on her wrist computer, then moved over to the machine in the corner. Before the Chief Scientist could stop her she had pulled the big red lever.

An utterly alien noise came from deep within the Machine, surging out into the cavern where it washed over the cavern walls, echoing and rumbling. It repeated itself over and over, the pitch rising ever so slightly.

A wheezing groaning sound.

* * *

'– a prototype TARDIS,' the Doctor concluded.

'Of course, Tegan, it all begins to fit into place. She fled Gallifrey in a TARDIS – one of the very earliest Types, I would imagine. Do you remember the turbulence that we encountered on the way here? That was her TARDIS passing ours in the Vortex – the scream was the sound of a mortally wounded TARDIS desperate to make landfall.'

'Does that explain why we were locked out?'

'Yes, yes, it must do. My TARDIS is protecting itself. The local Vortex must have been ripped to shreds.' The Doctor made a complicated motion with his hands by way of illustration.

'Angels and ministers of grace defend us!' Adam exclaimed. 'And the ghosts?'

'The disruption caused by a crippled TARDIS would be enough to break down the causal nexus. If someone were to try and operate the TARDIS, who knows what might happen? It might even destroy the Vortex. That's what they are doing. The Scientifica are trying to build a time machine from the wreckage, but they must not be allowed to succeed. If the damaged TARDIS is activated the consequences would be catastrophic. Time would be knocked out of joint. The ghosts are just the first symptom of that. The entire structure of the universe is at risk. All we can hope is that some madman doesn't try to activate the TARDIS before we can get there.'

The Doctor took a piece of chalk from his pocket and scratched a pictogram on a flat rock. That done, he drew a tight circle around himself and Adric. He replaced the chalk in his waistcoat pocket and consulted his fob watch. The Doctor stood his ground, his umbrella planted firmly in the rock in front of him. He looked around: they still weren't here, but it was nearly time. The wheezing groaning din filled the chamber. He could almost feel them around him. The wind was picking up now, whipping at his jacket. Adric was calling something, but it was lost to the gale. Down on the cavern floor, the research team were desperately trying to stop their equipment from scattering

189

in the wind. Just a few moments more. The Doctor broke into a broad grin and began to raise his hat, turning to face them.

And all around the planet, the ghosts began to appear, growing more solid with every moment.

Part Five

Breakthrough

13

Crossing the Line

The Doctor broke into a broad grin and began to raise his hat, turning to face them.

Although Adric had seen the ghosts on three previous occasions, this was the first time he'd been able to look at them properly. There were two of them and they were tall, a little more solid than before. Unlike his Doctor, this one seemed unafraid of them.

'We are perfectly safe inside the circle,' the Doctor said cheerily. The wind was howling around the chalk circle rather than through it. It was like being in the eye of a hurricane, or a diving bell.

The ghosts flickered towards them, growing larger and smaller with each step.

'You stand in our way.' The voice was soft, and like the wind it was all around them. It was a statement, not a threat.

'Ferutu. I am the Doctor,' the little man shouted over the roar of the wind. 'As you're not from round these parts, you won't have heard of me. Know then that I am a representative of the High Council of the Time Lords.'

The taller of the two ghosts drifted forward, watching the Doctor carefully. It found that it couldn't cross the chalk line and began to explore the extent of the invisible barrier.

'You are known to me,' it said, the whispers drifting effortlessly over the noise of the wind.

'I am?' the Doctor said, surprised. 'Then you have the advantage of me.'

The expression on the angular face did not change, the mouth did not move. Adric realized that its companion, the other ghost, had disappeared at some point. 'You do not know of us?'

The Doctor shook his head. 'Nothing but this rune.' He

193

indicated the symbol he had drawn on the ground. 'One of your kind drew it last night to anchor itself on this world. It's a binding symbol, isn't it? I wish to learn more.'

'Then I will show you.' It reached out its hand. 'First, you must step from the circle.'

'What assurance do I have that you will not destroy me?'

'None.'

Adric grabbed the Doctor's arm. The little man turned, and Adric saw that he was biting his lip. The wind was screaming around them like a flock of demons.

'Step from the circle,' the ghost repeated.

The Doctor nodded and took the step. Wind tore through the Doctor's clothes, forcing him to grab onto his hat. His jacket was whipping up, flapping as though it was trying to escape. The Doctor held out his free hand. The ghost clasped it.

The very moment they touched, both the ghost and the Doctor began to fade into nothingness. Then they were gone and Adric was alone on the plateau, in the eye of the hurricane, holding the Doctor's umbrella. The wind snapped off.

'Thank you for not trying to stop me.' The Adjudicator was staring into the glass dome, watching the lights dance around in a Brownian swirl.

Whitfield kept her expression neutral. 'I am curious to see what you are doing. Besides, you are wearing bio-electronic augmented armour, and are clearly combat-trained. I am a fifty-nine-year-old scientist.'

'I'd try not to kill you,' the woman assured her.

Whitfield smiled. 'Are you really an Adjudicator?'

'Of sorts. I stole this armour.' She consulted her chron-ometer again, then pulled the lever back to its former position. The noise of the engines gradually died down.

'One minute,' Whitfield noted. 'You activated the Mach-ine for exactly one minute.'

'Yes. And I'll be doing the same in quarter of an hour. I thank you in advance for your co-operation.'

'Bluerose bloom,' said Whitfield.

'I beg your –' It was as if the woman had been grabbed

from behind. She lost her grip on the holdall she was carrying, sank to her knees, gasped for breath.

'My dear child,' Whitfield began, 'if you are an Adjudicator, you'll know that they look after their property. And they set great store on crime prevention. This is what they call an "immobilizer". All the joints have locked, the computer's down, the radio's down, you're blind, and the air vents have closed. You've got about five minutes' supply – as long as you don't exert yourself.'

An armoured hand struggled to lift, the woman inside was clearly trying to release the catch on her helmet. Whitfield shook her head sadly. 'The system is voice activated. When the central computer discovers that a suit has been stolen, it flags it. Then, anyone who knows the codewords can immobilize the suit.' She reached down and unclipped the wrist computer. 'This has been recording your every move since you put the armour on. Shall we have a look at it back in my office?'

It had lasted only a minute, but reports were still coming in from everywhere on the planet. Sightings of ghosts, disruption to energy, water and information supplies. Provost-General Medford sat in one of the communications rooms of Icarus Station. Around him his most loyal personnel were at their screens, assimilating the information, trying to uncover any pattern to the disruption. The manifestations were limited to the planet's surface: there had been no sightings on the Skybase or on any of the ships in orbit.

Dattani's armada was an hour away, holding its position. During the attack the Provost-General had toyed with the idea of signalling for them, but he decided that he couldn't until the extent and nature of the alien threat was better known. Wait for the aliens to show their hand. They'd see the Adjudicator presence on the colony, they'd see this Skybase and they'd make assumptions about the planet's ability to defend itself. Then they would make their attack. Medford was the only person on the planet that was aware of the reinforcements. The Chief Scientist didn't know about them and the Scientifica computers and Bureau Databases both thought the Fleet was on patrol in another section of the Empire. It was a classic manoeuvre – not letting the enemy know the size of your forces.

There was an incoming call for him. He accepted it, and a full-sized hologram of Whitfield rezzed up by his side. Her uniform was as crisp as ever. Judging by her movements she only had a flatscreen monitor at her end.

''Lian, there's been a breakthrough.'

'Yes,' the Provost-General said.

'You know?' she asked.

'We have just been attacked, Juno.'

'Attacked? By terrorists?'

'By ghosts,' Medford said.

'There are no such things as ghosts,' she warned him sternly. 'Every recorded "ghost" has a perfectly rational explanation: ball lightning, optical illusions, freak cloud formations or movements of air.'

He didn't want to tell her that he'd seen them with his own eyes at the Scientifica, watched them slaughter his men. 'Seven hundred sightings in one minute? Sightings across the planet? Most were in the frostlands, as before, but there were some in the Strip.'

'One minute? When was this?'

'Fifteen minutes ago. Everything went crazy for exactly one minute.'

'That was when we activated the Machine.'

'You've got it working?'

'For exactly one minute. We've not processed all the data yet, but the initial findings are that the power fluctuations distorted the local time field. The rate it generates energy is incredible, if we can tap just a fraction –' Her voice was the most animated that he could remember, and he had known her since childhood.

The Machine must have been responsible for the ghost sightings. Medford tried to rationalize that idea. Had the device induced mass hysteria somehow? A thought struck him: the Machine could be a vast holographic projector, a giant archive of a lost civilization. But why would such a machine affect time?

Whitfield appeared bright, as if she had the explanation. 'My people reported atmospheric disturbances here in the cavern — that's all that happened. I've not confirmed the hypothesis yet, but I think they might have been a side effect of the time spillage: Manheim radiation perhaps, or Vendermann Flux. Temporal theory is one of the uncharted frontiers of science. At the moment we know so little about it.'

'Juno, you have to face the possibility that there really are ghosts. Call them what you want — this is the attack I've been warning you about. It looks as if they are linked to the Machine in some way. I'll send a battalion of my men to secure the chamber.'

'We're five miles underground. The Machine is an object for scientific study, not just some esoteric weapons system.'

'They can walk through walls, Juno, I saw —'

'Provost-General!'

Medford looked up, ready to admonish the officer who'd disturbed him. Instead his attention was taken by the main screen: the freighter was lifting from the launch pad, despite the futile efforts of a squad of his men. The fusion bombs were being stolen.

Chris took his position, pulling on a helmet. Nyssa sat in the co-pilot's seat, unsure what she should be doing. Half a dozen Adjudicators were firing at them, but the energy bolts just bounced harmlessly off the ship's hull. All around came the sound of docking clamps and fuel hoses disengaging.

'I can fly this thing solo,' Chris said, flicking switches above his head. The ship pitched around until it was facing deep space.

Nyssa replaced the dress strap which had fallen off her shoulder. 'Won't they just shoot us down as soon as we clear the station?'

'Nope,' Chris said. He pressed a button and the main engines engaged. The ship lurched forward, pushing Nyssa back into her padded seat.

'Hold your fire!' Medford shouted at the weapons officer. The Adjudicator lifted his hands from the keymat as though it had given him an electric shock.

197

The freighter was square in their sights, the computers matching the course as it began its descent. Only he and the crew of the freighter knew about the fusion bombs: whoever had hijacked the freighter must just be a thief who chanced upon it. Medford dismissed the thought: some terrorist had got lucky.

It accelerated away from the station, looking as though it was going to punch a jump to hyperspace, then at the last minute it dived down, tucking itself beneath the station. Now it was curving towards the planet.

'Sir, we have them,' the gunner complained.

'That ship is not to be fired upon.' There was little chance that the fusion charges would detonate, but Medford didn't feel like risking it. Besides, the charges were needed.

'Sir, it's heading over the horizon: they'll be out of our range in ninety seconds.'

'Do we have their course yet?'

'No, sir. The pilot isn't using the computer.'

'Launch an interceptor. Order it to shadow that freighter, but not shoot at it, regardless of provocation.'

'Aye sir. Grey One launched.'

'Prepare the Battle Platform. I'll transmat over.'

'— interceptor. Order it to —'

The link with Medford cut automatically and replaced with a PLEASE HOLD caption. Whitfield was transfixed by it for a moment, then she cut the connection.

'Lost in thought?'

Forrester had regained consciousness. Whitfield turned to look at her. She looked drugged, but that was just a residual effect of oxygen starvation. After immobilizing her in the Machine Room, Whitfield had called outside for a couple of scientists. They'd taken the unconscious woman back to the research dome on an antigrav trolley. There, they stripped off her stolen armour, replacing it with a grey kimono belonging to one of the physicists. They'd found a pair of handcuffs at the security post and put them round her wrists. Then they'd run the recorder on her armour and found out her name and how she'd fled the Scientifica.

'How much of that conversation did you hear?'

'You're a clever woman, Chief Scientist. If you didn't want me to overhear, you'd have gone to another room. Why was your boyfriend so keen to stop the freighter being shot down, do you think?'

'You really are an Adjudicator aren't you?' Bureau members were trained to read body language and read into nuances of speech. At times, Medford would know what she was thinking, could predict her actions, just from a word or the way she was sitting. There was no mystery about this: they had known each other since childhood, on and off, and had been lovers for over forty years.

Forrester smiled. She had perfect white teeth. 'Yes. And you've just used Standard Guilty Perp Tactic Number One: change the subject.'

Whitfield turned away, annoyed with herself, and tapped a control on the walltop next to the videophone. The screen lit up again, showing the Doctor in the middle of an animated conversation. The camera panned across, and showed Adric replying. These were pictures from earlier, from the transmat room. They were taken from Forrester's point of view, from the camera mounted in the helmet of her stolen armour. Without letting Forrester see what she was doing, Whitfield dialled up the Adjudicator database and searched for information on the stolen freighter.

'The Doctor has regenerated,' she told Forrester while she worked. 'Where is he now?'

'He looks even goofier with the sound turned down, doesn't he?'

'You've just changed the subject.'

'I need to get back to the Machine.'

'That's out of the question.'

'I was meant to activate it again after fifteen minutes.'

'You've missed that deadline already.'

'I know, but . . . has that freighter turned up on the register of stolen ships yet?'

The ship's registration details had just appeared, along with a message that no officers were to approach it. 'My people are searching the plateau. The Doctor will not be able to hide from them.'

Forrester was straining to look over her shoulder at the computer display. 'That ship's come from somewhere outside this system. Where?' Before Forrester had finished, the computer had supplied the answer: the freighter was assigned to the Third Fleet, so it ought to be on border patrol in the Seventh Galactic System. The Fleet was under the command of an Admiral Dattani.

Ten years ago at the All Worlds Science Fair on Dellah, Whitfield had been Senior Prorector and had led her planet's delegation. Medford had been there handling the security arrangements, a mutually beneficial arrangement, and the longest period that the two of them had been together for many years. One of his most loyal subordinates had been a Pakislovak called Dattani, a member of the Unitatus like 'Lian. Medford had told her many years later that Dattani had gone on to do well in the Space Fleet.

Whitfield felt a sense of betrayal. She isolated it at once, analysing the feeling in her stomach and right at the back of her head.

There was a commotion at the door.

Adric, the mathematician who had accompanied the Doctor, was there, being led in by a couple of her men, including the Prorector.

'We found him climbing down from the plateau, Chief Scientist.'

'He was alone?'

'Yes, ma'am. We took a couple of jetpacks up there. There's no sign of anyone else, but we found a second suit of Adjudicator armour.'

'Don't worry about that, it was only this lad's disguise,' Whitfield assured the Prorector. 'Where is the Doctor?' she asked Adric. The boy was exchanging worried glances with Forrester.

'We need to tell her, Roz.'

Forrester nodded. 'The Machine was only activated once,' she explained. 'So now the Doctor is trapped in another universe. We need your help to get him out.'

The Doctor was trying to explain the consequences of time travel to Tegan as Adam lead them down through the

200

bowels of the snowship. At first the Doctor had talked about tachyon tides and negative reality inversions. That might have been science, but it was gobbledegook to Tegan. So he'd resorted to an extended analogy: 'The Universe is like a human body, you see. A few cuts and bruises here and there don't hurt it. Not even major surgery if it's done properly by a good enough doctor. Paradoxes are just the scar tissue.' He paused. 'But if that damaged TARDIS was allowed to enter the Vortex it would be . . . a massive heart attack. Emergency treatment would be needed, followed by intensive care. The Universe would never fully recover, and there would always be the risk of a relapse.'

Tegan had always prided herself on having a cosmopolitan outlook. At school, her friends' ambitions had reached no further than the local factories and shops. Her classmates had always laughed at her when she said she wanted to see the world. She'd struggled to pass her HSC, they said, and so she would end up stacking shelves until she found the right man and married him, just like everyone else. But Tegan wanted to *travel*. She had studied languages, she'd learnt about Aboriginal culture, she'd spent her summers and all her money in foreign countries. She regretted some of her experiences and experiments now (and maybe ought to regret a few more of them) but all the time her frame of reference had been expanding. Moving to England as soon as she could, relishing the idea that every face she saw would be unfamiliar and that everything from car registration plates to the banknotes would all look different. With her new job, the world was her oyster.

But after only a few days travelling with the Doctor, Tegan had begun to question her wanderlust. It was like some crazy package tour. Four days, and as many alien worlds: the cool warmth of the TARDIS interior; the mud huts and pure mathematics of Logopolis; the recursive labyrinths of Castrovalva; and now this arctic colony. The day before yesterday Tegan had been witness to the dawn of creation itself. The cosmos was larger than she would ever be able to comprehend, and full of monsters and death. Everything out there wanted to kill her or destroy the universe. Tegan just wanted to go home and lock the door.

'Can you prescribe anything?' she asked wearily.

The Doctor's eyes were screwed shut as he tried to think of a solution. He had been staring death in the face, beating impossible odds, saving planets for centuries. How did he stay so cheerful?

Finally the Doctor clicked his fingers and looked her square in the eye. 'Temporal Fusion,' he said. 'We can send the TARDIS back along its original flightpath, undoing everything. You might say that the original flight is a stitch in time – well, we'll *un*stitch it!'

Another analogy.

'How's it done?' Adam asked. He was pretending to take it all in his stride, but Tegan could see he was as lost as she was. He was just some small-time crook, after all.

'Two Time Lords acting in concert would be able to navigate the Vortex. There have to be two – the mental strain would be too much for just one of us.'

'So we have to get you and Patience back to her TARDIS?' Adam asked. They had reached the top of some wooden steps. Quint climbed down them, Tegan followed him, trying to listen to the Doctor.

'Yes. We use the Time Control Unit. The telepathic interface ought to be undamaged, but even if it has been then I can rig something up from material from the TARDIS's central cortex.'

Quint helped Tegan down. 'So where is this TARDIS?' Adam asked the Doctor, who had reached the top of the steps.

'Well, that's just it, I'm not sure.' The Doctor stood up and straightened his frock coat.

Adam had been the last one to come down, now he was moving to a gleaming control panel.

Tegan looked around the room. The wood panelling had been replaced with chrome and white plastic. When she had been on holiday in Hong Kong two years before, Tegan had been invited to a party onboard a luxury yacht. That's what this reminded her of. A couple of people dressed in the same buccaneer style as Adam manned control panels, looking a few centuries out of place. All around were radar screens and instruments. The pilot obviously did everything by pressing buttons. They'd not been far off fly-by-wire in Tegan's time, but it was good to know that it had been perfected. Looking closer, Tegan saw patches of rust, and that some of the facings had been chipped. The ship was well-maintained, but it was old.

'Patience might be able to locate it, but, well . . . she's unconscious and I can't risk another telepathic conference. If I still had my time sensor . . .'

'Doctor, the conseque—'

'I am well aware of the consequences, Tegan,' the Doctor snapped. He returned to his musings. 'Now, I can't initiate temporal fusion by myself, so we need Patience conscious and relatively strong. So, I think we should keep heading for the Nightingale Facility.'

Adam nodded his assent. 'We cannot travel much further by ship: we'll be too big a target. We'll have to trek the last ten miles by foot. We'll be underground for most of the time.'

The Doctor looked around the room, taking in his surroundings for the first time. 'For people that reject science, you seem to have all the creature comforts,' he concluded.

'Who said that we rejected science?' Adam said. 'Living on this planet you need all the help you can get. What I reject is the arrogance of the Scientifica. They think that they can solve everything if they throw enough scientists at it. At the same time, they forbid research into a vast number of areas and they frown on individualism.'

'You sound bitter,' Tegan said. She of all people knew a grudge when she heard it. 'Anything personal?'

'I'm not some Scientifica reject, if that's what you mean. I come from a mining family. When my father was born, he knew that he'd have a job for life. By the time I came of age, a robot had my job.'

'So you hate robots?'

'No,' he laughed. 'You're quite the amateur psycho-analyst, aren't you? It's the Scientifica I hate. They run this planet. Their system is meant to run like clockwork, but it doesn't. So they ignore the uncomfortable facts to balance their precious "equations" and "calculations". Meanwhile a thousand people starve because they've missed off a decimal place. The world would be a lot better off without them.'

'What would you put in their place?'

The corner of Adam's mouth curled. 'A smoking crater, given half the chance.'

'And the government?'

'Anything would be better than the Scientifica, believe me. They called in three legions of Adjudicators to enforce their law. You should have seen them arrive in the frostlands, gunning down anyone in warpaint because they were traitors.'

'That doesn't excuse terrorism,' the Doctor said. 'You don't target railway stations and shopping centres if your dispute is with the military.'

'Don't believe everything you see on their holoscreens. You'd think that I was to blame for every crime on the planet. I'm a scapegoat, an easy solution.'

'You're really Robin Hood, then?' Tegan said sceptically.

'No,' he cackled, 'I'm usually robbing skitrains. I'm just a highwayman, a common thief. My friends are the pushers who sell the Scientifica's kids bleep and booster to perk up their nights out. I hang around with alien smugglers like Quint and his brother. I know I'm better than *them*, though. I don't think that justice is on my side, I don't think I've cracked the secret of the universe. I'm scum, just an ape who's got above himself. The difference is that I know it.'

Medford stepped from the lift onto the bridge of the Battle Platform. Three officers were manning the command post. They stopped what they were doing to salute him.

'Justice by your side!' they chanted.

'And fairness be your friend,' Medford replied. 'Is the response team ready?'

It was Dareau that answered. The Adjudicator-Lieutenant was a small man with a permanent sneer on his face. 'Yes sir. We can put them on the ground anywhere on the planet in two minutes.' This was an orbital platform designed as a command post. In the early stages of a conflict it would co-ordinate communications traffic and troop movements of a

204

battlezone. Normally it was a module of the Icarus Skybase, but in emergencies such as this it detached and took up a tighter orbit around the colony.

'Show me the freighter.'

The lighting in the control room dimmed and the hologram pit lit up. The freighter was ploughing along the tops of the clouds. By the side of the image, a tactical map appeared. The interceptor was following the freighter at a discreet distance. The picture was coming from a robot camera mounted on the nose of that plane.

'What are the sensors showing?'

'Three lifeforms. Apart from that, there's nothing: the hold's empty.'

Or shielded.

Medford asked the tactics officer to assess the skills of the person flying the freighter.

'He's good. Those Type Twelves are difficult to handle in an atmosphere, and he's managing to keep it steady even though he's not using the flight computer. He's also keeping us guessing – we've got no idea where he's planning to go.'

'He's just entered the northern frostlands. Sir, he's coming in to land.'

'You're kidding?'

They were planning to go outside into Antarctic conditions, but the outfit Adam handed her looked like her kid brother's tracksuit, complete with a double stripe down the arms and legs. The material was stained, and smelt stale.

Adam was already stripping off his furs. 'These coats are OK for short trips, but we'll be outside for at least an hour. We'll need these environment suits.' He was wearing the same sort of one-piece underwear she had been put in. Tegan was glad to see that the male version was equally tight. His suit had been patched up in half a dozen places.

The Doctor was saying something: 'The material is made up of hundreds of thin layers. The suit has microweave heat elements and warmth gets trapped in the air between them. A bit like double-glazing. Spacesuits aren't much thicker than this these days.' Despite his enthusiasm, he wasn't

205

changing out of his overcoat. Instead he was helping Tegan to find gloves and a balaclava that fitted her. The gloves he handed across looked like the ones surgeons use.

'Shouldn't it be tighter at the wrists?' Tegan suggested. 'To keep the cold out?'

'You'd cut off the circulation to your extremities doing that.' Adam had finished dressing. He looked faintly ridiculous, and it took a moment for Tegan to realize why: the skin-tight, ivory-white outfit he was wearing made him look like a ballet dancer. He was a slight figure, teenage thin. She looked down at herself. She looked no less ridiculous, but at least she had a better figure.

Quint came in, followed by a sled which was propelling itself. Patience lay on it, covered by a translucent white sheet. The thin plastic rose and fell regularly. There was a control box crudely welded to one corner. The casing was half-melted, as though it had been in a fire at some time in its long history.

'It saves us having to carry her,' Tegan observed.

'There are supplies on the sled, too. Including your clothes, Tegan.' The final item of the ensemble was the mask. It fitted tightly over her face, reaching the back of the ears, and it felt like a cross between a fencing mask and a hardhat. There weren't any airholes, but she could breathe.

'Porous?' she asked. The Doctor's expression of pleasant surprise was enough to confirm her guess had been right.

The door in front of them ground open. Quint passed each of them a small backpack. His was already strapped over his broad shoulders – the harness had been customized for him. When Tegan pulled hers on she judged that it weighed about ten pounds. 'These are emergency supplies. There's nothing that will show up on sensors. The cave mouth is fifty metres straight ahead.'

Outside, the wind had died down a little. The Doctor and Adam were already stepping down the ramp. Tegan followed the sled down, with Quint bringing up the rear. The Shark Person wasn't wearing a mask. Tegan was surprised how familiar he looked now, a mere hour or so after she'd screamed at the sight of him. When she got home would it be difficult to get used to the everyday things? It would take a couple of days, she was sure, to get used to living in a world where televisions only played flat images, telephones had rotary dials and earpieces and everyone she met was human.

As Quint reached the ground, the ramp was already lifting up. Around them were columns of ice, tinged with blue and carved smooth by the winds. The horizon was a little closer than it ought to be – or rather, than it would have been on Earth. Tegan realized that although the snow came over her ankles, she could barely feel the cold. She flexed her fingers. The Doctor watched her, smiling.

'It's quieter here than the waystation,' she said. *It was a young Asian man. His eyes were staring, pleading with her.*

'We're not in the mountains any more. There are no avalanches or glaciers here on the ice plains. Everything's nice and –'

Something the size of a house hurtled overhead.

A second after that, a smaller aircraft flew over.

They were travelling so fast that it took a second or two for the roar of their engines to catch up with them. When it did, the noise was enough to bowl Tegan, Adam and the Doctor over.

Tegan pulled herself to her feet and asked what the hell was going on.

'That was a freighter on a descent spiral being chased by an interceptor,' Adam told them. 'Let's get undercover before the Adjudicators arrive.' Behind them, the snowship had completed a one hundred and eighty degree turn and now it was setting off back into the blizzard.

Adam had reached the mouth of a pot-hole.

'Mining subsidence?' the Doctor asked.

'The whole area was overmined, the rock's like a honeycomb. It's impossible to map, there are rockfalls every day. Handy if you need to get around without anyone being able to find you.'

'You know a way to the hospital then?'

Quint grunted. 'The tunnels here are wide: we shouldn't have a problem getting the sled down them. It'll take a couple of hours.'

14

Convergence

'Program running,' Nyssa said. Data streamed across the readout above her head.

'I've just lost sensor definition,' Chris complained.

'Yes: half of the arrays are now looking for the Doctor, or rather his double heartbeat.' It had been a simple programming task. Nyssa was surprised how basic human computers were.

'That's like looking for a needle in a haystack.'

Nyssa frowned at the phrase. 'Considerably more complex than that, but well within the capabilities of the freighter's computers. Wherever the Doctor is, we should need to complete two orbits of the planet at most. What is the interceptor doing?'

'Holding its distance. It won't interfere. The Skybase knows that they can't bring us down without the risk of a fusion explosion.' Chris saw Nyssa's expression. 'No, don't worry: the bombs can't possibly go off unless they are armed. But they can't be sure that we haven't armed them.'

A buzzer sounded above Nyssa's head.

'We've found the Doctor!' she shouted. 'Two hundred kilometres ahead.'

Chris began the landing procedure. At the speeds they were travelling, it was quite a job to prevent the freighter from overshooting. The whine of the engines began to lower in pitch, and the white horizon dipped for the first time.

'We're on an automatic descent spiral. We'll have touchdown in four minutes, and we'll be within a kilometre of the Doctor's position. I'll find the suit locker and get a couple of environment suits. You gather up the fusion charges.'

Nyssa pulled herself from the co-pilot's seat and set off

down the length of the freighter to the cargo hold. The deck was pitching slightly as the freighter descended, but she retained her balance.

The hold was dark, the prone figure of the pilot still lay in the corner. She hadn't much time. There was a small box, a first aid kit, hanging from a hook by the door. She pulled it down and shook the contents out. They had already removed one of the fusion charges from its shelf. She took it from the coffin-like container, almost afraid to touch the evil thing, and laid it in the first aid box. An almost perfect fit. Moving over to the racking, she began to take the other containers down, one by one.

Adjudicator-Pilot El-Messawi sat suspended in his globepit, state-of-the-art gravitronics protecting him from G-forces that would have snapped his spine. He couldn't see outside: but he knew that he was sitting well back, almost at the tail of the tapered aircraft. His hands and fingers were coated in a million nanofilaments that translated the slightest nerve impulse into a complex aerial manoeuvre. His helmet fed him all the tactical and navigational information he needed.

The computer told him that the freighter had entered a descent spiral and showed him the point where it would land. Unlike the interceptor, the stolen vessel wasn't capable of a vertical landing in an atmosphere. Messawi cut through the freighter's flightpath, heading directly for the landing site.

As a precaution, Messawi activated the stealth mode. This was crude technology, rarely used in combat. It didn't make his ship invisible, it blinded the other man's sensors with a burst of energy. Most warships were protected against the tactics, but not an ordinary freighter.

The interceptor was over the landing point. As it hovered there, sensor beams flooded the snowswept landscape, looking for traps. Was the freighter rendezvousing with another vehicle here? Not by the look of it.

Satisfied, the pilot reconfigured his craft for land operations. Safe in his globepit, he didn't hear the fuselage slide back around him or the tail retract. The interceptor began dropping, its hoverchute ablating slightly in the atmosphere.

The wings folded out, elbow joints appearing halfway along their length. The engine cowlings twisted out of sight as the exoskeleton withdrew from its housing and locked into place. The nosecone rotated, the sensor arrays morphing to adjust to their new surroundings. Landing claws extended into feet and toes. The wing-mounted laser cannons rotated and extended forward until they resembled club-like hands.

In 'Walk' mode the interceptor was bipedal, the globepit mounted in the torso four metres above the ground. The head was packed with sensors, each arm was a powerful battery of weapons.

If anyone had been outside, they would have seen a squat humanoid shape, roughly eight metres high apparently straining to look up into the sky.

The computer flashed up a warning which the Adjudicator-Pilot didn't believe.

His ear filled with static as he opened up a coded comm-channel. 'Ah . . . Grey One to Battle Platform. I'm registering fusion charges ahead. Twenty-two of them. It must be a computer glitch.'

Nyssa had changed into a spacesuit. Cwej had already turned the thermostat up to maximum before she had put it on, and inside the freighter the heat was almost enough to scald her skin. Outside she suspected she would be grateful for every erg of energy. They were slotting the last two fusion charges into place as the ship landed.

'You carry the box,' Chris said. Nyssa closed the container, locked it shut with a tiny magnetic clamp and lifted it, not wanting to think what was inside. Cwej had drawn the pistol he had taken from the fallen pilot. He was still unsteady on his twisted ankle, and this was made worse when the ship lurched.

Chris looked up, wincing. 'What was that?'

The ground reverberated again. And again.

'Footsteps?' Nyssa asked.

'The Adjudicators are here already,' Chris said.

'It could be the Doctor.'

'Not unless he's put on a lot of weight. Come on!'

They left the hold, Nyssa clutching the box containing the bombs to her chest.

Just outside there was an external bulkhead. A square porthole gave them an excellent view of the snowblown landscape outside.

A giant was striding towards them through the blizzard: a robot ogre. Its hands, feet and head were crude, boxlike. Its skin was black and pale blue armour-plating. Searchlights swung around in all directions from mountings on the machine's hips, shoulders and head.

Chris studied it, calmly cataloguing its weapons and abilities. 'We're a sitting duck in here, we'll have to leave.'

'It's too big!' Nyssa said. 'We can't . . .'

'Hey, don't worry. We'll find a way. It can't risk shooting at us, remember?'

There was a cold blast of air as Chris popped open an access chute.

'I'll go first,' he said, easing himself through the hatch. The icy ground was only a metre or so below them. Chris lifted Nyssa down by the waist. They had the freighter between themselves and the robot, so had at least temporary cover.

Nyssa looked back. A massive hand grabbed on to the top of the freighter for support. The robot loomed over the starship, which was standing slightly askew. The robot peered down at them. Behind it, the clouds were black, and boiling.

'The sky . . .' she said.

'The weather is not the most pressing problem,' Chris said. He levelled his laser pistol and fired. A scarlet bolt sliced through the air, hitting the robot square in the chest. The armour absorbed the energy.

'Run!' shouted Chris.

Beneath the interceptor, the young man had stumbled over a knee-high clump of snow. The girl on his arm pulled him upright. Messawi took another step forward, enhancing the magnification on the viewer. He was gaining on them with each five-metre stride. The girl turned back, her mouth open in a scream that Messawi couldn't hear. She was

211

holding the box containing all the fusion sources. The man was a metre in front of her, clear space between them. He was turning to usher the girl on.

A green dot appeared on the man's chest. Instinctively, Messawi fired. The energy bolt hit the target just below the ribcage.

The young man pitched over, falling awkwardly. The front of his suit was red. He still had that laser pistol, but now he was firing wildly and the bolts were falling short of the interceptor's feet. Not one of them hit the craft, and even if they had they would have bounced off the armour.

Chris was on his back. The energy bolt had clipped his side, removing it. Blood poured from the wound. Nyssa tried to help him, but Chris held firm. He fired his pistol again, before losing his grip on it.

'We'll be killed,' she cried, close to tears.

'You'll be all right. Watch this,' he croaked.

The war machine took another step forward . . .

. . . and fell crashing into a hole in the ground, its gun arms flailing and firing.

Its weight had been too much for the unstable rock, especially when Chris's shots had weakened it further.

Chris made a disconcerting whooping noise which subsided into a cough.

'How did you know the ground was going to subside?'

He managed a smile. 'When the freighter landed there was that lurch, remember?'

'The weight of the ship caused the ground to shift slightly?'

'Strip-mining has weakened the underlying rock.'

'Don't talk,' she warned. 'Don't move. And don't look down.'

'I'm a mess. I feel cold.'

'You would: the suit's ripped.'

'Not that sort of cold.'

'Here.' Nyssa piled snow into the wound, causing Chris to squeal with pain. The cold would force the blood vessels to contract, slow the loss of blood. 'Keep it covered with snow. I'll get the first aid kit from the ship. The one that

212

came in that container.' Nyssa pointed to the box containing the fusion charges.

It wasn't there.

The tunnel was wide and, as Quint had said, the rocky floor hadn't proved an obstacle for the hoversled carrying the unconscious woman. After ten minutes, the Doctor had insisted that they stop to check her vital signs. Quint had joined him. They reported that according to the diagnostic computer the woman was still in a deep coma. Adam was glad for them.

'No change,' the Doctor said cheerfully.

'That's the trouble with this planet: nothing ever changes.'

'A very pessimistic view from one so young,' the Doctor admonished him from behind his half-moon spectacles.

'You're no older than I am, Doctor.'

The Doctor was thirty at the most, but was clearly annoyed by that observation. 'Appearances can be deceptive . . . people change.'

Tegan grimaced. 'The Doctor's living proof of that, if nothing else.' The Doctor's companion wasn't so self-conscious about her survival suit now, and seemed happy to be doing something other than sitting around and waiting. Adam realized that she didn't like him, which made him a little regretful, but he'd live.

'What's the future for this colony, then? All the minerals have gone, there's no money. Everyone who could afford to go has gone, the rest of us are stuck here. The mines are closed, we import virtually every manufactured item. Meanwhile, the Scientifica tell us that everything's going smoothly but we can't have any cucumbers to eat this year because they've used them all up trying to extract sunbeams.'

'They've what?' Tegan asked.

'It's a literary reference,' the Doctor explained. '*Gulliver's Travels*. Our friend here thinks that the Scientifica are involved in worthless scientific investigation.'

Adam smiled. 'They are magicians, trying to prove that magic doesn't exist.'

'Very poetic. What's it supposed to mean?'

213

'How's a transmat work, Tegan?'

'I don't know,' she growled. 'I'm still trying to work out why it's so light in this cave.'

'No one knows how a transmat works. They just sort of do – you ask a Scientifica technician and he'll talk about subspace, the space–time vortex and all manner of impress-ive-sounding ways of getting from A to B in zero time, but it'll soon become apparent that he might as well be talking about a flying carpet. It's pseudoscience. Technobabble. Science fiction.'

'Just because you don't understand . . .'

'*No one* understands, that's what I'm saying. It's not just transmats: nanoprocessors, fusion generators, hyperdrive, voice-recognition software. According to all the laws of physics these things shouldn't work, and no one really knows why or how they do. And that's just technology. Never mind the really complicated stuff like quantum particles, gravity, living organisms or sunlight. The universe is made from magic.'

'It's complicated, but there's a real scientific explanation in there somewhere.'

'Yeah sure. "Chaos Theory" – you know that people in the twentieth century thought that butterflies flapping their wings could start a hurricane on the other side of the world? It's true, twentieth-century literature is always going on about butterflies and hurricanes. OK: why do people go mad?'

'They're stuck in confined spaces for a long time with people who wind them up?' Tegan suggested pointedly.

'Very good. But you've fallen into the Scientifica trap: you're trying to explain everything away, reduce it to a simple cause-and-effect sequence of events. But you do that and you start using shorthand – "she had a hormonal imbalance", "the neurochemistry of his brain was unusual". That's just the scientific way of saying that he's possessed by the devil.'

'Hormones exist,' Tegan said.

'You've seen one, have you? The devil existed for most people until a few centuries ago. Science is a metaphor, not the truth. The Scientifica don't see that – they ignore the paranormal, rationalize away all the ghosts and UFOS.'

'You've seen a ghost, then?' Tegan asked scornfully.

'I have. And so have you, Tegan,' the Doctor said. Both he and Quint had been conspicuous by their absence in the conversation up to that point. Adam was about to ask the Doctor's views, but he was already asking a question of his own. 'Is that why the peacekeepers are here? To fight ghosts?'

Adam pointed at his own chest. 'The Adjudicators are here to combat the terrorist threat.'

'Three legions against a rackety old snowship? No disrespect, but you're not really worth it, are you? No, they're here for some other reason.'

Before Adam could reply, something weighing ten tonnes crashed through the roof.

Adam pulled Tegan down as the rock cascaded from the new hole in the ceiling, along with a huge black shape, like a tank. Adam lifted his head. It was a giant robot of some kind, built like a man. Its limbs were twisted. Hot hydraulic fluid was draining from one of the machine's joints. It looked like a warstrider of some kind: of course – the interceptor they had seen.

'Hurry, before it rights itself!' Quint shouted, running towards the machine. The Doctor was following close behind.

'It's a vehicle,' the Doctor shouted. 'With a driver.'

'I know. We have to get to him.' Stop him from contacting reinforcements.

The Doctor caught Adam's arm as they reached the machine. 'And do what?'

Adam glared at him. 'What do you think? Stop him from killing us.'

'Kill or be killed, is that it?'

'Yes.' Adam shook the Doctor off. They were standing next to a metal ball in the middle of the wreckage. It was about two metres in diameter made from a matt black material. There must be a way in. There was an unfamiliar whining noise. Adam followed it, and saw that the Doctor had managed to locate and open the hatch with some sort of tool. When the Doctor emerged his face was grave.

215

'We're too late for him. He's been electrocuted.' The Doctor closed the panel.

Adam couldn't be sorry. 'The distress beacon is active, then?'

'A man just died here.' Tegan had her hands on her hips and a scowl on her face.

'And another one just died somewhere else, what's your point?' Adam replied. 'This man is an Adjudicator, probably out looking for us. He wouldn't have shown us any mercy.'

There was a clattering from above. Someone up there. Adam and Quint drew their ceramic knives.

Forrester and Adric were sitting inside the Machine, managing to sip from their cups of tea despite their handcuffs. Adric had the plate of biscuits on his lap. The Chief Scientist thought that they looked out of place. Was this because they had told her that they were time travellers? Adric was from another universe, Forrester was an Adjudicator from a couple of centuries in the future. Adric had just said that the Doctor's race, the Time Lords, could travel freely in the fourth and fifth dimension.

'So this is a time machine?'

'It's a Time and Relative Dimension in Space machine,' Roz supplied. Now that Whitfield knew, the Machine had lost none of its awesome power. If anything, it was more impressive than before: this was something almost entirely new to human science. From the Martian invasion onwards, contact with the spacefaring races had boosted human technology. Alien technology had provided improvements to FTL drives, interstellar communications. An Arcturan broadcast picked up by a terrestrial radio telescope had included enough information to build a working transmat. A salvage team had recovered a starchart of the whole sector from a derelict Dalek saucer. Human scientists would have made all these discoveries in time, but not for many centuries. The Machine was – what? – ten thousand years ahead of current research. Would it prove *too* advanced? Give a man from the Neolithic a nanocomputer and he'd not understand it and he wouldn't have a use

216

for it. Would humanity, would she, be able to grasp even the basics of this machine's operation?

'This isn't helping the Doctor. He's trapped, and we can rescue him.'

'You can operate it?'

Roz laughed. 'All I know is we need to pull that red lever,' she said finally.

'I will not allow this Machine to be activated until I understand its functioning,' Whitfield stated. 'You travel with the Doctor – you must know at least the basic principles.'

Adric was looking around the cramped control room again. 'Just because we've travelled in the TARDIS it doesn't mean that we know how to fly it. This room doesn't look anything like the Doctor's ship.'

Roz muttered something to the same effect, then: 'Medford's a member of the Unitatus.'

'Yes, he is,' the Chief Scientist replied.

'The what?' Adric asked.

'It wasn't that difficult to figure out. My deduction was helped by the fact that he wears the symbol of the Unitatus on his armour. In my time they are a little more secretive.'

'What is the Unitatus?' Adric asked again. 'Some sort of religion?'

The Chief Scientist straightened. 'The Unitatus is a society based on an ancient organization that saw the military and scientists joining forces to defend Earth from alien attack. They are dedicated to that aim, even over national and governmental loyalties.'

'That's the theory anyway,' Roz said. 'By the thirtieth century they spend most of their time organizing charity events and arguing whether "Lethbridge-Stewart" was hyphenated or not. A few centuries ago – now – the Unitatus is still a growing political force. Many legions and colonial administrations have strong Unitatan traditions. A bit like the Christian and Mithraic cults in the late Roman Empire.'

The reference meant nothing to Adric. 'So that badge we saw on the statue of the Empress is the symbol of the Unitatus?' he asked.

217

'Yes, based on an ancient regimental design. As far as I am concerned, such superstition has no place in a modern organization, but many in the Empire have found that Unitatan membership furthers their career.'

'You're not a member. You're not part of the conspiracy. Medford's got something planned, Chief Scientist, and if he's not letting you in on it, then it can't be good for your planet.'

'You don't seem in any great hurry to save the Doctor,' Whitfield chided, unwilling to continue that line of conversation. 'Does anything look familiar? Does that?' The Chief Scientist indicated one of the instrument panels. There were various dials, criss-crossed by a string of lights.

Adric stepped over. 'It looks a bit like the navigation control station, I suppose.'

As Whitfield examined the panel again, the switches and levers began to make a little more sense. Unsure why, she slotted across one of the toggle controls. A string of numerals clacked into place on a digital readout.

'What are these?' She moved aside so that Adric could study the numbers.

The young mathematician tried to point out different areas of the equation, although the handcuffs restricted his movements. 'These look like space–time co-ordinates. I think that they represent the Machine's last journey. Those are the co-ordinates of this planet, I recognize them from when we landed. I . . . don't recognize the others.' He was lying.

'We don't have starcharts here. I'll have to access the archive at the Scientifica.' She pinched the control on her wrist communicator. There was no response. She asked the computer to explain the fault.

'Planetary weather conditions are affecting communication signals. Please try later.'

Whitfield dialled up a weather report.

Technician Kalraymia rubbed her eyes and looked up at the monitor again. It was the time of day when the foredroids rang in their reports. Although robot workmen did all the heavy labour these days, the rules were that a human had to supervise their work. This one was a battered old Class G maintenance 'bot that had been in service for four decades. Somehow, over the years, it had avoided all the routine personality overhauls. It had eccentricities that the Scientifica would not tolerate in a human being.

'Morning, love. Foredroid VKU474Y. Works Number: Twelve Alpha X. Location: Pryanishnikov Waystation. Job: Clearance to Scientifica Works Standard Three Kappa Pi Alpha Zed.'

'Go ahead with your report.'

'Ta, petal. Work to bring the Waystation back online is proceeding to schedule. We've dug the mass grave, and half filled it. One hundred per cent of the designated trees have been felled, eighty-seven per cent of the brickwork has been repaired. The skitrain station and line are open, and we've restored power, water and information supplies. Work in the main waystation building has been hampered by the materialization of the manifestations, but I confidently predict that we'll reach target and the station will be operational again in three hours.'

'The weather looks pretty rough out there,' she said, trying to make conversation. Behind the robot's triangular head there were stormclouds. Living in the Strip, Kalraymia never saw the raw weather they got out in the frostlands, the weather control system on the Icarus Skybase saw to that. Kalraymia shook herself awake. 'Wait a second: what do you mean "manifestations"?'

The robot paused for exactly a second before responding, it took Kalraymia slightly longer to work out why. 'Didn't you hear me, love? We're online for a bonus this financium.' Maintenance droids only ever had one thing on their mind.

'I heard you. Answer the question.'

The droid folded three of its arms. 'It's in the main building. Could you at least try to be a bit friendly-user?'

This was going to take a long time. 'What is in the main building?'

'Don't panic. Mind your suit, you don't want to rip it, believe me.'

Nyssa edged a little further down the rim of the crater. It was uneven ground, with a lot of sharp, flat stones. 'Chris, I've just lost enough explosives to obliterate a galaxy.' He had insisted that she looked for the bombs before returning to the freighter for the medical supplies. The snow around his wound was pink with blood.

'The box was sealed up pretty tight. A magnetic clamp doesn't just slip off.'

Nyssa looked back. She had retraced their footsteps, but as Nyssa had suspected, she must have dropped the box during the robot's attack. It had fallen down with it, and it could be under a mountain of rubble. Above them, the sky was seething, oily black cloud blanketed the sky as far as she could see in all directions. The cloud hadn't been like that when the freighter was in flight.

'The radiation detectors on our suits aren't picking up a leak. The box is still intact. And it goes without saying that none of the charges have gone off.'

'I'll get you back to the ship: there's a transmat on board. We'll beam to a hospital.'

'My injuries are too severe,' he whispered. Primitive transmats were often unable to copy serious wounds – if they tried to teleport Chris then there would be tiny duplication errors: chromosomes resequenced, nerves and neurons missing.

'I'll get those medical supplies. Then I'll signal for help.'

Chris didn't reply.

The hovercopter swept over the frostlands at the speed of sound. The navigation computer told the pilot to head for the crater nine kilometres south of their starting position. Above them, the clouds were growing and flickering like time-lapse photography.

The Doctor prised out a small silver box and smashed it against the side of the wreckage.

'Well, that's seen to the distress beacon.'

Tegan held up the first aid kit that she had just found. It had broken open. It must have come down in the rockfall. 'What do you make of this?' The box was filled with metal tubes that looked a bit like deodorant cans.

Tegan turned to get the Doctor, but he was already bounding over. He examined the contents of the box.

'You know, there are times when I wish I used expletives,' the Doctor concluded.

'Could you tell me what they are, please?' Tegan said. 'I hate not knowing what I'm panicking about.'

The Doctor was running his sonic screwdriver down the full length of one of the tubes. 'These are neutronic charges: fusion bombs.' He handed the cylinder over to her and pulled out another one.

'Grenades?' They looked a bit like stick grenades. She weighed it in her hand. It was light, almost as if it was hollow.

'Well, in a manner of speaking,' Adam said, coming over. 'Each one of those can destroy a city.'

Tegan's fingers went numb.

The tube slipped from her fingers.

It tumbled through the air, end over end.

Tegan flinched, her throat dry. There was a pulse at the back of her neck, a hindbrain instinct that told her to think nothing, to do nothing but push hard with her heel, to get away from the danger.

It hit the rock floor, bounced once and came to rest.

It didn't detonate.

'Jesus! Jesus Christ! Jesus Christ!'

'I don't know why you flinched – a *transmat* wouldn't have been fast enough to get you out of the blast radius,' Adam chuckled.

Tegan was still shaking. 'I'm surprised you can be so calm about it.' Quint was signalling his agreement.

'Well, I saw the Doctor disarm it with that magic wand of his, so I guessed we'd be safe.'

'You absolute –'

'Tegan! Is that you?' It was a girl's voice, coming from about fifteen feet above them.

Tegan looked up. 'Nyssa?' she said. The Doctor finished disarming another of the bombs and glanced up.

'Yes, Tegan, it's me. Is the Doctor with you? I need him.'

The Doctor had the sonic screwdriver in one hand, a fusion charge in the other. 'Yes. We're coming up.'

They clambered twenty feet up the scree. The ground shifted, but was stable enough to carry their weights. Between them, the Doctor and Tegan could support Patience's medical gurney, the anti-gravity device did the rest. Tegan reached the top after the Doctor. The sky was horror-film dark, thick with black clouds. Twenty feet away, Nyssa was kneeling over a wounded man. Both were wearing close-fitting dark grey spacesuits. As the Doctor approached, Nyssa stood, brushing the snow from her legs.

'I like your outfit, Nyssa.'

The young woman looked Tegan up and down. 'I prefer yours.' She managed a short laugh, and the two hugged. It felt odd: inside their insulated outfits they couldn't feel the heat of each other's bodies, or the softness of skin. They parted a little clumsily.

The Doctor was bending over the fallen man. 'Don't worry, I'm the Doctor.'

The man paused. 'No you aren't,' he concluded sadly.

There was an embarrassed silence.

'He *isn't*,' the man insisted, using precious energy doing so.

Tegan knelt down. She knew some basic first aid. The most important thing in these cases was to keep the patient conscious. This man was already delirious: she had to start a conversation. 'Hello, I'm Tegan. Wait a minute: you're the sex maniac!'

The Doctor raised an eyebrow.

'I met him at the Imperial. He's a crim: he keeps shifty-looking company. His name is Bruce.'

Nyssa put a hand on her shoulder. 'He's explained all that, Tegan. It's a long story. His real name is Chris. He knows the Doctor.'

'Well, I don't know him,' the Doctor said. 'Are these yours, by the way?' The Doctor patted the kit box and slid it over to her.

'The fusion bombs!' Nyssa exclaimed. 'You got the magnetic clamp off.'

222

The Doctor frowned. 'How on earth did you get hold of such an impressive arsenal, hmmm?'

'That's another long story. Doctor: Chris needs help.'

Tegan had been examining him the whole time. She looked up, shaking her head. He'd already lost pints of blood, the shock alone would be enough to kill him.

'Where are Adam and Quint?' the Doctor asked suddenly. They weren't here, and now he mentioned it, Tegan couldn't remember seeing them climb up.

'Adam?' Chris coughed. 'Are Forrester and Gemboyle here, too?'

The Doctor tilted his head to one side. 'Gemboyle? That name rings a bell.' Before continuing his train of thought, he winced. The Doctor could hear something, Tegan realized. After a moment, she could too: a siren.

A hovercopter was heading towards them over the horizon, a searchlight probing the ground.

'Sir, cloud cover is now one hundred per cent. There is massive electrical activity, and it's interfering with our sensors, transmats and communication beams.'

'What is the origin of the storm?'

'Unknown. There is no meteorological reason.'

'We're getting pictures from Pryanishnikov, sir.'

'Pictures? What do you mean?'

The holopit lit up.

There was a flash of lightning.

A tall, angular figure faded into view an inch above the floor of the main dining hall.

'These are pictures that were taken by a maintenance droid, sir. According to the timecode they are an hour old.'

The same time that the Machine was activated, Medford noted. On the screen, the ghostly figure raised its hand, then brought it down swiftly. A line of flame appeared in its wake. The apparition trailed his fingers through the fire, drawing a swirling pattern with the flames. The picture focused on the symbol which hung, burning in the air.

The apparition stepped down onto the floor. There was a rumble somewhere in the distance. The new arrival

223

cocked his head, as if it was the first time he'd ever heard thunder, then continued his work.

The robot maintained its surveillance. The figure bent down, and spat on the ground. It drew a symbol like a cross from the saliva, then ran its index finger down his forehead.

'Translation rune placed.' The figure was male, now, his features were softer. He flexed his fingers, tested his weight in this new gravity.

Join me.

The room was suddenly full of them: men and women in stiff, high-collared robes. They stretched and shook as if they had woken from a deep sleep.

'We must secure this world.'

Some of them began clearing a space in one corner of the room. The others were drawing patterns on the floor and walls, even into the air. An elaborate design emerged, a fractal spiderweb with a clear focal point. That done, six of them moved towards the centre of the design, sprinkling water on the ground from their fingers. They took their places, chanting words of power. The fractal web began to hum with energy.

Medford pressed a control on his wrist. A coded signal ricocheted from his communicator to the nearest tele-communications console, then broadcast thirty miles to a military communications satellite. After a couple of microseconds' pause, it was re-routed to the Icarus Skybase. There the communications centre picked up the command and sent a request to the hyperlink relay. Less than a second after he pressed the switch, the hyperlink whirred into life and broadcast a prearranged signal along a quark-thin beam into hyperspace. A second later the message was complete. Silently the computer erased all trace that the message had ever existed.

'They are here,' he whispered. 'The invasion has begun.'

15

Downtime

There was the rumble of thunder outside. The storm had started two hours ago, just as the hovercopter was coming over the horizon. It had been an ambulance from the Nightingale Facility, the very place the Doctor had needed to take Patience. It had taken a little persuasion to convince the paramedics that they were passengers on the space freighter which had been hijacked by terrorists, that the criminals had brought the ship down in the frostlands and that they had made their escape with all their identification and belongings. But Chris and Patience clearly needed emergency help, and both Tegan and Nyssa were also injured, so the paramedics had accepted the situation. The Doctor and his companions had been loaded aboard the ambulance and rushed to the Facility. By the time they had arrived, the storm was beginning to interfere with radio signals, and so the staff there were unable to check the Doctor's story with the Scientifica. By another stroke of luck, there were no Adjudicators stationed at the Facility, they'd been called away. For the moment at least, the Doctor and his companions were safe.

'Doctor?'

He looked up at the word, aware that in a hospital it wasn't always someone calling his name. The Head of the Facility, Director Fletcher, was standing over the Doctor, holding an electronic clipboard. He was a tubby little man with a neatly clipped moustache. His face was almost as florid as his medical tunic.

'Your friends are all out of danger. Miss Nyssa was uninjured; Mrs Jovanka was suffering only from bruising. Her husband's injuries are healing nicely. Your own wife's injuries were complex, involving a little brain damage. That has been repaired now, and she has regained consciousness.'

The Doctor decided that explaining his companions' relationship to himself and to each other would both waste time and invite further questions. Instead he thanked the Director and asked whether he might see them.

'Of course. Your wife is upstairs, but the others are in ward five, just down this corridor.' He indicated the direction.

The Doctor struck up a conversation. 'This seems a very unusual location for a hospital.'

The Director nodded. 'We're right in the heart of the old jabolite fields. We used to provide emergency care for miners. These days, we still have emergency facilities, but most of our work is medical research.'

'In what area?'

The Director held a door open for the Doctor. 'Mental illness. At any given time there are about two hundred patients here being processed for correction.'

The Doctor could well imagine what 'correction' involved, and he doubted that any psychiatrist from Tegan's time would recognize the conditions being treated. No psychiatrist outside the Soviet Union, anyway. The concrete-floored corridor suddenly felt a lot colder.

The Doctor could hear Tegan, and she was grumbling. As he turned the corner, he discovered why: she, Nyssa and Chris had been allocated beds in the same small ward. She sat tightly wrapped up in one bed, Nyssa was sitting on the end of the young man's. Both girls were wearing flannel pyjamas, Chris was only wearing his boxer shorts.

'A unisex ward, I mean it's just not right. I want somewhere to change back into my clothes.' She held up her uniform blouse.

The Director tried to be soothing. 'What precisely is your complaint, Mrs Jovanka? Offworlders sometimes have unusual customs regarding gender-segregation, I know, but what possible objection can you have to sharing a ward with your own husband?'

'He keeps showing me his operation scars,' Tegan muttered.

'I don't. That's what I'm saying: there aren't any. The skin's just pink and hairless.' The lad was practically bouncing up and down with delight. The Doctor found himself smiling at the enthusiasm.

'I'd rather not know,' Tegan told the room.

'If you like,' the Director suggested, 'I could appoint a marriage guidance counsellor.'

While the two continued their discussion, the Doctor crossed the room and unclipped the simboard from the end of Chris's bed. 'You seem to have made a full recovery, Mr Cwej.' There was no sign at all of the stomach wound.

'You pronounced it right . . . yeah, I have. A lucky escape. They even fixed my ankle. Are you really the Doctor?'

'Yes,' the Doctor said a little warily.

'You're a Time Lord who travels around time and space with your companions in your TARDIS. Fighting injustices, defeating evil? Neither cruel nor cowardly?'

'Er . . . yes. I didn't realize I had a fan club. On this planet, my reputation seems to have preceded me.'

Chris clammed up, clearly occupied by some thought or other. The Doctor chose not to press the point.

On the other side of the room, Tegan had rounded on the Director. 'I thought that this place was run on logical lines. Why on earth do you still have weddings?'

The Director attempted to stand his ground. 'A pair-bond often has beneficial social advantages and can actually improve worker-productivity. Marriage is encouraged among certain grades, although the Scientifica take a neutral stance on the issue. Most of the members of the Scientifica, myself included, are unmarried.'

The Doctor turned away, smiling. 'Where's Adric?' Nyssa asked him.

'Adric?' Chris said. 'But I thought that he was the one that . . . came from Alzarius,' he finished quickly.

The Doctor frowned. 'I don't know where Adric is,' he admitted. 'We were split up at the Scientifica.'

'Do you have the first aid box?' Nyssa asked.

'Underneath my coat,' the Doctor said softly. The overcoat was draped over his arm. 'Don't worry, I've disabled them.'

'How?'

'It's a technique beyond the science of the Humanian

227

Era: I reversed the polarity of the neutron flow. Anyone who tries to use the bombs now is going to be rather disappointed.' He checked that the Director wasn't looking, then passed the box over to them.

'What are we supposed to do with these?' Chris asked.

The Doctor shrugged. 'You're a resourceful chap, I can tell. I'm sure you'll think of something. Tegan,' he called over, 'why don't you come with me? We'll find you somewhere to change, and then we'll pay a visit to Patience.'

The screens were awash with static. All around the bridge of the Battle Platform, Adjudicators sat trying to decipher the scratchy, indistinct images coming from the colony. Up here in space, there was no interference. Anxious transmissions from Icarus Skybase punctuated the Adjudicator's work. Their instruments suggested that the activity in the clouds was 'not conventional electricity', whatever that meant. There was still one reliable line of communication open from the planet: technicians at the Scientifica had managed to rig up a device that could send out pulses of neutrinos. The Adjudicator-Lieutenant stationed at the pyramid had sent a Morse message that all appeared well on the planet. As a precaution, Adjudicator units had been deployed planetwide under the cover of anti-terrorist operations.

Medford sat in the centre of the room, brooding. The Scientifica prided themselves on the constant monitoring of the population: close circuit cameras on every corner, concealed microphones in most public places. The justification for this wasn't crime prevention, that was just a useful side benefit. The mass of data collected allowed the Scientifica to predict social and economic trends. Housing and transport needs could quickly and accurately be assessed. Public opinion could also be instantly gauged. On most worlds in the Empire, even the Corporate Belt, such invasion of privacy would be intolerable. Most people on this colony didn't even notice it.

But with the microphones not working, rumours would be spreading. Without their news broadcasts, the population would be making up stories by themselves. Ghost stories.

On one screen the last pictures relayed from Pryanish-nikov before the blackout were silently replaying them-selves over and over. Half a dozen robed figures were chanting something, surrounded by gossamer-thin cables that glowed and pulsed with white light.

A couple of hours ago, when the image had been fresh, every Adjudicator in the room had fixed their attention on it. Now they hardly noticed the aliens in the corner of their room.

The Quartermaster-Fiscal informed the room that the signal booster was ready. Medford pulled himself upright. Things were moving at last. Now they could do a sensor sweep of the planet and know the movements of the enemy forces. As a team of Adjudicators prepared the scanware, Provost-General Medford realized that in the next few moments, humanity might discover that it had already lost the war. Painfully slowly a holographic globe appeared, tides of pixels sweeping around the virtual surface, improv-ing the resolution with every orbit. The computer was marking off the settlements in black, Adjudicator units in blue, enemy units in red.

There wasn't a single red dot.

The computer buzzed a warning as a cluster of tiny yellow triangles appeared at one location in the northern hemisphere.

'What are those?' Medford asked.

Adjudicator-Lieutenant Dareau was consulting the auto-manual. 'The yellow triangles are fusion charges,' he said after a moment. Medford admired the way he managed to keep the surprise out of his voice. Knowing Dareau, he was relishing the prospect of mass-destruction. The Lieutenant had friends in the Senate, and he got results. Medford was of the old school that valued means over ends.

'They are concentrated at the Nightingale Facility. And there's the freighter. Are you sure there are no enemy units in the area?'

The Quartermaster twisted a control and the map became speckled with grey. 'That is every piece of metal in the area weighing more than ten kilos, Provost-General. Derelict mining equipment, crashed snowships, pipelines. The only military machinery down there is ours.'

Medford tapped the map, making it ripple. 'That's the nearest ground unit?'

'Yes, sir. A hovertank squadron. They were based at Nightingale, but they are en route to Pryanishnikov.'

Medford spread his hand. It wasn't large enough to bridge the gap between the tanks and the hospital.

'They are a little over half an hour away at full burst,' Dareau answered, before Medford could ask.

'What's the status of the transmat network?'

He already knew the answer. 'Intermittent. The Scientifica have imposed restrictions on all non-essential journeys.'

'I want two hundred Adjudicators at Nightingale.'

'You'll have to send three hundred, then. The others will vanish somewhere between de- and remat. If they are lucky.'

Medford considered the odds, just for a moment. He'd seen a transmat accident once. Ten years ago, during the Kalkravian Revolution. They had been beaming out hostages when the EMP from a fundamentalist bomb had hit: all of a sudden the people on the platform had become twisted, mutilated things. There was a sound that still haunted him: shrieking, warbling half-formed words and screams.

There was another option. It would commit a large proportion of his forces, but they would not win the war without the fusion charges.

'Prepare for orbital drop.'

The officers began shouting at their subordinates or into their microphones. 'Crash stations!'

'Full armour, everyone.'

'Hoverchutes cast.'

'Put this station down at the Nightingale Facility.'

When the Doctor and Tegan found her, Patience was sitting by the window, staring out at the raging storm. She was impossibly beautiful now that the colour had returned to her face. Even in a hospital gown, without makeup, she put Jerry Hall to shame.

'G'day,' Tegan whispered. It was like talking to a work of art.

'Hello.' Tegan wasn't surprised that Patience had an English accent, although perhaps she ought to have been. The tone of Patience's voice and smile had been calculated to make her feel at ease, but Tegan only saw a perfect row of teeth. She felt self-conscious in her polyester stewardess's uniform.

'Has your memory returned?' the Doctor asked gently.

'Not all of it,' she said. 'But I think that is for the best. I remember my husband and my eldest son.'

'Your name?'

'And yours,' she replied, smiling. The Doctor looked away, almost coyly.

'Your TARDIS?' Tegan prompted. She hadn't forgotten the Doctor's apocalyptic warnings. The sooner they could get this 'Temporal Fusion' sorted out, the better. Patience hadn't understood the question, which didn't inspire much confidence.

'The name was coined after your time,' the Doctor said. 'Tegan means your time capsule.'

'Not mine: my husband's. It is near here.' She rubbed her temple, as if she could hear it calling to her.

'We need to initiate temporal fusion,' the Doctor told Patience. He explained the procedure to her, rattling off a string of long words that Tegan didn't even try to understand. Patience listened, nodding every so often.

'I can't return home,' Patience told him.

'I know.' The Doctor placed his hand on Patience's thigh, so casually that it took a moment for Tegan to be surprised by the intimacy. It wasn't the sort of thing the Doctor did. 'We can remove the Time Control Unit from your husband's TARDIS and operate it remotely. It will return to Gallifrey, and you can remain here, with me. All traces of your journey will be erased.'

Patience smiled, placing her hand over his.

'Doctor – look!' Tegan called out.

Outside, the cloud pulsed and rippled.

'What's that?' the Doctor asked. The sky reminded Tegan of the surface of a duckpond just after a stone had been thrown into it. When she told the Doctor as much, he grabbed her arm.

'Run, Tegan! Find Nyssa!'

* * *

231

There was a dot of light at the epicentre of the hole in the clouds. It was growing, glinting in the light.

In the distance, all around, there was a faint rumbling. It was growing louder, second by second, but there was no way of saying where it was coming from.

The wind was picking up, soon reaching gale force.

The shape in the sky was large enough to see, now. It was a globe, pale blue. Impossible to judge the scale of anything that far up – like trying to work out how large a cloud is by relating it to things on the ground.

The size of a marble now, sonic booms reverberating all around as it punches through the stratosphere. Clouds parting like the Red Sea, thick beams of sunlight forming leaning columns of light from the heavens to the ground – a spotlight on the falling object.

The size of a tennis ball. It's pale blue, with markings all over the surface. Flames dance on the lower hemisphere as the friction burns the metal hull.

The size of a melon, but still impossibly high. It's artificial, not a meteor. But it isn't a conventional spacecraft: they skip across the levels of the atmosphere, like a flat stone on the sea. Spacecraft descend in gentle parabolas, they glide in, slowing down as they go by deploying parachutes, retro rockets or antigravs.

The size of a football, and still among the clouds, so it's bigger than the largest aircraft or hot-air balloon. There's a burning line scored in the sky. In the wake of the object the sky has caught fire.

Beachball. It's dropped beneath the clouds and now it fills the sky. The wind is screaming as the air is sliced in half. Doubling in size every second, it's now possible to judge that it is the size of ten cathedrals.

Antigravs fire at the last possible second, the underside of the Battle Platform barely clears the roof of the Nightingale Facility. It dwarfs the hospital, eclipsing the sun.

For a moment it hangs there.

Night had fallen, along with the sky.

The floor was carpeted with shards of glass. They crunched and tinkled as Tegan ran over them. Chris and

Nyssa were ahead of her, at a double door at the end of the corridor. The glowbes that lined the ceilings were automatically adjusting their lighting levels.

There were screams: men and women, above and below. Tegan found herself sharing their fear and incomprehension. She refused to succumb to it, concentrating on catching up with Nyssa and her friend. He was trying to trip an electric lock with some device or other. Both had got dressed while she and the Doctor had been away: Cwej was in his tuxedo, Nyssa in a green silk dress that left little to the imagination.

'Who's screaming?' she asked.

'The inmates here,' Chris said. 'This place is a mental institution.'

The door clicked open.

'An insane asylum?' Nyssa said absently. Such things had long vanished on Traken, and only featured in the most melodramatic literature.

'That's not a nice phrase,' Tegan lectured her. Behind the doors was a large storeroom. Cwej was hurrying down the aisles, checking the plastic bins. 'The Adjudicators will be swarming around this place. We need to hide the bombs.'

'In here?'

'I was hoping to find some of that material that shields stuff from sensors.' Tegan had no idea what he was talking about.

'The Doctor has disabled the bombs,' Nyssa reminded him.

Chris turned. 'They'll still show up on scanners. Even if the Doctor's right and Medford can't undisable them, we can't just hand them over to him without a fight, he'd get suspicious.'

Nyssa stopped. 'My people have a proverb: the best place to hide a light is in the sun.'

'Are you suggesting that we put the bombs in plain view?' Tegan said, trying not to sound too exasperated.

Chris was nodding. 'This facility has a fusion generator. We put the bombs in there and the fusion signature of the power plant will disguise them.'

'Then what are we waiting for?'

* * *

233

The first Adjudicators were sappers, on the rooftop almost before the gravity ladders had finished unfurling. They set up the laserwire that cut the holes in the roof and disabled the satellite dish that relayed radio and transmat signals.

The second wave of Adjudicators were the troops in full armour. They went into the building under strict radio silence, moving swiftly. The suits had the full schematics of the Facility in their archive. The troops spread through the wards, barely noticing the inmates cower from them. There were twelve crucial points: exits, garages, lifts and stairways, the armoury, environmental control and suchlike. These were to be secured first.

Outside, the Battle Platform's gun batteries came online, sliding smoothly from their housings. Anything, absolutely anything, that came out of the building beneath them would be atomized. There was no room for human error: the procedure was computer-controlled, and would be over before any of the Adjudicators onboard the Platform would even be able to register the target.

The assault team had secured the strategic points. They picked up two prisoners in the ventilation ducts: a male and a female, both unarmed. A sensor sweep showed that the fusion charges had disappeared.

The Doctor and his companion were in a holding area in the vast hangar deck of the Battle Platform. The Provost-General had left the flight deck with two bodyguards to interrogate them. Adjudicators and their equipment filled the hangar. Although there were no windows, there was a sense of movement. Shortly after they had been brought aboard, the Platform had lifted, then began to drift. Medford imagined the vast structure floating above the ground, oblivious to trivia such as the laws of aerodynamics and gravity.

Bright yellow loaderdroids were ferrying missiles and power plants to the squadron of sleek fighter aircraft. A technical team were refitting all the hovercopters with particle cannons. At the far end of the room half a dozen hovertanks were jostling for position with about twice as many large wardroids. The air was filled with the sound of

234

sirens, welding beams and shouted orders. As he and his bodyguards passed through the throng it parted around him. He came to a halt in front of the bars of the cell door.

The Doctor and the Patient were deep in conversation at one end of the cell. She had fully recovered, and stood with a composure that matched the Doctor's own. It was difficult to believe that this was the wizened corpse that Juno's team had discovered, almost fossilized, in the rock around the Machine. The Patient had sat in cryogenic suspension in the research dome for a year, doing little more than gather a little more dust. The Scientifica had long run out of tests to conduct on the body – every possible measurement and observation had been made. At the same time, the Imperial Council were getting restless: peacekeeping operations on the planet had quickly proved successful and what little subversion and unrest that existed was easy to confine. The 'alien threat' he had so urgently reported had yet to make its presence known, and there were elements at Court who were suspicious of the real motives of the Unitatus. Openly, the expense of maintaining three legions on the planet was beginning to be questioned. Reluctantly the Chief Scientist had released the Patient into the care of the Adjudicators' Bureau. When evidence of the Machine and its Pilot were unveiled in the Court itself, that would have brought home the nature of the threat.

That was before the enemy had started massing at the Waystation, only a couple of hundred kilometres away. Medford had been unable to contact Whitfield at the research dome. The Machine may have already fallen into the hands of the enemy.

The Doctor began calling to him as soon as he was within earshot. 'Provost-General, you must listen to me. There is a dangerous piece of machinery on this planet. You know of it: you found Patience there, and the Scientifica are running experiments on it.'

Medford's face remained stony. He was face to face with the Doctor now. 'You know what the Machine is?'

'It was built by our people,' Patience said.

Medford nodded, as though he had known all along. 'And what is it?'

The Doctor seemed to consider his options for a moment. 'It's a time machine,' he admitted, 'a broken one.'

The Adjudicator considered this for a couple of seconds. 'Can you fix it?'

'I not only can, I must,' the Doctor insisted. 'The TARDIS has already been activated on a number of occasions and it's caused damage to the structure of time. If you check with the Chief Scientist, you'll find that the ghosts only appeared for as long as the TARDIS was active. If the Scientifica attempt a full-scale flight, then . . . well, I don't know what the consequences would be.' He was telling the truth, or was a skilled liar.

'The logical thing to do would be to destroy the Machine,' Medford concluded.

The Doctor paused for a moment. 'It's indestructible.'

'Nothing's indestructible, Doctor.'

'There is a better way,' Patience said. 'We can return the TARDIS home.'

'Home?' Medford asked casually, trying to get her to reveal more. She was clearly an intelligent woman, but seemed naive in comparison with the Doctor. Five minutes' talking, and she'd tell him everything he needed to know about the alien threat: the level of technology, the types of weapons, strategy and philosophy.

'To Gallifrey, the moment it left,' she explained. 'If guided properly, the flight would undo all the damage that has already been done. It's called temporal fusion.'

Medford had checked the name 'Gallifrey' with the Imperial Datanet – the Doctor had used it before. The planet was not listed anywhere, not even in the Blue Book of the Unitatus or the most obscure of the discredited early deep space travelogues. 'And you can perform this temporal fusion?'

'I've not seen the state of the TARDIS yet, but it's had millions of years to recover. It should be fairly close to working order by now. You must take me to the research station.'

Medford smiled. 'But of course.'

The wallscreen beside was buzzing with disjointed reports of military action across the planet. The terrorists were taking full advantage of the freak weather, but the peace-keeping force was more than a match for them. Forrester had made her opinion clear: she didn't believe a word of it.

The scientists had adjourned to the research dome for the night. Before they had finished, they had managed to identify more of the instruments in the control room of the Machine. Whitfield had made some solemn speech to the effect that humanity was taking its first steps to a full understanding of the Time Machine and its operating principles. Then she'd ordered that Roz and Adric were taken to one of the spare bunkrooms and locked up for the night.

The Scientifica technician given the task bent over Adric and fluffed up his pillow. The boy had already complained that the cuffs were chafing his wrists, and the only thing he could do to relieve the itching was to rest his hands in his lap.

'You're not the most experienced security guard, are you?' Forrester asked the technician.

He chuckled at that. 'I'm a particle physicist,' he admitted. He was only in his early twenties, with a floppy black hairstyle that made him look even younger.

'You've locked us up in a room right next door to the transmat.'

'We've changed the codes, so you won't be able to use it. Besides, you're handcuffed.'

Roz nodded, accepting the answer. 'There aren't any Adjudicators here?'

The technician seemed gratified by Roz's interest in him. She had relaxed a little. He bent over her, refreshing her glass of water. 'A standing order of the Chief Scientist. It was one of the preconditions laid down when the peacekeeping force arrived that this project would be allowed to continue without interference from Earth. We get the occasional observer or messenger, but by order of the Empress herself none bear arms. We're eight kilometres underground here, and the only way in is the transmat, so we're pretty safe from attack. The best type of security is secrecy. Only seventeen people in the universe know about this research station, present company excepted.'

Roz's face and the technician's were level, and only

inches apart. 'A cigarette's out of the question, I know, but can I stretch my legs?'

'Sure. You're in handcuffs.'

He moved back, and watched as Forrester stood, her hands about level with her belt. She shifted from one hip to the other. 'You don't use those robot 'cuffs the Bureau use.'

'No,' he laughed almost apologetically. 'I didn't realize you were a connoisseur.'

Forrester clasped her hands together, as if she was trying to squeeze life back into them. 'Autocuffs do have one advantage.'

'Yes?'

'Yeah. They wouldn't have let you tie my hands together at the front.'

'What's wrong wi–' Forrester threw her hands up like a club, catching the technician on the chin. He reeled, and was quite unprepared when the hands swung back down and connected with the back of his neck.

'I thought you'd never ask,' Forrester told him. 'If my hands were tied at the back, I wouldn't have been able to do that. Think of this as a learning experience, and be glad that I didn't garrotte you.' She bent down and fished the keycard from the prone technician's tunic. Adric positioned himself so that she could release him, then reciprocated. Both sets of handcuffs clattered to the floor.

Forrester picked up one of the sets and cuffed the technician to one of the chair legs. 'Let's get back out to that TARDIS. There might still be time to save the Doctor.'

'Wait,' Adric warned. They stopped, listened as the transmat chamber next door activated with a whine.

'Incoming,' Roz noted. 'We've got visitors.'

There were dozens of footsteps. Adric couldn't see them, of course, but could hear the clattering of their plastic armour-plating. They were marching resolutely towards them, until the last minute when they turned a corner. From then, the noise gradually subsided. Forrester had been listening intently.

'Adjudicators,' Forrester said. 'Over a dozen of them. That'll make it more difficult to get to the Machine.' A thought struck her. 'Not impossible, though. We need to get to a computer.'

Next door, the transmat activated again. Another group of people in armour.

'That man just said that your Empress banned Adjudicators from coming here.'

'It looks like there's been a change of policy.'

Part Six

Deus Ex Machina

16

The Empire Strikes Back

'It looks like there's been a change of policy,' the Prorector said.

He found Whitfield in the bunk in her office, woke her and told her about the Adjudicators. She was on her feet before he had finished speaking, sealing up her tunic.

'Where are they now?'

'All over the place, Chief Scientist. There are dozens of them.' Sure enough there were a couple of Adjudicators in full armour at the end of the corridor, guarding the lift.

'You there! Explain yourself.' As they got nearer, the two scientists were dwarfed by the armoured figures.

The Prorector looked the nearest Adjudicator up and down. 'You dare to bring weaponry here?'

Neither of the soldiers spoke.

Whitfield took a step back. 'This is in direct violation of the Imperial Mandate. The Court will hear about this.' The threat was meaningless for the moment – the weather conditions on the surface meant that the staff at the research dome couldn't even contact the Scientifica. The Prorector wondered how they had managed to beam in: they must have access to some truly state-of-the-art equipment, and even then there must have been risks. The Adjudicators seemed unworried by the thought that they were disobeying their Empress. This disturbed the Prorector: the Adjudicators' Bureau prided itself on its loyalty and impartiality. Now they were acting as if they were a law unto themselves.

The lift door slid smoothly open. Provost-General Tertullian Medford stepped forward.

''Lian!' Whitfield exclaimed. It was an open secret among the Scientifica that the Chief Scientist and Provost-General were lovers. This was the first time that the

Prorector had seen the two of them together. Medford let her approach him, but hardly reacted to acknowledge her.

There were other people in the liftshaft: two hulking Adjudicators with drawn blasters and a couple of oddly dressed civilians, a man and a woman. He wore a cream frock coat lined in a vivid red. If that was not eccentric enough, there was a rather limp plant, one of the *Umbelliferae*, pinned to his lapel. The woman wore just a thin cotton nightshirt, probably hospital issue. She had flowing blonde hair and exquisitely long legs.

'Doctor?' Whitfield said, expressing some surprise, as though it wasn't quite who she'd expected. 'We meet again. And this is the lovely Patient?'

The Prorector realized he was staring. Instinctively he knew that this was indeed the near-corpse they had discovered at the foot of the Machine. He remembered studying the body. He had been the first to realize that it was still alive. How could such a leathery, sexless thing be transformed into the goddess before him now? She smiled at him, and he found it impossible to ask the question.

'Why are you here?' Whitfield asked.

'The Doctor can repair the time machine,' Medford said. 'The security implications of that are obvious. There has to be a military presence here when the Machine is made operational. Besides, the enemy have manifested on the surface. It can only be a matter of time before this cavern is attacked.'

'You chose not to discuss this with me first?'

'There is nothing to discuss. Under the terms of the Defence of the Realm Act, this planet is now under Martial Law.'

'If you are using this planet in some Unitatus power struggle –'

'It goes far further than that, Juno. The Empire will fall tonight if I don't do this.'

The fusion reactor door was three inches thick and between them and the Adjudicators. It seemed like an ideal place to dig down, but Cwej knew standard Bureau tactics. He had told Nyssa and Tegan that a squad would already have been sent to

244

secure the generator. The three of them would have to move quickly to hide the fusion bombs.

The generator was a stubby glass tube about the size of a kettle sitting in a nest of cables. The container was full of little metal beads in a clear, boiling, liquid. Nyssa opened up the first aid box containing the bombs and began handing them to Chris and Tegan. They found a hiding place for each: the charges were so nondescript that they could easily have been components of the generator.

Nyssa handed the last one over to Chris. Something was wrong. 'There are only twenty-one charges.'

'Are you sure?' Chris checked for himself, but Nyssa was right. 'There *were* twenty-two before, weren't there?'

Nyssa wanted to say that she had miscounted, that really there had only ever been twenty-one, but she knew otherwise. 'The other one was there when we packed them, but after that . . .'

'It must have fallen out when the robot fell. I wasn't really in a position to keep track of things after that.'

'The box was sealed with a magnetic clamp,' she noted.

'Not when we caught up with the Doctor.' Chris was trying to piece together what had happened, using his police training to assemble the facts in a logical order. Nyssa found that all she could remember was hugging Tegan and a feeling of overwhelming relief when she saw the Doctor.

Tegan's eyes were wide open. 'Adam!' she declared.

'The Doctor mentioned a man called Adam,' Nyssa said, 'and someone else: Kent . . . Clint?'

'Quint,' Tegan confirmed. 'They were people that stood up against the Adjudicators and the Scientifica.'

'The terrorist leader? The bomber?' She'd heard the name on the car radio, when they'd been driving to Cwej's flat.

'That's how the newscasts here portray him. To his followers he's a revolutionary, fighting against the cruelty of the Scientifica and the Adjudicators. My partner, Roz Forrester, has met him, and she's convinced that he's really only a small-time crook.'

'For what it's worth, he agrees,' said Tegan.

'He has bombed civilians?'

Chris nodded. 'Yeah, those associated with the presence of the peacekeepers: support staff, bars and hotels. The usual stuff.' Nyssa shuddered at the thought that humans could take such atrocities for granted.

'So what would he do with a fusion bomb?' she asked.

'If you'd met him, you'd know,' Tegan said quietly. 'He hates the Scientifica. That bomb would completely annihilate their pyramid, and everything around it.'

Chris shook his head. 'The Doctor disarmed the bombs, remember?'

'Adam was right there when the Doctor started to defuse them,' Tegan informed them. 'He wouldn't have taken one that had already been disarmed. He had the opportunity to palm one before the Doctor could get to it.'

Chris's face was pale. 'We have to warn them.'

'They'll kill him,' Nyssa objected. 'The Adjudicators are the ones that brought the bombs to the planet in the first place.'

Tegan nodded. 'If we don't tell them, Adam will kill thousands of people. Now I've seen at first hand what the Adjudicators have done here, but no one deserves to die like that. The upper echelons might have made the decisions, but that doesn't mean that every lab technician, maintenance man and cleaner in the pyramid has to die too.' Tegan began walking to the door. 'There isn't even a choice to make. You had better get away from here. Only one of us has to go.'

Nyssa shook her head. 'We're coming with you.' Chris nodded his agreement.

The squadron of hovertanks rounded the mountainside and came to a halt. The Waystation sat on a raised area of ground. There was evidence of the struggle earlier that day. The brickwork was streaked with soot in places, unusually pristine in others. A group of workdroids sat well away from the buildings, biding their time.

There were six tanks in the squadron, but only one had a human occupant. It sat at the back of the group, indistinguishable from the teletanks. The Control Tank would co-ordinate the others in the event of an encounter with the enemy. Since the Galactic Wars, a series of arms treaties restricted the capability and sophistication of combat robots: something the size of a tank with full autonomy was banned, but if it was controlled – however tenuously – by an organic operator, that was fine. After half a millennium of enforcing the law, the Bureau of Adjudicators were perhaps the most proficient organization in the quadrant at finding such little loopholes.

Lieutenant Solim, the driver, tried the communicator one more time. However much she altered the settings, there was nothing there but white noise. It had been the same for nearly two hours. She sat back, considering her options.

There was a tap on the hatch.

'Look mate, are you coming out, or what?' It sounded like one of the robots. Solim activated the periscope. The workdroids had made their way over to her tank and were now gathered in a semicircle around it. They'd left caterpillar tracks, footprints and other imprints and trails in the snow. There were half a dozen droids in all. The foreman was the only one that was anything like humanoid. A couple of bulky yellow loaders sat at either side, next to that were a decoratoid and a robobrickie. Squatting at the back was an autosmelter roughly half the size of her tank. They'd somehow managed to distinguish the Control Tank from the others, which was meant to be impossible. These droids had blown her cover: if there really was an enemy presence in the Waystation, they'd know which tank to target first.

There seemed little reason to stay in the tank. Solim unplugged herself, pulling a transmitten on over her right hand. It would allow her remote control of the entire squadron if needed.

She jumped down, cursing herself for forgetting to reset her armour's thermostat. While she corrected her mistake, the foredroid trundled over. 'They've gone.'

'Are you in charge?'

'Aye, lass.'

'Who's gone?' Hopefully it meant the enemy.

'The Skybase, the Scientifica, even Nightingale. Wiped out.'

'It's just the storm,' she scolded.

247

'A storm doesn't stop *radio* waves, duck.'

'Not on Earth, but this is an alien planet. Do you know what's in the atmosphere?' Solim didn't have a clue herself, but she knew that extremely low temperatures could affect conductivity.

'Look, love, I've worked here all me life, and there's been nowt like this before. The clouds are dust from a nuclear winter. The debris from the explosions sticks in t'upper atmosphere and blocks out the sun.'

She checked her wrist computer. 'The radiation counter registers normal.'

'We're thousands of kilometres from the Strip, it'll be days before the radiation clouds get up here.' Strange how a standard speech synthesizer could be made to sound patronizing.

'What about the ghosts?'

'They're still there. If you ask me, they don't seem interested in interfering with us. I don't see why me and my men can't just get on with our work.'

'You know where they are?'

'Main Hall.'

'Come and show me.' All the robots edged forward. 'Just the foredroid.'

He shrugged as the others clanked to a halt. Solim took in the Waystation, trying to get a sense of the lie of the land.

'If you're right and there's been a nuclear attack, that won't have affected the Skybase. Could you convert that transmat mast into a ground-to-space radio beacon?'

'I'm a fully qualified engineer, love, not some bootleg piece of rubbish.'

'Is that a yes?'

'If I had an emergency works order, yes I could do it. It's a ten-minute job.'

'OK, I give you an emergency order –'

'No, lass, I'll need the form. I'm not authorized to do anything without a signed form with a Fault Number, Date and Priority.' Its chestprinter began whirring into life.

Solim sighed, and hoped she could find a pen in the Waystation building.

* * *

They turned the corner, their hands raised.

The two Adjudicators brought up their blasters, caught unawares by them. Tegan flinched, half-expecting to be shot there and then.

'We surrender,' Cwej announced. 'We are unarmed, but we know where the fusion bombs are.'

The Adjudicators kept their distance, wary that this was a trap.

'The Scientifica is at risk, you must listen to us,' Nyssa insisted.

The guards stepped forward.

A group of Adjudicators, Scientifica technicians and the Doctor and Patience walked steadily towards the Machine. The Provost-General and Chief Scientist brought up the rear. Medford looked down at Juno. She had not spoken a word for over ten minutes, and he recognized that she was using every ounce of her self-control to suppress her emotions. He was having to do the same. If he had an opportunity afterwards – if there was an afterwards – then he'd apologize to her.

Ahead of them, the Machine rose up like a mountain. Medford had seen it only half a dozen times before, always from the safety of the research dome. Seeing it up close only made it more disturbing. The twisted, almost organic, shapes defied gravity and logic. The architects of the Doctor's race clearly had no aesthetic sense.

The doorway was a square of light set into the thick metal. The Doctor and Patience were the first through, with Whitfield closely behind. Just as Medford was about to cross the threshold, his wrist computer bleeped. He checked the display, but it only stood at 00:12:07. This was something else. He told the group to continue without him.

It was the Quatermaster-Fiscal. 'We have them, Provost-General. All but one of them.'

Medford acknowledged the report and signed off. When he followed Whitfield, the Doctor and the Patient into the Machine, there was a broad grin on his face. His expression soon changed: this was the first time he had been inside, although he had seen holographs and read all the reports that Whitfield had chosen to release. The room was so mundane compared to the outward appearance of the Machine, almost suspiciously so. It was also a mess: it looked like the aftermath of an electronics firm's Christmas party, with wires and equipment strewn around the room apparently at random.

'It's smaller on the inside,' he stated.

'That's because it is dimensionally immanent,' the Doctor said casually. Medford frowned.

'He means that it's smaller on the inside,' Whitfield said impatiently. 'I would prefer a more scientific explanation. I would also ask how and why you have reverted to your original appearance.'

Patience supplied the answer, to the first question at least: 'In electrokinetic theory space expands to accommodate the time necessary to encompass its dimensions.'

'Isn't that what I said?' the Doctor asked glibly. His attention was occupied by one of the pieces of machinery lining the walls, a large transparent dome. He and Patience moved over to it, and between them they pulled the glass back.

The Doctor reached inside. 'Might I have my sonic screwdriver back?'

Medford nodded and handed it over. 'No tricks,' he warned.

The Doctor smiled, and began to detach one of the mechanisms on the inside rim of the dome. Patience was unclipping wires and cables that ran into it, rerouting them. They had clearly planned this procedure.

'What are you going to do?'

The Doctor held up a gold sphere. It was about the size of a cricket ball with an elaborate swirling pattern shimmering on the surface. 'I've already finished. This is the Time Control Unit.'

'You can control the entire Machine through that?' Medford asked.

'Yes.'

'How?' Whitfield asked.

'I'll show you outside. In fact we'll have to get to a safe

250

distance: these early models are prone to leakage.'

'To avoid time pollution TARDISes are grown in space, well away from Gallifrey itself,' Patience said. The Doctor nodded sagely.

Whitfield's eyes were fixed on the Time Control Unit. 'That has enough range to work from the research dome?'

The Doctor chuckled. 'From the other side of the universe.' He looked over to Whitfield. 'Put simply, the Stattenheim signals are broadcast along the time contours in the Vortex that accommodate the Eye of Harmony simultaneously on Gallifrey and within each TARDIS. Elementary chronon transduction, really, but a very neat solution.'

'Give it to me,' Medford demanded.

'Unless you are a Gallifreyan, it's not much use to you,' the young man informed him as he handed it over.

'You *are* Gallifreyan, Doctor,' Medford replied, 'but while I have this, you can't use it.' The Doctor's face fell.

The observation gallery was a plastic bubble on the side of the research dome, with an awe-inspiring vista of the crashed TARDIS. The room was lined with high-backed chairs. There were two Adjudicators guarding the door.

'Might we have two of those chairs together in the centre of the room?' Medford confirmed the order, and the service drone burbled over to the chairs. When that was done, the drone slotted back into its recharge point. The Doctor and Patience took a chair each. They sat facing each other for a moment, mentally preparing themselves for the task ahead. Finally Medford handed the Time Control Unit to the Doctor, who placed it on the floor between them, careful not to let it roll away.

'Now what?' Medford asked. He glanced at his wrist computer which had reached 00:02:11.

'We need to concentrate. This process will be quite tiring.' In unison, the Doctor and Patience closed their eyes and took a deep breath.

'Contact.'

The sphere twitched, then sprouted open, morphing upwards, filling out until it resembled a small tree, a sapling. Medford glanced out at the Machine. The new apparatus almost resembled the crashed TARDIS in miniature. Branches curled out towards the Doctor and Patience, delicately wrapping themselves around their heads like crowns. The process could have been a violation, but instead it was almost tender. After moments, the Doctor opened his eyes and began breathing again.

'There.'

'It's done?'

'The TARDIS is now primed.' The Doctor was bent over Patience, checking that there was contact between the metal branch and the woman's skin.

'Explain precisely what you have done,' Whitfield said.

'A TARDIS and its owner are almost symbiotically linked. Before any flight, a TARDIS needs a little telepathic coaxing. In this case, the ship hasn't operated for aeons, poor chap, so the process was even more complicated than it might have been.' He ran fingers across the circlet around his own head, then withdrew them, apparently satisfied.

'You have successfully booted up the TARDIS's mainframe and programmed its navigation computer with the co-ordinates of the planet Gallifrey,' Whitfield said coldly.

'Indeed.' The Doctor held his palm against a portion of the frame, and a tiny switch appeared. 'The dematerialization control,' he said. 'Now, once I'm connected up again, I'll lapse back into a telepathic trance. All you'll have to do is flick this and the crashed TARDIS will head back to the exact point in time and space from which it originated.'

'How long will the journey take?' Medford asked.

'Oh, a good ten minutes,' the Doctor guessed.

His hand hovered over the switch.

There was someone else in the room, one of the ghosts.

Medford recognized it as the first to materialize at the Waystation. Although he couldn't be certain of it, this looked like the ghost he had confronted in the life support chamber at the Scientifica pyramid. It was solid now, somehow more human than before. It stood on the ground, rather than hovering.

'Doctor,' the ghost said, its voice a calm whisper. Its skin was pale, drawn.

The Gallifreyan stepped forward, feigning surprise. 'You know me? Then you have the advantage of me.'

The ghost cocked his head to one side, confused by the question. 'You do not know of us?'

Medford moved forward, interposing himself between the Doctor and the ghost. 'I am Provost-General Medford, the commander of the military forces on this planet. Once again, I ask you to state your business here.'

'You do not concern me,' the ghost stated, matter-of-factly. It was looking straight through him at the Doctor. 'Only the time machine concerns me.' It took a step forward.

Medford didn't move. 'This planet and everything on it is under the protection of the Divine Empress. If you attempt to interfere with the Machine or this colony, then I will destroy you.'

The ghost watched him for a moment, measured his response. Medford stood perfectly still. The ghost was hairless, with thin, almost transparent, skin. Other than that it might have passed as human.

'You threaten us?' it asked finally. Its tone was more one of curiosity than anger.

'If force is needed to remove you from this world, then I shall not hesitate to use that force.'

The ghost's expression hadn't changed. Then there was a sudden movement. The left arm lashed out.

The other two Adjudicators in the room had drawn their sidearms when they had first registered the ghost's presence. Now they fired.

The energy bolts streaked towards their target at the speed of light. But they were slowing down, along with everything else in the room. The Doctor and Patience were reeling in slow motion, the others were statues.

Medford looked around at the tableau. There was a bubble of air around him, outside it time had stopped. The energy bolts continued inexorably towards the ghost, but now they were crawling through the air no faster than a snail would.

253

The ghost cocked its head to one side, watching the energy bolts for a moment. Then it waved a hand and the Adjudicators who had fired the bolts were caught in a glowing energy field. Medford watched as their armour began to tarnish and fade. Rust spread from cracks in the breastplate, half-congealed hydraulic fluid spilled from the joints. As the helmets crumbled away, Medford realized that the occupants had aged to death long ago. Both sets of armour crashed dustily to the ground.

'You threaten us, we who are the lords of time?'

Medford turned to face the apparition. 'You have psionic control over time? You can manipulate the Time Vortex with your mind?'

'It is magic.' Its finger scratched a rune in the air, and Medford was on his knees, gasping for breath. He could almost feel his heart missing beats and his lungs misfiring.

'Advanced technology,' he managed to gasp, 'nothing more.'

'Magic,' the ghost repeated. 'You speak of nothing. You are nothing: a creature of shit and blood and dreaming. You cannot comprehend what we are, you cannot stop what we are.' It seemed oblivious to his distress, even though it was responsible.

'This is your last chance to withdraw,' the Provost-General coughed. 'Leave now or be destroyed.'

'Chimpanzee arrogance!' the ghost said. 'You cannot threaten me, Provost-General, you can hold no secrets from me.'

The ghost leant forward. Medford suddenly felt his mind open out and his memories unfurl. He could see the ghost study his thoughts, discarding those that did not interest it: his Asteroid Express PIN number: 8414; his childhood on the family farm on the slopes of Mount Bedford; the sickly-spice taste of Danbweldian wormcake; Jaltarra's winning goal for Earth in the '84 Worlds Cup from twenty-five metres; the reason his mother had chosen his forename; lying alongside Juno for the first time, her body as cool as a spring breeze. She was nineteen, five years his senior.

That was ignored, in favour of the military codes, the tactical information, the scientific and intelligence data.

Everything he knew of history, art and literature. Earth's defences and those of Ponten and Oberon. The secrets of the Unitatus Guild, the meanings of the Bureau's innermost rituals. The locations of every secret weapons research project in human space. The ghost took it all, yet hardly seemed interested in what it found.

Medford's wrist computer bleeped once. The display was flashing 00:00:00. The Provost-General smiled, remembering.

'No . . .' the ghost said.

Twenty thousand kilometres out from the Icarus Skybase space was twisting. The darkness folded in on itself and began to pulse and seethe. Chinks of light appeared, great four-dimensional cracks in reality.

The *Ark Royal* was the first out of hyperspace. There had been a warship of that name for a millennium and a quarter, but the latest was by far the largest. A cylinder over three kilometres long from bow to stern, it bore few external features. The retro rockets began firing, the ion drives began to engage, allowing it to move in normal space. All along the flank of the *Ark Royal* hangar bays clanked open and missile batteries deployed. The first fighter squadrons were already spaceborne by the time the next few ships arrived.

These were perimeter defence craft, their hulls dull green barrels bristling with weapons. They came out of warp at the edge of the system, sketching in the boundary of the battlefield with trails of photon mines laid in five dimensions.

A dozen carriers came next. These were ugly ships, little more than slabs of grey metal. Even before they had fully slowed down, the ancillary vessels had begun to pour from the hangar bays: shuttlecraft, tugs, workpods, tankers, messenger buoys and their fighter escorts.

Wave after wave of flat-sided cruisers and wide-bodied frigates were arriving, taking up carefully pre-planned positions. Medical and salvage ships brought up the rear. The ether buzzed with comm signals as the battlecomputers talked to each other, agreeing on the topology of the warzone, relaying maps and stats to each other. The ships flicked and darted around each other like a flock of birds or a shoal of fish.

Admiral Dattani stood at the centre of the *Ark Royal*'s flight deck. His white hair was thin, now, but this only emphasized his high forehead and aquiline nose. The holoscreen in front of him was filled with the white disk of the planet, which was rotating at a leisurely sixteen miles a second.

'The entire fleet has arrived, Admiral,' Bil reported. 'They confirm battle-readiness.' The weapons officer at the station directly behind him was from Procyon, one of the few of his race to serve in the fleet. He was blue-skinned, with heavy ridges on his cheekbones and fronds instead of ears. Many would have considered that Bil looked out of place in a Space Fleet uniform, but in that respect Dattani was a progressive: he wouldn't deny a talented individual a place on the *Ark Royal* just because he was differently human. 'The fleet has arrived safely, sir. All ships are now at their allotted position. They are awaiting further instructions.'

'Admiral, the Skybase is signalling us,' the communications officer said.

A young man in a Scientifica tunic appeared in one corner of the screen. As Dattani identified himself, the computer picked out the Skybase on the main image. It appeared as a tiny white dot over the northern hemisphere. The scientist quickly explained about the abnormal cloud cover which was blocking all attempts to probe it. The technical details were transmitted to the *Ark Royal*'s science station.

'Where's the Provost-General?'

'*He was onboard the Battle Platform when it made its orbital drop. It was aiming for the Nightingale Facility, a hospital in the northern frostlands. It was chasing a stolen Type Twelve freighter. That was a little under two hours ago.*'

Just after he had signalled for the fleet. There weren't any Type Twelves assigned to this system, it could only be the ship that had brought Medford his fusion bombs. 'Understood,' the Admiral concluded.

'*That was about the time the storms started.*'

'Has there been any contact with the enemy?' Bil asked, sensing that his commanding officer was deep in thought.

'*Only the pictures from Pryanishnikov Waystation.*' The screen flickered, and the image of a darkened room appeared. There were half a dozen figures in the centre, surrounded by glowing white lines. They were chanting and swaying. It looked like a ritual from a primitive religion. '*There were no reports of military activity anywhere. This is the only permanent record of them that we have.*'

Dattani leant forward. 'Focus our sensors on that area of the planet's surface.' He searched the image for clues.

Dominic, the communications officer, was hunched over his instruments, straining to hear something.

'What is it, Lieutenant?'

'A transmission from the Waystation on an Adjudicator emergency channel.'

'Put it on the screen.'

A pretty young woman with long jet-black hair in Adjudicator battlearmour appeared, filling the screen. '*This is Solim, Twelfth Tank Division. Thank the Goddess, I thought I was the only one left alive down here. I'm at the Pryanishnikov Waystation, which has been occupied by enemy forces.*' She was in her mid-twenties, the expression on her face reminded Dattani a little of Celestine, his late wife. The Admiral stepped forward, although he needn't have done for the microphones to pick up his voice. 'I am Admiral Dattani, of the *Ark Royal*. Report.'

'*I've rigged up a drone here with a camera. Are you ready SAM?*'

'*ReADY, MA'am.*'

The picture snapped to an image of the main hall. The six figures were still there, still moving. They seemed oblivious to Solim and her drone. The cabling, or power lines or whatever they were around them were larger, more intricate than before and hummed with energy.

'*They seem to be drawing power from somewhere. The pulsing of this web stuff coincides with the rhythm of their chanting. More than that, the power they collect is being transmitted elsewhere. I think this must be the enemy nerve centre.*'

257

'I think you must be right,' Dattani whispered. He turned to the weapons officer. 'Arm the anti-matter beams. Target that Waystation and fire.' He paused. 'I'm so sorry, my dear.'

The radio had gone dead again. Solim shook it, although she knew intellectually that the action would have no effect on the nanocircuits inside the device. She moved over to the hole in the wall, where the foredroid was waiting for her.

'Weather's clearing,' it informed her.

Solim looked up. A neat circle of pale blue daylight had appeared in the black clouds directly above them.

The drone they had found bobbed between them. 'WARning: IT's –'

White light surrounded everything, shining through the droids, the brickwork, even the mountains. Solim made a reflex action with her hand, but before the hovertanks even received the command they burst open and evaporated, along with everything else.

The ghost saw the plan, built up over the last year, to assemble legions of Adjudicators and an armada of war rockets. An elite military force dedicated to the Unitatus, humanity and the destruction of Earth's enemies, operating in secret, able to deploy ultimate weapons. The largest military force assembled since the dying days of the Galactic Wars, composed of the finest military minds in human space.

It felt its comrades as they were attacked. The ghost screamed, clutching itself.

'Regroup! Withdraw!' A flame began to run the length of its arm. Before it had reached the shoulder, the apparition had vanished.

Time started again. Two energy bolts sliced the thin air in front of Medford, who fell to the floor rubbing his throat. To the Doctor's astonishment, the Provost-General was grinning, looking his most avuncular. Whitfield and one of his officers moved to help him up. The Doctor tried to move forward, then remembered that he was still linked to the Time Control Unit.

'What happened?' the Chief Scientist asked him.

'A visit from the enemy,' Medford said, giving the Doctor a look that worried him, 'an attack. But we repulsed it. Now it's time to take the fight to them.'

The Doctor stepped forward. 'That'll be very nice for you, I'm sure. Now, if we could just get this TARDIS underway, then I'd be happy to help you.' The Doctor pointed at the switch again, for added emphasis.

'Stand away,' Medford ordered, drawing his pistol. The Doctor took a step back.

'Provost-General. I appreciate that you are having a little local difficulty here, but whatever it is, whatever the true nature of these ghosts, it pales into insignificance compared with the damage this TARDIS has already done.'

'I know exactly what damage this TARDIS can do,' Medford said. He tapped at his wrist communicator. 'Quartermaster, are you ready?'

'*We are outside the Machine now, sir.*' The Doctor looked out of the observation dome. A small group of Adjudicators were by the door of the crashed TARDIS. There was something else there, too: a trolley of some kind.

'Set them to detonate on rematerialization.'

'*Aye, sir.*' As the Doctor watched, the trolley rolled through the doorway. The door swung shut automatically.

'We recovered all but one of them, Doctor, and your companions told us about the other one.'

The Doctor frowned. 'Where are they?'

'That need not concern you. We've been aware of the alien threat for a year now, Doctor. That's plenty of time to plan.'

' 'Lian, what are you talking about?' the Chief Scientist was clearly not in on the whole scheme.

'Your friend the Provost-General has assembled quite an arsenal, including two dozen fusion bombs. He's about to use them.'

'Is this true?' Whitfield's question was barely whispered.

'I'm sorry, Juno,' and from his tone of voice, the Doctor thought that Medford genuinely might be, 'but these are desperate times . . . the peacekeeping force was never going to be enough. The Unitatus –'

'I don't care about your stupid men-only secret societies. What was that about fusion bombs?'

Medford looked out of the observation port. 'They are primed and ready. Now they are loaded aboard that time machine and in ten minutes they will detonate, destroying the Doctor's home planet and with it the entire Time Lord invasion force.' The Doctor suppressed a smile. If he told Medford that the fusion bombs had been deactivated, it might break the mood. Worse than that, the Provost-General might abort the launch. He feigned horror: 'No, you mustn't.'

'Too late, Doctor.' Medford leant over and flicked the switch.

The Doctor's eyes snapped shut as the telepathic link was established, but he could hear a tremendous wheezing, groaning noise from outside the dome and could feel the joy of the TARDIS as it entered the Time Vortex.

A rumbling noise had started outside.

The Doctor opened his eyes. Removing the Machine that had been a feature of the cavern for so long had weakened the rock, and boulders were crashing down to the floor. The Doctor smiled, relieved.

Medford was standing over Patience, who was also conscious. He had not holstered his pistol.

'Kneel down.' She did as he asked, dropping her hands into her lap. She looked over to the Doctor for reassurance.

Medford plucked the crown from her head with his free hand.

Without Patience, the telepathic link was difficult to maintain. The Doctor sat down, concentrating on the TARDIS, trying to picture it spinning through the Vortex. It was still there, and as it continued along its flightpath he could almost feel the damage done on its first journey being repaired.

He winced. An unexpected surge of energy. But temporal fusion was working, and now it was underway, as long as he concentrated, he would be able to regulate the process himself.

'It is not too late to stop this war from happening!' the Doctor cried out, using precious fragments of his mental energy. 'We can help you.'

'You've helped us already, thank you. Now, though, keeping you alive any longer is just a threat to security.' The Provost-General held up the pistol, a projectile weapon. 'If the brain is destroyed, you can't regenerate. That's what you said, isn't it?'

The Doctor nodded, unable to think. Just a few moments more and the Machine would be free of the damaged sections of the Vortex.

Medford placed the pistol to the back of Patience's head. His hand was still on her shoulder. She kept her eyes open, staring ahead, mouthing a plea to her husband.

'No!' the Doctor shouted. He found himself closing his eyes. For a moment the Machine swam away from his view. It was on the brink of safety, so close to sanctuary.

There was a gunshot.

But there wasn't the sound of a body falling to the ground.

The Machine was away, with a clear path home to Gallifrey. The damage to the Time Vortex was mended.

The Doctor opened his eyes, filled with irrational hope.

Patience still knelt there.

Medford released his grip on her shoulder. She pitched over. The Doctor lurched forward, snapping his connection with the Machine, but catching Patience. He crouched, cradling the back of her head. Her blue eyes were open, but empty. The Doctor's fingertips had found the edge of the moist hole in the back of the skull. A warm liquid was dripping through his fingers.

Patience slowly faded out of existence. The Doctor uttered a short prayer in a language he couldn't remember learning as she became lighter and lighter. She was gone now, and the Doctor was left clutching a bloodsoaked nightgown. He stared at it through wet eyes. Then he realized that the Provost-General was aiming the pistol at him.

Its muzzle was flecked with blood. The Doctor was unable and unwilling to move.

The pistol was six inches from his forehead. 'There's a bullet here with your name on it, Doctor.'

261

17

The Face of the Enemy

The pistol was six inches from his forehead. 'There's a bullet here with your name on it, Doctor.'

'Fire away, it only has a fifty-fifty chance of hitting him.' The owner of the voice stepped forward from behind them, raising his hat.

Medford swung round, levelling the pistol at the speaker. Whitfield flinched, then realized that she recognized the little man: this was the regenerated Doctor who had been speaking to Forrester and Adric. As the Chief Scientist tried to work out what both of the Doctors were doing in the same room, the new arrival was rounding on Medford. 'You think that you can solve everything with a gun, don't you? That everything's black and white. Good or bad, legal or illegal, unfair or just, war or peace. Dead or alive. That's what you want, isn't it?' As he spoke, the Doctor was stepping closer and closer to Medford. 'Life would be so much simpler with me dead, wouldn't it? What are you waiting for? Shoot first and ask questions later.'

Medford pulled the trigger.

A bloodstained hand yanked the gun down, and the bullet impacted into the floor. The ground was still rever-berating from that as the younger Doctor wrestled with the Provost-General. Despite being middle-aged, Medford was the stronger man, shoving the Doctor aside with little effort. Whitfield had never been proud that her lover was a soldier, she had never quite reconciled the gentle man she talked to in the still of the night with the man who had killed people with his bare hands. As he raised his arm, ready to pistol-whip his opponent, she felt only shame, which turned to relief when she realized that the pistol was no longer in his hand.

The little Doctor was holding it gingerly by the barrel, as

if the gun was radioactive. 'But life's never that simple, is it?' he concluded sadly.

Medford whirled around, and began striding towards him. 'Give me the gun,' the Provost-General snarled.

The Doctor tossed the gun in the air, over Medford's head, just too high for him to reach up and grab it. As it arced back down, the other Doctor caught it. Medford advanced on the Doctor with the gun. The door to the corridor outside opened automatically as Medford passed it. There were a couple of people in the doorway. Whitfield thought at first that they were Adjudicator reinforcements, although she couldn't remember the Provost-General calling for them. Instead, a large angular shape came flying in, connecting with Medford's back.

Whitfield realized that it was Roz Forrester, performing some martial arts manoeuvre or other. Both she and Medford were pulling themselves up, bringing their arms up into defensive poses. Forrester was still in her kimono, and looked about half the size of the Provost-General in his armour. She wasn't that much younger than him, either, but somehow they looked almost evenly-matched. Adric was behind them, coming through the door, edging round them.

'Out the way, both of you!' the younger Doctor shouted.

Whitfield calmly registered the following sequence of events:

The entire room turned to face the Doctor. He was holding Medford's pistol in both hands, aiming it squarely at its owner's chest. His eyes were narrow.

Forrester and Adric dived for cover in opposite directions.

The Doctor fired the pistol.

The bullet slammed into Medford's stomach, lifting him off the ground and throwing him back a metre into the air, straight through the door.

The air was filled with the sound and smell of the gun-shot.

The other Doctor was the first to his feet. Before anyone else had even reacted he was by the doorway, slapping the control. The door slammed resoundingly shut.

Forrester was at the walltop computer, pulling her

kimono back into place. 'By authority of Provost-General Forrester, R S, raise the security screens around the observation dome.' The perspex bubble became opaque. Outside, Whitfield could hear metal shutters clanking into place. There was a low buzzing in the air, a forcewall. 'This order can only be countermanded by myself.'

'Provost-General?' the little Doctor scowled.

'I'm overdue for a promotion,' Roz said simply.

Adric handed the Doctor back his umbrella. 'We hacked into the computer and upped our security clearance. We're both Provost-Generals.'

'You do not become Provost-General by killing the incumbent,' the Chief Scientist noted. She was alone in here now, sealed in with two Doctors and two of his companions. They were all staring at her.

'Medford's not dead,' the younger Doctor stated. He was standing at a table, emptying the bullets from the pistol. 'Projectile weaponry is very effective against civilians, but not anyone wearing armour. But even if you are wearing inch-thick pontenium alloy you have to obey Newton's Third Law of Motion.'

'For every action there is an equal and opposite reaction,' the other Doctor supplied, rather redundantly, considering who he was addressing.

'Indeed,' the younger one continued, 'he was thrown backwards by the force, and he's probably got a nasty bruise on his stomach, but other than that he'll be fine. Now, perhaps we could get on.'

'Not before you explain exactly what is happening here,' Whitfield announced, trying to keep a lid on her feelings of relief. 'You are both the same Time Lord? You have crossed your own timestream?'

The younger one set the gun down. 'Yes, Chief Scientist, I am the fifth incarnation and this chap is . . .'

'The seventh,' the other replied, 'and don't let anyone tell you anything different. Are you all right, old chap?' He produced a silk handkerchief from his pocket and proceeded to dust his former self down.

'You could have been killed, provoking the Provost-General like that,' the fifth Doctor said accusingly.

264

The little man smiled thinly. 'Yes, I could. But then again, from a certain perspective, we've already died: me, you, Roz and Adric. From another, we never really existed, we don't count and this isn't happening.'

'Thanks for that cheery thought,' Forrester said, stepping forwards. She introduced herself to the younger Doctor. 'I hate it when he goes all melancholy.'

'We've met,' the Doctor said, shaking her hand, 'at the skitrain station.'

'Yeah, sorry about that. If I'd known you were the Doctor, I'd have . . .' she broke into a grin, 'thought twice before doing it.' Whitfield wasn't sure what had happened, but Forrester had just admitted being the terrorist who had attacked the skitrain carrying the Patient's cryotube as it was transported from here to the pyramid. The Chief Scientist looked down at the bloody rag that was all that remained of the female Gallifreyan. The fifth Doctor caught her eye, and a sad smile flickered across his face. The Chief Scientist looked away.

Adric was tapping Bob, the drone that sat in the corner, as if it was the first time he'd ever seen a robot. Bob was the only automaton at the research dome, and did much of the handiwork. Unlike a couple of her colleagues, the Chief Scientist had never been emotionally attached to it. Forrester's Doctor was examining the Time Control apparatus. He prodded it experimentally with his umbrella.

'Be careful with that,' the fifth Doctor said irritably, 'it's a very delicate piece of equipment.'

'We don't really need it now, though, do we? The Machine is on course for Gallifrey, temporal fusion is working and the bombs have been defused. You've done very well, all things considered.'

'What do you mean by that?'

'Well, you didn't really plan it this way, did you?'

Adric nodded. 'The Doctor's right, er, Doctor . . .' his voice faded away as the young man stared at him.

'The other thing, of course,' the seventh Doctor began, 'is that in all the fuss, you've forgotten about –'

'– Adam!' the fifth Doctor blurted. 'He must have the

other bomb. Chief Scientist, you must listen to me. Adam will already be on his way to the Scientifica with a fusion device. You must find a way to warn them.'

Whitfield shook her head, her mind racing. The terrorist leader had one of the fusion bombs. He'd be able to detonate it anywhere on the planet, potentially killing millions. 'Not possible. All the communications links are down: there's some sort of atmospheric effect interfering with stuff up there.'

'We must find a way,' the Doctor declared.

'We've told you everything we know, we've told you it three times.'

Tegan's anger was slowly dissipating into a weary acceptance that the questions would continue regardless of the answers she gave. Cwej stood by more stoically, but he was also becoming restless. Nyssa – who had kept quiet, unable to add anything – had watched as the officer questioning them had become more aggressive, challenging the details of their stories, even threatening them. They hadn't been allowed to sit down, and had already been told that sleep and a meal were out of the question.

'You must have recovered the twenty-one fusion bombs by now. There's one missing. You have to warn the Scientifica. Adam only needs a couple of seconds to plant the bomb.' Cwej spoke softly but firmly.

They were in the director's office at the facility. For some reason the lieutenant hadn't transferred them up to the Battle Platform. Nyssa suspected that this was for psychological reasons. At first assessment, escape seemed more likely from the hospital than the vast war machine that hovered above it. The doors were thin, and plastic, camera surveillance was minimal. Then you realized that escape was impossible with the Battle Platform above you, capable of blasting the entire facility into atoms. One step outside and you'd be killed instantly.

The communications panel on the desk was crackling. The Adjudicator technician working at it looked up and confirmed what Nyssa had suspected: 'The communications blackout seems to be easing.'

266

The Adjudicator-Lieutenant, Dareau, halted the interrogation for a moment to listen to the broadcast.

'—tfic— —cast— —all clea— —lobal— —gency—.' The half-words were punctuated by crackles and bursts of white noise.

'Is that the best we can do?'

'Yes, sir, but it's an improvement over what we've had before. The blackout is lessening. It also means that a short-pulse transmat might be possible.'

'Now you can warn the Scientifica,' Tegan insisted.

Dareau ignored her. 'Would you risk transmat yourself, technician?'

'No, sir,' his subordinate admitted.

'Then don't presume to risk the lives of my men.'

'For God's sake,' Tegan said, '*I'll* go, if it'll help save those people's lives.'

Chris shared Nyssa's horror at the idea. 'No!' he shouted, but the Adjudicator-Lieutenant was smiling.

'An excellent idea.'

Tegan picked up the tone of his voice. 'What's wrong?'

'It's best that you don't know,' Nyssa assured her.

'Oh, but look at her expression,' Dareau said. 'I'm sure that she does want to know. Tell her.'

Nyssa swallowed. 'The transmat signal has to be completely free of interference. If there is even a slight signal distortion, your DNA would be resequenced. If the signal breaks up more, then you could arrive without vital organs, or a nervous system.'

The radio crackled again, as if to emphasize how poor the communications link was.

Tegan was wide-eyed.

'And the best thing of all,' Dareau said, 'is that you volunteered, so sending you is perfectly legal. Perhaps your death will inspire your companions to tell the truth about their terrorist activities.'

The Provost-General pulled himself back against the wall, struggling for breath. He tried to unclasp the breastplate of his armour, but his fingers were clumsy in his gloves. He reached for his wrist, breaking the seal, tugging the glove from his hand. Reaching over again, he could lift away the armour, placing it to one side. His stomach was a huge square bruise.

Medford exhaled, tried to ignore the pain, wished he was twenty years younger.

The door to the observation gallery had closed. Now he watched as the security shutters came down and the force-wall activated.

'Provost-General!' One of the Adjudicators, Medford couldn't identify which, was running towards him.

'I'm all right,' Medford gasped. 'Get a laser cannon down here. I want that door open.'

Adam slit the transmat operator's throat, wiping his ceramic blade on the woman's green tunic. Quint wasn't here. Glancing at the instrument panel, Adam saw that at least he'd been lucky: the map of the transmat grid was faint, broken in places. It was a planetwide problem, and it was affecting virtually all aspects of life. 'Severe weather conditions', according to the computer. There was no sign of the Shliman in the system – not surprising when the computers only gave a one in three chance of successful teleportation. It was a good job they hadn't done what they usually did when travelling on the public system: the standard tactic to avoid detection was to bounce around the system from node to node before getting to their destination. With half the system down, they'd both have ended up nowhere.

Adam broke into a smile, imagining the chaos that a single storm was bringing to the Scientifica. He unzipped his bag and removed the fusion charge. It was about the size of a cigar. He wondered for a moment where he should plant the bomb for maximum effect. Then he remembered the blast radius of the bomb and realized that he didn't have to be too fussy.

'What are you doing?' a distinctive Celtic voice asked.

The Doctor turned, still not yet used to the idea that the small, scruffily dressed man represented his own future. 'Trying to find a way to boost the signal. That way we can send a warning to the pyramid.'

268

The smaller Doctor nodded thoughtfully, pursing his lips. 'Hmmm. Yes. It might work.'

The fifth Doctor peered at him over his glasses. 'Look, if you don't want to help, then don't, but please don't get in my way. Time is rather pressing.' He returned to the innards of the machine, locating what looked like the signal booster. If he could find a way to increase its power supply without burning it out . . .

There was a tap on his shoulder. The Doctor whirled round and loomed over his future self, making him blink. 'Now look, things are getting critical here, and there isn't any time to lose. If you want to make yourself useful, then check that apparatus. It's a remote control for a TARDIS and in a couple of minutes, we'll need to –'

'– double check that temporal fusion has worked and that the Machine is on course, yes, very good,' the little man said. 'Sorry, but this is all getting a bit convoluted. Could you explain something for me?'

'Quickly,' the Doctor snapped, turning back to his work.

'Fine, fine, quickly. I'll try to be concise. Er . . .' he paused, apparently to deliberately infuriate his earlier self. 'That's it: what's Adam got?'

'A fusion bomb.' The signal booster was quite fragile, a nanochip with a crystalline structure.

'How do you know that it's a fusion bomb?'

'I was there when he got it,' the Doctor used the tone he usually used to talk to small children, or Tegan. He removed the booster, and reconfigured the surface with the sonic screwdriver.

The seventh Doctor tutted. 'Careless. You should have stopped him from getting hold of it. Or better still, you should have defused it.'

The booster slotted easily back into place and began warming up. 'Adam took a bomb before I had a chance to,' the Doctor explained patiently.

Tegan screamed all the way to the transmat chamber, and had to be carried. Nyssa and Chris were more subdued. One Adjudicator placed her on the transmat platform, two others restrained her companions.

269

'I'm sorry,' she told them, trying to compose herself.

Chris shook his head. 'I feel the same way.'

'Goodbye, Tegan,' Nyssa said quietly. From her tone of voice, Tegan could guess that she had little confidence in the transmat process. Dareau just smiled.

'I thought the Adjudicators enforced justice,' Tegan said defiantly. The Adjudicator-Lieutenant's face had set into a permanent expression of cruel indifference. Everything about his appearance, from his cropped hair to the glint in his dark brown eyes, suggested that he revelled in his sadistic image.

'There have always been fanatics in the Guild,' Chris said, 'always a few who are more interested in the punishment than the crime.'

Dareau was watching him with contempt. 'A pretty speech. I won't ask where you got it from.'

'Do it if you're going to,' Tegan said defiantly, straightening herself.

'Tegan,' Chris said, 'remember your rights.'

Dareau pressed the dematerialization control.

Tegan screamed.

Then realized she had arrived at the pyramid.

A Scientifica technician was lying in a pool of blood in the middle of the room. Adam was by a control panel, looking up at the source of the noise. Now he turned his attention back to the bomb in his hand.

'No he didn't.'

The fifth Doctor frowned, finally looking back. 'What do you mean?'

'I defused it,' his future self said joyfully. 'I was in a cave when I nearly got hit by a rockfall. Among the rubble I found a medical kit sealed up with a magnetic clamp. That sparked off my curiosity, so I opened it up and discovered that it was full of fusion bombs. It only took a minute or so with my sonic screwdriver, but it was easy enough to render them all harmless. So,' he concluded, grinning from ear to ear, 'everything's under control and there's no need for all this flapping around.'

'How did you defuse them?' his earlier self asked. The

Doctor had never realized just how youthful he had looked: to human eyes he wasn't even Benny's age, and Roz was almost old enough to be his mother. It diffused his authority, making him look petulant rather than stern.

He was happy to explain. 'I used a technique unknown in the Humanian Era: I reversed the polarity of the neutron flow.'

'You did what?' his fifth incarnation scowled. The expression looked out of place on such a pleasant face.

'You must remember: it's a tried and trusted method.'

'I know perfectly well what it entails: I did it myself. To those bombs.'

'You reversed the polarity *back*?' the Doctor spluttered.

'Yes, it rather seems that I did.'

'Well, didn't you check?'

'Did you?'

'I didn't *need* to.'

'Well, I didn't think that *I* did.'

'So you've rearmed all the bombs?'

Tegan leapt at Adam as he turned around, bringing her elbow down on his nose. It was a lesson she'd learnt in a self-defence class, but this was the first time she'd ever put it into practice. Adam stumbled backwards, still keeping hold of the bomb. 'Drop it!' she yelled. 'You've lost now, you'll never get away.'

Adam smiled. 'Here goes nothing.' He twisted the cap.

Adric shook his head. 'Not all of them.'

They both turned to face him. 'It's logical enough,' he explained, 'you' – the seventh Doctor – 'defused all the bombs. You' – the fifth – 'found the bombs, and accidentally rearmed them all. Except the one Adam took before you could get to it. Now he is planning to blow up the Scientifica using the only bomb that isn't working.'

Nothing happened. Adam looked up.

Tegan punched him hard in the face, and almost felt sorry for him as he collapsed to the floor. Almost.

She prised the bomb from his fingers. He'd primed it: she

271

could see that the cap had been twisted over to 'ACTIVE'. But the bomb hadn't gone off. After all that, the thing had been a dud. She turned the cap back anyway and slumped to the floor, trying to catch her breath.

The door slid open and an Adjudicator burst through, pressing his blaster to Tegan's head. 'Drop the bomb, drop the bomb or I fire.' His voice was so fast and loud that the helmet speaker distorted it. Tegan hardly heard it.

She put the bomb down, too exhausted to argue.

'You're under arrest,' he hissed.

'How ironic,' Roz noted dryly.

'So the Scientifica is safe?' Whitfield asked.

'It might well be,' Adric reminded them, 'but now there's a TARDIS loaded full of armed fusion bombs heading back to Gallifrey.'

The fifth Doctor ran over to the Time Control apparatus, but the seventh Doctor merely consulted his pocket watch. 'It won't arrive for another six minutes, so there's still time to explain.'

'You know that Gallifrey is safe anyway,' Whitfield said. 'The Machine is heading to the past. If your home planet had been destroyed back then you wouldn't be standing here now.'

'Time travel doesn't work like that,' Adric said disdainfully. 'There are rules that have to be adhered to.'

The seventh Doctor's expression flickered for a moment. 'As I was saying before I was so rudely interrupted, my illustrious counterpart here has forgotten all about the Ferutu.'

'The what?'

'The *ghosts*.'

The laser cannon was having no effect on the forcefield-augmented door to the observation dome. The energy was simply absorbed. Medford doubted whether the Doctor and his colleagues who were keeping Whitfield hostage inside even knew that they were trying to get in.

The Adjudicators massed by the door ready to burst in and take out the Doctor and his followers were shifting around. The Provost-General was about to berate them for their restlessness, but realized that they were reacting to something behind him. Medford turned to see what it was.

There were thirteen of them, more or less fully materialized. They were advancing towards the door of the observation dome, not worried by the line of rifle-bearing Adjudicators. Their height and stiff cloaks made their physical presence all the more commanding.

'What are they?'

'They're probably other incarnations of the Doctor, too,' Forrester observed acidly.

The Doctor leant against the grey wall of the observation dome. He couldn't see anything outside, only his former self and companions reflected in the perspex. They looked pale and insubstantial, like ghosts. He spoke softly. 'In a billion years' time, on a distant planet, a race of humanoids will have evolved to a point where they have become the most advanced race that the universe has ever known. These are the Ferutu. Their lives are governed by what humans would call magic. By scratching runes in the air and by performing rituals, the Ferutu were the first race to discover the secrets of Time. Because time and space are linked, this means that they can control matter and energy. This power makes their frail humanoid bodies immortal, it allows them to travel anywhere in the universe, at any point in time.

'The Ferutu stepped between the stars, oblivious to such mundane restraints as "distance" and "causality", and they discovered that it was teeming with life. Some of the races the Ferutu encountered – those so primitive they still used spacecraft to travel between stars – thought of them as sorcerers, or gods. They are the Lords of Time.'

'That's the ancestral role of Gallifrey,' Roz noted.

'Ah, but there is one difference: the Ferutu use their great powers. They equip the forces of good, supplying them with advanced technology and weapons, they intervene in history, gently bending the course of time. Wherever or whenever the forces of evil threaten a helpless people, a Ferutu arrives from nowhere and beats them back.'

273

'There's one small flaw in all this,' the fifth Doctor noted. 'It's just not true. You know the policy of the High Council: time experiments above a certain level are absolutely forbidden. If the Ferutu are intervening on this sort of scale, then why haven't the Time Lords tried to stop them?'

'I asked the leader of the Ferutu that same question as he showed me their history. He simply looked at me with a puzzled expression. He had never heard of Gallifrey. Then he recalled that he had once heard the name Rassilon. He showed me the starless gulf called Rassilon's Rift on the edge of the galaxy. Some travellers speculate that in the distant past there was some great catastrophe that destroyed all matter in the area.'

'An alternative timeline,' the fifth Doctor whispered. 'They come from a version of history where Gallifrey was destroyed.'

The seventh Doctor nodded. 'Somehow, the damage caused to the crashed TARDIS has broken down the structure of time and allowed hints of their alternative timeline to appear in our universe. When the Machine was activated, the gap between the two domains was so narrow that you could walk between them.'

'The ghosts?'

'That's right. They are almost shadows of the Ferutu, merely crude flickerings compared to their true form.'

'Like the TARDISes on Mars?' Forrester asked. The Doctor nodded, but didn't have time to explain the reference to the bewildered Whitfield and Adric.

'I've been to their universe, that's where their leader took me. Ferutu rule is absolute. Darkness remains on the fringes of the cosmos, where the War still rages. There are Daleks and Vampires there, and worse. But the rest . . .' his voice trailed off for a moment. 'Mile-high palaces of gold and crystal, set in lush parkland surrounded by unspoilt forests and seas that teem with life. Eternal summer, entire galaxies where poverty, greed and want have been unknown since the dawn of time.'

'All under the watchful eye of the Ferutu?' Roz said.

'No. They are a solitary race, as a rule, and don't even understand what political power or ambition is. Their subjects, if that's what you want to call them, are whatever they want to be: poets, philosophers, athletes, artists. I have seen them, talked to them, walked amongst them.' He looked around the small group. 'I've been to utopia before, but there's always been a serpent lurking in the under-growth. Not there.'

'Hang on a second,' Roz said jokingly, 'whose side are you on here?'

The Doctor looked at her. 'The side of justice and fair-ness, as always,' he whispered.

'From what we have seen,' the fifth Doctor said, 'the Ferutu can be savage: they've killed people in cold blood.'

'They are fighting for their survival. As we are. They are having to put their moral qualms aside. As we are.'

Adric was frowning. 'How do we beat them if they're all-powerful?'

The Doctors both shook their heads. 'The rituals they perform become increasingly complex,' the seventh Doctor explained. 'It needs a group of them – a coven – to draw up the more complex sigils, and the material requirements needed to compose a totem become more esoteric. In their universe, entire planetary populations act as, well, magic capacitors: they generate and store energy, ready to use it. With billions of Ferutu acting in concert, they can restruc-ture matter on a galactic scale. But one Ferutu on its own is just a petty conjuror, capable only of minor feats of tele-kinesis and telepathy.'

'That's why there's always been more than one when they manifest,' Whitfield said.

The Doctor nodded. 'You believe me, then?'

'You are describing a scientific system: an advanced one, but a system none the less. Clarke's Law: "any sufficiently advanced form of technology is indistinguishable from magic." A capacitor is a piece of technology, not sorcery, regardless of what energy it ultimately collects.'

'Arthur didn't rule out the possibility that magic exists,' the older Doctor noted. 'I am simply translating the words the Ferutu use into terms that we all understand. Make no mistake, they are magicians.'

The ground was rocking. The gun, a glass full of fruit juice and a couple of other loose items clattered off the desk. The Time Control apparatus was rattling like a chandelier.

'An earthquake?' Whitfield said. 'But no seismic activity has ever been recorded in this area.'

The Doctor smiled.

Dattani sat in the command chair, listening to the Adjudicator in charge of the forces stationed at the Scientifica. The cloud cover was still almost total, but now radio signals were penetrating it. The state-of-the-art communications software aboard the *Ark Royal* was allowing almost perfect reception. Although they could now receive messages, the news from the planet hardly made their effort worthwhile: there was no sign of the Provost-General and the Chief Scientist was on business elsewhere on the planet when the emergency was declared.

'Admiral, the sensors have located a pocket of enemy activity. Thirteen lifesigns matching those at the Way-station.'

'Where?'

'Eight kilometres beneath the planet's surface. A cave system in the northern hemisphere.'

The tactical display came up on the main screen. Dattani scratched his chin.

'What's down there?'

'If we can trust the sensor readings, then a metal dome, about two hundred metres in diameter. There are various signatures down there of energy weapons and forcewall generators.'

Dattani broke into a rare smile. 'Congratulations, every-one, we've just found the enemy base.' He pointed out one of the heavy cruiser groups on the display. 'Move those ships into position. Tell them we need a hole digging.'

The six heavy cruisers moved into their geostationary positions and began to pour streams of anti-matter onto the designated point. Anything that had been on the surface was instantly vaporized, along with the cloud and snow. There was little soil to burn off, and within seconds the beams were annihilating the bedrock.

* * *

As one, the ghosts snapped their heads upwards at the rumbling noise. Medford didn't recognize the sound either, but kept his attention fixed on the enemy.

'Stop them,' their leader hissed. One of the apparitions faded away.

Dattani watched the tactical display as the anti-matter beams tunnelled down at the rate of about a mile a minute. Any faster might trigger fusion and fission reactions, according to the scientists. Nevertheless, the progress of the drilling had a sense of inevitability to it.

'Ready the bomber squadrons. When we've dug the hole we're going to drop a couple of photon charges down there.'

The flight deck was suddenly quiet. Dattani turned.

His weapons officer was lying in a pool of his own blue blood. Every other man and woman on the bridge was also slumped, their throats slit. Dattani examined Kellerston, the nearest.

A woman's hand held up a bloodstained knife in front of his face.

'A more primitive weapon than your anti-matter beams, but effective.'

Dattani pulled back. She was one of the enemy, a ghost. She wore a stiff dark blue robe, through which he could see the twinkling lights of the battlecomputers. She was hairless, flat-chested and taller than he was, but she was undoubtedly female. Her voice came from all around him.

'How did you do this?'

'We are Ferutu, the Lords of Time. It was a simple matter to halt the flow of time and kill your crew, one by one.'

'The *entire* crew?'

'Yourself excepted.' There were over two thousand people onboard the *Ark Royal*. Her robe and hands didn't have a single drop of blood on them.

'Why spare me?'

The Ferutu woman smiled, pointing at the screen. 'So that you could see this.'

Dattani watched as each of the ships in the fleet exploded

in turn. The smaller were first, the fighters and shuttles popping like firecrackers. Then the cruisers and frigates burst open, their reactors exploding. The Admiral watched as their armour-plating peeled and blistered away leaving only the skeletal framework beneath. One of the carriers, possibly the *Restoration*, tried to escape but only managed to collide with the Skybase. Both were consumed in a raging atomic fire.

The screen was suddenly dark again.

'What has happened?' The view outside was a bare starscape, with no sign of the starships. *It was an illusion, the fleet is unharmed.*

'Adjust the viewer,' she requested. Dattani leant over the control panel and did so. The planet sat there, serene as ever. There was no spaceborne activity.

'Where is the fleet?' he asked.

'Long gone,' she said. 'Now we are in the posthistoric future.' Behind the planet, a swollen red sun was dawning. 'Do not mourn your race's passing. They were never meant to have been. To us, your galaxy is known as the Mutters' Spiral, the home of a benevolent mutant insect species. Life never evolved on your Earth. Goodbye, Admiral.'

And she was gone.

18

The Day After Yesterday

The storm was clearing, the clouds melting away almost as fast as they had appeared. With the end of the storm came the end of the blackout. The airwaves quickly became jammed with emergency broadcasts. Technicians hurried to repair the damage to the transmat network, the computers in the Scientifica pyramid hummed with activity as they began to collate damage reports.

Aircraft and skimmers had crashed and all the hospitals were full of accident and crime victims. There had been limited looting and vandalism in some sectors of the Strip. The atmospheric disturbance had tripped the circuits of a thousand droids and sensors. The Pryanishnikov Waystation and the mountain it had been built on had vanished. The Provost-General and Chief Scientist were missing. The Battle Platform from the Icarus Skybase was alongside the Nightingale Facility.

When one of the computers tried to contact the Icarus Skybase, it registered something akin to panic. The entire planet was surrounded by millions of tonnes of shrapnel. Much of the debris was already caught in the gravity well, explaining the marked increase in meteorite activity. The rest was a radioactive mass of scrap metal that posed a major navigation hazard. The computer projected that an armada equivalent in size to one of the Earth Fleets had been utterly destroyed.

Unmanned probe droids were sent up from the spaceport to examine the wreckage. Every single fragment it examined was Terran, and virtually all of the organic matter was human, too. Some of the pieces were identified as the remains of the Skybase. Surviving flight recorders suggested that the entire Third Fleet had warped into orbit during the blackout before being wiped out by forces unknown.

The military strategy subprogram advised that the colony should surrender immediately. The intelligence-gatherers reported that there was no enemy to surrender to. Both computers crashed.

'The Scientifica report that the prisoner arrived safely,' the Adjudicator at the transmat controls announced.

Nyssa and Chris hugged each other. Nyssa pulled back. The way Dareau was looking at her made her feel cold.

'They also report that the transmat and communication networks are coming back online. The only problem now is hardware: a lot of transmat platforms and communicators were overloaded. There is no contact with the Skybase as yet.'

The transmat platform lit up. Tegan materialized, three Adjudicators behind her. Without even acknowledging her friends, she fixed her sights on Dareau.

'That's the man,' she announced calmly. 'Dareau.'

'Adjudicator-Lieutenant Dareau, you are under arrest for torturing a suspect.' The officer in charge of the group read him his rights: 'I am obliged to inform you that your words, gestures and postures are being recorded and may form part of any judicial action taken against you. You have the right to consult legalware.'

Tegan went over to Chris and Nyssa, who had their arms around one another again. 'Thank you,' she told Chris. 'I consulted the legalware. It's an encyclopedia of law, on a computer databank,' she explained to Nyssa. 'Like a robot lawyer.'

'And you found Volume 12, Paragraph 9, Subsection 4 of the Adjudicator Code banning all forms of torture, physical force and mental cruelty when questioning a subject. It's one of the Guild's most sacred tenets, and a tradition that we are proud of: Dareau will get a mandatory ten years.' Chris smiled, satisfied that justice had been done. Nyssa did the same.

'Are you all right now, Tegan?' she asked.

Tegan grinned, her eyes flashing. 'Oh yeah. I've just saved the planet, broken the nose of the terrorist leader and sent down a bent copper. All in the space of five minutes. Who needs the Doctor, anyway?'

The drone poured the fifth Doctor a cup of tea. The other was already sipping his through a curly straw he'd produced from his jacket. Roz was examining the contents of her own teacup with some suspicion. Bob had poured Adric's tea first, and he had already finished it. The laser cannon outside had stopped firing. This ought to have been reassuring, but Forrester had the nagging feeling that it meant that the Adjudicators had thought of another way in.

'Do you have biscuits?' the little Doctor asked. 'My favourite are chocolate Hob Nobs.' Bob didn't reply, interpreting the remark as a joke.

Roz wasn't feeling so generous. 'How much longer before the bombs explode?'

'They arrive in Gallifreyan timespace in four minutes,' the younger Doctor answered, without consulting his watch. 'Don't worry, we've not forgotten.' Something about him irritated her, probably the realization that she was getting old: when the *Doctor* looks younger than you, then you're past it.

'Have I got this right?' Adric asked, passing the drawing pad over to the other Doctor. In the absence of anything better to do, Forrester watched the pair of them. The Doctor was more relaxed around Adric than anyone else she'd ever seen. He watched him, was interested in what he was doing. Like a grandfather playing with his grandson. But there was more to it than that. The Doctor's eyes betrayed a sadness of some kind, some deep regret that he was leaving unvoiced. The younger Doctor had noticed it, too, Roz could tell.

Her Doctor examined the drawing carefully, then produced a pen of his own. 'Just a little bit curlier with the cross-bar . . . there.'

He held up the symbol.

'It's what he drew outside when he summoned the Ferutu leader,' Adric explained.

'A binding rune,' the Doctor added. 'Any circle drawn around this symbol acts as a barrier that the Ferutu can't

281

cross, either physically or with their magic.'

'Laser guns can't harm the Ferutu and they can walk through walls, but draw that on a piece of paper and we are safe?' Whitfield snorted.

'Yes,' the Doctor said simply. 'In their universe, even the CyberHost recognize the logic in wearing such designs on their armour.'

'So we just carry one of these each and we're safe?' Adric asked.

'It isn't that easy, as you probably suspected: there would be nothing to stop the Ferutu from resorting to physical attacks: using their magic indirectly to, say, drop a boulder on our heads or they could just pick up one of the many guns lying around the place and shoot us with it.'

'It's a useful weapon, though,' Roz conceded. 'How do we use it?'

'We have *three* weapons at our disposal,' the seventh Doctor announced. 'A time machine capable of delivering a vast fusion payload to almost any point in space or time, this rune, and my – our – legendary powers of persuasion.' He absent-mindedly tore the piece of paper with the rune on it off the drawing pad.

'Balancing that, we have three problems,' the fifth Doctor responded. 'We can't leave this room without Medford shooting us or communicate with the outside world by radio. The Machine will explode wherever it materializes, and regardless of where that is, the consequences will be catastrophic. Then there are the Ferutu, a race of sorcerers willing and able to alter the flow of time to survive.'

'Could we materialize the TARDIS in the Vortex?' Adric suggested.

'Not without severely damaging the structure of space–time, no,' the Doctor replied.

'We could send a warning back to Gallifrey,' Roz suggested. 'Either now or in the past: wouldn't they be able to timeloop it?'

'That's just the sort of interference that we are trying to prevent,' the fifth Doctor lectured sternly.

'Yeah, but it isn't the sort of interference that amputates

one of the galaxy's spiral arms,' she pointed out. *Don't talk to me like I'm three years old.*

'Two wrongs don't make a right,' the young Doctor informed her.

The seventh Doctor rubbed his forehead wearily. 'The entire universe is at stake and I'm locked in here with another incarnation of myself, and not even one of the *good* ones. Your plan has its merits, Roz, but I'm afraid the fusion explosion would be enough to rupture any timeloop, even if one could be established quickly enough.'

'I don't hear any suggestions from you,' the fifth Doctor said, clearly more than a little annoyed by the Doctor's dismissal of him.

'It's a shame we can't buy a little more time,' Adric muttered.

The Doctors looked at each other.

'Do you think their leader will agree?' the fifth Doctor asked.

'We won't give it a choice,' the seventh said grimly. 'Quickly now, everyone. Adric: we need a white circle drawing, about four metres in diameter. Just there, in the middle of the room.' He tossed the boy a piece of chalk. 'Chief Scientist: help my former self with the Time Control apparatus, I'll join you in a minute. Roz, a word in your ear.'

She came over and bent close to him. 'What's up?'

'My former self: he's prone to suicidal acts of selfless heroism.'

'Aren't we all? So?'

Forrester glanced down. The Doctor was holding a piece of paper in his hand, and was folding it in half without looking at it. 'It might be necessary to render him unconscious.'

'OK. I don't trust him anyway.'

'Whyever not?'

She tried to rationalize her feelings. 'He's just so damn . . . trustworthy. It's suspicious. How will I know when you want him clonked?'

'I'll give you a signal. I'll tap the side of my nose. Give him a swift blow to the back of the head. And please try not to kill him, that would complicate matters even more and might take some explaining.' His instructions finished, the Doctor stepped over to the apparatus that sat at one end of the room.

The fifth Doctor and Whitfield assured him that everything was still working. Together the Doctors helped each other to connect up to the machine. They sat facing each other.

'Ready?'

'Ready.'

They closed their eyes.

Roz turned to Whitfield and Adric. 'Does anyone have a clue what's going on around here? What's that equipment?'

'It controls the flight of the Machine. The Doctor sent it back to Gallifrey.'

'I'd gathered that much,' Roz snapped. 'What are they doing it for?'

'Is that where the Patient has got to?' Adric asked. 'I wondered where she was.'

Whitfield ignored him. Forrester looked around. She'd forgotten all about the Patient.

Medford's wrist communicator buzzed. He took his eyes off the enemy to answer it.

It was the Battle Platform, but it was the Quartermaster-Fiscal, not Dareau.

'Sir, I –'

Whatever he was about to say wasn't important. 'Get the Platform over to the research dome. The enemy are here.'

The ghosts walked straight past him, paying him no attention. Then all twelve passed through the door, into the observation dome.

Adric finished drawing the circle and moved back over to the Time Control apparatus. The Doctors sat facing each other, their eyes closed. Their faces were set in expressions of grim determination, sweat trickled down both their brows. It was odd: they looked almost entirely unlike one another, but he could tell they were the same person.

The fifth Doctor's eyes opened. 'We have regained control of the Machine. Gallifrey is safe.' Adric suspected that the process had been a great deal more complicated than the simple statement suggested.

'So what have you done with the Machine?' Whitfield asked.

'It's heading back this way,' the seventh Doctor announced, frantically folding up the piece of paper in his hand. 'We're using a shortcut through the Vortex. Now, that isn't going to please –'

As one, the Ferutu stepped through the wall and strode into the middle of the room.

'You're trapped,' Adric announced triumphantly.

The Ferutu leader looked down. It was standing in the middle of the circle that Adric had just drawn. It moved its foot forward, over the line. 'Without the rune, this is simply a geometric shape. You fail to understand our ways.' It flicked its wrist and a bolt of energy shot from it. Adric was thrown back across the floor, every nerve in his body screaming.

Forrester bent over him. 'Only stunned,' she was telling everyone else. Adric shook himself awake, not wanting to miss what happened next. Forrester helped him up.

'Coo-ee!' the seventh Doctor called from the other side of the room. For a moment Adric thought that the little man was calling to him, not the ghosts. With a flick of his wrist, the Doctor released the paper dart he had been preparing. It glided over to the Ferutu, one of whom caught it without effort.

'What is this?' it asked curiously. 'Is this the best weapon your universe can deploy?'

'Open it,' the fifth Doctor suggested. The Ferutu did as requested.

When it saw the rune it roared. 'No! This cannot be!' The leader tried to move, but couldn't: the foot it had placed over the line was now stuck to the floor as if it had been glued there.

The Doctors scrambled over to the trapped ghosts, disconnecting themselves from the apparatus around their heads.

The fifth Doctor was first over. Adric noticed that Roz was careful to take up position behind him. 'We've averted the destruction of Gallifrey. My people will be the first to master Time, and yours will cease to exist.'

'You have come to gloat?' the Ferutu asked. Adric was on his feet. He began hobbling over to the middle of the room.

'No. We have come to ask you a favour,' the seventh Doctor said. 'The Machine will detonate when it re-materializes. It's en route back here.'

'It will destroy this galaxy,' the Ferutu said, licking its lips.

'Yes,' the fifth Doctor said, 'but if the Machine explodes anywhere other than Gallifrey, then your timeline will snap out of existence.'

The other Doctor stepped forward, and when he spoke there was more than a little menace in his voice. 'We will die, the entire human race will die, the Daleks and Cyber-men will die. But it will be worse for you: if that bomb goes off here, then you and everything you have ever known will never have existed. Can you face the thought of all those billions of years of history and striving that you showed me vanishing forever? Not even we will be left to remember it. Everything you have ever known, everything you have even heard about will be gone.'

'Why are you doing this?' There was an expression of anguish on the leader's face. Adric was the only other person in the room who knew what it was like to be marooned in another universe, far away from everything he'd ever known. He could sense the emptiness, the hol-lowness in the Ferutu leader's voice.

'You can prevent the bombs from exploding,' the fifth Doctor said. 'Focus your mind on the Vortex.'

They did as they were asked.

'Can you see the Machine?'

An image was appearing in the circle, an illusion or hologram. It was now possible to see the vast Machine rotating as it moved through the time spiral. It was huge, but dwarfed by the walls of the Vortex itself. There were patterns there: five-dimensional optical illusions that made it impossible to judge scale, or direction of movement.

'We see it.'

It was coming closer. The bombs were heading back to the cavern. How long was it now before they would explode? Adric guessed about three minutes.

'You can stop the Machine,' the fifth Doctor shouted. 'Use your magic to halt the flow of time around it. Freeze it in the Vortex.'

The Machine ploughed through the Vortex like a hurricane or a tidal wave, a force of nature. It was unstoppable.

'That would be difficult,' the Ferutu leader admitted. 'It would require great effort and a complex ceremony.'

'Two minutes, ten seconds before materialization,' the little Doctor announced. 'Now, by my calculations, to stop the Machine you'll need a ritual that takes two minutes and twelve Ferutu. Now, there's a coincidence. Which is it to be?'

The Ferutu leader stood impassively for a moment. 'There isn't a choice.'

'There is always a choice,' the fifth Doctor snapped. 'This one is the most fundamental of all: to be or not to be. Stop the Machine and the two universes will be able to co-exist. Let those bombs detonate and one of them will be wiped out.'

The Machine was hurtling closer with every second.

'It's like flipping a coin,' the other Doctor said. 'Until the bombs explode, we don't know whether it will be heads or tails, your universe or ours. Using your magic you can keep the coin in the air forever, barring accidents.'

The Machine was nearly here.

The Ferutu leader scrutinized them. 'Agreed,' it said finally. The Ferutu began their ceremony.

The fifth Doctor leant over his future self. 'Do they have enough time?'

The little man nodded, but was biting his lip.

The Ferutu were chanting a simple mantra. Those on the edge of the group were making slow, sweeping gestures. The mantra grew louder, almost hypnotic. Outside the circle, Adric could see both the Ferutu's ritual and the Machine, one superimposed over the other. The sides of the Vortex were crackling with a new form of energy now, one that Whitfield and her fellow members of the

Scientifica could not even acknowledge existed.

'It is done,' the Ferutu leader announced, 'equilibrium has been achieved.'

The Machine hung in the Vortex, flickering slightly. It was so close, Adric felt he could almost reach out and touch it. The other Ferutu were locked in position, their hands twisted into warding signs.

The doors to the observation dome hissed open, and Adjudicators poured in, pulling up their rifles. Adric edged behind one of the tables, ready to pull himself down for cover.

'Don't shoot!' Whitfield ordered. 'And don't cross that white line.'

Medford stepped through the door and over to her. 'Are you safe?'

She nodded and he kissed her forehead. 'I'm afraid that the explanations will take quite a while.' She sketched in the broad detail of what had happened.

The Provost–General edged around the circle, looking up at the Ferutu, who were still locked in concentration. He rested his hand on the younger Doctor's shoulder. 'You trapped them?'

'Yes.'

'Then you have saved the planet. It seems that I have misjudged you.' He turned to Forrester. 'And that was a nice move. If you ever want a place in the Guild, I'm sure that the Board of Admission on Ponten would accept my reference.'

'Thank you.' The praise was honest, although Adric detected more than a note of scorn in Forrester's reply.

Adric looked back at the Ferutu, who were still frozen in concentration.

There was a tap on his shoulder. The Chief Scientist had been scribbling down something on the sketchpad. Now she handed it over to Adric. It was a series of formulae, one that took him a couple of seconds' hard concentration to decode. He took Whitfield's pen and jotted down a couple of corrections, passing them over for verification. They looked up at the same time.

'What happened here can't be stable,' Adric began.

Both Doctors looked annoyed. 'And why not?' the fifth Doctor said haughtily.

'In effect you've created a new universe out of nothing,' the Chief Scientist stated. 'Whatever happened to the Law of the Conservation of Energy?'

The seventh Doctor allowed himself a thin smile. 'It's about to be enforced. Watch.'

Adric turned back to the image hanging in the circle. Another Machine was surging through the Vortex in a straight five-dimensional curve.

'The Machine's past is about to catch up with it,' the fifth Doctor said softly. There was nothing he could do.

'Have you ever wondered what would happen if an irresistible force met an immovable object, Chief Scientist?'

'No,' Whitfield said. 'The problem is one of semantics rather than physics: an immovable object is one that can't be moved, however great the force. An irresistible force is one that can displace any object. By definition, both cannot exist simultaneously.'

'Besides,' Forrester noted, 'one of them is packed to the gunnels with F-Bombs.'

'This is not what we agreed,' the fifth Doctor snapped suddenly. The other raised his finger, and Adric was surprised to see Roz snap to attention behind his Doctor.

'You have betrayed us!' the Ferutu leader howled. It was in anguish, like a caged animal.

The young Doctor whirled around. 'Try to —'

The two Machines collided. The frozen Machine was dislodged, slamming it out of position. Time started around it.

There was a white flash.

When the light had died down, one of the Machines had vanished, and the remaining half of the other was spinning out of control, ricocheting from the walls of the Vortex, tearing chunks from it.

The image faded, leaving just the Ferutu standing there in silence.

The fifth Doctor stared at the image. 'The damage to space—time . . .'

'There isn't any,' the seventh Doctor said. 'You repaired

it, remember? Temporal Fusion. Neat to use the instrument that did the damage to repair it.'

'Why are they still here?' Medford asked.

'Inside the circle they are protected,' Whitfield explained. 'But if they ever managed to break the power of the rune then they would instantly snap out of existence. They are the only survivors of their universe.'

'A fitting punishment for what they did,' Medford said. He explained about the destroyed Skybase and Fleet, the twenty thousand men they had killed. 'Once we have left, defence drones will be placed down here and the transmat link will be destroyed. This chamber will be sealed. How long do Ferutu live?'

'They are immortal,' the fifth Doctor said automatically. 'They will still be here when the star that this colony orbits has become a red giant.' He seemed rooted to the spot, his senses dulled. Adric watched him as everyone else in the room began to relax and draw breath.

Medford was still on edge. 'They will escape then?'

'That won't be our problem,' Whitfield said. 'That will be eight billion years from now.' She was sipping from her tea, which was still warm.

The seventh Doctor rested his hands on his umbrella. 'Humanity is long dead by then, this galaxy has been abandoned by all sentient life, for reasons I had better not go into. There won't be any passing spacecraft to rescue the Ferutu, and they'll drift for eternity, only dying with our universe.'

'They were only fighting for their survival,' the fifth Doctor said.

'So were we, Doctor. The difference is that we won.' There was the barest hint of remorse in the Provost-General's voice, though.

'Have we?' Whitfield asked. 'With the Machine gone, the Senate will withdraw your peacekeeping force and all their research grants.'

Medford put his arm around her, and began to lead her out of the observation dome. 'We're not going anywhere for the moment, Juno, the planet is surrounded by a billion tonnes of radioactive shrapnel. The peacekeeping force will help you to rebuild. Besides, Earth will see us as traitors, now. It's as well that they can't get to us just yet.'

'Thank the Goddess for radioactive shrapnel,' Forrester said archly.

The Chief Scientist seemed almost broken, and didn't react to Medford's attempts to comfort her. 'I'm not sure I can trust you, 'Lian.'

'I did this for you,' he said, aware how weak the words sounded. Whitfield didn't react, simply walking from the room. Medford hurried after her, oblivious to everyone else.

Forrester and the seventh Doctor were following them out of the observation dome. Adric paused at the doorway. His Doctor was standing in front of the Ferutu.

'Could you do me a favour, Adric?' he said softly. 'Could you get back to the Scientifica and round up Tegan and Nyssa.'

'What will you be doing?' Adric asked.

'I have a little unfinished business here,' the Doctor replied.

The Ferutu were silent, some were asleep. Their leader was standing, watching over them. The chamber was dark, lit only by dull blue emergency lamps.

'You are still here.' Its voice was calm.

'Yes. I didn't know what he was planning, really I didn't. I will do everything in my power to release you.'

The Ferutu's expression didn't change. 'You know your future. You use your knowledge to imprison us and destroy all that we have known. That promise was broken before you made it.'

The Doctor nodded sadly, remembering the future. 'I'm sorry. But I am a Time Lord: I have many destinies, many future selves. He won't be the last.'

'We would have done the same as him. If we were released we would find a way to re-establish the true course of time. We know that today, like ourselves, you have also lost your past and future.'

The Doctor nodded, picturing Patience framed in the window of the Nightingale Facility, the weak light behind

291

her blonde hair. Then he saw his future self sneering as he condemned an entire universe to death.

He picked up her nightgown. The blood had dried into Rorschach patterns: question marks and owls and stars.

'It is not the first time you have met her, it will not be the last.'

The thought filled the Doctor with hope. 'Thank you. Tell me of your people.'

'I have, I will.'

The Doctor nodded. 'I have to go now. He is not my only future.'

He hesitated before folding up the nightgown. He would take it with him. The Doctor left the observation dome, keying the sequence that closed and locked the door. As the chamber sealed behind him, the Doctor did not look back.

The Doctors lifted the panel back into place on the side of the transmat control terminal. The seventh Doctor bent over and fastened it shut with his sonic screwdriver.

Chris materialized on the platform. 'Hello, everyone,' he said cheerily. They had restored the radio link a quarter of an hour ago and quickly established that everyone was all right. The Provost-General and the Chief Scientist had left, separately.

Cwej helped up the fifth Doctor. The young Time Lord thanked him. Roz passed him back his frock coat.

'There's something I don't understand,' Cwej said.

'Hmmm?'

'Well, if he's your future self, why don't you remember all this from first time round?'

'Does everything have to have a reason?' Forrester asked. 'Perhaps it's magic.'

'No, no,' the fifth Doctor said, 'the rules of time travel are very precise, and Mr Cwej here has a good point. Now, on both occasions that we met Omega, that was straightforward Blinovitch Conservation.'

'That was true all three times, yes, but it doesn't apply here,' the other Doctor noted from underneath the console.

'Yes, yes, I know that. Now, Zodin erased our brains with mind rubbers.'

'I remember it well.'

'But that hasn't happened this time. The crashed TARDIS might have had misphased Relativity Displacers.'

'It might,' the seventh Doctor conceded, 'but it didn't.'

'Tachyon Backflush?' the fifth Doctor suggested.

Chris sniggered. 'Sorry – it's just that it sounds rude.'

Forrester shook her head disbelievingly. Her Doctor stood, brushing himself off and taking his umbrella back from his past self.

The fifth Doctor straightened. 'There is another possibility.'

'Go on.'

'You *do* remember. You've remembered all along.'

The Doctor smiled enigmatically and tapped the side of his nose.

At the pre-arranged signal, Forrester knocked out the fifth Doctor with a swift blow to the back of the head.

The seventh Doctor bent over his past self, but rubbed his own skull. 'A palpable hit,' he said. Cwej was looking bewildered.

'Sorry,' Roz said, biting her lip, 'I wasn't sure whether you still wanted me to –'

'Not at all,' the Doctor replied quickly. 'I don't remember feeling a thing.' He looked down at his prone former self. 'I think we'd better leave, though.' He was at the transmat console, twisting dials and pulling levers.

'The transmat network is fixed now, is it?'

'Oh yes. It should beam us straight over to the apartment we rented.' The Doctor tapped in a final command and joined Cwej and Forrester on the transmat platform. 'We'll tie up the loose ends, then get back to the TARDIS. Wolsey will be wondering where we've got to.'

The transmat activated and all three disappeared from view.

Available in the *Doctor Who — New Adventures* series:

GODENGINE by Craig Hinton
CHRISTMAS ON A RATIONAL PLANET by Lawrence Miles
RETURN OF THE LIVING DAD by Kate Orman
THE DEATH OF ART by Simon Bucher-Jones
DAMAGED GOODS by Russell T Davies
SO VILE A SIN by Ben Aaronovitch
BAD THERAPY by Matthew Jones

The next Missing Adventure is *Burning Heart* by Dave Stone, featuring the sixth Doctor and Peri.